All the

One of the reasons I love *Three Reasons to Say Yes* so much is that Clevenger wrote such strong secondary characters in Kate and Mo. I fell for them almost as much as the main characters, so to have them get their own book I was excited. This is a story about two best friends since college that have a ton of chemistry but have never done anything about it. ...If you are looking for a well written, angsty romance, look no further. This is an easy romance for me to recommend. I think with this series, Clevenger is at the top of her writing game and I can't wait to see what she puts out next.

-Lex Kent's Reviews, *goodreads*

This book is the second installment in Clevenger's Paradise Romance series. It's not necessary to read the first book, *Three Reasons to Say Yes*, to enjoy Kate and Mo's story... *All the Reasons I Need* is a thoughtful summer romance full of emotion. It let me imagine myself on a tropical beach, napping in a hammock, and sipping an exotic drink with a little umbrella in it. There's just something about beautiful sunsets and waves crashing on the beach that make falling in love seem easy.

-*The Lesbian Review*

Three Reasons to Say Yes

This is without a doubt my new favourite Jaime Clevenger novel. Honestly I couldn't put it down from the first chapter. ...All in all this book has the potential to be my book of the year. Truly, books like this don't come around often that suit my reading tastes to a tee.

-*Les Rêveur*

…this one was totally my cup of tea with its charming relationship and family dynamics, great chemistry between two likable protagonists, a very convincing romance, some angst, drama and tension to the right extent and in all the right moments, and some very nice secondary characters. On top of that, the writing is technically very good, with all elements done properly. Sincerely recommended.

Pin's Reviews, *goodreads*

This was a really easy story to get into. I sank right in and wanted to stay there, because reading about other people on vacation is kind of like taking a mini vacation from the world!

It's sweet and lovely, and while it has some angst, it's not going to hurt you. Instead, it's going to take you away from it all so you can come back with a smile on your face.

-The Lesbian Review

Party Favors

This book has one of the best characters ever. Me. Or rather you. It's quite a strange and startling experience at first to be in a book, especially one with as many hot, sexy, beautiful women in it who, incidentally, all seem to want you. But believe me, you'll soon get used to it. …In a word, this book was FUN. It made me smile, and laugh, and tease my wife. I definitely recommend it to everyone, with the caveat that if you don't like erotica you should probably give it a pass. But not only read it, enjoy it, experience it, also find a friend, or a spouse, or even a book buddy online to talk to about it. Because you'll want to, it's that great.

-The Lesbian Review

I've read this book a few times and each time changed my decisions to find new and inviting destinations each time. This is a book you can read time and time again with a different journey. If you're looking for a fun Saturday night read that's sexy and hot as hell then this book is 100% for you! Go buy it now. 5 Stars.

-*Les Rêveur*

The story is told in the second person, present tense, whichis ambitious in itself—it takes great skill to make that work and for the reader, who is now the narrator, to really connect to the thoughts and actions that are being attributed to them. Not all of the scenes will turn everyone on, as we all have different tastes, but I am pretty sure there is something for everyone in here. And if you do as you're told and follow the structure the author uses, you can dip into this book as much or as little as you wish. An interesting read with some pretty hot interactions.

-*Rainbow Book Reviews*

Just One Reason

Other Books by Jaime Clevenger

Bella Books
Call Shotgun
A Fugitive's Kiss
All the Reasons I Need
Moonstone
Party Favors
Sign on the Line
Sweet, Sweet Wine
Three Reasons to Say Yes
The Unknown Mile
Waiting for a Love Song
Whiskey and Oak Leaves

Spinsters Ink
All Bets Off

About the Author

Jaime Clevenger lives in Colorado with her family. She spends her days working as a veterinarian, but also enjoys swimming, teaching karate, playing with her kids, and snuggling the foster kittens and puppies that often fill her home. She loves to hear a good story and hopes that if you ever meet her, you'll tell her your favorite. Feel free to embellish the details.

Just One Reason

Jaime Clevenger

BELLA
B O O K S
2020

Bella Books, Inc.
P.O. Box 10543
Tallahassee, FL 32302

Printed in the United States of America on acid-free paper.

First Bella Books Edition 2020

Editor: Medora MacDougall
Cover Designer: Judith Fellows

ISBN: 978-1-64247-154-0

Acknowledgment

Thank you to all of my beta readers and writer friends. I appreciate you so very much, and this story is infinitely better because of your advice. Thank you, Corina, for always being willing to read a scene one more time. You make me a better storyteller—and better person in general. Thank you, Katie, for pushing me to think more deeply about relationship dynamics. Thank you, Dawn, for reminding me of the benefits of good timing and pacing. Thank you, Sandy, for convincing me to go for those happily ever afters. Thank you, Medora, for another fabulous editing experience. Thank you, Jessica, for letting me use my own picture for the cover. I can't tell you how happy it makes me to know that it's the same beach where these two fall in love. And finally, thank you, dear reader. I love that you are willing to go on another adventure with me and I truly hope you find your own paradise.

CHAPTER ONE

Between *yes* and *no* there were a whole line of *maybes*. That one seemingly innocent word had gotten Terri Anderson into more trouble than any other. But never had *maybe* gotten her signed up for a ballroom dance class.

"You promised."

"I didn't promise. I said *maybe*." Terri rubbed the back of her neck, willing away a headache. The last thing she wanted to do tonight was learn how to waltz. If she ever got to the bottom of the stack of charts she needed to write, she still had at least an hour's worth of patient phone calls to make. "Besides, I don't see why you need me. You'll have Julia."

"And I need you for moral support. Please? Pretty please?"

Terri smiled, not that Reed could see. "You sound like one of your kids. Just don't say with a cherry on top."

"Pretty please with a cherry on top?" Reed chuckled. "You can't stop me. We aren't even on the same floor. I'm all the way up on seventh and you're probably stuck on third."

"You should see how fast I run those stairs. I'm like a little billy goat. Wait, what do they call girl goats? Hold on a minute." Terri held the phone away from her ear and motioned to the intern who had popped out of room 306. "We need a urine sample from that patient. Did you remind her?"

"She says she doesn't need to pee."

Terri struggled to remember the intern's name. Too many new faces had appeared in the last month. July was always barely managed chaos. A fresh class of interns filled the halls, tempers flared along with the heat—welcome to Sacramento General—and there were no slow days. "She might not feel like she has to pee, but after two liters of fluid she needs to pee. Trust me."

Terri held the phone back up to her ear. "I've had a hell of a day, Reed, but I'm saying yes because I owe you for that carcinoma case. How you spotted that lesion, I'll never know—"

"You're the best, Terri. By the way, girls are called nanny goats. Can you make it by seven?"

"Nanny goats?"

"I read it in one of my kids' books. Bryn decided she wanted to move to a farm, but Carly had a breakdown because she's terrified of chickens. We compromised by getting all the library books on farming. The good news is I finally understand crop rotation and I'm pretty sure I could milk a cow."

"Seriously, no one knows more useless facts than you."

"So you'll be there?"

Terri glanced at her watch. Half past five. If everything went according to plan, she'd have enough time to race home for a shower. "I'll make it. But I still think you can do this without me."

"You've seen me dance. I need my personal physician on standby. And my therapist. You happen to be both."

Terri almost felt bad for Reed. Except she was engaged to an amazing woman and only needed to get through one song. "You might be making this into a bigger deal than it is."

"Everyone's gonna be staring at us. What if I choke and forget how to move my feet?"

"Better than stepping on Julia's feet."

"Very funny," Reed grumbled. "We're meeting at the pub next to the dance studio for drinks first. I'll text you the address."

"You hoping alcohol is going to make you Fred Astaire?"

"No. I gotta be realistic. I'm hoping I'll look like one of those inflatable tube men at a car lot."

Terri laughed loud enough to get a sharp look from the nursing station. She waved off the eye roll from JoAnne, her favorite stodgy nurse.

"Excuse me, Dr. Anderson?" The intern had reappeared in the hallway. Her scrubs were wet and she tugged on the fabric with a look that promised tears were on their way.

"Reed, I gotta go. See you tonight." Terri ended the call and studied the intern. "Looks like that didn't go so well."

"I was helping her out of bed and she peed. On me."

"Did you catch any?"

"No." She dropped her gaze to study her shiny new Danskos.

"It's okay. We'll get that sample." Terri sighed. "Why don't you go get changed and grab something to eat. You still want to be a doctor, right?"

Slow nod.

They'd both had a long day and she couldn't run the kid too hard. "Get your patient some juice and then sit down and talk. Eventually your new friend will pee."

* * *

Ten minutes into the walk and beads of sweat dripped down her back. The city seemed subdued, as if all of Sacramento was considering a siesta. Even on Sixteenth Street the traffic seemed to only inch along.

Terri longed to go back to the cool shower she'd raced through or at least her living room with the A/C blasting. After another twelve-hour day, kicking her feet up on the sofa for a Netflix binge sounded perfect. Instead…ballroom dancing.

She crossed at the intersection, her tank top already sticking to her damp skin, and angled toward a blinking neon sign advertising the pub with a giant bottle of beer. The dance studio next door had a more subtle sign.

"Terri!" Julia, Reed's fiancée, waved as she hurried up the sidewalk. "I'd give you a hug but it's too hot."

"No joke. When is July going to be over?" Of course August wouldn't be any better. At this rate, the heat would last until the pumpkin spice lattes appeared. "You look fabulous. New skirt?"

Julia nodded. "I told Reed I'd wear something to distract her. She's been stressing all week about this. And I don't know what she said to get you here, but thank you."

"This is probably good for me. I keep saying I need to get out more, but then I come home and take my shoes off and the rest of the night is history."

"Maybe you'll meet someone tonight."

"While waltzing? Highly unlikely." She'd given up on randomly meeting anyone. She'd also given up on her online prospects. Once she'd settled on being happily single, reentry in the dating world seemed more hassle than it was worth. "If we get Reed through this dance class, I'll call the evening a win."

"We'll both call it a win," Julia agreed. "I told her that a wedding dance was no big deal, but she insisted we needed a class. Then after we were signed up, she started worrying that everyone else would be straight."

"I don't think it's the straight people she has to worry about. Have you seen her dance?"

"I have." Julia frowned. "She has many, many other talents."

They stepped inside and a wall of delicious icy air greeted them. Terri took a moment to adjust to the dim lighting. If only they could spend the rest of the evening here.

"Mo and Kate said they might come, but then they both had work commitments tonight..." Julia scanned the crowd. "Reed did manage to convince one of her residents."

"She asked a resident?"

"Her name's Sam. Reed says she's Family, but that's all I know. Oh, there's Reed." Julia gave a soft moan. "Sometimes I don't know how I got so lucky."

Terri would have teased her for the moan, but she was stuck on the detail that Reed had invited a resident. No amount of air conditioning could make her interested in small talk with a resident. Later she'd give Reed a hard time for not warning her.

Reed pushed her Clark Kent glasses up on her nose and headed their way. In a few strides, she'd passed the other tables to wrap her arms around Julia. The two shared a big kiss, seemingly uncaring of any onlookers. Tall, slightly nerdy, and enough of a butch to make her irresistible, Reed was a polar opposite to Julia, who fit the bill of a curvy, fashionable femme with an extrovert's ability to win over anyone. But they were a perfect couple.

After another deep kiss, Terri cleared her throat. "All right, you two lovebirds. Save it for the wedding."

Reed pulled back. She at least had the decency to look extremely satisfied with her luck in love.

"I brought you a surprise," Reed said.

Terri cocked her head. "You brought me a surprise?"

"Think of it as the cherry on top. You're going to hate me at first for it, but then I know you're gonna thank me later."

"Okay, now I'm worried."

"You probably should be. I've never tried matchmaking."

"Oh, no." In one second it clicked. The resident. "Reed, please say you didn't."

"But I did." Reed grinned, clearly pleased with herself.

Terri wanted to grab Reed by her tie and pull her out of the pub to give her a piece of her mind. Sure, plenty of attendings dated residents, even if it was heartily discouraged. The problem was her history. It simply couldn't happen again.

She had no time to argue. Reed started to their table with Julia's hand locked in hers and, steeling herself for who she might see, Terri glanced to the back corner. A blush immediately shot up to her cheeks.

Of course it's her.

Reed had found the one resident that could easily grace the cover of a lesbian *GQ*. Terri had spent the past year actively trying not to notice her. Unfortunately there were only so many butch women in the hospital, and none of them were as hot as Elizabeth Samuels.

Tonight her scrubs had been exchanged for a pair of tailored dark gray slacks and a collared paisley shirt with sleeves rolled up to her elbows. The top two buttons of her shirt were undone in a casual look that only made her more appealing. She kept her short brown hair in a messy cut that Terri could almost imagine running her fingers through. But it was her broad shoulders and fit athletic build that really were the problem. No doubt she could pin someone on a bed. For whatever reason.

Terri's mouth went dry when she met her gaze and smiled. Of course she had a perfect smile. Probably she was an amazing kisser too. But that didn't mean she'd be interesting. Or even nice. With luck, she'd be an annoying know-it-all.

As soon as they reached the table, Reed made quick introductions. Elizabeth Samuels went by Sam. She shook Julia's hand first and then turned to Terri.

"Hi."

Dark blue eyes settled on her and Terri couldn't hide a fresh blush. She tried to keep her pulse in check as she reached across the table to clasp Sam's hand. Smooth skin and a firm grip—the universe clearly had it out for her. *I'm not dating a resident. Not again.*

"I'm happy to finally meet you," Sam said. "I keep hearing your name around the hospital."

Reed coughed and Terri's eyes darted to her. Oh, she'd definitely pay her back later for this.

"And not only from a certain radiology guru," Sam added.

"Really? Who else?" Terri wished she'd thought before the question slipped out. She didn't want, or need, to hear accolades, but now it sounded as if she were fishing for exactly that.

"My friend Carter told me I should pay attention to you and then I heard the same thing from about a half a dozen other residents. And Shellhammer over in ICU calls you the boss-diggity-dog."

"Shellhammer's right," Reed agreed. Her wink across the table at Terri wasn't subtle. "Boss-diggity."

Reed pulled out a chair for Julia and promptly sat down next to her. The only remaining seat was the one next to Sam's. Terri felt Sam waiting. Sitting down next to her would only add to the feeling of being on a double date. She looked up from the empty seat and Sam's eyes caught hers. A warmth swept through her body, and she quickly took her seat, knowing her cheeks had betrayed her again. Sam sat down, and Terri avoided looking her direction.

"Didn't you say that Shellhammer told you to spy on Terri?" Reed asked.

"He did," Sam said.

"So did you actually spy on her?" Julia asked.

"Well, not creepy stalking or anything. I checked out a few cases and talked to some residents."

Julia raised an eyebrow. "Yeah, that sounds like spying."

Sam's smile was sheepish. "Dr. Anderson's got a reputation for being the best internist in pediatrics. I wanted to know why."

"You can call me Terri. We're not in the hospital." Terri wasn't sure what to say about the spying part, however. And was it better or worse that Sam was buttering her up with compliments? She had enough to worry about with the tingling sensation that zipped through her body every time Sam looked her way.

"Terri's rep is well earned," Reed said. "She's saved a lot of lives."

"You have a lot to do with that," Terri returned. "It's nice to have a radiologist who doubles as a rock star internist on speed dial."

"Which is the only reason you agreed to ballroom dancing."

"True." Terri wanted to add that Reed owed her double for letting a resident tag along. Especially this particular resident.

"I need both of you on speed dial when I'm seeing my own cases," Sam said.

"For the next two years, you'll have us," Reed said. "After that…"

"After that, you might have to block my number 'cause I'm gonna keep calling." Sam looked over at Terri. "Is now a good time to ask for yours?"

Reed chuckled. "You gotta work on your pickup lines, my friend."

Finally it was Sam's turn to blush. "That's not what I meant. I mean I would ask for your number but…not like that." She blew out a breath and added, "I promise I'm cooler than I seem right now."

"That's too bad," Terri said. "I was starting to think you were tolerable."

"Well, I'm not that much cooler."

Terri couldn't help smiling. Being the recipient of Sam's attempts to impress wasn't completely awful. It wasn't going to work of course, but still.

"I've got a Cherry Coke and a margarita?" The waitress glanced from Julia to Terri since Reed and Sam both already had drinks.

"The margarita's mine." Julia leaned close and kissed Reed. "Thanks for ordering for me, sweetie."

"Then I'm guessing the Cherry Coke's for you." The waitress placed the soda in front of Terri with a smile.

"Thank you." Terri reached for the glass. Reed inviting Sam was akin to handing her a cool soda after a long walk in the desert. *So tempting*. The soda she wouldn't say no to, but Sam she had to resist.

"So, Sam, how'd Reed convince you to come dancing?"

Reed spoke up before Sam could: "Someone kind of invited herself."

"Only because you were tripping about being the only woman in a tie at a straight dance class. And then I didn't have time to go home and get my tie."

The image of Sam in a tie was not what she needed to think about. She sucked down a big sip of the soda, thankful no one could read her thoughts.

"I don't usually invite myself to things. But I love dancing and my friends all got stuck working late."

"Benefits of radiology," Reed said. "We know when to call it a day and go home."

"Or go out dancing," Julia added.

"Or do that." Reed wrapped an arm around Julia's chair. "Gosh, I can't wait to waltz with you."

"Gosh?" Julia leaned close and pecked Reed's cheek. "Sweetie, no one believes you want to do this, but there's a possibility you might like it."

"There's also a possibility I'll injure one of us." Reed countered. "We could skip the wedding, you know, and go on a longer honeymoon."

"You want to miss your wedding night with me?" Julia waggled her eyebrows.

"Not when you put it that way." Reed returned the waggling eyebrows, laughing as she did.

"When's the wedding?" Sam asked.

"October."

"Do you two have a photographer? Before med school, that was my full-time job. I've shot a lot of weddings."

Terri wondered how old Sam might be. She seemed more mature than a lot of the residents, and there was a chance she was older if she'd had the photography gig for a while. But how much older? Probably not enough.

Julia looked at Reed and then back at Sam. "We don't. Are you offering?"

"I'd love to. Assuming I can get away from the hospital."

"I can pull some strings," Reed said. "You won't need that much time off anyway. The wedding's going to be close. We're getting married at a little winery in Napa."

"You get me the time off and I'll take the pictures."

Julia clapped her hands together. "This is perfect! Reed kept saying all of our friends could take pictures, but I wanted a real photographer."

"You know it's all about what the bride wants," Sam said, clinking Reed's bottle against hers. "Didn't you get that memo?"

"Apparently not."

"So, let me get this right," Julia started. "You're a photographer, a doctor, and you waltz? Do you put all of that on your dating profile?"

"Usually I lead with a bit about stamp collecting." Sam grinned. "I don't get a whole lot of matches."

"Stamp collecting? Are you serious?" Reed squinted at Sam. "How old are you? Eighty-seven?"

"Close. Thirty-one. And you can see my stamp collection whenever you want. But tonight I'm gonna wow you all with my completely uncool waltzing." Sam struck a pose and everyone laughed.

Terri's body warmed when Sam joined in. She held onto Sam's gaze even when she knew she ought to look away. Someone who could poke fun at themselves got major points in her book. But a resident was automatically disqualified, she reminded herself. And thirty-one? *No way.*

"How'd you get into ballroom dancing?" Julia asked.

"My folks sent me to an all-girls private school and ballroom dancing was required. Since I was tall and not exactly girly, I got picked for lead all the time. I didn't think I'd like it at first, but there's nothing like having a beautiful girl put her hands on your body and ask you to make the next move."

Reed scratched her head. "Maybe I need to reframe this waltzing thing in my mind."

Julia bumped against her shoulder. "Ahem. Suddenly you're realizing that it won't be so awful to dance with me?"

"So where do you fall, Terri?" Sam asked. "Are you a dancing queen or only here 'cause Reed sounded pathetic when she called you?" Sam ducked when Reed playfully swatted at her.

"Definitely not a dancing queen. I like to dance, but I have to be in the mood."

"Meaning the right partner?"

Terri shrugged. She didn't want to take Sam's bait. "More the right scene. I like dance clubs."

"Lots of sweaty sexy bodies and a nice hard beat?"

The tone of Sam's voice wasn't suggestive, but her words had Terri stumbling for an answer. It didn't help that Sam's eyes were locked on hers and the smile on her lips had a wicked certainty to it.

Terri cocked her head. "You spying on me in dance clubs too? You should probably stop."

The confidence in Sam's eyes slipped away. Maybe she didn't fully understand the risks, but Terri knew all too well. Setting boundaries was for the best.

"I really haven't been spying. I mean, I did follow some of your cases, but only because Weiss and Shellhammer both told me I should."

"Wait, Weiss told you to spy on me too?" David Weiss was the chief of medicine—effectively Terri's boss as well as everyone else's.

"Weiss is an old family friend. He was close with my grandpa. Anyway, my point was that he thinks highly of you." Sam held Terri's gaze. "I'm sorry if I was out of line with that dance club stuff."

The concern on Sam's face was obvious, and Terri decided she'd made her sweat enough. "Okay. Apology accepted."

"I can't wait to see you two in rounds together." Reed leaned across the table to pat Sam's shoulder. "Be prepared to get whipped, my friend."

"I don't think whipping will be necessary." A flush went through Terri and she didn't dare look in Sam's direction. *Whipping? Seriously?* Hoping to deflect, she quickly added, "How long are you in Radiology?"

"Two more weeks. Then I'm on Med-Peds."

"Med-Peds?" Julia's eyebrows bunched together.

"Internal medicine-pediatrics," Reed answered.

While every resident cycled through internal medicine and most spent at least a month in pediatrics, not every resident ended up working with her. With any luck, Sam would be scheduled with McReynolds. "Who's schedule are you on?"

"Yours."

Shit. Terri cleared her throat. Now she really had a problem on her hands. "I shouldn't have made that whipping comment. It was inappropriate and—"

"And funny," Sam finished. "Now we're even."

Even? Terri wasn't sure what was worse—that she needed to have the upper hand with Sam or that part of her liked when she lost it.

"Sometimes I'd like to be a fly on the wall in that hospital of yours," Julia said.

Reed shook her head. "Terri would grab a fly swatter and take you out in two seconds flat."

"I would. Sorry, Julia. I'm a hard ass. I do my job and expect everyone else to do theirs." She hoped Sam understood exactly what she meant by that.

"In the meantime, lives get saved but the flies are screwed." Reed tipped back her bottle, finishing the last of her beer. She eyed her watch. "All right. Time to face the gallows."

Terri carefully avoided bumping Sam's chair as she stood up. Gallows might be an exaggeration, but she wanted to skip the dance class as much as Reed did. And yet she wondered exactly what she was dreading.

No harm would come from one dance class. Even if someone from the hospital saw them together, she could easily explain it. All she needed to do was get through the evening—then promptly forget any attraction to Elizabeth Samuels.

CHAPTER TWO

Who knew that Dr. Anderson—Terri—had tattoos? And not simply a rose or a little butterfly on a shoulder or an ankle. Some artist had spent some serious time on her arms and back, and although the dark green tank top concealed some skin, the wing of a bird peeked out where the fabric scooped low over her cleavage, making it even harder for Sam not to stare at her chest.

The pub had been a near-complete disaster. Not only had she talked too much, she'd taken things too far with the dance club comments. The look on Terri's face then had spoken volumes. Now she had to get through the next hour without saying, or doing, something stupid.

Probably she had no business going for the aloof powerhouse that ruled the third floor of the hospital in the first place. But despite all the ways she'd screwed up, her body stirred with arousal when the dance teacher had motioned for Terri to stand next to her.

"Can I ask a favor?"

Terri glanced up from her purse. She'd gone to check her phone again—the third text notification in ten minutes. But this time, Sam noticed, she hadn't responded and instead turned her phone on silent.

"Sure." Terri tucked the phone into the front pocket of her purse and then straightened up. "What is it?"

"For the next hour, can we pretend that you're not an attending and I'm not a resident?" It was a ridiculous request, but she had to ask anyway. When Terri didn't respond right off, Sam added, "There's a chance I'll step on your toes."

"So it's not that you're worried about all of this ending up on your review?" A hint of a smile crossed Terri's lips.

"That too."

She rocked her head side to side as if weighing her options. "Okay. One hour off the record. But step lightly. I'm wearing sandals."

Sam let out the breath she'd been holding. "You got it."

So far, they'd only gone through hand positions and the footsteps for a basic box step. The dance instructor had stopped there to go around the room and check in with everyone. Then she'd started chatting. Sam wished she'd hurry up so she could get over the hurdle of taking Terri's hand.

It hadn't taken Weiss or Shellhammer's advice to get her to pay attention to Terri. Between the long curly red hair hardly tamed by the clip at the back of her slender neck, arresting green eyes, and a confidence that roared through her, Terri was impossible not to notice. Sam couldn't keep her eyes off of her.

As far as hospital gossip went, the jury was out on if she was dating anyone. Aside from Reed, she seemed to keep to herself. One nurse let it slide that she'd dated both men and women in the past and a rumor circulated that she'd been in a love triangle with two residents years ago, but most of the details sounded too crazy to believe.

"So I'm guessing you don't usually make a habit of taking dance classes with residents?"

"Not since that last twerking episode."

"Twerking?"

Terri's smile finally cracked. "I'm trying to lighten the mood."

"For a minute there I had this image of you—"

Terri held up her hands. "Please erase that image."

Sam laughed. "I don't think I can." Joking was definitely progress. And when Terri relaxed and really smiled, she was even more attractive.

"Hey, one hour off the record applies to me too."

"Okay, okay." Sam stopped laughing. "Honestly after you jumped on me about the spying thing I thought you were a tight ass, but one joke about twerking and you've completely changed my mind."

"I didn't jump on you. Let's not start that rumor too."

Immediately Sam thought of the love triangle rumor. Could it be true?

Terri continued, "I'm sorry I was harsh earlier, but I didn't want to give you the wrong idea. Reed socializes with residents. I don't. It's nothing personal."

Nothing personal. Terri certainly knew how to slap her ego. But Sam wasn't giving up that easy. "Good thing I'm not a resident for the next fifty-three minutes."

"Smooth. Very smooth."

"And while we're off the record, would you mind if I get something off my chest?"

"Fifty-two minutes and counting. Now's your chance."

"I like club dancing better than ballroom."

"So the crowded dance club with the sexy sweaty bodies is actually your thing?"

"I'd say it's a shared thing," Sam returned. "Dance club later?"

"Not a chance—but nice try." Terri continued, "I kind of liked the image of teenage Sam stuck in a private school ballroom making all the preppy girls swoon better than dance club Sam."

"I don't think any swooning happened."

"Oh, I'm sure there was some. You've got the suave debonair thing down. How many girlfriends did you have back then?"

"One."

"Only one?"

Sam nodded. "Her parents found out and pulled her from school. Honestly I don't have the best luck with relationships. Lately I've settled for the friends with benefits thing."

"There's nothing wrong with that. Nothing wrong with the sex with strangers thing either. Residents have a hard schedule. You can't expect it's going to work dating a normal person."

"Sex with strangers? You've done that?"

"Because we both know that we're going to remember this conversation, even if it's off the record, I'm not going to answer that. All I'll say is that I don't fault anyone for their choices as long as everyone's consenting."

Sam wasn't sure why she was surprised at the thought of Terri having sex with strangers. Maybe because she seemed like the type of woman that someone would try and tie down. *Figuratively or literally.* Sam swallowed as her thoughts tumbled that direction. Terri, in handcuffs, on her bed…

"Did I say too much? You've got this look on your face that has me worried." Terri pursed her lips. "This one hour off the record thing might be a bad idea."

"I was only thinking…I'm not sure I'd want to have sex with strangers. If it's good sex, I wouldn't want them to stay strangers."

"Some people don't want commitment." Terri looked as if she wanted to say more, but the instructor had finished going around the room and clapped her hands to get everyone's attention.

"Leads, please take your partner's hand."

Sam took a deep breath and held out her hand. "Remember, this doesn't go on my review."

"What if you're good?"

Sam grinned. "There are so many things I could say in response to that."

"Very funny. But I only meant dancing."

The first notes of "The Blue Danube" filled the space, and Sam shifted in front of Terri. Her heart raced as Terri's palm pressed against hers, and she hoped she'd remember the dance moves. She placed her other hand on the smooth line of Terri's shoulder blade. Nerves fired at every point their skin made contact.

"This okay?"

Terri dipped her head. The nod was subtle, but the effect—no words, only acquiescence—kicked up Sam's arousal. Terri's hand settled on her upper arm, and Sam immediately wondered what her lips would feel like. She stepped forward and they were in motion.

Sam fell into the steps, letting the music carry her, and before long the room slipped away. She forgot about everything except the place where Terri's hand rested on her arm and the feeling in her body when Terri's eyes held hers.

"I don't think you need this class," Terri said. She moved close as they stepped around another couple and the scent of her perfume caught Sam's attention.

"I'll take that compliment." Sam shifted their path toward a space in the center of the room.

"You should. I don't give compliments out often, so you might want to hold onto it."

"So you're never going to tell me that my records are stellar or that I have amazing diagnostic abilities?"

"Unlikely."

"Then after a long day seeing patients, I'll have to remember that at least I'm good at waltzing. I'm sure it'll come in handy at some point."

Sam congratulated herself on Terri's smirk. She added, "This isn't your first time either. Or you're a quick study."

"I'm a quick study on a lot of things."

The innuendo lit through Sam. "Why am I not surprised? You know, I fully expect you'll ignore me after tonight, but this is nice."

"As long as we're on the same page," Terri returned.

Sam knew she didn't have much of a chance, but the way Terri looked at her, her gaze an open challenge, made her want to try even harder to win her over.

They passed by Reed and Julia who still hadn't moved from their starting spot. "You two doing okay?" Sam asked.

Julia pursed her lips. "We're getting there."

"Okay, so it goes: one-two-three. Right?" Reed's brow furrowed as she studied her feet.

"Sweetie, it's possible you're overthinking this," Julia said. "Maybe we could try it without saying the numbers at all."

"I heard somewhere that everyone looks at the bride anyway. What if I stand in one spot and you dance around me?"

Julia shook her head. "The fact that you're sexy is not enough to get you out of this dancing thing."

"I could try to be sexier."

"Not possible." Julia stood on her tip-toes and pecked Reed's cheek.

Sam looked back at Terri. "They're adorable."

"And perfect for each other. Some people get lucky in life."

"But at the moment it looks like she'd rather be passing a kidney stone."

Terri squinted at the pair. "Which one?"

Sam laughed. Terri's subtle sarcastic humor wasn't something she'd expected. Then again, she'd had no idea what to expect from tonight. The instructor switched off the music, ending on an open note that would likely have made Strauss turn in his grave, and Sam reluctantly let go of Terri's hand.

"Let's try this again with new partners," the instructor announced, quickly pointing off pairs.

Sam swallowed her disappointment and made her way over to where her new partner waited. She shook the woman's hand and then glanced back at Terri. Her new partner said something to make her smile, and although Sam knew she had no claim to her, she felt a flush of jealousy when he took Terri's hand.

Sam held out her hand and her new partner clasped it. The feel of the stranger's grip on her arm confirmed that she didn't want to dance with anyone except Terri.

As it turned out, they never finished "The Blue Danube." The instructor kept switching from song to song and changing up dance partners nearly as frequently. Sam only made it back to Terri for the last song and before she'd relaxed enough to try chatting, the instructor ended class.

Terri let go of her hand and took a step back. "That was more fun than I thought it'd be."

"Does that mean you're converted to ballroom dancing?"

"Not quite. I still prefer club dancing." She paused. "You're a way better dancer than any of the other partners I had tonight. That must have been some boarding school education."

"Never thought it'd pay off." Sam nodded to the handful of folks talking to the instructor about the next class. "So, I take it you're not signing up for a full semester?"

"I'm at that point in my life where I can't even commit to a magazine subscription. You?"

"Most nights I'm not out of the hospital before ten." Although if Terri had said she'd sign up for the classes, Sam would have found a way to make it happen. "These past few weeks on Radiology have definitely been an exception."

"Enjoy it while it lasts."

Sam knew the early evenings would be over as soon as she began working with Terri, but she couldn't wait to start. Radiology, and Reed specifically, had been a surprise bright spot in an otherwise terrible year. She'd pressed through a lot of it, thinking about how close she was to the month she'd be working in Med-Peds.

When the instructor started in with announcements for the next few classes, Terri went over to her purse and picked up her phone. She frowned at the screen and then cussed under her breath.

"Everything okay?"

"I have to go back to the hospital." Terri quickly tapped out a text and then tossed the phone back in her purse.

"Do you want company?"

Terri raised an eyebrow. "No."

Sam shrugged. "Worth a shot." And she didn't regret asking. Terri's rejection wasn't as icy as it'd been at the pub, and her expression had a playful look of exasperation that made Sam wish the night wasn't ending. If she had another hour, maybe she could convince Terri to give her a chance.

"See you around." Terri swung her purse over her shoulder.

Sam didn't have time to stammer out a goodbye. She watched Terri hug Reed and Julia and the next moment she'd slipped outside. The other couples still milled about the room and their chatter filled the space, but Sam stared at the door wondering what would happen if she tried to catch up with Terri. Reed clapped her shoulder, startling her out of her thoughts.

"Thanks for coming tonight."

"Yeah, no problem." Sam forced a smile.

"I actually did have fun," Reed said. "Not a lot of fun, but it wasn't horrible."

"A couple more classes and you're gonna be ready for pro."

"Sure—if I had your feet. You made it look easy. I told Julia it's a good thing we're going first otherwise I'd be even more of a joke out there."

"You're gonna be fine. Though another class or two wouldn't hurt."

"Julia's signing us up for another month." Reed motioned to Julia, who was chatting with the instructor. "Maybe you and Terri can sign up too?"

"I did try to ask, but…"

"Turned down before you could even get the words out?"

Sam sighed. "How'd you know?"

"'Cause I know Terri. Trust me, she likes you. I've seen her around enough people to know. If you like her, I wouldn't give up quite yet."

Sam thought of how fast Terri had split. "You really think I might have a chance?"

"I think you wouldn't lose anything asking her out on a date." Reed reached into her pocket for her phone. "She's gonna kill me for this, but I'm texting you her number."

"Wait, don't. I can't call her if I didn't ask for her number. If she kills you just for giving me the number, think of what she'll do to me."

"You've clearly figured Terri out." Reed slipped her phone back in her pocket. "But it's too late. I already sent you the number. Thanks again for coming tonight."

Sam imagined the tongue-lashing she'd receive from Terri simply for calling. She'd have to delete Reed's text. If she kept Terri's number, sooner or later she'd be tempted to call.

Julia came over and slipped her arm around Reed. "Hey, sexy. Can I take you home?"

"Yes, please." Reed turned back to Sam. "I think you should call her. What do you have to lose?"

"I do have to work with her, you know."

Reed nodded. "But we both know you want to call her anyway."

Reed was right, but Sam didn't say as much.

After they'd gone, Sam took out her phone. She stepped outside and read the text from Reed. Her finger hovered over Terri's number, ready to delete. Before she had time to second-guess, she touched the call button instead.

The line went right to voice mail and she tried not to feel deflated. Terri probably didn't answer numbers she didn't recognize. After a moment's indecision about leaving a message, she ended the call.

Why the heck was she hung up on Terri anyway? She knew where to find a date for the evening if she wanted it. She wasn't desperate. And she didn't need to be chasing someone who clearly didn't want to give her the time of day.

Her phone rang, and it took her a moment to realize Terri was calling her back. She answered on the second ring, her heart racing.

"Sam?"

"Hi." *Think.* But all thoughts had slipped out of her mind with the sound of Terri's voice.

"Did you mean to call me?"

"Yeah. Sort of. I mean, not sort of. I meant to call. But now I'm thinking it was probably a bad idea. Well, I knew it was a bad idea before." Sam paced in a circle in front of the dance studio.

She needed to sound intelligent ten seconds ago. "I didn't ask Reed for your number. She texted it to me, but I told her not to. Not because I didn't want it, but because you didn't give it to me. So I wasn't going to call because you didn't give me your number and I didn't ask. And I figured that you wouldn't want me to call but then—"

"Okay, stop." Terri laughed. "You know how you said you were cool?"

"Actually I said I'm really not cool." At least Terri was laughing. That was something.

"Reed texted me your number too. That's how I knew it was you."

"Oh. Right."

"Did you have something you wanted to say?"

"Yeah. I did. I still do." Sam stopped pacing, wishing she'd planned out what to say before she'd tried calling. "It's a nice night and I don't want it to be over yet. I thought maybe… maybe you'd want to meet up after you finish whatever you need to do at the hospital."

There was a long pause before Terri said, "What time is it?"

"Quarter to nine."

"Does that mean our free hour is up?"

"Ten minutes ago." Sam wished she'd made better use of that time.

"Tonight was fun. But I meant what I said."

"The part about me not being cool or the part about you not socializing with residents?" When Terri didn't answer, Sam knew. "I should have called ten minutes ago, huh?"

"Reed shouldn't have given you my number."

Sam wanted to say that there were a lot of things people shouldn't do but did anyway. But the words didn't come out.

"I have to go, Sam. I'll see you around."

For a long moment after Terri ended the call, Sam stared at the screen. There would have been no point in asking her out to dinner, but she wished that she had anyway. And it was too late to argue that she was only a resident for another two years. She had to forget about a date and go back to referring to Terri as Dr. Anderson.

Before she'd made it to her car, her phone beeped with a text. She immediately hoped it was Terri. It wasn't.

Megan: *Can I have you tonight?*

Megan's timing was either shitty or perfect. Sam drummed her fingers on the side of the phone, debating her answer. She might be terrible company, thinking of Terri the whole time. Or maybe Megan would manage to get Terri off her mind for a while. Either way, she wouldn't hurt Megan's feelings.

All Megan wanted was no-strings-attached sex. Wanting more than that felt ridiculous, but Sam couldn't help it. The same rule applied to so many things. She didn't want what everyone thought she should want. No matter how hard she tried.

CHAPTER THREE

Aside from feeling like she was walking on eggshells, the first day with Elizabeth Samuels on her team went perfectly. As did the day after. Terri found herself relaxing when a week passed without any mention of the dance class or any mention of the phone call afterward. Well, she'd relaxed as much as she could around someone who made her distracted with one look. She got through each day by keeping a razor-sharp focus on their cases and was quickly impressed when Sam did the same.

So, two weeks in, the bouquet of flowers in front of her office completely blindsided her. Terri unlocked the door and picked up the vase, unable to help herself from admiring the delicate purple irises interspersed with daisies and a handful of sunset-colored calla lilies. Simply put, they were gorgeous.

McReynolds had the office next to hers, and he'd already informed her that he'd spotted Samuels delivering the flowers. Terri didn't respond to his questioning smile and instead asked if he had settled on his choice of vacation days. The distraction tactic had worked, and McReynolds was back in his office with the door closed, probably thinking of his plans for Tahiti in January.

She set the arrangement on her desk and the space immediately brightened as if she'd thrown open a curtain. Fortunately it wasn't a dozen long-stemmed red roses. But still. What the hell was she going to say to Sam?

Forcing away the impulse to check for a card, she put her purse in the usual drawer and then reached for the desk phone to check voice mail. Surprisingly, she had no messages. She hung up the line and pulled the vase closer, poking through the leaves to find a card. Nothing. She pushed the vase to the other side of her computer and sat down in her chair.

"Knock, knock."

Terri looked up to see Reed's outline in the doorway. She blamed the flowers for the fact that she'd completely forgotten to close the door. At least it was only Reed. Anyone else would have gotten the stink-eye for bothering her before seven. "Hey."

"Nice flowers. Got a minute?"

"For you I always have a minute. What's up?" Hopefully Reed wouldn't ask where the flowers had come from, but at least she could honestly say they didn't come with a card.

Reed held up a sticky note. "Julia put this on my morning coffee. She said I had to give it to you first thing."

Terri reached for the note and smiled. It was a drawing of a kidney complete with anatomic labels for the different parts. A cartoon heart had been added around it and "Thank you" was written in bubble letters below. "I'm guessing this is from Carly?"

Reed nodded.

"She's got mad skills with crayons."

"You're the one with the mad skills." Reed paused. "Sometimes I scoop her up to give her a hug and it hits me how close I came to losing her. You have no idea how many times I've silently thanked you."

"You thanked me enough when it happened. And you know I would have given her my own kidney if it would've helped. I love Carly. Both of your kids." Terri had treated Carly a few years back and she loved the thank you notes she still got. Nothing was better than a note from a kid she'd helped. "Tell her I'm impressed she remembered the renal artery and vein."

"I will. By the way, she keeps bugging me about having you over for a barbeque."

"Carly does?"

"Apparently you told her you liked barbeques. I'm sure it was months ago, but that kid doesn't forget a damn thing. Anyway, I was thinking next Sunday could work. Not this weekend—we're going down to see Mo and Kate at their new place."

Terri had a vague recollection of a conversation with Carly about liking barbequed chicken. Clearly Carly had misunderstood her, but now she was stuck. A barbeque at Reed's was a half-day project. "Reed, my schedule is a nightmare for the next month."

Reed nodded as if she'd expected Terri to decline.

"Can I let you know?"

"I should make you tell Carly that."

Terri sighed. "You know how crazy work is right now."

"I know. And I also know you can't be at work every day. It's not good for you." Reed glanced at the flowers. "Were those delivered? It's a wonder they got past the front desk."

Terri didn't say she knew whoever had brought them had snuck them in. A delivery person wouldn't have access to the sixth floor in the first place. "What can I bring?"

"To the barbeque?"

"Don't act so surprised. Yes, to the barbeque." Terri stuck the kidney picture to her file cabinet. "It's been too long since I've seen Carly and Bryn. I miss your kids."

Reed's smile stretched across her face. "They're gonna be so happy. Maybe you can come over early and help chop stuff? Oh, if you have an extra stethoscope, bring that. Not your favorite one. The girls made up a new variation on the telephone game. It's hilarious."

"I can't wait." Now that she'd made the decision she already was looking forward to it. Reed was right. She shouldn't be at work every day. She could take a Sunday off.

Reed closed the door on her way out and Terri leaned back in her seat. She eyed the flowers again. What was Sam thinking giving her flowers? *Samuels, not Sam,* she reminded herself. She'd been censoring herself since the ballroom dance class but now that they were working together, she couldn't allow any slips.

It was impossible to deny the attraction she felt to Sam. She noticed her as soon as she walked into a room. The scent of Sam's cologne wasn't strong, but it was distinctly her, with a hint of leather and vanilla. And something earthy that Terri couldn't put her finger on. Whatever it was, Sam smelled delicious and had caught Terri off-guard more than once. She also managed to look sexy every damn day. Even at the end of a long shift. Her messy haircut only got more disheveled, her eyes a little heavy-lidded, and her scrubs wrinkled. For better or worse, that only made Terri think of what she'd look like after a night together.

But so far Sam had done nothing to make her worry about the chemistry between them. She conducted herself like all the other residents—always respectful and carefully distant. And she couldn't deny that Sam was one of the best residents she'd come across in years.

Being smart got a resident points but with Sam that was only the beginning. She instinctively knew how to talk to patients, quickly winning over their trust, and she always did her homework on her cases. Even in stressful situations, she remained calm. And not once had Terri heard her complain about putting in the hours. She charmed the staff, including some of the tougher nurses, and the other residents clearly liked her.

Dammit, why had she brought flowers?

Terri brushed her fingertip along the silky smooth edge of a calla lily. She could pretend she hadn't gotten the flowers or she could casually say thank you. Maybe Sam would get the hint without a big conversation about it? There was a slim chance the flowers had come from someone else and Sam had only delivered them to her door, but Terri couldn't think of who.

A knock sounded and Terri felt the heat rise to her cheeks. Would Sam drop by uninvited? "Come in."

David Weiss smiled over his coffee cup. "Morning, Terri. I was on my way to the break room for a donut, but I saw Reed pop out of your office and thought I'd bother you as well."

"It's not a bother at all." Terri stood up. As head of the hospital, Weiss was technically her boss. She couldn't exactly tell him to buzz off even if her thoughts were completely distracted from work. She motioned to the chair opposite her desk, and Weiss sank heavily into it.

"I don't need the calories, but have you tried those vending machine donuts?"

"Yes. They're addictive." Terri sat back down, wondering what Weiss could possibly want. She respected Weiss and had, more than once, sought out his advice. But he rarely came looking for her.

After they'd exhausted the subject of the weather and updates on his grandchildren, Weiss cleared his throat and said, "So, how's Elizabeth doing?"

It took Terri a moment to realize Weiss was talking about Sam. *Samuels.* "She's doing well. Why do you ask?"

Sam had mentioned a connection with Weiss, but she couldn't recall the details now. It certainly wasn't standard for Weiss to ask about a resident. Weiss rubbed his gray-whiskered chin.

"Maybe before I tell you, I should say Elizabeth received no special favors. In fact I didn't know she'd matched here until all was said and done. That said, I was good friends with Elizabeth's grandfather. Al and I were in med school together back in the age of the dinosaurs."

Weiss clasped his hands over his belly. "After we graduated, Al started a family practice down in San Jose, and well, you know what happened to me. Probably would have lost touch, but our wives were friends and soon we both had kids. Before you know it, the kids were grown and grandkids were on the way.

"When I heard Elizabeth matched here, I gave her a call. Told her how much I admired her grandfather and how I missed him." Weiss paused. "He passed away a few years before she started med school. I know he was a big reason she went into this…but she's told me she's had second thoughts along the way. She took several years off after college, and even after she started the residency, she said she wasn't certain medicine was a fit."

"I'm surprised to hear that." Blown away was more like it. "She said she wanted to do family practice. She seems perfect for it."

"I agree." Weiss sighed. "And I thought she'd finally gotten past her hesitations. Then last week she came to talk to me. Said she didn't want to disappoint anyone, but she wasn't sure she should finish the residency. We had a long talk and I thought I'd changed her mind. But I got an email from her last night."

"She's quitting?"

"Effective January first." Weiss cleared his throat. "Now I'm not asking you to make any allowances. You've got a well-earned reputation for expecting your residents to be top-notch. We both know how much they learn because of that. And I know she respects you. She said as much in the email. Which is why I was thinking maybe you could talk to her."

Respect? Well, Terri would take that over other things that Sam could have told Weiss. But it didn't make sense that Sam could be considering leaving the residency. In fact, the thought of it made her sick. Had she been pushing too hard? Certainly she'd held Sam to a higher standard, but that was only because she was clearly a rock star.

"But she already gave you notice."

"Yes…and I think someone could still change her mind."

Someone. But should it be her? She couldn't exactly explain to Weiss the possible conflict of interest if she directly asked Sam to stay.

"She keeps surprising me by how good she is." Terri shook her head. "But I will say, she works longer hours than almost everyone else. And she never gives less than a hundred percent. It could be burnout." It wasn't unheard of. Residents worked longer hours than anyone else in the hospital; more often than not it was sheer exhaustion that broke them.

Weiss nodded. "I suggested she take some time off. She wasn't interested. Said she didn't want to let anyone down."

"Quitting the residency would let more people down."

"And I'd be letting her grandfather down. Carol and I had her over to the house for dinner when she first started here. She's a lovely young woman and would make an excellent physician. I know her grandfather's practice is holding a position for her."

"If she leaves the residency, she throws away her whole career." And for what reason?

"So you'll talk to her?"

Terri had looked over her file. There was nothing to suggest Sam hadn't earned her spot in a competitive residency through her own merit and she was nearly halfway done with perfect reviews so far. It didn't make sense. Personal issues aside, she couldn't live with herself if she didn't at least try to convince Sam not to quit.

"I'll talk to her. I'm not saying I can convince her, but I'll try."

"Maybe remind her there's life after she finishes here."

Not that the pressure would be any less once she had her own practice, but at least the hours were more manageable. Terri had a clear memory only of the sheer exhaustion of her residency years. Yes, she clocked more hours in bed now, but the responsibilities had only grown.

"And if there's anything you need from me, schedule changes or whatever, let me know." Weiss reached for his coffee and stood, signaling the end of their meeting. "Turns out I still want those sinful powdery donuts."

"Take the stairs to run off the sugar."

Weiss chuckled. "Thanks for the advice, doc."

* * *

There was no opportunity to pull Sam aside after rounds. A patient in the ER had pulled a gun on a nurse and the whole hospital went on lockdown. Even after the cops had settled everything, excess adrenaline seemed to waft through the air.

The staff teetered on edge, and Terri had to step in on more than one argument.

That on top of a full caseload meant no one left early. Terri tried to keep her crew focused, but she wasn't exactly on it herself. She couldn't wrap her mind around why Sam wanted to quit. Sure, it wasn't unheard of for residents to make that decision, but red flags were usually easy to see. She'd been paying plenty of attention and hadn't noticed anything to suggest that Sam wasn't happy. The more she tried to rationalize what might be going on, the more she wanted a chance to talk privately with Sam.

It wasn't until evening that she found Sam alone. Terri had sent everyone to grab food before evening rounds, and she spotted Sam in the cafeteria waiting in line to pay for a sandwich. As soon as she noticed Sam, she headed right toward her, practicing the lines she'd thought of earlier: *We need to talk. Can you come to my office later?*

Terri was nearly to the sandwich line when she saw Megan Gresham walk up to Sam. Gresham was another resident and had been on Terri's team up until a few weeks ago. Terri didn't usually have a problem with residents getting friendly, but she felt a sting when Gresham not-so-subtly caressed the low of Sam's back.

Terri immediately turned toward the line for the grill. Suddenly she needed fries and a burger more than a sandwich. It was ridiculous to be jealous and yet the feeling was there all the same. Gresham was practically a kid. Maybe twenty-seven at most. If Megan Gresham was her type, no way was Sam into her. Not that her attraction mattered since nothing could happen. *But still.* She placed her order, deliberately avoiding any look back at the sandwich line, and then checked her phone while she waited.

"Dr. Anderson?"

Terri looked up from the screen. Probably Sam had seen her approach earlier and was wondering why she'd abruptly changed direction. "Yes?"

"I dropped off some flowers at your office this morning, but I forgot all about the card." She held out an envelope.

Terri wondered at the fancy handwriting on the envelope. Swirly cursive wasn't what she'd expected from Sam. "The flowers were beautiful. Are beautiful. McReynolds mentioned you'd left them, but I didn't say anything because…well…I wasn't exactly sure why you'd give me flowers."

"Oh, they aren't from me. You remember the Cortez family? Roberto left yesterday. His parents were so happy they wanted to thank you in person, but by the time we got discharge papers ready, you'd already left for the night. When they said they had flowers for you, I didn't have the heart to tell them flowers weren't allowed. I snuck them into my locker last night and then slipped them up to your office this morning."

"That's sweet of Roberto's folks." Terri knew her face was flushed. She felt like an idiot for thinking the flowers were from Sam. "But you deserved the flowers. You spent way more time with them than I did."

"I was happy with hugs. I'm not really a flower person." Sam scrunched up her face.

If Sam was going to let her off the hook about thinking the flowers were from her, she had to roll with it. "You know, taking flowers from a patient's family wouldn't mean you lose your butch card."

"I think that depends on who you ask." Sam smiled.

Since Sam had joined her team, Terri had successfully guarded against any interactions that might be perceived as flirtatious. She knew she was walking a fine line now, but the whole situation was already weird.

"I should probably go get my dinner before they give it away," Sam said, nodding at the sandwich counter.

"Enjoy your meal." Terri thought of the conversation she'd had with Weiss and added, "Oh, can you stop by my office before you leave tonight?"

"Uh, sure." Sam paused. "Did I do something wrong?"

Behind Terri, a cook called out: "Turkey burger and fries?"

Terri glanced at the counter and then back at Sam. "That's mine. You didn't do anything wrong."

"You use that same tone with the interns when they screw something up."

Terri met Sam's gaze. The stirring in her body reminded her she had to tread carefully. "We'll talk about it."

Sam didn't seem satisfied with Terri's answer but said, "Okay, I'll wait for you after rounds then. In your office?"

When Sam restated it, the request sounded almost inappropriate. But Terri nodded, reminding herself that nothing inappropriate was going to happen. The fact that she was asking a resident up to her office for a private meeting might be an issue for her, but Weiss had asked for her help and she had an obligation to him.

"If tonight's a problem for you, we can set up a different time."

"No. Tonight's fine. I'll be there."

Terri didn't let herself watch Sam return to the table where Megan Gresham was waiting. She picked up her food and made a beeline out of the cafeteria. Under most circumstances she didn't have a problem with PDA. The fact that she didn't want to see it now was proof that she cared if Sam had a girlfriend.

CHAPTER FOUR

Sam picked at her sandwich. Normally the cafeteria food tasted decent, but she had no appetite for it now. Instead of eating, she wanted to curl up in a ball and close her eyes.

Sleep sounded so tempting. Lately every night she'd hit her mattress with her shoes still on, only to wake up in the same position with the alarm ringing. She couldn't remember the last time she'd slept for more than five hours. But exhaustion had nothing to do with why she wanted the escape of sleep now. For once she longed to simply be tired.

Weiss hadn't replied to her. After she'd sent the email, she'd tried to push her decision out of her mind along with all the ramifications that came with it. Everything had hit her like a rock when the Cortez family had all hugged her. They were too generous with their praise. She wasn't as good as they thought, but she stopped herself from saying that. Already the guilt was threatening to make her change her mind.

And now Terri Anderson wanted to talk to her. Sam racked her mind for what she could have done wrong—or what else

Terri could have heard. But she knew it had to be about the email. Weiss must have passed on the news.

The question now was how much to tell Terri. Admittedly, there were parts of being a doctor that she liked. But her reasons for going to med school in the first place had been suspect at best, and she couldn't follow through on a career that felt like a life sentence. Not now. Not after all the things she'd learned about her grandfather. She wasn't ready to talk about that, however, and Terri didn't need to know details. She'd keep it simple. Anyway, none of it would affect Terri. She'd committed to staying another four months and she'd be off Terri's schedule in two weeks.

"I heard Jerry finally had to do an enema. Got totally sprayed and then had a breakdown about it." Megan popped a chip in her mouth and crunched. "He acts like an entitled toddler sometimes. I don't know what Ellie sees in him."

Sam hadn't told Megan about her decision. She hadn't told anyone except Weiss. "It's a little messed up that we joke about enemas over dinner. You know that, right?"

Megan grinned. "We could talk about other things that involve lube."

"Do you ever not think about sex?"

"Hmm. Let me think. No." Megan held two curved potato chips together. "What does this look like to you?"

"A duck bill?"

"It's a vulva. Can't you see it?" Megan turned it to show off a different angle. "I figured you'd be all over that considering how much you like to eat out."

Sam pushed away the chips, shaking her head as Megan held them up closer. "You act like a sixteen-year-old boy sometimes."

"Lucky for you, I'm twenty-six. Otherwise you'd have a lot of explaining to do." Megan crunched the chips. "Speaking of, I think you need to get laid more often."

"More often than every other night?" Sam reached over and snagged a chip off Megan's plate. "Sex doesn't fix everything."

"But have you ever had sex with someone and felt worse after?"

"Yes."

Megan gave an exaggerated sigh. "I don't know what's up with you lately. You've been acting like someone took your dog to the pound."

"Which would suck—if I had a dog." And since when was Megan perceptive? Maybe Sam hadn't been pretending everything was fine quite as well as she'd thought. "I'm tired. That's all."

"Well, I know where you could sleep. Wanna drop by tonight?"

Sam shook her head. "I need sleep more than sex. I've finally reached that turning point."

"That may be the saddest thing I've heard all day. So this is what happens in your thirties, huh?"

Sam nodded. "And I have to meet with Dr. Anderson after rounds."

"Tonight? Why?"

"She wouldn't tell me."

Megan crunched another chip. "Maybe she finally figured out you have a mad crush on her."

"I don't have a crush." Sam shifted back in her seat as she ran her hand through her hair. Megan didn't know about the ballroom dance class or that Terri had already soundly turned her down.

"You do that when you're lying." Megan mimed looking off to one side and then running her hand through her hair. Her eyes darted back to Sam's with a knowing smile. "Liar."

"Okay, maybe I'm attracted to her. And you've got a thing for Shellhammer in ICU. It doesn't mean that either of us are gonna get lucky."

Megan laughed. "I'd totally do Shellhammer. How'd you know?"

"It's obvious. You hover in ICU whenever he's around and bat your eyes any chance you get."

"I wouldn't actually date him. It'd only be about sex if something happened. Wait, are you jealous?"

"No." Sam wasn't. If Megan started sleeping with him, however, it would end their arrangement. "But tell me before anything happens."

"I will. And you'll tell me before you sleep with Dr. Anderson, right?"

"That's not happening. But you know I wouldn't break our rule." The beauty of what they had partly came from both of them being honest about it. Since neither of them had anyone else at the moment, they kept each other company. Once that changed, they'd agreed to move on without any hard feelings. Or STDs. Sam glanced at her watch.

"Shit, it's almost eight. I've gotta go." She downed the last sip of soda and stood up. "See you tomorrow night?"

Megan shrugged. "If I don't have a new fuck buddy by then. Clearly I need someone hornier than you."

"Clearly." Sam chuckled as Megan stuck out her tongue.

Rounds lasted way too long. Terri insisted on morning and evening rounds in addition to the midday Grand Rounds that all residents attended and then allowed extra time for anyone to ask questions. Most of the time Sam appreciated her thoroughness. No patients slipped through the cracks. But tonight Sam couldn't focus and kept eyeing the clock on the wall. She wanted the conversation with Terri to be over and done with so the knot in her stomach would finally go away.

It was close to ten by the time the last question had been asked and the other residents filed out of the break room, most of them stifling yawns or rubbing their eyes. Sam hung back, waiting for Terri to look her way.

"Want to head up to my office now?" Terri pointed at the chart in Sam's hands. "Or do you have things to finish up still?"

Sam wished she had a patient to check on or paperwork to complete. Anything to get her out of the conversation. But knowing Terri, she'd only stay late waiting for her.

She hung the chart on the wall along with the others and faced Terri. "I'm ready."

They didn't talk as they rode the elevator up and no one got on with them. The silence only messed with Sam's head more. She stared at the silver door, willing some emergency to stop them. But at nearly ten o'clock on a Thursday evening, the place was finally quiet.

When the door opened, Terri stepped out first. Sam followed her down the hall. Over fifteen hours ago she'd been in the same hallway holding the Cortez flowers. She'd thought then of how much she'd love to be bringing Terri flowers that she'd picked out herself. Of course she couldn't do that but the thought reminded her how her attraction wasn't going anywhere. She could long for her all she wanted, find countless ways to fall harder for her, but Terri's answer wouldn't change.

Terri unlocked the office door, walked in, slipped off her stethoscope, and pointed to a chair. "Have a seat."

Sam sat, watching Terri take off her ever-present white lab coat and hang it with the stethoscope. Toned, slim frame, every movement perfectly controlled. The coat concealed her tattoos and even though Sam had already seen the artwork, had already brushed her hand over the skin, she found herself staring. God, she was beautiful.

"You seemed surprised earlier that I'd want to talk to you, but I'm wondering if you figured out why. You were pretty quiet all through rounds."

Terri's words snapped Sam back to reality. She was in Terri's office for one reason only. "I'm guessing Weiss talked to you."

Terri nodded. "But honestly I don't understand." She sat down—not in the seat behind the desk where she would be far enough away that Sam could pretend this was only a professional meeting—but on the desk itself and only a few feet away. "So. Tell me. What's going on in your head, Samuels?"

It was one thing writing the email to Weiss, but saying it all aloud would mean it was real. She was going through with it. On one hand, there was relief. On the other, regret was already stalking her. But was it regret that she'd gone to med school at all? Or regret that she was quitting with so many of the boxes already checked?

"I'm leaving January 1st." She needed to cut to the chase. The last thing she wanted was for Terri to try talking her out of her plan and the more details she knew, the harder she'd try to do exactly that. "I want to make sure I don't mess up anyone's holiday plans and I'm already committed on the schedule through the New Year."

"So you'll be quitting the residency when you'll only have a year and a half remaining?"

"And I've told Weiss how sorry I am to be letting everyone down," Sam added.

"Sounds like you've already made up your mind on this." Terri exhaled. "I take it there's nothing I can say that will make you reconsider?"

Sam hesitated. The way Terri was looking at her, a mix of disappointment and anger but obvious desire too, made Sam think all over again that she was making a mistake. She wished Weiss hadn't told Terri. Or that she'd waited two weeks to send the email. Then Terri wouldn't be the one she was letting down. By then she'd be working with a different attending—one she wasn't impossibly attracted to. And yet she hadn't been able to wait another second. The decision had been eating up all of her thoughts, and she'd hardly been able to concentrate on her cases.

"This has been a long time coming." That statement simplified things, but she didn't need to tell Terri the more complicated version. Up until a few weeks ago, she'd been committed to becoming a doctor and following her grandfather's plan, even if it wasn't ever what she wanted for her life. She'd had plenty of doubts, but she'd ignored them for the most part. Then everything had come crashing down.

She'd had a weekend off after her rotation in Radiology and before starting on Med-Peds. Instead of staying in town, she'd driven down to her beach house—her grandmother's beach house that was now hers. One box of letters with one folder of receipts. That's all it took. If she'd never seen the proof of who her grandfather really was, she'd still be trying to live up to his expectations.

"You're throwing away your entire career." Terri's voice raised, and her anger hit Sam like a slap. "What the fuck are you thinking?"

Sam straightened up and, fighting the impulse to match Terri's volume, said quietly, "Dr. Anderson, you have no idea what I'm throwing away. It's a lot more than a career."

Terri muttered something about a waste of time, and Sam had the insane desire to stand up, kiss her, and then walk out. But instead she held Terri's gaze, facing down all the anger she saw reflected. In the past few weeks she'd seen Terri get mad more than once and certainly heard her swear. She wasn't a prude. But she'd only sworn at herself or when the system let her down. Lab results taking too long. A diagnosis of cancer when she'd been hoping for infection. Insurance not covering a medication she needed to prescribe. This was different.

"Tell me you've got one hell of a reason."

"I've got one hell of a reason." This was her choice. What anyone else thought didn't matter.

"You could take time off. I looked over your file. Your reviews have all been glowing. But you haven't requested any vacation. You're allotted four weeks that you can use at any point during the residency."

"If I take any of those weeks off, I won't come back."

"Why not?"

Sam shook her head. While it was true she didn't owe Terri an explanation, she also didn't know where she could even start. That this wasn't her dream was the easiest answer. But it wasn't about dreams anymore. She couldn't keep putting everything else she wanted on hold for something she'd never wanted at all. Seconds stretched into at least a minute and still Terri waited. Sam had to give her credit for being stubborn, but it wouldn't change anything.

"No answer, huh?" Terri's steely gaze bored through Sam. "Then I guess we're done here."

She pushed off the desk and stood up. She was close enough that she could have touched Sam, and for one crazy moment, it seemed like she might. Sam didn't breathe. Terri had to know how much she wanted to reach for her. A long second passed and then Terri walked around to the other side of the desk and sat down.

Sam stood. "I'll see you at morning rounds?"

Terri didn't respond. She didn't even look up at her. The jaw muscles in her face clenched.

"I'm sorry."

"Don't apologize to me. This is your life you're fucking up, not mine."

Sam took the stairs instead of the elevator, on the off chance she'd see someone she knew. All she wanted was to be in her bed already asleep. Then she wouldn't have to think, wouldn't second guess. Tomorrow would be a repeat of today, but now at least there was an end in sight. January 1st.

CHAPTER FIVE

"Who gets up at five in the morning to work out?" Terri held her plank position, sweat dripping on the mat under her.

"We do." Julia grunted. "Some people like working out early."

"Freaks of nature."

Julia dropped onto her knees with a grin. "My thoughts exactly. And you don't even like yoga. What happened to the spin class you were taking?"

"I still go on Saturdays. But I can't swing a six o'clock start through the week." Terri glanced at the instructor and changed her position. "I need time for a shower before rounds."

Julia looked sideways at Terri. "Are you engaging your core?"

Terri stuck out her tongue. "Thanks for the reminder." She tensed her abdomen and scowled at the blue mat. Lately her yoga mat was seeing more action than her bed. She'd convinced herself she was okay with her paltry sex life until Sam had appeared on the scene. *Samuels*. And God what a mess that turned into.

Since their conversation a week ago, someone had kidnapped her rock star resident and handed her back a facsimile that was a total dud. If she didn't know, she would have wondered what the hell had happened. Before she'd described Sam as brilliant and meticulous. Now distracted and sloppy fit better.

True, she'd only dropped the ball on little things so far—forgetting to order morning labs on a stable patient being the worst of it—but it was the "so far" part that gnawed at Terri. She had a bad feeling that something critical would be missed before Sam woke up and realized the mistake she was making.

In some ways, she wished Sam hadn't committed to staying on to the end of the year. If she wanted to quit, why not give two weeks' notice and walk out? As it was, she had one foot in the door and one foot out. Nothing could be more frustrating. Well, there was one thing—how her body still responded when Sam walked into the room. She hated that the attraction hadn't ebbed despite everything.

"You okay over there?" Julia whispered. "Get stuck in downward dog?"

Terri glanced from Julia to the front of the class and quickly dropped onto her butt. She reached for her toes and mouthed, "Thank you."

From what she could tell, Sam hadn't told anyone else about quitting. The news would have run through the hospital if she had. At least the other residents would be talking about it, and Terri had enough experience with gossip to always have one ear on the ground. But everyone around Sam acted as if nothing had changed.

During rounds she'd come up with a perfect plan for a case that had stumped everyone else, and then a half hour later Terri would catch her staring out a window as if she was already on the other side of it. Terri could deal with know-it-alls and she'd had her fair share of hotheads. But smart people who weren't focused didn't belong practicing medicine, and she certainly didn't want to carry them on her team.

She went back and forth on telling Sam to leave now, but she was still holding out hope that she'd snap out of her funk. But maybe that line of thought was her own mistake.

"Where are you today?" Julia whispered.

"Already at work apparently," Terri said drily. She'd missed another move.

Unfortunately, the class had moved onto a pelvic lift. Engaging her thighs while she lay on her back with her hips jutted up in the air didn't help get thoughts of Sam out of her mind. She tried to focus on the ceiling fan. Sam had a little over a week left on her rotation. Then she'd move on to be someone else's headache. If only she could simply feel good about that.

* * *

As it turned out, yoga was the bright spot of the day. Considering how poorly that had gone, Terri decided she should have given up then and gone back to bed. Instead she'd dutifully gone to work. Could she call in sick now? She certainly felt sick.

Even before she reviewed the chart, she knew what had gone wrong. A simple miscalculation. She also didn't need to be told who had written the orders. And now that she'd made certain the patient was stable—the seven-year-old boy snoozed with his grandmother on one side of the bed and his mother on the other—she wasn't going to wait on delivering her reckoning.

Terri stopped at the nurses' station and JoAnne looked up without smiling. "Yes?"

That was JoAnne, all business, no humor. Thank God she'd been the one to double check the dose of insulin before loading the syringe pump. "Thank you. You know how badly that could have gone."

"Only doing my job," JoAnne returned.

"Well, I appreciate how well you do it. He's sleeping now. Can you buzz me when he wakes?"

"You got it." JoAnne checked her watch and then added a note to the record. "Should I let Dr. Samuels know as well? She's asked to be notified of any developments."

"Please do. But tell me first." She couldn't let another screwup happen.

JoAnne gave one cursory nod and turned back to her chart. Crisis averted, she had other fires to tend.

Terri, however, wasn't done with this particular blaze. She headed for the elevator, her brain still churning with all the what-ifs. JoAnne had caught the error; no overdose had been administered. But what if it'd been an inexperienced nurse who only followed what Sam had ordered? Terri fully intended on asking Sam that question. If Sam knew what was good for her, she'd be waiting in the office as requested with an apology on her lips.

Goddammit. She'd seen this coming. Not this mistake exactly but something big. She'd even considered pulling Sam aside that morning and telling her to get her head back in the game or leave. And if she'd been treating her like any other resident, she'd have done exactly that. Which was why she shared in the blame now. She'd known better.

The elevator pinged and she stepped inside, grateful for a moment alone. She took a deep breath. Her wrath had gotten her as far as pounding out a text to Sam with a quick rundown on the case, where she'd screwed up, and a clear command to be in the Residents' Office in twenty minutes. But now she needed a plan. What exactly should she say? That she didn't deserve to be practicing medicine if she didn't double check her damn math? Everyone made mistakes. Everyone. Including her.

The elevator opened on the seventh floor and Terri stepped out. No patients were on the seventh floor and she had a break from nurses with questions as well. She made her way past the admin offices and hoped she'd clear the conference room without seeing any other docs wanting to chat. Until she saw Sam's face and gauged how contrite she was about this mess, she couldn't think about anything else.

"Hey." Reed stopped mid-stride. "What are you doing all the way up in my world? And why do you look like you're about to throat punch someone?"

"I'd never do that. The bruise would be way too visible."

Reed laughed and Terri felt her anger drop a notch. She exhaled. Leave it to Reed to know exactly what to say. "I wish I could say I was coming to hang out with you. I have to go yell at one of my residents. You heading home already?"

"I promised Julia I'd be home in time for dinner. She mentioned she saw you in yoga this morning. Said you seemed a little distracted."

"You'd be distracted too. Five a.m. and a bunch of sweaty yoga butts?"

"Depends entirely on the butt." Reed grinned. "But that is early even for a cute butt. We still on for this Sunday?"

"Sunday?"

"Barbeque. Remember? You're coming over early to entertain the kiddos. Or help me make kabobs. I invited Sam too. Hope that's okay. She's off your service at the end of this week anyway, right?"

"No. She's got one more week." Unless she decided to quit early. But Terri didn't want her to quit. Not really. "I wish you hadn't invited her."

Reed scratched her head. "If you want I'll un-invite her."

"Don't do that. It'll be fine." After all, she'd survived dancing. Certainly a barbeque would be less intimate. But tonight was a perfect example of why she needed careful lines between socializing and work.

"So I take it things aren't going well?"

Terri sighed. "I'm starting to think of her as an attractive stomach ulcer."

"At least you're admitting you're into her."

"It's not happening." Terri wanted to say more, but she resisted. Reed didn't know about Sam leaving. She'd kept it to herself partly because she still hoped Sam would change her mind. The note she'd sent to Weiss only said that the conversation hadn't gone well, but she wasn't ready to give up yet. But after today… "The truth is, having her on my team hasn't been all roses."

"She's sharp, but she needs someone tough like you to ride her ass."

Is that what Sam needed? Terri wasn't certain of anything anymore. And as much as she'd been ready to have it out with Sam earlier, both about the case and her attitude, now she only wanted to delay the inevitable. "How's the rest of the wedding prep going?"

"I had no idea it was going to be so much work. There's all these little details… At least we got Sam nailed down as our photographer. She showed me some of her stuff online. She's amazing. All this artsy stuff. I had no idea. Honestly, I think she could be big if she stuck with it."

"Do you think she made a mistake going into medicine instead?" Terri had gone through all the possible reasons of why Sam could have had a change of heart about the career, but nothing made sense. Why come this far and then quit?

Reed's forehead creased. "No, of course not. She can always do the photography on the side. Plenty of us have hobbies. Even you. Although does work really count as a hobby?"

"Trust me, I'd like to have other hobbies."

"Sam could be a hobby."

"A person can't be a hobby. Besides, she's my resident." And at the moment she needed to focus on giving her a lecture about insulin.

"I know I'm probably pushing too hard. But, seriously, what's your hang-up with her? Is it because of everything with Kayla?"

Terri had mostly pushed the fiasco called her second marriage out of her mind, but not enough time had passed to where she could laugh it off. "I need to keep work separate from my social life."

"But you're always at work. You can't keep holding yourself back from another relationship." Another doctor passed in the hall, and Reed waited until she was out of earshot to add, "Even if it's not happening with you and Sam, my point is, you need to start dating again. You'd be happier with someone."

"That's arguable."

"Okay, fine. We can argue it later. I'll let you go for now." Reed opened her arms. "Quick hug."

Terri stepped into the hug, thankful that Reed knew what she needed even if she'd never admit it. She exhaled, enjoying the sensation of being held, but stepping back before her emotions got to her. "Thanks for being you. Especially tonight."

"Whatever you have to tell Sam, go easy. You always take it harder than your residents."

"How'd you know it was her that I have to talk to?"

Reed shrugged. "Lucky guess."

Terri watched Reed leave, wishing she could follow. Instead, she had to deal with Sam. She started for the Residents' Office, but her phone rang before she made it two steps.

"What's up?"

"You still here or did you blow this popsicle stand?" Travis Shellhammer's drawl made it sound like they were all at a medic outpost in an old Western movie.

"I'm here."

"Got a case I was hoping you'd take a look at. Only if you have time though. I think I saw McReynolds around somewhere…"

"He already left. How critical?"

"Well, we're not bleeding out, but we don't look good."

From Shellhammer, that was saying a lot. Terri didn't know how long the conversation with Samuels would take, but she doubted she'd be up for going back to ICU after. "I'll be right there."

She sent a quick text to Sam explaining the delay and then turned back to the elevator. Tonight was long from being over.

CHAPTER SIX

Waiting in the principal's office had felt a lot like this. Sam remembered the first time she'd landed herself there. She was eight and the agony of waiting eclipsed all else that followed. Her mistake then had seemed monumental—she'd kissed Jennifer Livingston in front of half the playground. A teacher had seen them and called both girls over in the midst of hooting and jeers from their classmates.

Even before she'd heard the teacher's whistle, she'd realized that she should have waited until after school to lock lips. But a dare was a dare and she'd enjoyed the hell out of the kiss. So had Jennifer Livingston. And yet Jennifer had escaped punishment by claiming she hadn't known Sam was going to kiss her. She'd known all right. She'd been the one to offer the dare.

If only this was about a kiss. Sam's stomach rumbled. When had she last eaten? A bagel during rounds that morning? No, she'd had two Reese's peanut butter cups for lunch along with a third cup of coffee. Lately, that counted as a rounded meal.

She stared at the computer screen trying to recall the rule-outs for elevated potassium. Usually random facts like that were on instant recall, the page number of the textbook imprinted in her mind along with an image of a list and all she had to do was scroll down. But not tonight. *Hyperkalemia*. Why couldn't she think?

Something had happened the day she'd told Terri about her decision to quit. All the pages in her mind that she'd depended on had gone blank. It was as if she'd been released from all that burden. Unfortunately, that release came several months too early.

Ignoring another rumble from her belly, she pulled up the Internet. One more record and she'd be finished for the night. But what about Jack? She closed her eyes, remembering the little boy's face as he'd told her about making origami hats. God, what had she done?

As much as she'd wanted to charge down to the third floor where Jack and his family were, pull the chart and see her own notes, confirm that Dr. Anderson was right about the mistake she'd made, and then if so, apologize to everyone in the room, she hadn't done that. Instead she'd dutifully gone to the Residents' Office to wait.

Twenty minutes had never lasted so long and now she'd have to wait even longer. Terri's text had been brief: *Shellhammer needs me on a case. Give me another twenty minutes.* Of course whatever Shellhammer needed help with took precedence, but she wished Terri would at least tell her if Jack was okay.

And for once, the Residents' Office was deserted. Where the hell was everyone? Purgatory couldn't be this empty. She figured she wouldn't feel quite as sick if she could talk to someone about what had happened. But maybe talking about it would only make it worse.

She still hadn't told any of her friends that she was leaving. No one even knew the real reason why she'd gone to medical school. She'd made a habit of not talking about personal things and didn't want to start now. All she wanted to do was walk away. Disappear.

The door popped open and Sam immediately straightened, expecting Dr. Anderson.

Megan smiled. "There you are."

"You've been looking for me?"

"Always." Megan winked. "You're a breath of fresh air in this place. What are you doing tonight?"

"Megan-speak decoded: want to fuck?"

"You broke my super secret code?" Megan feigned a look of surprise. "You know I'll have to kill you now."

Sam didn't have the energy to laugh. And she definitely didn't have the energy for sex. "I appreciate the offer, but I've got records."

"If you keep turning me down, I'll start thinking it's me and not that you've gone celibate."

"Don't knock celibacy. We'd probably be a lot more productive if we didn't need to get laid." Sam finished typing and clicked on the search icon. "But it's not you. I promise."

Sex might relieve some tension, but her libido had gone missing. Even thinking about it sounded like too much work. And while sleeping with Megan had short-term benefits, lately it only left her aching for more.

Megan dropped into the seat next to Sam and peered over her arm at the computer screen. She smelled like strawberry bubblegum. "Why are you looking up hyperkalemia? Got a cool case?"

"Not really." Sam wondered if she could bring up Jack and her mistake and then decided against it. She ran her hands through her hair, knowing it was a disheveled mess. Along with a day off, she needed a shower. "Are you finished for the night?"

"Yep. Off early, but Miles wants us back here at six in the morning. Who has rounds before sunrise?" Megan grumbled. "So how's it going with you and your Dr. Hot-stuff Anderson?"

"It's not going." Sam eyed Megan. "But are we okay?"

"What do you mean?"

"You sound a little jealous."

"Whatever. I'm not jealous."

Sam had heard that "not jealous" line before and it usually meant exactly the opposite. Her arrangement with Megan didn't include emotional attachment, but she well knew how that could change for someone.

"We screw around," Megan said. "We're both in it for the same thing. That's why I'm not jealous."

Sam cocked her head. "Then why do you sound jealous?"

"'Cause someday I want someone to look at me the way you look at Dr. Anderson."

"How's that?"

"Like they want to fuck me senseless and worship me after. Not necessarily you someone, just someone." Megan shrugged. "Don't freak out on me, Samuels. We. Only. Fuck. We're on the same page."

"Okay. Not freaking out." Sam smiled at Megan's finger gestures depicting what they did in bed. She might be crass, and young, but she had a sweet side that she had trouble hiding for long. "All right, you can stop with the motions. I get the idea. You know, Charlie looks at you like he wants to worship you after a good—"

"Uh-uh. Nope. Not talking about Charlie until I'm done asking you about Terri Anderson. You sidetracked me there, but I have more questions. Are you still into her three weeks after having to put up with her attitude?"

"She's a hard ass, but she's almost always right. Everyone knows it. And she's the best internist here. I respect her."

"Respect, huh? Which is why you get those puppy dog eyes every time you see her in the hallway and your voice goes all funny?" Megan rolled her eyes when Sam started to argue. "Don't try to talk your way out of this. I've seen it more than once. And I've seen how she looks back at you."

"What do you mean?"

"She likes you."

"She puts up with me. Barely." When she'd started on Med-Peds, Sam thought Terri liked having her on her team. Terri had made it clear at the beginning that she wasn't going to cross any lines, but they seemed to at least have an understanding that there was something—chemistry or whatever—between them. But after Sam had told her she was quitting, that all vanished.

Terri's coldness had taken Sam by surprise. She'd tried to get back in her good graces only to screw up over and over again. And now Jack. Her mistake there wasn't little like the others and she figured there'd be no coming back from it. Terri might not even acknowledge her after she'd finished chewing her out.

"Maybe you should tell her how good you are under the covers."

"Not gonna happen. She'd never sleep with me."

"Never say never." Megan reached down to stroke a hand up Sam's thigh. "Do you think about her when we have sex?"

Sam pushed Megan's hand off. "Seriously, sometimes I wonder about you. Your relationship with sex is kind of messed up."

"There's a lot of things that are messed up about me. Why are you picking on sex?" Megan jabbed Sam's arm playfully. "All I'm saying is that I think she'd be into you if circumstances were different. You probably don't have much of a chance until after you finish your residency. She's no Dr. Copeland screwing in the OR. But I get why you're into her. She's hot for someone who's probably almost forty."

"Almost forty isn't that old."

"Speak for yourself." Megan pointed at herself. "Twenty-six, remember?"

"Right. You're a baby. This is why we have different ideas about sex."

"Says the geriatric thirty-one-year-old." Megan leaned over and kissed Sam's cheek.

The peck was quick, but it carried an obvious hint. Megan still wanted sex even if that was all that Sam could offer. "Geriatric might be going a little far."

"How about older and wiser?"

"That I'll take."

"Then lose those sad eyes and take me home. I'd love a good hard fuck from you tonight."

Megan hadn't asked why Sam was down. Maybe she didn't care. Did it matter if their relationship only centered on sex? Before Sam could decide on an answer—it was almost painful turning down a request for sex despite how lousy she felt— Megan's phone buzzed. She reached into her pocket and smiled.

"Charlie wants to meet up for pizza. Want to come?"

"I can't." Sam motioned to her laptop. "I'm stuck here with my records."

"He's been sending me all these texts. I know you said you liked being up in Radiology with Reed, but he says he's never been so bored."

"Tell him that even if he's not getting covered in blood he can still save lives. And he should be paying more attention to Reed. That woman's brilliant."

"You sure you don't want to join us? You can convince him in person. Besides, your records aren't going anywhere."

"There's this case I messed up on…" Sam felt a lump in her throat. She clenched her jaw, clamping down on the emotion, and then cleared her throat. "I have to talk to Dr. Anderson about it."

"Is it a big deal?"

"Maybe. I hope not." Yes. It was a huge deal.

"That's what the sad eyes are about?"

Sam shrugged. That and everything else. *Shit.* What the hell was she going to say to Terri? Maybe Terri would do all the talking. Maybe she'd yell or tell her to get out. Sam could take that punishment.

"We all make mistakes, Sam. That's why we have an attending to fix things. How about this: talk to your Dr. Anderson, aka Hot-stuff. Apologize and get over whatever is making you look like Eeyore. Then call me. I want pizza, but I also want your hands on me." Megan reached down and caressed Sam's middle finger. "And in me." Her touch was so light it sent a shiver up Sam's arm. "Sometimes we work too much, you know? We both could use a little release."

"You're probably right."

"I know I'm right. You'll call me?"

Sam nodded.

"Good. Add that to the list of why I like you. You're easy."

"Do I want to know what else is on the list?"

"Your eyes got me from the start." Megan traced Sam's eyebrow lightly. "These belong on a model. Along with your long eyelashes. God wasn't messing around on you."

"I hope God was paying more attention to my brain than my eyelashes."

"Jury's out there."

"Ouch." Sam chuckled. She didn't think it'd be possible to get out of her funk but leave it to Megan.

"And don't ask me how Dr. Anderson isn't all hot and bothered with your eyes undressing her all the time. I ought to tell her that your long lashes look even better when you're going down—"

"Okay, stop," Sam said, laughing again. "It's not happening with me and Dr. Anderson. But you and Charlie have potential. He likes you."

"Yeah. I know." Megan stood up and went over to the bay of lockers. She slipped off her lab coat and stared at the contents of her locker. "Sometimes I think I'll marry him."

"Wait, what? If you like him that much why do you mess around with me?" Suddenly Sam felt a wash of guilt. Charlie was trans and a total sweetheart despite the fact that he had a bit of a one-track mind for orthopedic surgery. "I didn't think you were that interested. I mean you guys are always going out, but you said it wasn't anything."

"He won't have sex with me unless I agree to a date. Being friends with benefits isn't his thing."

"So agree," Sam said immediately.

"You make it sound simple." Megan swung her purse over her shoulder. "You want me to bring you back a slice? Veggie, right?"

"I don't think we should have sex until you decide yes or no on Charlie."

"Now you're gonna hold out on me too?"

"I'm serious. I like Charlie. You two would be perfect together. Go have a pizza date."

Megan leaned against her locker. "What if I want pizza and no commitment?"

"Charlie wants a date, not a marriage license, right?" When Megan didn't argue, Sam continued, "I think this means you get your pizza and you get to eat it too. You know, like cake."

"Cake? That's a terrible line. Don't use that the next time you want to get laid."

"How about I stick to batting my eyelashes?"

"Worked for me." Megan's phone buzzed again and she glanced at the screen. "It's Charlie again. He's ordering half veggie and half meat lover's special. He says I should invite whoever wants to come." She hesitated. "What if I'm not sure about wanting anything more than sex?"

Sam stopped herself from saying there was nothing wrong with that. Lately she wasn't so sure. "What are you scared of?"

"Charlie's perfect. I don't want to screw around with him."

"Start with a date, Meg. He's an adult. He can figure things out on his own. Not dating him because you're worried about breaking his heart is dumb."

"Gee, I feel so much better."

"You know how to do sarcasm justice." Sam smiled. But what business did she have to give anyone advice anyway? "I don't see what you have to lose."

"Maybe nothing." Megan eyed her phone again. "Okay. I'm gonna ask him if he really wants me to invite other people." A moment later she added: "Shit that was fast. He says: 'I'd rather only share with you.'"

"This is a good thing."

"Tell me about it. I could so eat half a pizza right now. Dammit. I do want to date him. You really think I should?"

"Yes. And I'm crossing my fingers Charlie gets lucky tonight." Sam held up her crossed fingers as proof.

"You're the best. I mean it. I should tell Dr. Anderson." She dropped her phone in her purse. "Wish me luck."

After Megan had gone, the quiet of the room bothered Sam more than before. She tried to focus on her last record and managed to finish it, knowing it was one of the worst she'd written in a long time. What was taking Dr. Anderson so long? Over an hour had passed since she'd gotten her first text. Something must have gone wrong. What if something had happened to Jack?

CHAPTER SEVEN

Terri knocked on the Residents' Office door at half past eight. She had to squint at her watch twice, not believing so much time could have passed. Most sane people were home having dinner. Her stomach growled, reminding her that she should be having dinner too. Or finished with dinner and enjoying a show. In a perfect world, she'd be snuggled on the couch watching that show with someone.

"It's unlocked. Oh, wait, it's not. Hold on a minute."

She recognized Sam's voice—more strained maybe than usual but still the same sexy low tone that had comfortably eased its way into the short list of sounds she longed to hear every day. Some things she couldn't fight.

Sam opened the door. "Sorry. The last person must have locked the door on their way out." She lifted her chin enough to make eye contact with Terri and then slunk back, holding the door open.

If Sam had long flowing tresses and wore a toga, she'd be a dead ringer for a Grecian statue with the solemn expression she had on her face. And if Terri had met Sam in a bar, she'd go home with her in a hot second. Then she'd wake up to those midnight blue eyes and long dark lashes. But Sam wasn't a stranger in a bar.

Terri cleared her throat. She tried to focus on Sam while at the same time not focusing as she deliberated her opening line. That was when she noticed the trembling lip. Sam had grabbed a hold of the edge of a nearby chair like she needed a life raft.

"Is he okay?"

Terri felt a rush of sympathy. For her, the delay had been a good thing. Between her conversation with Reed and then helping Shellhammer, she'd had time to simmer down. She'd also had time to check the most recent lab results and knew the patient was stable. But Sam had been relegated to the seventh floor and had no idea. "He's fine. He was sleeping when I left him and JoAnne's on tonight so we'll hear if anything changes. His numbers are already better."

"Thank God." Sam exhaled. "I don't know how I made that mistake. I check and double check everything. I don't see how it was even possible…" Her voice trailed. "But somehow it happened. I'm so, so, sorry. You sure Jack's okay?"

Terri nodded. The boy's name was Jack. She had a head for numbers and patterns. Names not so much. Mostly it didn't matter—as long as she had the right chart.

"I promise he's fine. JoAnne caught the error before she'd even loaded the pump."

"She's good."

"She's the best," Terri added.

Sam let out a shaky breath. "Can I go down there and apologize to Maureen?"

"Maureen?"

"Jack's mom. And Rita too."

"Rita's the grandma?" Terri guessed.

Sam nodded. It was one thing to learn the patient's name, but she'd gotten everyone in the family as well? That was impressive. Terri had lost count of how many patients they'd seen that day. No way could she name them all, let alone the family members.

Suddenly it occurred to her that if Sam had some connection to the family, she could have been distracted when she was writing up orders. Obviously it wasn't an excuse but it was something to consider. "Do you know this family? If so, you should have mentioned that."

"I don't know them. At least I didn't. I met them when Jack was admitted. But now… God, I don't know what I'm going to tell Maureen."

"You're not going to tell her anything. The correct dose of insulin is being infused."

"But—"

Terri cut her off with a raised hand. "I realize this is hard, but the family needs to trust that we are taking care of Jack. And we are."

Sam sank into the chair she'd been holding onto. "I kept hoping that you were going to send me another text saying that you'd read the chart wrong. That everything was fine after all."

"You screwed up, Sam." She took a deep breath. "I know it feels awful when it happens. We've all been there. You should have double checked your math. That's all."

Sam nodded and her shoulders slumped. After a moment, she dropped her head in her hands. "Thank you for fixing everything."

"Thank JoAnne."

Sam's head bobbed, but she didn't look up. Terri wanted to reach out and fix Sam's messy hair, but she shoved her hands in her coat pockets instead. "Remembering names is a good skill. Patients can tell if you're scanning a chart before you walk in the door or if you remember who they are."

"Jack's in first grade. His teacher's Ms. Olson. He likes recess and making paper hats. He got a little origami book for his birthday." She rubbed her eyes but didn't look up at Terri. "I like to get to know my patients. And I like to apologize to them when I make a mistake."

While that might be the right thing to want, Terri couldn't let her apologize. When she shook her head, she half-expected Sam to challenge her. Her remorse was palpable. "I'm hard on my team. Everyone knows it. I don't like these kind of things to ever happen, but none of us are perfect. You made a math error and your nurse caught it. End of story."

"I could have killed him."

All Terri wanted to do was go to Sam and wrap her in a hug. But she pushed away the thought of even reaching out a hand. Lines were in place for a reason. Sure, Weiss could have her over for dinner—that was a collegial favor to an old classmate's grandkid. And Reed could take her out for drinks, but they had a butch bond. If she pulled Sam into an embrace now, even she wouldn't believe it was entirely innocent.

"Everyone makes mistakes, Samuels. Everyone. I guarantee you won't make this one again." She folded her arms. All the better not to forget and accidentally reach out to fix Sam's unruly hair. Or caress her neck. Anything to comfort her. "What you do now is thank your lucky stars that you work with a team that watches out for each other. Tomorrow you show up and prove you deserve to be on that team. Show up the way you did for the first two weeks. And it never hurts to thank your nurses. They remember."

"I don't deserve to be on your team." Sam straightened up. Her gaze held Terri's. She wasn't crying, but her eyes were moist. "I thought I could hang on until January but…I shouldn't have signed up for this residency in the first place and it's a mistake for me to stay any longer."

"You quitting is a mistake." Terri had been ready to boot Sam out earlier, but now she'd seen a different side of her. She was more certain than ever she needed to fight to keep her. "When did you last eat?"

Sam didn't answer. After a moment of indecision, Terri unfolded her arms and reached out to touch her shoulder. She didn't expect Sam to lean into her hand. When she did, Terri's body instantly responded, begging to be allowed to pull her close. She stepped back instead and cleared her throat.

"So I'm going to assume that the last thing you ate were those Reese's peanut butter cups I saw you popping after we checked in on that dialysis case."

"Jenny Armada—that's the name of the dialysis patient."

"But what's her grandmother's name?"

For a second Sam looked concerned that she should know that tidbit as well. She relaxed as soon as she caught Terri's half-smile. Her own smile in return was weak at best. "Thanks. Kick me while I'm down."

"So those Reese's were the last thing you ate?"

Sam nodded.

"I don't know how you look so good when all you eat is crap." Terri swallowed as soon as Sam looked up at her. Yes, the words had slipped out. She should have filtered her thoughts, but she was tired and hungry and it had been a hell of a day. And Sam did still look hot despite everything. Why cover with a lie? With Sam's eyes locked on her she couldn't think of one anyway.

"Reese's aren't crap. They're like little balanced meals—protein, carbs, fat. And I could cite more than one study confirming the health benefits of chocolate." Sam gave Terri another half smile. The effort it took was obvious. "I hate to do this to you, to everyone, but I can't keep this up anymore. I'm done."

Sam went over to the locker bay. She pulled off her scrub top. The navy blue tank top she wore underneath showed off shoulders that belonged on a crew team. "You know, I didn't want to quit while I was on your rotation."

"Then don't." Terri paused. Sam had turned around to face her, and she had to push herself to go on. "Earlier today I would have let you walk away. I've been so frustrated with you I probably would have helped you clean out your locker. Why stay 'til the end of the year when you've already emotionally quit, right?

"You've been a pain in my ass ever since we talked last week. And I don't carry dead weight on my team. But after all of this with Jack… You've changed my mind. You have so much damn potential. And so much heart. When you focus, you're an amazing doctor. I can't let you quit." Now it was more than making Weiss happy. Way more.

Sam turned back to her locker. She fished out her wallet and keys and then closed the door. "I've known for a while now that I'm not meant for this job. I kept pretending—for a lot of reasons. But if I learned anything today it's that I need to get out before I screw up again. What if no one had caught my mistake?"

"You're not quitting while you're on my team." Sam started to argue, but Terri held up her hand. "You're hungry and tired. And we all want to give up after a hard day. Especially when we mess up. But I'm not letting you. And you're still my resident which means I get to tell you what to do."

"If I didn't feel like crap, I'd say something inappropriate in response to that."

Terri had hoped Sam wouldn't make any comment about the double entendre that was her last sentence. In fact, given everything that had happened tonight and how professional Sam had been for the past three weeks, she was surprised she'd gone there.

Sam continued, "It's hard pretending I'm not attracted to you."

Terri sucked in a breath. Declarations like that wouldn't help either of them, but her honesty was endearing. "I need you to focus, Samuels. Quitting is a mistake. You have to realize that."

Sam leaned back against her locker. "You can't tell me not to quit."

"Sure I can. And for the record, I've been pretending that I'm not attracted to you too."

"I know."

Of course Sam knew. A flush went through Terri as Sam's gaze refused to leave hers. One minute she wanted to shake Sam and the next she wanted to step into her kiss. But she had to be the mature one in all of this. And no part of her decision to stop Sam from quitting could be about how much she wanted her to stay for her own sake.

"Do you like sushi?"

Sam cocked her head. "I love sushi."

"Good. I'm going to drop off my things at my office and then we're going to dinner. Meet me in the lobby in ten minutes." Dinner was risky, but the conversation couldn't be over yet. She needed to convince Sam to stay. "And just so we're clear, I'm not asking you out. But we're both starving and it's been a shitty day."

CHAPTER EIGHT

Terri had picked the sushi restaurant six blocks away from the hospital partly because she didn't want to chance seeing anyone from work. A walk also seemed like a good idea. They stepped out of the hospital and into the warm evening. After they'd crossed two streets, Terri slipped off her light jacket.

Sam glanced at her, seemingly about to say something and then looked away.

"What?"

"At work you're always careful to keep covered up." Sam hesitated. "It's nice to see your skin. But I probably shouldn't say that."

"People complain about a doctor with too many tattoos." Terri decided not to comment about what Sam should or shouldn't say. She certainly appreciated seeing Sam's shoulders exposed. "I figure we're far enough away now that I'm safe. Especially at ten o'clock at night."

Sam nodded but didn't say more. Terri would have to work on getting her to open up—after they had some food.

As soon as they stepped into the restaurant, one of the chefs looked up and smiled. He called out to the other chef who raised his knife in a friendly greeting.

"You're a regular here?" Sam guessed.

"Best sushi in town. And they're open until midnight." Without asking Sam, Terri headed for the bar. She wanted to avoid a table and any suggestion of a romantic dinner.

Little red boats, each carrying a plate of sushi rolls, floated in a narrow stream in front of their seats. Terri waited for several boats to pass before making her selection.

"Sitting at the bar may be a bad idea," Sam said. She'd already eaten most of her first roll and now eyed the passing boats, clearly planning her next choice. "I think I could eat everything in front of me."

"But sitting at the bar means you don't have to look at me when I ask you hard questions."

Sam slowed her chopsticks, a piece of sushi dangling mid-air. "I read up on diabetes and hyperkalemia."

"I don't want to talk about Jack's case. I know you're smart and I don't need to tell you what could have happened." Terri dipped her sushi in wasabi-laced soy sauce. "Maybe I should tell you some stories of my own dumb mistakes to make you feel better. But I want to talk about something else."

Sam waited for her to go on. She'd set her chopsticks down and the same somber expression she'd had when Terri first walked into the Residents' Office had returned.

"What are you going to do after you leave?"

"Surf." Sam's answer came immediately. "It's been too long since I was in the water. And I've got a lot of sleep to catch up on. My bed's missed me. I need a few days off and then I'll look into getting my old job back."

"Okay, I didn't expect surfing." But it did explain where she'd gotten those gorgeous shoulders. "So that's one of your hobbies along with the stamp collecting and the photography?"

"Photography's not a hobby."

Terri tilted her head. She'd clearly hit a nerve. "That's the old job?"

Sam nodded.

Terri decided to try the less sensitive subject first. "Where do you surf?"

"Santa Cruz mostly. I've got a place down there." Sam glanced at her. "Do you surf?"

"No...but I've always wanted to learn."

"I could teach you."

"I'm scared of sharks. And I have no free time to learn anything. But that's a different subject. Are you leaving medicine because you love photography more? You don't think you can do both?"

"It's more complicated than that."

Terri waited. She had a feeling Sam wanted to open up and the less she said, the more that might happen. "Want to tell me why?"

"No one dies if you screw up on a photo shoot." Sam's smile slipped off her lips as fast as it had appeared. "Sorry. Coping mechanism." She eyed her plate. "The truth is, photography's what I love. And you have to go all in if you want to make a living doing it. When I went to med school, I let my business partner—the guy I'd hired to help me shoot—take over. He doesn't like to work as hard as I do and things have been slow.

"We can do two weddings a weekend through the summer if I get us back on the map. With family photo shoots and corporate gigs on the side, we can stay plenty busy. And if all that happens, I can get back to my own projects. That's the goal."

Giving up medicine when she'd already gotten this far seemed unfathomable but Terri held back those words. "Reed mentioned you'd shown her your portfolio. She was impressed. She called it artsy, but that's probably the wrong word."

"Well, it's not the worst word I've heard." Sam leaned back on the barstool. "Can I ask you something?" When Terri nodded, she said, "How do you come back to work the next day when you make a mistake? A big mistake."

"After I sit down and cry?" Terri exhaled. "I call Reed. Talk everything over. Tell myself I'll learn from it. And then I cry some more."

"I hate the responsibility of having someone's life in my hands. I want to help people, but it's too much. I know people make mistakes and move on, but I can't. It's not only Jack. I nearly messed up with Alexa Peters—that little girl who came in vomiting blood. If you hadn't made me run another electrolyte panel on her, I don't know if she would have pulled through. And that kid with lymphadenopathy. Isiah Wilkenson. I didn't even think of—"

"My job is to help you. Of course I'm going to think of things you don't. You can't keep a list of every time you make a judgment error."

"This is more than judgment errors." Sam shook her head. "Every night I go to bed and I think back over the day. I lie there going through the details of every case. Did I miss something? What else could I have done?"

"We all make mistakes, Sam. None of us are perfect."

"You're calling me Sam now?"

Terri swallowed. She'd slipped up. Although she'd often called her Sam in her mind, she'd been careful to say Samuels out loud. "Samuels."

"Generally I like Sam better. Although when you say Samuels I feel like I'm in trouble and I kind of like it when you're a little mad at me."

"You've been in luck lately. I spent most of this past week being completely pissed at you."

"I noticed. How are you feeling now?"

Her anger had slipped away as soon as she'd realized how sorry Sam was about everything. Now? "I'm not sure."

"I guess that's fair." Sam picked up her chopsticks again. "Can I ask you another question?"

"Yes, but with that tone I reserve the right not to answer."

Sam smiled. "You don't miss much." She picked up a piece of sushi and dipped it, seemingly delaying as she decided whether or not to ask her question. "Why don't you date residents?"

Terri wanted to answer. With all the rumors that had gone round about her and her ex-wife and the other resident that had formed the alleged love triangle, she wanted to be able to tell her side of the story. Given how the gossip mill worked, she knew Sam had probably heard at least something. But it felt wrong to give any of the tall tales credence. And she didn't want to give Sam some half-assed excuse. She polished off the last piece of sushi on her plate and pushed it to the side. "Try a different question."

"Are you in a relationship?"

"No."

"But you date women."

"Yes. And men." Terri held Sam's gaze. "What are you getting at?"

"I want to ask you out. What do I have to do?"

"First off, you have bad timing." Terri was flattered nonetheless. "Second, it's not happening."

"All right. I get it." Sam pushed her empty plate to the side and took a sip of her water.

"Tell me why you went to med school."

Sam stared at the line of sushi boats for a moment and then shifted in her chair to face Terri. "You sure you really want to know? You'll probably think less of me for it." When Terri nodded, Sam said, "Well, I didn't go to medical school because I wanted to be a doctor."

"Okay, I'll bite but only because that might be the weirdest thing I've heard all day. Let me guess—you're an international spy. Are there people watching us right now?"

Sam's smile creased her eyes. For the first time all night it was a real smile—and it took Terri's breath away.

"How'd you know?"

"Well, it was either a spy or a high-end escort."

"An escort for med students specifically?" Sam laughed. "Would you date me then?"

"Maybe."

Sam smirked, but her expression quickly turned serious again. "I did it for money—which I know is about the shittiest reason you could become a doctor."

"I don't believe you." Plenty of people went into medicine because it promised a stable paycheck, but Terri had gotten good at spotting those doctors who were only in it for the money. "You care about your patients more than any resident I've had on my team. No way is it about the money."

"I do care about them. But I don't want to be their doctor." Sam paused. "I never knew exactly how well-off my grandparents were until after they died. My grandfather wrote me a letter that his lawyer gave to me at the funeral… If I went to med school, took over his old job as a family practice doc, I'd inherit forty-one million."

"Holy shit!"

"Yeah, that was pretty much my response." Sam continued, "Most of it is my grandmother's money. She inherited a lot from her parents and kept investing it. Apparently Grandma was cutthroat on the stock market. As far as I knew, she was an eccentric old lady who liked to paint."

"Were you close to her?"

Sam nodded. "We used to spend every summer together at her beach house. I was closer to her than to my parents."

"I'm sorry. I'm still stuck on the forty-one million part."

"I was too for a long time. Long enough to convince myself to go back to college and take the pre-reqs I'd missed for med school, apply to med school, graduate, and get into a residency. Then I realized it was only money."

"Yeah—but a lot of money." Terri had turned in her seat so their knees were almost bumping. The downside of sitting at the bar meant they were closer than if they'd gone to a table. When she looked at how close Sam's legs were to hers, she knew she should change her position. But she didn't want to. "What happens if you don't work at your grandfather's practice?"

"I get the rest of my life back."

Terri cocked her head. "I mean what happens to the money."

"It goes to some big anti-gay religious foundation. I think he figured that knowing where the money would go if I didn't follow his plan would be one more reason I'd do everything he wanted." Sam shook her head. "He knew I was a lesbian and didn't like it. But he didn't approve of a lot of things about me. And, yet, for some dumb reason, I still wanted to impress him. I looked up to him. He was this great doctor that everyone loved."

"So if you give up, you lose all the inheritance?"

"All the money anyway. Technically I own my grandmother's beach house. That was in her will, not his, but I can hardly afford the taxes on it with all the student loans I have to pay back."

"Your family didn't help you there?"

"According to the will, I had to pay for medical school and everything on my own. Then any loans are repaid when I start working at the practice—in monthly allotments—along with the inheritance. My grandfather wanted complete control."

"What do your parents think about all of this? Of you quitting?"

"They don't know. If I told them, they'd want me to finish, but we don't really talk… They have their own money so that part doesn't probably matter much to them. They're both successful lawyers."

"They don't have forty-one million dollars."

"No." Sam sighed. "But who needs that much money?"

"Any other grandkids?"

"Just me."

Something passed over Sam's face, and Terri decided not to push more. "I can't believe you did it only for the money. Forget about that list of mistakes you're keeping in your head—can you honestly say that you don't like being a doctor? You're so good at it."

"Remember how you weren't going to give me any more compliments after I wowed you with my box step?"

"Dammit, I forgot." Terri smiled when Sam shot her a cocky look. Her eyes sparkled, and the heat between them shot up a dozen degrees. Terri moved her knee so they weren't quite as close. If she was trying to get Sam to focus, she had to do her part too. "What bothers me is that you're really good at being a doctor. I can't believe that's all an act. That you don't actually like helping people."

"I *do* like helping people. I like figuring out what's wrong, figuring how to make them feel better. And if I ignore this week's mistakes, part of me thinks I could still be good at it."

"So who wins if you quit?"

Sam's brow furrowed. "What do you mean?"

"If you don't go through with this, do you win because you get your old life back? Or does your grandfather win because maybe he knew all along you weren't going to follow through?" Terri waited. When Sam didn't answer, she said, "Maybe he wanted that money to go to that anti-gay foundation all along."

"Maybe." Sam blew out a breath. "Then I guess he wins."

"And you're okay with that?"

"No. But it's not that black and white." Sam was quiet for a moment and then said, "What would you do?"

"I'd stick it out. But I love being a doctor. I'm the wrong person to ask. I also hate losing."

"Somehow I'm not surprised. You might be one of the most stubborn people I've met. It's a good thing when you're trying to save someone's life…"

"But?"

Sam grinned. "When someone is trying to get you to go out with them and you've made up your mind against it only on principle, the stubborn thing is a little frustrating."

Terri had to give Sam credit for trying. "Answer's still no. What else you got?"

"I could have lots of money."

"I've got plenty." Terri returned Sam's smile. For better or worse, she liked it when they were back to flirting. But she had to keep it in check. "And you don't actually have the money if you quit."

"So basically I'm screwed."

"Or not." Terri knew she'd overstepped, but Sam only laughed. When the other diners turned to look in their direction, Terri wished they were alone. But that would definitely complicate matters. She reached for her water and took a long sip. No matter how tempting Sam was, she couldn't go thinking about what it would feel like to be under her.

"So what's your family like?" Sam asked. "Sisters, brothers? Crazy-rich grandparents?"

"No crazy-rich anybody. Two sisters, divorced parents."

"That's all I get?"

Sharing personal details about her family wasn't part of the script, but she felt like she owed Sam a little. "Mom got pregnant with me when she was a teenager. Dad split. Then a handful of years later he came back and Mom got pregnant again. And again. Cue lots of parental fighting. Dad split for good and Mom raised us working two jobs."

"How old are your sisters?"

"Thirty-three and thirty-one." Terri wondered if Sam had guessed her age. It wouldn't be impossible to figure out—a simple Google search would show when she'd graduated college and med school. Although Sam was nothing like her younger sister, she couldn't help thinking that they were the same age and that nearly ten years separated them. She wondered if Sam would be flirting as hard if she knew that detail, but she couldn't exactly blurt out her age.

"Are you close to them?"

"We see each other for the holidays and talk when we can. But we're all busy. Kelly manages a boutique hotel in San Francisco and Bianca's in Reno, married with three kids. It usually takes some life crisis to get one of us to pick up the phone…"

"I'm guessing you're the one they come to for help."

Terri nodded. "Growing up I took care of them a lot. The divorce wasn't finalized until I was fourteen, but my dad skipped out way before then. Mom had to work all the time so I took over parenting. Made dinners, made sure everyone did their homework, that sort of thing."

"Sounds like you had to grow up fast."

"I did. But I don't have any regrets—not about that anyway."

"What's one of your regrets?"

Terri leaned back in her seat. Sam was easy to talk to, but she had to remember boundaries were still there for a reason. "I think that's enough about me."

"Come on. One regret. I'm sure the wise Dr. Anderson learned something the hard way."

"Oh, plenty." Terri sighed. "But as for regrets… Well, I guess I regret that my younger self let people talk me into things that weren't right for me. And here I am trying to talk you into something. Maybe you shouldn't listen to me."

"What'd you get talked into?"

"Marriage."

Sam looked as if she didn't believe her. "And I can't even talk you into a date."

Terri smiled. "I've become a hard ass in my old age."

"Someone seriously talked you into marrying them when you didn't want to?"

"Twice. But don't worry I learned my lesson. I wouldn't do it again even if someone paid me."

"Huh. I wasn't expecting that."

"Okay, my turn." Terri took a deep breath. "I don't want to tell you what to do. I really don't. But I want you to have time to think this over. So I'm going to ask you for a favor. Take some time off. You've been working yourself too hard—and that's coming from me."

Sam's shoulders dropped. She looked down at her hands, folded in her lap. "Time off won't change my decision."

"What if it did? What's the worst thing that would happen?" When Sam didn't argue, Terri added, "I don't want you to quit—because you're a damn good doctor. And you don't want to lose forty-one million dollars. I know you say it's only money, but it's a lot of money, money that some anti-gay foundation doesn't need. You at least have to admit that much is true."

Sam still didn't respond so Terri continued. "A couple more years of the residency and then go work at your grandpa's practice part-time. There's no stipulation on that part, is there?"

Sam shook her head.

"Then you could still make it work with the photography. You're so close. What if you only need a break for a few weeks?"

"I need more than that."

"Are you sure?" Terri pressed. "Tell me that there isn't some part of you that's questioning your decision."

Sam didn't say anything for a long moment and Terri knew she wasn't certain. Some part of her had to be doubting her choice.

"I already gave Weiss my written notice," Sam said finally.

"And he'll shred it if you change your mind."

Sam shook her head again, but Terri was determined. "I want you to show up for rounds tomorrow morning. We both need to check on Jack. And then I want you to go up to Weiss' office and talk to him about taking some time off."

"You think Jack's going to be okay?"

"I know he is. And you need to give yourself a break." Terri reached out and touched Sam's shoulder. She'd only intended a little pat, but the contact of her palm against Sam's skin sent off flares in her brain. She pulled her hand back as she felt the temptation to slide it all the way down Sam's toned arm. She straightened up. "We should probably go. Tomorrow's gonna be a long day."

CHAPTER NINE

For a day in competition for worst ever, it had ended better than expected. After they'd finished dinner, Sam offered to walk Terri home. She knew the answer would be no and the added eye roll came as no surprise. But she left the restaurant with the memory of Terri's hand caressing her shoulder. It had taken all of her control to not show any response to the touch that had lit through her body.

On the drive home, her thoughts bounced from Jack, who was still stable when she'd called to check in, to where she'd take Terri on a date. A date wasn't happening, but she liked the fantasy anyway. And for someone who was adamantly against dating, Terri had tried awfully hard to convince her not to quit. But she couldn't stay on simply because Terri wanted her to.

After she pulled into the apartment complex, she sat in her car for a few minutes. Now that Terri wasn't sitting next to her, convincing her she should finish the residency, all of her doubts had returned in full force. She didn't want to go up to her apartment, but where else could she go tonight?

Reluctantly she forced herself out of the car and up the steps, ignoring the barking dog that had spotted her. The apartment still didn't feel like home. She even had trouble remembering the address when she had to fill out forms. One nondescript brown building in a sea of brown apartment buildings surrounded by freeways and strip malls. She'd never intended to stay long. Like so many other things, the place was temporary. A stepping stone in a river full of them. But where would she be in two years' time? Working at her grandfather's clinic?

She unlocked the door and set her wallet and keys in the basket, wondering how many more nights she'd repeat that move. If she could be anywhere, she'd be back in the beach house in a heartbeat. But maybe she needed to listen to Terri and ask Weiss for time off. God knows she didn't need the time to think—she'd done plenty of that. But a break might at least clear her mind.

"You're home late. Want a beer? Kylie replenished our stock." Daniel was sitting cross-legged too close to the TV with a video game controller in one hand and a bottle of beer in the other.

"Not so you could drink it all in one night, however." Kylie came out of the kitchen. She had two bottles of beer, both open, and without asking, handed one to Sam. "You look exhausted. Shitty day?"

Sam shrugged. "No worse than the last 400."

"Truth." Kylie sighed. "I wonder how much money I would have saved on beer if I hadn't decided on oncology."

"Don't start budgeting now," Daniel said, his eyes still on the screen.

Sam took a long sip and dropped onto the couch. Kylie settled in at the other end. She sipped her beer slowly and trained her gaze on Sam. Squinting at her, she said, "You sure you're okay?"

"Not really. I'm so tired lately I can't sleep." Sam didn't want to admit the rest.

"You've been acting off for weeks now," Kylie pressed.

"Yeah. Since I've been on Med-Peds with Dr. Anderson."

"Which means she's barely surviving hell." Daniel blasted an alien, cussing as a meteor came out of nowhere and exploded the screen. The image of the red planet reformed a moment later. "Give her a break, Ky. You were a mess when you were on Med-Peds, too."

Kylie ignored Daniel and said, "It started before that. After you spent that weekend in Santa Cruz... I'm worried about you."

"She's concerned about your mental health," Daniel said, practicing his formal British accent. "Would you care to set up an appointment to discuss your feelings?"

"Shut up, you." Kylie tossed a pillow at Daniel's head. "I'm being serious."

"I appreciate the fact that I live with someone who cares about my mental health. But at the moment my mental health wants to drink this beer and fall asleep. Can we do a therapy session another day, maybe?"

After a long minute with Kylie still eyeing her, Sam thought of getting up and going to bed. But she was too tired to move. Kylie was right. She'd been holding everything together until her last trip down to Santa Cruz. That was when she'd found the box of letters and receipts and her world had been upturned.

Kylie tapped her knee. "I'll get it out of you eventually."

One damn box. A month ago she'd thought she'd known what the rest of her life would look like. Now she was swimming in the middle of the ocean with no land in sight. Although she'd never wanted it, she'd thought she could be a doctor. And maybe even be good at it. But now the last thing she wanted to do was follow in her grandfather's footsteps.

And yet Terri had almost convinced her that she should finish anyway. Maybe taking the job in her grandfather's practice would be the biggest F.U. she could give him. If she quit, she'd go back to her old life, but what about where the money went? Could she actually let that money go to an anti-gay foundation?

Kylie tapped her knee again. When Sam didn't respond, she exhaled and finally looked away. They watched Daniel's video game in silence until Kylie complained about early morning rounds. Sam let Kylie get up and head to her bedroom, but she still didn't move.

After another long sip of her beer, she closed her eyes. For a moment, she didn't want to think of what came next. She let herself rest with Daniel's video game monsters attacking each other as the soundtrack for her numb mind. A few minutes of numbness and then she'd take a shower and climb into bed.

* * *

The next morning, Terri gave no indication that anything had changed between them. She was brusque as usual during rounds and after the others had gone to check on their respective patients, she'd turned to Sam and curtly said: "Weiss told me he's expecting you at nine."

Jack was doing well—thank God. By his mother's words, he felt better than he had in weeks. By his own words, he was hungry and wanted pancakes. After she'd convinced him to try the sausage and eggs instead, she went to see Weiss.

In a half hour it was all decided. She'd finish out her time in Med-Peds, continue on to the two weeks in Emergency as scheduled, but then take a week off before starting her month in Cardiology. She couldn't help worrying who would take on an extra load for that week, but she agreed to the plan anyway.

Weiss clapped her back enthusiastically as she left his office, and Sam tried to ignore the nagging doubt that she might still let him down.

CHAPTER TEN

A loud buzzing woke Sam from a dead sleep. Eyes closed, she pawed the nightstand until she found her phone and silenced the alarm. She slumped back on the pillows, wondering what day it was and what the alarm was for.

Shit. Reed's barbeque.

She scrambled out of bed. She had to shower, pick up the ingredients for a fruit salad, and drive to Reed's. In under an hour. Why hadn't she'd given herself more time? And what was she going to wear? All of her clothes were in the laundry basket—or on the floor.

On any ordinary Sunday, she'd have done all her laundry. But after working all week in Med-Peds with Terri, she'd been called in to ICU on Friday night. Forty hours later, she'd finally left the hospital that morning. By the time she got home, she'd had no energy to do anything more than stumble into bed.

Rummaging through her dresser, she found black board shorts and a *Ghostbusters* T-shirt. Not an outfit that would impress anyone—least of all Terri—but at least she'd be clean.

Reed's place was a cute bungalow with kid stuff littering the yard. Sam had swung by a roadside farmers market for a bag of peaches and a flat of strawberries, and she picked her way up the front walk with her hands full. Her mother would have given her a hard time for not coming with the fruit salad prepared, but her mother had also never worked two overnight shifts after a full work week.

Before she had a chance to ring the bell, the door popped open and a kid with brown curls scowled up at her. "Who are you?"

"Sam."

"I don't know you. What's in your bag?"

"Peaches." Sam tried not to feel intimidated by the hard stare. When the kid crossed her arms, she realized she wasn't getting in the door. She held up the tray of strawberries. "I've also got some yummy-looking berries."

The strawberries got a slightly more interested look, but the kid still wouldn't budge. "Those aren't berries. They're strawberries."

"Well, strawberries *are* berries, right? So…can I come in?"

"No, they're not. Berries are different."

Sam scanned the entryway and the hallway beyond it for some sign of an adult. Why was she even arguing with this punk? She tried for a lighter tone. "If I say that strawberries aren't berries can I come in?"

"You're a stranger."

"Yeah, but I know your moms. They invited me." This was getting ridiculous. She clearly needed help. "Hello? Julia? Reed? It's me. Sam."

"Hey, Sam," Reed called. After a moment, she popped her head into the hallway and grinned. "Sam, meet Bryn. She's our guard dog."

On cue, Bryn barred her teeth and growled.

"Guard dog, huh? That's pretty scary." Sam tried smiling, hoping she might still win over the kid. "Do guard dogs like strawberries?"

Bryn lunged forward and Sam jumped back. Her flip-flops caught on the edge of the doormat and she stumbled, nearly dropping the peaches, and then bumped into something behind her. An arm caught her waist and she turned in time to see Terri.

"You okay?"

"Yeah, I'm fine." Sam straightened up as Terri's hand slid off her. Getting scared by a kid and then nearly falling was about as unsmooth as she'd ever been. Thank God Terri was the one blushing. "Thanks for catching me."

"I scared her," Bryn said, cackling with laughter. Two seconds later she threw herself at Terri.

Terri caught the kid, spun her in a circle, and then deposited her on the threshold with a kiss on the top of her head. "Kids can be pretty scary. But you, Bryn, are the worst. Congratulations."

Bryn soaked up the compliment. She grinned, showing way too many teeth, and then took off squealing down the hall. As soon as she'd gone, Terri said, "She grows on you."

"Like what? Resistant bacteria?"

Terri laughed. "Yes. Exactly like that."

"I'm usually not scared of kids."

"Sure." Terri winked. "Don't worry. I won't tell anyone."

Sam was about to argue, but the look in Terri's eyes stopped her. "Hey, I wanted to thank you for dinner on Thursday. For talking to me and, well, for everything."

Terri continued to hold Sam's gaze and the air between them seemed to grow hotter by the second. Finally Terri nodded and said simply, "You're welcome."

Sam knew she still didn't have a chance—Terri was too damn stubborn—but something was different in the way she looked at her tonight. Suddenly she wanted to convince her that they could skip this barbeque and go somewhere alone. A cafe or a park maybe. Somewhere to talk. But not about work. Since their dinner, she'd come up with about a hundred more questions she'd thought of asking. Before she got up the courage to say anything at all, Terri brushed past her and stepped into the entryway.

"I wouldn't stay out here alone if I were you. Bryn can smell fear."

Sam watched Terri's hips swing as she walked down the hall. Her flowery skirt swished with every step, and Sam had to push away the thought of how easy it would be to slip a hand under the material. In fact, it wouldn't be easy at all. Another woman wearing that skirt, maybe. Not Terri Anderson.

The hall opened up to the kitchen where Reed was pouring barbeque sauce over a rack of ribs. She had on an apron with "Kiss The Cook" emblazoned on the chest and Julia was at her side in a matching apron.

"Sorry I'm late for helping," Terri said. "I got called in this afternoon... But I brought cheesecake for dessert."

"Perfect. We saved the veggies for you to chop for the kabobs." Reed nodded to a pile of mushrooms, onions, tomatoes, and bell peppers.

"Hey, Sam. Welcome." Julia held up a barbeque-mitted hand. "Bryn told us she already managed to scare you."

"I wasn't really scared—"

"Oh, you're not the only one," Reed interrupted. "The mailman's convinced she's a gremlin."

"She's actually very sweet," Julia said. "It's mostly an act. And Carly's even sweeter—wherever she's hiding. Do you need a serving bowl for those strawberries?"

"And a cutting board. I brought peaches too."

Julia went over to a cabinet and pulled out a glass serving bowl. She set this next to a cutting board and pointed out the block of knives. Reed's kitchen looked like the playground for a serious chef and Sam wondered who did most of the cooking.

Reed held up the pan of ribs. "We better get this on the grill. You two gonna be okay if we abandon you for a minute?"

"I think we'll manage," Terri said.

"You sure?" Reed exchanged a glance with Terri, and Sam quickly turned to set the fruit on the counter, pretending not to notice that Terri's cheeks were red again.

"Come on, you," Julia said, pushing Reed toward the open screen door. "Sam, watch out for anyone under five feet. They attack without notice."

"Thanks for the warning."

The moment the screen door closed, Bryn and another smaller kid with blond braids popped up from behind the couch near the sliding glass door. Bryn took one look at Sam, screeched, and took off running. The smaller kid stayed behind, her eyes and nose only a few inches above the sofa back cushions.

"Hi, Carly," Terri said. "Wanna help?"

"Maybe later." Carly had a voice a fraction as loud as her sister and a sweet smile. She glanced at Sam, blushed as red as Terri had earlier and then dropped back down behind the sofa.

"Okay, now that one I could handle," Sam said.

"Yeah, you and Carly would get along."

"Why?"

"You both like spying."

Sam opened her mouth to argue that she hadn't really spied despite what she'd said, but the glint in Terri's eye stopped her.

"What?"

Terri shrugged. "Nothing. I like you this way."

"Which way is that?" There was something about Terri's tone and the way she didn't answer the question that made Sam feel both self conscious and turned on at the same time. She looked down at the outfit she'd put together. "You a *Ghostbusters* fan?"

"It's not the clothes. Although you do have a nice butt in those shorts—which I was not going to tell you." Terri reached for a colander and started pulling peaches out of the bag Sam had brought. "What I meant was I like this relaxed version of Sam. You work last night?"

"And the night before. After our full week. And I didn't sleep much in between." Sam turned on the water and started rinsing off the strawberries. "Thanks for telling me you like my butt. Can I say I like you in a skirt?"

Terri rocked her head side to side, her focus still on the peaches. "Probably not a good idea."

Bryn appeared at the back door, screaming for her sister to come outside and Carly crawled out from behind the couch. She waved, specifically at Sam, and then ran after her sister.

"How long does it take for the other one to grow on you?"

"She got me on the first day. But she was a tiny little baby then." Terri handed Sam the colander filled with peaches. "You want to wash everything and I'll start chopping?"

After they'd finished with the fruit, they started in on the veggies. Sam hoped that Reed and Julia would stay outside for a while longer. As often as they worked together in the hospital, they were rarely alone and everything about tonight felt different.

"Do you like cooking?" Sam asked.

"As long as I don't have to follow a recipe." Terri handed her a bell pepper.

"Because you don't like being told what to do?" Sam rinsed the bell pepper and then took a tomato from Terri.

"That depends."

"On what?" The question slipped out before Sam realized Terri's innuendo. Instead of some cool response, Sam only managed. "Never mind. I get it. I'm a little sleepy."

"I can tell. You're supposed to be washing that tomato."

"Yeah, but you distracted me and now I'm having a hard time focusing on a tomato." Sam held the tomato under the water and then turned to hand it to Terri.

Terri didn't take it. "What are you thinking about?"

"Same thing I've been thinking about since we went out for sushi. That I like you way more than I should."

"Way more, huh?" Terri held her gaze. "Sorry about that."

"You're different tonight too."

"I'm not in work mode," Terri said.

"It's more than that."

Terri finally took the tomato and chopped it, added the slices to the pile, and then looked back at Sam. "You look like you want to say something. What is it?"

"Something I probably shouldn't say." Sam paused. Terri had leaned back against the counter to face her, the outline of her nipples barely visible through the thin material of her blouse. "You know, we wouldn't have to date. And I wouldn't tell anyone if that's what you're worried about. I'm good at keeping secrets."

"We went out for sushi for work reasons."

"I know. But we wouldn't have to date," Sam repeated.

"So just a fuck? That's what you're looking for?"

Heat went straight to Sam's core as Terri's challenging gaze held hers. The desire to slide between her legs blotted out every other thought. She swallowed. "I'm not gonna lie. I want more. And you keep being all professional, but…"

"But what?"

"I know I'm not the only one who wants it." Sam also knew the chance she was taking. "You say you can't date me. But what I'm saying is we wouldn't have to date. I wouldn't tell anyone and neither would you." She paused, half expecting Terri to immediately shoot her down. When that didn't happen, she added, "I know nothing can happen while we're working together, but I start on Emergency in a week."

After a long minute, Terri said, "I'm not going to say you're completely wrong." She turned to the cutting board and started slicing a bell pepper. When she finished with the pepper, she reached for a second tomato. "You gonna start cleaning the rest of the mushrooms?"

"I'd rather watch you," Sam admitted.

Terri raised an eyebrow but for once had no response. Sam took a step toward her, knowing full well she might get stopped. Terri's knife stalled. She looked up at Sam, still not saying a word. The air between them sparked with electricity.

Sam was close enough to kiss her, close enough to sense how they were both holding their breath. She slipped the knife out of Terri's grasp and set it on the cutting board, then rested her hand over Terri's—the smooth skin warm under her palm. Desire flooded her senses.

Terri's lips parted as Sam leaned toward her.

"Boo!" Bryn's voice was as loud as a cowbell clanging in an empty church.

Sam stepped back quickly, letting go of Terri's hand.

"Were you going to kiss her, Aunt Terri? Bleh!" Bryn's face puckered like she'd sucked on a lemon. "Kissing is so gross."

Sam wanted to find Bryn's volume control button. There was a chance that Reed and Julia hadn't heard but only a slim one. Maybe she could bribe her not to say anything more. As soon as she had that thought, however, Bryn darted outside and

Sam's stomach sank as she heard: "Aunt Terri almost got kissed! On the lips!"

"Shit." Terri reached for a kitchen towel, dried off her hands, and then picked up the filled tray of kabobs. "I'll take these out to the grill if you want to finish up the rest."

Sam nodded, but Terri wasn't looking at her now. She watched her leave, knowing she should say something. What the hell could she say?

After too long deliberating, she picked up the knife Terri had left and quartered the tomato, then reached for the mushrooms. Her body was on auto-pilot as her thoughts raced from leaving to going after Terri. Even though she'd had no doubt Terri had wanted her kiss, she was clearly upset that they'd been caught. The only thing worse than getting interrupted during a kiss was never getting it in the first place—and still getting in trouble.

Reed came in from the backyard. "I'm sorry. I talked to Bryn and told her she had no business spying on you."

"It's fine."

"It's not." Reed sighed. "She's a difficult kid. She can be amazing too but sometimes I'm not sure how to parent her. And she's really protective of Terri."

"Maybe I should leave."

"You're gonna leave Terri alone to weather this? I'd like to say that Bryn won't bring it up again, but the truth is, I can't promise that."

Sam exhaled. "Is Terri pissed?"

"No. She's…frazzled. And—" The doorbell rang, breaking off the rest of Reed's sentence. "That'll be Mo and Kate. Don't worry. As soon as Bryn sees Mo, she won't pay attention to anyone else for the rest of the night. She's had a kid crush on Mo since the first moment she saw her."

With the addition of Mo and Kate, who Sam quickly learned were Julia's college roommates and who had recently become a couple, the noise in the house quadrupled. Bryn was truly infatuated with Mo and tailed her like a yipping puppy dog. Even Carly came out of her shell, squealing when Kate pretended to chase her. Sam kept to the periphery, chatting with Mo while she finished off the kabobs and then answering questions from Kate about work as they all stood around the grill. She tried not to focus on Terri, but it was impossible not to be aware of her. Every so often, Terri's gaze would settle on her and Sam was desperate then for a moment alone. It wasn't clear that she was upset, but she didn't look exactly happy either.

They ate dinner outside in a backyard that clearly got more kid time than adult time. Between the patch of overgrown grass, a sprawling tree laden with dozens and dozens of green apples, and a swing set badly in need of a coat of paint, there was a raised garden bed that clearly hosted more snails than plants, a rickety kids' picnic table, and an odd assortment of patio furniture. Something about the yard and the lack of formality in the dinner as well—with everyone grabbing what they wanted off the grill—made Sam finally relax.

Terri sat with the kids and Mo at the picnic table. Julia and Kate each took lounge chairs. Reed sat on a folding chair clearly meant for the beach, and Sam settled in on a swinging bench with a torn canvas overhang.

The conversation ranged from the upcoming wedding to stories from a recent trip to Mexico that they'd all gone on together. Sam listened, grateful that for the most part she wasn't expected to add anything. Between the adults' conversation and the kids', there was no such thing as a quiet moment and the closeness of the group made Sam aware that she was the one outsider. Normally she would have risen to the occasion and joined in, but she felt Terri's gaze on her too often and was stuck wondering if she'd screwed up again with her.

"You got quiet over here. Everything okay?" Reed held out her hand for Sam's plate.

Julia and Kate had their heads together as they chatted, and the kids had run off with Mo and Terri for a game of hide and seek. Lost in thought, Sam hadn't noticed Reed get up to gather everyone's plates.

"I'll help you with the dishes," Sam said, standing.

"I won't say no." Reed smiled. "But I might ask you what you were over here brooding about."

"Brooding?" Sam got up and picked up the last few dishes that Reed had missed.

"You don't like brooding? How about ruminating?

Sam grinned. "Ruminating's not any better."

"You're right. I've been reading a lot of farming books and I think it's starting to wear off. Cow anatomy is pretty interesting. I knew they had four stomachs, but there's a lot more to it."

"How does Julia put up with you?" Sam asked, chuckling as she held the screen door open for Reed.

"I'm really not sure." Reed headed past her into the kitchen. She set her stack of dishes in the sink and turned on the water. "While we load the dishwasher, you can tell me if you're brooding about what happened with Terri."

"Maybe." Sam added the dishes she'd collected to the pile in the sink. "I like her. A lot."

"I know you like her. And she likes you."

From her tone, Sam knew Reed was holding something back. "But?"

"She's my best friend. Don't screw up with her."

"I can't screw up. She won't even say yes to a date. And I'm not going to tell you how much I want to do other things, but it doesn't seem right to just mess around. Not this time. I've slept with plenty of women—"

Reed held up her hand. "You can guess how much I don't want to know about the rest of your sex life. My advice is don't rush this. She's been pushed into relationships too many times."

They loaded the dishwasher, but Reed didn't say more after Kate and Julia came into the kitchen. Sam had more questions, mostly about Terri's past relationships, but she guessed Reed wouldn't answer her directly. She'd have to ask Terri.

The after-dinner entertainment included Reed's kids convincing everyone to lip synch to a pop song and then a round of Telephone played with the addition of stethoscopes. Instead of simply whispering a phrase to your neighbor and waiting for the last person in the circle to make a fool of themselves as they said aloud whatever they'd thought they'd heard, Reed's kids had added the rule that you had to wear a stethoscope and someone whispered the phrase into the bell.

The "Stethoscope" version of Telephone was good for several rounds of laughs. It wasn't until it was Sam's turn to be last that she got nervous. Terri had started the round, and her eyes were on Sam as Kate whispered into the bell of her stethoscope. When Kate finished, Sam took the stethoscope off. She scratched her head, wondering if what she'd heard was in fact what Terri had said or if one of the kids had jumbled the phrase—possibly on purpose.

Sam shook her head. "I can't say that."

"You have to say what you heard," Bryn said. "That's the rules."

"Okay, fine." Sam could feel the blush on her cheeks, but she cleared her throat and said, "I can never find a good way to kiss her."

Terri laughed immediately. "That's not what I said—I swear." She was still laughing as she clarified, "I can never find a good pair of scissors!"

"What?" Mo, who was on the other side of Terri, shook her head. "I swear I heard *kiss her*."

"Scissors. I said scissors."

"But why?" Mo was laughing now too. "It's not like it's that hard to find a good pair of scissors."

"Is anyone surprised that Mo heard something about kissing?" Julia asked, laughing as well.

"No one." Kate stood up and went over to the sofa where Mo was sitting and planted a big kiss on Mo's lips. "No one."

Bryn had her eyes covered, avoiding the kiss. "Grown-ups make everything about kissing."

"On that note, I think it's my bedtime." Mo stood up and caught Kate's hand. "Want to go home with me and look for a good pair of scissors?"

"You know I do."

Terri's phone rang and she went upstairs to take the call as the kids begged Mo and Kate to stay longer. After ten minutes, they managed to get out the door promising an overnight stay soon. Sam decided to leave then as well, though she wondered if she should say something to Terri before going.

She eyed the stairs, debating. The call was probably from someone at the hospital, and there was no guarantee how long she'd be on the phone. Waiting for her would probably be weird and what would she say anyway? Sorry I almost kissed you and the kid saw?

Finally she decided to leave without saying anything. At the door, Reed handed her a care package with a few of the leftover ribs and grilled veggies, along with a slice of the cheesecake. She thanked Reed and Julia and then stepped outside. The street was quiet compared to the noise of Reed's kids, and she took her time walking the half-block to her car, too many thoughts kicking round in her head.

"Gonna leave without saying goodbye?"

Sam let go of the car door handle. Terri stood on the sidewalk, her arms crossed.

"I didn't want to make things weird for you," Sam said.

"It might be weirder if you leave without saying anything about trying to kiss me earlier."

She had a point. Sam nodded slowly. "I should probably say that I'm sorry I tried to kiss you."

"But you're not sorry."

"No."

"Then don't say it." Terri walked the last few steps to Sam's car. "You're still a resident. My resident."

"I am. So you can't kiss me?"

"I can't. But you don't have to be sorry about what you want. I want it too." Terri looked at the road as a car passed. She waited until the sound of the engine had faded and then said, "In case you're worried, I'm not mad."

"I won't be your resident for much longer, you know. After that…" Reed's words repeated in Sam's head. *Don't rush her.*

"After that, what? You haven't decided if you're even staying around." Terri shook her head when Sam didn't argue. "Get some sleep, Samuels. You've got one more week on my schedule and I'm not going easy on you."

CHAPTER ELEVEN

Terri spun around before the impulse to kiss Sam won over her self-control. She crossed Reed's lawn, went up the front steps and then inside without chancing a glance back at Sam's car. As soon as she closed the door behind her, she exhaled.

"You didn't kiss her." Reed leaned against the stair bannister. "You're almost as bad a spy as your kids."

"I wasn't watching you. But I know that if you'd kissed her, you would have gotten in her car."

"Are you saying I'm loose?" Terri arched an eyebrow. "You're right, but still it's a little funny coming from you."

"I'm not loose anymore." Reed looked up the stairwell. "Julia's putting the kids to bed. Wanna stay and talk for a minute?"

"I should already be driving home."

"But you won't sleep anyway," Reed said. "Come on."

Terri followed Reed into the living room and sank onto the couch. "Why do I feel like I'm about to get a lecture?"

"No lecture. Promise."

Terri eyed the seat where Sam had sat earlier. She wished Sam hadn't left already. "What happened with Kayla...and Rebecca...I can't have a repeat of that."

"Sam's not Kayla. And she's definitely not Rebecca."

"You're right. But she's a resident."

Reed kicked her legs up on the ottoman and leaned back. "This hard rule you have about not dating residents is dumb."

"Dumb?"

"Kayla loved drama. And attention. She also liked you a hell of a lot more than you ever liked her."

Terri couldn't argue. "You know, you could have told me all this five years ago—before I married her."

Reed shook her head. "You knew what you were getting into with her. Were you actually surprised when she started sleeping with Rebecca?"

"We'd agreed to an open relationship."

"And to talking about things first. And to not sleeping with anyone from work. She wanted to make you mad. But more than that, she wanted to make a scene." Reed paused. "You know what pissed her off the most? That you wouldn't address any of the rumors."

"How long have you been waiting to tell me your analysis of my failed marriage?"

"For a while. But my point is, Sam's discreet. No one would know. If you two didn't work out, she wouldn't say anything to anyone."

"She's not that discreet." Terri thought of how Megan Gresham had sidled up to Sam in the cafeteria and rubbed her back. It wasn't an overt PDA like a kiss on the lips, but Sam hadn't moved away from her either. Anyone in the vicinity would have guessed they had a relationship. Even if it was only a friends-with-benefits thing, the point remained that caresses in the cafeteria weren't subtle. "Anyway, it doesn't matter. I'm happy single. I've got a full life and good friends. I don't want a relationship."

Reed didn't say anything in response. She crossed her ankles and stared up at the ceiling fan.

"What?"

Reed lifted her shoulders. "Nothing."

"Not everyone needs to be in a relationship," Terri argued.

"You've told me that before. My answer is still that while that may be true, *you* need to be in a relationship. And you're lying when you say you're happy. I know you aren't. You haven't been happy for a while."

"Why do I have such an annoying friend?" Terri closed her eyes. "Okay, let's say you're right. Maybe it's been a while since I've been happy. But I'm also exhausted and adding a relationship to my plate isn't going to help."

"You've been working way too much. You need a vacation. You're still going on that Costa Rica trip, right?"

"Yes, although after this week, September feels like about ten years from now." Terri hadn't forgotten about the week-long eco trip in the jungle, but she'd been too busy to think that far ahead. "Everything's been so crazy I don't know how I can take any time off."

"The hospital will be fine. The place didn't collapse when we went to Mexico, right? I mean, not completely anyway." Reed gave her a wry grin. "And this time it won't be both of us gone. I'll be around to keep an eye on everything… I know you don't like anyone telling you what you need, but you really need a break. You work through every holiday, and it takes someone getting married for you to even do a long weekend."

"You're right." Terri could admit that she had no life outside of the hospital. While that kept her from feeling like crap about her relationship skills, it wasn't healthy. As for Costa Rica, she hadn't managed to do anything more than book the trip. All the things she'd heard about it from everyone who had gone made it sound like the kind of place where planning ahead was important. But she doubted she'd have the luxury of even opening the travel book she'd bought until she was on the plane.

"I know you can handle the stress of the hospital better than anyone, but I think you're burning the candle at both ends. There's gonna be a point when there's nothing left."

"You're a bundle of positive energy tonight, aren't you?"

"I'm honest and direct. Part of my charm. That's what Julia tells me anyway.

Have you thought anymore about that private practice job in San Jose?"

Terri nodded. As much as she didn't want to admit she couldn't keep up, she needed a break from the pace that had been building speed all summer. More than once she'd let herself consider leaving the hospital. She'd gotten plenty of offers over the years, but she'd never truly considered it until this past spring. One of her colleagues had joined a group practice that wanted another internist. The perks included a schedule where she'd work three days a week. She might actually take time off and not have the entire place collapse without her.

"Even if you didn't take that other job, you could set better boundaries. Go on dates. Take more than a week off…"

Terri knew it was possible to do all those things. For other people, in other jobs. The problem was she loved parts of her job, but being needed all the time was exhausting. "What would you do about Sam?"

"If I were you? Well, for starters I would have kissed her when I chased her out to her car tonight instead of letting her drive away."

Terri let out an exasperated sigh. "I'm being serious. I need help."

"What do you want to do about Sam? Forget the resident thing for a minute because we both know that's only an excuse. When you close your eyes, what do you want?"

"I want to kiss her."

"See? We're making progress."

Terri pictured the kitchen that afternoon and Sam leaning against the counter. The playful banter had turned to something more so quickly she hadn't had time to set up her boundaries. But she hadn't wanted to. She could still remember the sensation of Sam's hand on hers. Her heart had seemed to stop as she'd waited for the kiss she knew was coming.

"I don't know, Reed. I think I've failed at this too many times."

"So you're scared of failing again. Too scared to even try. How novel—no one's ever felt that before."

"You're such a pain in the ass."

"Tell me something I don't know." Reed grinned. "The thing is, I think you're also scared because you know Sam could be good for you. She's sane, which is more than you can say for most people you've dated, she's smart, and she's got direction in life. What's more, she's actually a challenge for you. Besides, she won't be a resident forever."

Sam might be sane and she definitely was a challenge. But the direction thing wasn't completely true. Terri thought of telling Reed about the inheritance and how Sam didn't even want to be a doctor. Sam hadn't made her promise not to say anything, and yet she wasn't sure she wanted Reed to know.

"I really wish Bryn hadn't stopped her from kissing me." Terri dropped her head back on the couch pillows. "Damn, I wanted that kiss."

"You know that's okay, right?"

"I've never had it this bad for someone. Never. I go to bed thinking about her and wake up still thinking about her."

"Do you remember what you told me when I said the same thing about Julia? I almost didn't drive to her apartment that day—I had all these excuses. Carly still wasn't feeling that great, Bryn was being difficult, and I told myself that Julia didn't need my messed-up head. You told me to let her decide."

"Actually I think my exact words were 'get your head out of your ass and go after her,'" Terri said.

"You may have said that too. And it was good advice." Reed chuckled. "You know, you could do something crazy like text her. You have her number."

"I can't. If something happens and there's a trail of texts…"

Reed set her hand on Terri's knee. "Try trusting her. I dare you."

"Screw you." Terri laughed. "You can't dare me on something like this."

"Why not?"

By the time Terri finally got into bed, it was nearly midnight. She set her alarm, wishing she'd actually had a weekend away from work. After leaving Reed's, she'd gone back to the hospital to check on the case Shellhammer had called her about and in six hours she'd be back in the hospital to start another week.

As much as she needed to go straight to sleep when her head hit the pillow, that didn't happen. Instead, she started thinking of Sam as soon as she closed her eyes. After ten minutes, she sat up in bed and switched on the bedside lamp. She reached for her phone.

It's possible I'm lying here wishing I'd kissed you tonight.

Sam's response was faster than she'd expected: *It's possible that makes me really happy.*

Okay. They were doing this.

But I can't be thinking about kissing you.

Sam: *Does that mean I can't be thinking about taking off your clothes? Or all the other things I've been thinking about doing?*

Terri stared at Sam's text. She was wide awake now. They'd gone too far already for her to say this exchange was innocent.

I want you to tell me what you've been thinking, but that would definitely cross a line.

Sam: *Then I won't tell you how easy it would be to push up that skirt you were wearing. Or unbutton your blouse.*

There was a break and then Sam added: *I also won't tell you how I want to trace that tattoo on your chest. How I want to trace all your tattoos. And I won't say how my body wants to feel you under me.*

Terri swallowed. This was definitely too far. She'd opened the door, but Sam had quickly taken over and she was too turned on to ask her to stop. But she definitely needed to.

Terri: *I should tell you to stop but I don't want to*

Sam: *Then don't tell me. And I won't tell you how much I want to see you naked.*

Terri stared at the words, her heart racing. She set the phone face down and took a deep breath. What the hell was she doing not stopping her? They had to work together tomorrow. Her phone buzzed with a new text and she immediately flipped it over to read the words.

Sam: *Reed told me to wait for you. Did you know that? But I don't want to wait. I want to come over tonight. I want you to open the door and take me to your bed. Then I want you to spread your legs. And ask me to fuck you. I want you so much I wouldn't let you get any sleep. Course I won't tell you any of that. Because...lines.*

Terri could hardly breathe. She set the phone back down and reached between her legs. Damn, she was already wet. She let her finger circle her clit and her body responded with a firm clench. Every part of her wanted Sam inside her.

Wiping off her finger, she reached for the phone again. It wasn't fair that Sam had done this and she couldn't ask her to come finish what she'd started. She tapped out the words she didn't want to say: *We can't do this. I shouldn't have messaged you.*

Sam: *Whose lines are you worried about crossing?*

When Terri didn't answer, Sam texted again: *Neither of us are going to tell anyone. Say I'm wrong and you don't want me to come over.*

Terri: *I have to go. Good night.*

Terri tossed the phone on the night stand and then switched off the lamp. She could find her vibrator in the top drawer without the light on. Tonight it was a far cry from what she wanted, but Sam had given her plenty to imagine.

CHAPTER TWELVE

Sam could hardly breathe when she set her phone down. Had she really texted Terri all of that? And Terri hadn't stopped her. God, what'd she do for one night with her.

She got out of bed and went to the kitchen for a glass of water. No one was around to talk to, both of her roommates were long since asleep, but she couldn't tell anyone about the exchange anyway. And if things went any further with Terri, it would all have to stay a secret.

She looked out the little window above the sink. Another brown apartment building, illuminated by the parking lot lights, stared back at her. A dog barked somewhere and the sound echoed. With the thin walls and the ever-present freeway noise, the apartment was never truly quiet. But the noise didn't stop her from feeling lonely and longing to have someone to talk to. Maybe her roommates would listen. Maybe Megan would too. But what advice could they give?

If she stayed, she'd make everyone happy. Her parents, her friends, Weiss, and now Terri. If she left, she'd have the ocean to look at every day. But she'd give up forty-one million dollars and, worse, let everyone down. And how would she pay back all of the loans she'd taken out? She took a long sip of water and then added her glass to the pile of dishes that overfilled the sink.

The box from the beach house still sat in the middle of her room where she'd left it. She opened it now, took out one of the letters she hadn't yet read, and sat down on the floor. She'd gotten used to Paul Samuels' slanting cursive, but his handwriting in this particular letter wavered more. He started off with a colorful story about one of his neighbors, a drag queen with a day job as an accountant who'd forgotten to take off his bright red nail polish before heading into work one day. Sam found herself smiling despite the rest of the letter's somber tone. Paul's chest cold hadn't responded to antibiotics yet, and, in his words, his cough threatened to blow off the apartment's roof. He had a sense of humor, despite everything, and she could almost hear him laughing.

When she reached the end of the letter, tracing the swirly capital "l" in the word love, she leaned back against the bed and closed her eyes. From the letters, she'd quickly gathered that Paul Samuels was her uncle. After she'd figured that much out, she'd gone online and done some hunting. Then she'd come back to the box and pored over the letters and receipts to map out a story no one had ever told her.

Paul Samuels had died in 1989 in a little apartment in San Francisco that his mother, her grandmother, had been paying the rent for. Along with the rent, her grandmother had also been paying all of his medical bills. According to the newspaper obituary, which Sam had found on top of all the letters, Paul had died of pneumonia. But there was no doubt in her mind that AIDS had sealed his fate. And she'd figured out why no one had ever told her about him. Her grandfather, the same man who everyone touted as the perfect doctor, had disowned his son for being gay. Paul had written about it in one of the letters. He'd also forbade his wife, her grandmother, from talking to Paul. Of course she hadn't listened.

Sam carefully refolded the letter and slipped it back in the envelope. She'd found the box in the beach house's guest bedroom closet, buried under trays of oil paints and a pair of old shoes. The tattered brown box had escaped her notice for years, but she'd had a full weekend off between Radiology and Med-Peds and decided to take the time to finally clear out the room.

She'd been working on cleaning the whole house, when she had the time, for a few years, but everything took longer than it should since she couldn't bring herself to simply toss her grandma's stuff without sorting through it. The first time she'd read Paul's name, scribbled on the lid of the box, she'd stared at it dumbly, thinking she had no relative by that name. Then a lump formed in her throat as she read the name again. She knew they must have some connection, and before reading anything inside the box, she'd had a sense that something awful had happened.

But the box had given her more than the story of her uncle's tragic death. She'd learned what no one had ever told her about her grandfather. And knowing all that, could she truly follow in his footsteps and take over his old job?

She stayed on the floor until she felt chilled and then climbed into bed. The clock blinked two a.m. but she didn't feel tired. Picking up her phone, she pulled her sheets up to her chin and then read through the series of texts she'd exchanged with Terri. She couldn't help smiling when she got to the last few lines.

* * *

Morning rounds passed without any stray glances from Terri. Sam hoped for some hint that things had changed between them, but the only thing she noticed was that Terri pointedly avoided looking in her direction. And while everyone else chowed down on the donuts Sam had picked up, Terri slipped out to take a call from Shellhammer.

There was no break for lunch and again Sam had no excuse to catch Terri alone. She thought of sending a text and then changed her mind. By four her stomach rumbled loud enough to get a questioning look from a patient and after she'd finished with him, she went down to the breakroom. The food from the machines was tolerable at best, but she didn't have time for a run to the cafeteria.

After staring at the row of turkey and cheese sandwiches that she knew would taste stale, she punched in the code for an apple, promising her stomach a real meal in a few hours.

"Branching out from Reese's?"

Sam spun around at Terri's voice. "Hey." She'd waited all day for a chance to talk to her and "hey" was the best she could come up with? Sam glanced down at the apple. "I want pad thai. With a side of spring rolls. Unfortunately I haven't found that in a vending machine."

Terri reached for the apple. She took a bite, chewed with a furrowed brow, and then swallowed. "This is terrible."

"That's what you get for stealing someone's lunch." Sam went over to the next dispensing machine and punched the code for a bag of Reese's, then went to the next machine and paid for a Coke.

When the Coke dropped, she turned and handed it to Terri. "Want to have dinner with me tonight?"

Terri ignored the question. She popped open the Coke, took a long sip, and then tapped her nails on the can. "How'd you know this is what I came here for?"

"Because you live on caffeine. So you didn't follow me down here?"

"I did follow you. But I planned on using the Coke for my excuse."

Terri's coy smile hit Sam full in the chest. "Can I buy you anything else to keep you here longer?"

"You know I can't go to dinner with you. And I'm not saying I didn't like the texts you sent last night but...that can't happen again. Right now nothing can happen."

"Next week I won't be working with you."

Terri shook her head. "You'll still be a resident."

"You want me to wait almost two years to ask you out?"

"I wouldn't tell you to wait for anyone. But you have to decide if you want to be here at all and I don't want to complicate that." Terri eyed the package of Reese's. "You gonna eat all of those?"

Sam opened the package and handed her one. "So that's your final decision? You don't want to complicate my life?"

"Why are these things so damn good?"

"I think they slip crack in the chocolate."

Terri raised an eyebrow. "Now you tell me."

"I can do complicated, you know. What if I promise to figure out my shit without factoring you into it?"

"You could do that?"

"Probably better than you can relax around me."

Terri rolled her eyes. "You've seen how much caffeine I drink. I don't do relaxed." She paused. "I want you to make your decision first. Then we'll talk."

CHAPTER THIRTEEN

By some gift from the gods, the week was quiet—though no one dared say that word aloud. Although Terri had told Sam it wouldn't happen, she did try her best to relax. Both about the question of Sam leaving and the question of their attraction. Sam helped some by going back to being the all-star she'd been at the start, winning over patients and impressing everyone else.

Terri even gave her a few compliments but only because they were truly earned; once when she'd stepped in and offered to hold a screaming infant so the mother could comfort her sick toddler and then when she'd caught another resident's mistake and subtly pulled the resident aside without attracting anyone else's notice. For all she tried, Terri couldn't not notice her.

She'd reread the texts Sam had sent the night after the barbeque enough times to have the lines memorized, but she didn't dare text her again to restart the conversation. They'd reached an agreement, however tenuous it felt when Sam stood a little too close during rounds, and she intended to stick by it.

Sam finished her Med-Peds rotation and moved on to Emergency. Days passed and they rarely saw each other. Terri wanted to let Sam focus and she had her own work to do, but not seeing her only made her think about her more.

On a few occasions she went down to the Emergency Room when she knew Sam would be there. One look confirmed Sam's desire hadn't gone away. One look also made Terri wish she hadn't promised never to sleep with a resident again. Instantly being turned on in Sam's presence was bad enough. But then came the end of Sam's rotation in Emergency.

Terri knew Sam had gone to the beach house that she'd mentioned and after only a few days the distance to Santa Cruz felt insurmountable. She counted down the days of Sam's week off, hoping each night that she'd get a text from her, even though she knew she wouldn't, and planning what she'd say when Sam got back. As tempting as it was to simply call her, she didn't let herself. Sam wasn't simply on vacation. She was figuring out the rest of her life.

On the last day of Sam's week off, Terri got a message from Amos Hardinger, one of the cardiologists. He wanted to talk about a shared patient. Instead of calling him, she took the stairs down to the second floor after rounds. She didn't spend too much time on the second floor and it was a good excuse to make an appearance before Sam would be there—in case anyone happened to notice that she suddenly started frequenting the floor when Sam was around.

As soon as she walked into the cardiology suite, Amos gave her a wide smile. Amos loved to talk and more than once Terri had to steer him back to the case he had a question about—a patient in liver failure who'd had a heart attack. She felt antsy, wishing Sam were already back and wishing she knew her decision. But she told herself that Sam couldn't possibly decide not to finish the residency.

"Well, I appreciate your advice on that one," Amos said. He clapped his hand on her shoulder. "Want to take over a few of my cases so I can get a breather?"

"I hear you're down a resident." As soon as Terri spoke, she hoped Amos wouldn't ask how she knew that information.

Amos grimaced. "Yeah and looks like we might be shorthanded for the rest of the month."

"What do you mean?"

"Weiss sent me an email this morning. Our missing resident had some kind of family emergency and might be gone for longer than we expected."

"Wait, this is Elizabeth Samuels?"

Amos nodded. "You know her?"

"She was on rotation in Med-Peds last month."

"I've heard from others that she's good. But some of these kids can't swing it. Who knows if it's actually a family emergency... Leaves me in a tight spot, I'll tell you that much. But I won't bother you with my headache. I'm sure you've got plenty of your own."

Terri's mind spun with questions. She wished Sam had called or told her what the emergency was, but they weren't exactly close. And was it even a family emergency or was that a line from Weiss to cover for Sam? "I could probably shift around some residents to fill in if that would help."

"Ah, no, we'll make it work."

Terri left Amos with a final word that if he changed his mind, he should call her. She hoped her response didn't reveal the swell of emotions that had caught her off-guard. If Sam had made a decision and told Weiss without saying anything to her, whatever connection Terri thought they had didn't exist.

Goddammit. That curse slipped off her tongue followed by several more before she made it to the stairwell. She couldn't take the elevator pissed—with her luck, she'd bump into a resident or a patient or both.

As she climbed, she swore under her breath at every step. She shouldn't care if Sam quit. But she did. And the fact that Sam hadn't told her, hadn't even bothered to reach out, made her furious. But not at Sam. At herself for thinking Sam would want to tell her.

But what if there had been some emergency? That thought led her all the way up to Weiss's office. She needed to ask him what Sam had said. Weiss might be covering for Sam, but if he wasn't she needed to know what had happened. Her questions couldn't wait to be answered in an email, and she didn't want a paper trail of the conversation anyway.

Fortunately, the hall was clear. Terri paused long enough to catch her breath and steady her emotions. Weiss might be older than dirt by his own words, but he could be annoyingly perceptive. And she cared about his opinion of her. If he guessed she had an interest in Sam outside of the hospital, she'd have a bigger problem on her hands.

At her knock, Weiss's friendly greeting boomed: "Come on in."

Weiss stood up when Terri came in. "Well, speak of the devil." He pointed her to a worn leather sofa opposite his desk and then sank into his own chair. "I was about to send you an email. I don't suppose Elizabeth talked to you?"

"No."

Weiss had asked her to talk to Sam before, but did he expect Elizabeth to confide in her in the event of a family emergency—or in the event that she'd decided to quit after all?

"Then you're here about something else." Weiss sighed. "I'm sorry. I've had a lot on my mind this morning."

"Actually I am here about Elizabeth," Terri couldn't lie. Not to Weiss. But she could keep plenty to herself. "I went over to talk to Amos about a case and he mentioned he was going to be down a resident for the next month."

"Yeah, he's not happy."

"I offered to try shifting residents around since we've had a fairly light caseload and he's been slammed… He said Elizabeth had a family emergency?"

"I may have invented that part." Weiss pushed a stack of papers out of his way to clear a place for his coffee mug. "When she came to ask for time off last month, I knew there was a very real possibility she wouldn't come back. I took the gamble. Figured it was either a week off now and maybe she'd get her head unscrambled, or we lost a resident."

Terri kept her responses measured as Weiss explained he'd sent an email to Sam to check in and she'd written back to say she still hadn't decided. He'd offered one additional week as a last favor to her grandfather.

"She did say she felt terrible about letting you down."

"Me?"

"She mentioned you specifically. That's why I was going to email you." Weiss leaned back and his old leather chair creaked. "Do you think you could talk to her? I have her number and the address of where she's staying."

"If she's worried about letting me down, it sounds like she's already decided."

"Maybe. Maybe not." He sighed. "This isn't the first time I've had to let a good resident go. But circumstances are different this time and Elizabeth's particularly hard for me to let go of."

Terri wanted to say she understood. He had no idea how much she shared that sentiment.

CHAPTER FOURTEEN

Water crested over the nose of the board, splashing Sam's face with the chill of the Pacific Ocean. She dug her hands through the water, letting her board buoy her weight over the swells. At ten in the morning, the sun hadn't burned off the fog, but there was no wind and the tide was coming in. Even better, only a handful of surfers dotted the water. She couldn't ask for much more.

A perfect day on the water and nowhere else to be should have made her happy. But her chest felt heavy. She paddled through the rolling breakers, annoyed when she caught a mouthful of saltwater and then annoyed at herself for not laughing it off.

Easing up on her stroke, she searched out a spot to wait for a wave. The first few waves came and went. She used the excuse that she needed more time to check the mood of the ocean. Every day, every hour, it changed, and at the moment it seemed to be holding its breath. Or maybe she was the one holding her breath.

She watched the other surfers near her catch a ride before she decided to take the next one regardless of how it looked. As the swell rose up behind her, she paddled hard. Seconds later she pushed up onto her feet. The wave lifted her and the sensation of flying took over. Flying on top of the world. She took a deep breath, inhaling the salty ocean spray and trying to breathe out the funk she hadn't been able to shake for days.

Rocks rose up out of the water straight ahead. She grabbed the rails of her board and turned. Unfortunately she was a fraction of a second too late. The nose of her board dipped and her feet flew up in the air as she plunged into the water.

The ocean slapped her flat on the chest. She tried to relax, rolling with the wave instead of worrying about breathing as her board leash tugged at her ankle. Fighting the water never helped. All she could do was make a silent prayer that she'd dropped in further from the rocks than she thought.

After a long moment, the rolling stopped. She surfaced and sucked in a deep breath. The wave had gone. She'd been coughed up and spit out, and now the endless stretch of blue stared back at her as smooth as a lake. Between sets anyone could be fooled.

She looked back at the shore and a flash of panic coursed through her. The rocks she'd tried to avoid poked their heads above the water only feet away. If she stayed long enough to catch her breath, the next wave would crash her right onto them. It'd be some irony if she ended up back in the hospital after all. *As a patient.* Skull fracture, multiple contusions…she could almost see the report. With a few hard strokes, she caught up to her board, scanned for any dents, and then scrambled on.

* * *

"What can I get you?"

"Slice of pepperoni."

"You got it." The kid turned to pull a crispy pie out of the brick oven behind the counter and started slicing.

Sam had exchanged her wetsuit for a dry T-shirt and shorts and her board waited for her outside, balanced against a wall with a handful of others. After a few too many rolls in the waves, she'd given up and decided lunch was in order.

"Sam!" Danielle pushed past a couple waiting for their order and gave Sam a crushing hug, promptly followed by a kiss on the cheek. "I thought I saw you out there on the water, but I wasn't sure. Then I saw your board outside and knew! Can't miss those tiger stripes."

Sam grinned. "It's good to see you." Really good, in fact. She hadn't want to admit how much she needed a friend, but the way her body melted into the hug confirmed she couldn't stay a hermit for much longer.

"How long you in town?"

"Maybe forever. Were you surfing this morning? I didn't see you."

"Forever?" Danielle gave a "Woot!" loud enough to get the kid behind the counter's attention. He smiled as he slid Sam's pepperoni slice onto a paper plate.

"But what about the residency? I thought you signed up for three years of torture."

"I did. And it's a long story that I totally don't want to talk about. My goal is to surf enough that I'm too exhausted to think."

Danielle laughed. "How's that working out so far?"

"I think I got the exhausted part down." Unfortunately, her brain wouldn't turn off no matter how hard she tried.

"Well, I'm happy to have you back in town." Danielle gave Sam another squeeze. "I gotta run, but come see me later. You're gonna need free coffee if you don't plan on working."

Danielle stuck out her tongue when Sam rolled her eyes. They'd practically grown up together, spending every summer on the beach, and Sam's heart swelled knowing she still had a friend in town. A good friend.

Danielle headed for the door, waving and hollering, "Welcome home, Sam."

Home. Santa Cruz had always felt like home. And now she'd finally said out loud that she might never leave. But the realization of what that meant was bittersweet.

For the first few days back, she'd only surfed and slept, eating canned soup and anything else she could rummage from the nearly empty pantry. Then she'd decided to go to the grocery store and restock. Strangely that step had cemented in her mind that she could in fact stay in the cottage.

She hadn't told her parents. Aside from Weiss, she'd only contacted her roommates back in the Sacramento apartment, promising to clear out her things and pay her part of the rent until they found someone to take her place. If she didn't come back. *If.*

Megan had texted a handful of times, but Sam had evaded all her questions. Terri hadn't called or texted even once. Clearly she was leaving her alone to figure things out. Sam was mostly glad for that. She didn't want to talk things out with anyone. But she missed Terri and wondered if she knew that she'd become part of the decision. Giving up forty-one million dollars that had never felt like her money in the first place was one thing, but the thought of not seeing Terri again?

"Here's your pizza. And welcome home."

"Thanks." Sam slid her money across the counter and took the paper plate. The kid had given her an extra large slice and a third of it hung over the edge of the plate.

She ate the first few bites on the street corner where she could keep an eye on her board, but once the hunger subsided, she tossed the plate and folded the pizza in half to eat as she walked home.

The cottage wasn't far, but Sam didn't rush the walk. As soon as she spotted the bright blue panels with white trim she smiled. Perched on a cliff above the ocean, the land itself was worth way more than the little house, but she loved it still. Memories of carefree summers spent there were part of that. The whole thing sorely needed a remodel, and it wasn't much to look at inside. Just two small bedrooms upstairs along with a tiny bathroom, a kitchen so outdated it could be called retro, a powder room off the hallway, and a living room with a sagging brown couch and one equally sad love seat. But the view couldn't be beat. At night, with the windows open, the sound of the waves lulled her to sleep and every morning she woke to the salty smell of the ocean.

Since she'd left Sacramento, the insomnia she'd fought for the past several years had vanished. Seals would jostle her from a dream sometimes, but she could drift off again even with their barking, and the cry of the gulls made a perfect alarm clock.

Sam gave her board and wetsuit a quick rinse in the outdoor shower and then stripped down to shower salt and sand out of her hair. The neighbors could see her if they looked over the fence, but no one did. After toweling off, she tugged the same T-shirt and shorts back on before she got numb. Even in late summer, Santa Cruz was never truly hot and the temperature had dropped when the fog rolled in.

Out of habit, she checked her phone when she came into the kitchen. She'd had few texts and fewer calls since leaving Sacramento, and this time she had only one missed call. Doug. She'd talked to him the day before about possibly coming back to work with him and he'd been happy to hear the news. His message detailed an upcoming wedding he needed help with and then a family photo shoot he could pass on to her if she wanted it.

Saying yes to the photo shoot would make it official. Forty-one million dollars gone. But she couldn't keep pushing off the decision with an empty bank account. Before long, she'd need cash in her pocket.

She started to call Doug and then felt a wave of nausea. Without stopping to process her thoughts, she pulled up Terri's number and quickly pressed the call button. She waited as the line rang, her heart thumping fast in her chest. The voice mail picked up and she debated what to say. On a Friday afternoon, Terri was probably too swamped with patients to take a call.

"Hey. It's me…Sam. But you already know that 'cause you have my number." She took a deep breath and started over. "I need to talk to you. I know you're probably busy, but can you call me?"

She paced between the couch and the love seat. "I thought it'd be easier to make this decision. It's not easy at all." Nor was leaving all of her thoughts on a voice mail. "Anyway. Can you give me a call back? I'd really appreciate it."

She stopped pacing and tossed the phone on the coffee table. Terri might not call her back for hours. And after they talked, what then? What did she even have with Terri? Crazy distracting chemistry. And yet she knew there could be more.

She stared out at the ocean. The water was gray now with the fog hovering close and the waves were cresting higher than when she'd been out earlier, but she didn't want to get her board again. She was spent. Her morning workout didn't hold a candle to all the handwringing over the decision, the emails back and forth to Weiss, the anticipation of telling Terri, and then the realization of what her choice meant. She sank down on the couch wishing she had something that had to be done, something she was needed for to distract her thoughts.

Aside from surfing and sleeping, the only other accomplishments she'd managed that week had been to finish sorting through the boxes of her grandmother's things. She'd gotten the guest room and the closet entirely cleaned and then bought a new mattress and bedroom furniture. The other bedroom—her grandmother's—still had too many boxes and paintings to think about so she kept the door closed.

Her grandfather never liked the cottage. He said it was too small for his taste, and he didn't like the beach anyway. But Sam knew the real reason he had never spent time there. The cottage belonged solely to her grandmother and she claimed the space as her own, with unfinished artwork and knick-knacks cluttering every corner.

Despite being married for nearly fifty years, she'd kept the cottage as her own world. She'd come to paint, to hide away from the world, and to have a space where she could be truly herself. After she'd passed, a lawyer had given Sam the deed to the cottage and the keys. He'd explained how she'd be responsible for the taxes and the insurance. Everything inside the cottage belonged to her—the artwork, the knick-knacks, and the meticulously maintained Aston Martin that had been strictly used for driving on Highway One. All of it. Her grandmother had been very clear in her will that her grandfather was to have no say in any of this. Everything belonged to Sam.

At the time, Sam had been living in San Jose with her then girlfriend. Despite the fact that they were nearby, her grandfather had refused to speak to her because of the relationship and because he thought she was being ridiculous trying to make it as a photographer. But her grandmother had been proud of her for chasing a dream. Sam had held on to that.

Then a year later her grandfather had died. When she heard how much money she could inherit, as long as she followed his stipulations, she'd given up everything. All of her camera equipment went into storage and she'd gone back to school. The girlfriend moved on to women who had more time on their hands, which was probably for the best. Sam had no time for her, let alone anyone new. Then came the residency in Sacramento and what little life she'd thought she'd had was gone completely. All of those steps, all of those sacrifices, all for forty-one million dollars.

But now what she stood to lose was even more complicated. She eyed her phone, willing it to ring. When it didn't, she leaned her head back on the couch and closed her eyes.

CHAPTER FIFTEEN

"Can you talk?" Terri hadn't wanted to bother Reed, but she needed someone to reason with her. Someone who wouldn't judge.

"Sure, what's up?"

"No…I mean, in person. Can you meet me somewhere?" Terri paced the landing of the stairwell. She'd made it back to the third floor, managed to see a few patients and even round with her residents, but then she'd gotten Sam's message.

"Tell me when and where."

Thank God for Reed. "My office in twenty minutes?"

"I'll be there."

Terri let out the breath she'd been holding. "Thanks."

Reed hadn't asked why Terri wanted the sudden meeting, but twenty minutes later, the question was clearly on her mind. "How worried about you should I be?"

Terri unlocked her office door and held it open. "I don't know. Probably a lot. I swear to God, I promised myself I wouldn't fall for a resident ever again."

"Well, that was a dumb promise. You can't stop yourself from feeling things."

"I need you to be the voice of reason here." Terri crossed her arms. "Sam's probably quitting the residency."

"Seriously?"

Terri nodded. "And I don't want her to. Obviously. But I can't decide if that's because I really think she should be a doctor or if it's because I really want to sleep with her."

"I can't believe she's quitting. Why?" Reed scratched her head. "You said she needed some time off to deal with some family things."

"Yeah, well, I may have covered for her. It's a long story. I'm the one who suggested she ask for time off. She told me she was quitting and I convinced her to take some time to think it over. Anyway, Weiss just told me. He asked me to talk to her, but I don't see the point of trying again."

Reed sank down in the chair by the desk. "You don't see the point because you don't think she'd listen to you? Or because if you take the chance and she still says no, then she's turning you down too?"

"You're supposed to be the voice of reason—not my subconscious."

Reed gave her a look bordering on pity. "I'm sorry. Look, I get that you don't want her to quit but…What do you want out of this?"

"What do you mean?"

Reed sighed. "I know you're upset. But is it only because you think she should finish the residency? Or because if she leaves then you miss out on what you could have had together?"

"Yeah, still not helping."

"Okay. I'll make it simple. What do you want to do right now?"

"I want to see her," Terri said immediately. "But I can't decide if I want to talk to her, or strangle her, or kiss her. Or all three."

Reed smiled. "You've got it bad."

"I'm not joking."

"I know you aren't. That's why it's funny." Reed leaned back in the chair, clearly thinking. "So you picked me to be the voice of reason 'cause you thought I wouldn't tell you to sleep with her?"

"I didn't say I wanted to sleep with her. I said I couldn't decide if I wanted to kiss her."

"Well, we both know where that would lead. Terri, I'm the one who introduced you two. If you're expecting me to tell you to forget about her, I'm not going to. I still think you'd be perfect for each other."

"I don't want her to quit. That has nothing to do with whether or not I kiss her."

Reed cocked her head. "Are you sure?"

"No." Terri cussed. "I can't understand how she could walk away from this. From being a doctor. She's gone through all the steps. And now she decides to quit?"

"You can't understand it because you would never quit." Reed paused. "She probably didn't have a single mom like you did who sacrificed to make sure she got to college. And scrimped when she could to send a care package when she was in med school. She probably doesn't have anyone asking her to send money when times get hard like your sisters do. And how many times have you paid your mom's rent? Having people need you changes things. You can't tell me there aren't days where you consider walking away from it all."

"Of course there are days."

"But you stay because when it comes down to it, you want to be a doctor. We both know it's not for everyone."

Terri pressed her hand to her forehead. "Tell me what you'd do."

"I'd go find her. Talk to her. And then probably kiss her. I mean, if I were you."

"What if that kiss leads to more?" Terri shook her head. "Then this becomes a bigger mess."

"*When* that kiss leads to more, you'll figure it out."

"What if I can't?" Terri worried that Reed was right. She hadn't stopped thinking of Sam. Distance hadn't made her desires any less. But that was a problem too. What if she liked her more after a night together?

"You need to get her out of your system. Get in your car and go find her. Spend the night. Either you'll leave in the morning and never see her again or you'll convince her not to quit. If that happens, then you have to deal with the question of whether or not you're ready to be in a relationship again."

Terri exhaled. She didn't see any other option. The thought of never seeing Sam again made her feel sick. But she couldn't talk to her on the phone. She'd only yell and that wouldn't make anything better. "What is it with me and residents?"

"I'd say this time wasn't entirely your fault. She has it bad for you too. But I don't blame her. You're pretty amazing."

"I tried to ignore her."

"Yeah, but that was dumb." Reed snorted when Terri glared at her. "You know how you're always doing what's right for other people? Maybe this time you should think about what's right for you."

CHAPTER SIXTEEN

Sam rubbed her eyes as a ringing jostled her awake. She reached for her phone and then realized the sound wasn't coming from that. When it occurred to her it was the doorbell, she called out, "Hold on a minute." Not once had she heard the doorbell ring in all the summers she'd spent at the cottage. Everyone always knocked or let themselves in.

She opened the door and stared dumbfounded for a full second at Terri. "How'd you find me?"

"Weiss gave me the address." Terri's lips were a tight line. Normally she was a hard read but this… Impossible.

Sam suddenly worried what might have happened at the hospital. "Is everything okay?"

"I have to pee. Can I come in?"

"Sorry. Yeah. Of course. Come in. It's a long drive." Sam wished she weren't stammering. It was dark outside. How long had she slept? She opened the door wider. "The bathroom's down the hall on the left."

"Thanks."

Terri stepped past her and a whiff of her perfume caught Sam's attention. This was no dream. Terri was here—in a pair of dress pants and a light pink blouse. Sam had seen her in the same outfit at the hospital, which meant she'd come straight from work. And she'd driven three hours to see her instead of calling. The only thing that made sense was that Weiss had sent her here.

The bathroom door opened and Terri came out. She looked at Sam for a moment and then, before it was clear what she was thinking, turned into the living room. She didn't sit down but instead walked past the sofa to stare out the window. The fog hadn't lifted and little was visible past the circles of orange-yellow under the streetlamps.

"You can't tell right now, but it's a nice view of the ocean. We're up on the cliffs above the water..." Sam's voice trailed when Terri turned to face her. She wanted to go to Terri then, wanted to kiss her more than ever, but she held back. "Did you get my call?"

Terri nodded. "And I should have simply called you back. But I'm here."

"Why?"

"I'm not exactly sure." Terri held Sam's gaze. Still unreadable.

"Did Weiss send you down here?"

"That'd be asking a lot. He did suggest I talk to you. But, no, I came because I wanted to."

Question after question filled Sam's mind. What would Terri say when she told her about quitting? "I'm glad you're here."

"Have you already made up your mind?"

Sam nodded. She hated to say the words, but she could tell Terri already knew. Maybe had guessed as soon as she'd walked in the door. "I'm not going back. I'm done."

Terri seemed to take the information in slowly. She didn't say anything for a moment, then walked closer to the window, eyeing the gray again. Sam started to explain that she'd wanted to tell her first, before anyone else, but before she got half the words out, Terri cut her off.

"So you've got a nice view, huh? Is that it? Throw everything away for a fucking view? Goddammit, Sam. You're making a huge mistake and you know it."

"I threw away the life I had. I want it back." Sam tried to keep her tone in check but Terri's sudden anger rocked her. "You only know part of the story." Even if she thought she knew everything, what gave her the right to judge?

"How many people have given their time to help you become a doctor? How many sacrifices did they make? How many have you made? And how many lives could you save if you didn't give up? You're a damn good doctor—one of the best residents I've ever had—and you're going to throw it all away. Why? Because you don't like the fact that someone told you what to do. That it wasn't your choice."

"If you came all this way to tell me how to live my life—"

"That's not why I came." Terri interrupted again, her voice raised. "But now, sure, I'll take that on. Clearly someone needs to tell you that you're fucking everything up."

"This is my life to fuck up." Sam couldn't keep her temper in check any longer. Not with Terri acting like the only grown-up in the room. What the hell kind of nerve did she have? "I know you tell people what to do all the time. But I'm not your resident anymore. This isn't your hospital. You don't run this show."

"Screw you."

"If only that was why you were here," Sam returned. She cussed under her breath and then said, "Weiss told you to convince me. So here you are. And now you're upset that you can't be the one who fixes this like you fix everything else."

Terri laughed, but the sound cut like a knife. She crossed the room and stopped a foot in front of Sam. "You have everything all figured out, don't you? Ever consider that you might not know everything?"

"I don't want a lecture right now." Sam clenched her teeth as the desire to kiss Terri burned through her. How could she still want her?

"I'm so damn mad at you," Terri breathed.

Sam held her gaze. She knew Terri wasn't lying. Anger radiated from her, but it was all Sam could do not to reach for her. "If you're so mad, why do you want to kiss me?"

"Who said I wanted to kiss you?"

"I can tell. You put up this big front, but I can see through it."

"You're wrong about a lot of things." Terri pressed her palm against Sam's chest like she was trying to hold her back. "I wish you were wrong about this." She leaned forward and met Sam's lips.

The kiss shouldn't be happening, but it was. Terri's lips pressed hot against hers. Exactly what she wanted. Sam gave in, opening her lips as Terri's hand moved from her chest to her neck. She pulled her closer, deepening the kiss, and the demand in her lips sent heat flooding through Sam's body.

When Sam couldn't hold back any longer, she spun Terri around and pushed her up against the wall. Not letting up on the kiss, she slid a hand under Terri's blouse to feel her smooth skin.

One kiss and then another even more crushing. But it wasn't enough. She undid Terri's bra and took a breast in each hand. As soon as she touched the nipples, pinching the tips, Terri moaned. The sound seemed to slip out involuntarily, but then Terri clutched Sam's hands hard against her.

Sam's arousal spiked. She moved against Terri, grinding her desire. Kissing Terri, having her hands on her body, all of it felt too good to be true.

"Do you have a bed, asshole?" Terri said, her lips on Sam's neck. "Or are you planning on fucking me against the wall?"

"Hadn't really thought about it," Sam said, between kisses. Something about the fact that Terri was still mad turned her on even more. She didn't feel like making love—she felt like proving a point. "Bed's upstairs."

"I want a bed," Terri said.

She let Sam kiss her again, harder this time, and gave in when Sam took another kiss before she could take a breath. Sam could feel Terri's anger fighting her desire. Every time she tried to push Sam back, she pulled closer in the next moment. At least that emotion went both ways.

Sam got Terri to the stairwell, nipping at her lips every few steps. Before they'd made it to the top of the stairs, she had her shirt off and Terri's as well. She kicked open the door as she undid Terri's pants, then tugged off the underwear along with the pants. Terri managed to get Sam's board shorts untied, but that was as far as she got.

The sheets weren't turned down, but Sam didn't care. She needed Terri now and couldn't wait. She pushed her onto the bed and moved on top of her, kissing her again. Her hands trailed up and down—from Terri's breasts to her hips and lower to her thighs. She held back from touching her center, wanting to save that for last.

Terri massaged her way down from Sam's shoulders to her back and then to her butt. She pushed Sam's shorts off all the way and cupped her butt cheeks, moaning against Sam's ear.

Sam paused between kisses. "You like my butt, don't you?"

"I'm not answering that. I like too many damn things about you." Terri gripped Sam's butt harder and pushed up her hips. The contact of Terri's clipped hair against hers was adding fire to the blaze. "But I'm getting you out of my system tonight."

Sam pushed up on her hands, holding herself away from Terri so the feel of her skin wouldn't be a distraction. "Is that what you really want? One night with me, and then you can move on?"

"You got a problem with that? You're the one who's quitting."

Sam didn't answer. She knew then that Terri wasn't only mad about her leaving the residency. For all she said about not wanting to date, Sam knew the truth. She hadn't come because of Weiss. She'd come because she'd wanted this. But was that all?

"Don't start thinking now," Terri said. "Just fuck me."

Terri's red curls cascaded over the pillow. In the dim light, Sam couldn't make out the detail on all of her tattoos, but the mosaic of colors was gorgeous against Terri's pale skin. "You're beautiful."

"Put your damn hand between my legs."

"You still think you can tell me what to do, huh?" Sam shook her head. "You're wrong. You're not in charge here, remember?"

Terri parted her knees further and Sam felt a surge at her clit.

"But I know what you want." Terri pumped her hips off the mattress. "And you know what I want. So give me your hand. Then we both move on and we don't have to look back."

Desire ripped through Sam's body and she had to clench her hands into fists to stop herself from reaching for Terri. She didn't want to be someone Terri moved on from and forgot. But what choice did she have? And the truth was, if this was all she could get, she wanted at least that.

"Unless you're the kind of butch who's got a cock in the nightstand drawer. I'd take that too."

"Maybe I am." But Sam wanted Terri without any toys first. She could get her strap-on later. She shifted onto her side and touched Terri's lips with a fingertip. "But you won't be able to get me out of your system with one good fuck. And I like femmes to say please."

The last line was a gamble. She drew a slow line from Terri's lips, over her chin, down the center of her chest, and then stopped an inch below her belly button. She traced the triangle of trimmed hair, deliberately pressing lightly where she knew Terri wanted more. "If we do this, I'm in charge."

Terri sucked in a breath. "Screw you."

"I know you want me."

"And you want me." Terri's knees parted further, and she pushed her hips up again, bumping Sam's hand. "Fuck me."

Terri's words came out like a hiss, but Sam only smiled. "When you say please I will."

Terri shook her head, but she held Sam's gaze. Her anger was a smoldering heat now. Sam could hardly wait any longer.

"I know you want to say it." Sam stroked up the inside of Terri's thigh, waiting for the word. "I think secretly you want someone who'll tell you what to do. Wanna tell me I'm wrong?"

Terri shifted, trying to push herself onto Sam's fingers. When Sam stroked down her thigh instead, she let out a frustrated growl and grabbed Sam's wrist. She pulled Sam back to her center as her hips jutted up. "Fine. I'll play your game. *Please*. Happy?"

It was more of an order than a request, but Sam was too hot to be picky. "I am. And you're gonna say it again. You won't be able to stop yourself."

Sam pushed inside and Terri's breasts heaved. For the first few thrusts, Terri tried to keep hold of Sam's wrist, tried to control her, arching up every time Sam pushed and letting loose a string of curse words, but she finally gave in and let go. Collapsing back on the pillows, she spread her legs and let Sam work. "Fuck me. That feels so damn good."

"Happy you said please?"

"Yes. So much yes." Terri closed her eyes, moaning softly.

"You want more, don't you?"

Terri nodded, eyes still closed. Sam moved on top of her. Wetness covered her hand and the warm vault tightened around her fingers. She pumped hard, figuring out quickly how much Terri could take and then giving a little more. Terri's moans only encouraged her to go harder. Her thumb rode Terri's swollen clit. A few strokes over the tip and she was on the verge of coming. Sam pushed another finger inside, and Terri gripped her forearm.

"Don't stop… Please. Please."

The added "please" was music to Sam's ears. Terri wanted to say it. She wanted this. Sam had known it all along—but now she could feel it. She shifted so she could reach Terri's lips, kissing her as she stroked faster.

When the orgasm came, Terri's nails sank into her skin. Sam held her as she cried out, not releasing the pressure on her clit. Terri clenched down on her, and Sam rotated a few degrees, then pushed a little deeper.

"Oh… Like that."

Terri grabbed at Sam's wrist, trying to hold her in place as her body clenched again and again. When the orgasm was over, Sam slowly pulled her fingers out. Terri reached for her, wrapping her arms around Sam's chest and murmuring swear words against her shoulder.

"You can cuss all you want. The truth is you came here tonight because you wanted that."

"You didn't even offer me a drink."

"I don't have any Coke," Sam returned. "I have other things but…sometime I'm going to ask you why you don't drink alcohol."

"Don't ask me now." Terri exhaled. "I was hoping you wouldn't be good in bed."

"So what's the verdict?"

"I'm not going to say it out loud because I know you're already gloating. And I'm still mad at you. It sucks that this has to be a one-time thing." Terri shifted against Sam, kissing her neck. "I'm thirsty."

"It doesn't have to be a one-time thing."

"We both know it does." Terri sighed. "Water?"

Sam moved Terri's arm off her chest and got up. Now wasn't the time for a deep conversation about connection, but she hated that Terri was convinced they had no chance.

CHAPTER SEVENTEEN

When she got back to the room, Terri was sitting up. She took a sip of water and then set the glass on the nightstand.

"Don't get back in bed."

Sam cocked her head. "You know this is my house, right?"

Terri slid her legs over the edge of the bed and stood up. "I know. And you're in charge and all of that. But there's something I've been wanting for a while now."

Terri slid her hand down the front of Sam's chest and then dropped onto her knees.

"Whoa. What are you doing?"

Sam barely got the question out before Terri's mouth was on her. She nearly came when Terri sucked her clit between her lips. She gasped, but Terri didn't let up.

"Damn." Sam took a shaky breath, moving her legs apart as Terri's tongue dove inside. "You're good at that."

Terri pulled away long enough to say, "You like me on my knees."

"More than you could imagine." Sam moaned as Terri's tongue slid up the inside of her thigh and then dove inside again.

Maybe it was only sex that Terri wanted. Maybe after tonight, Terri would never want to see her again. Sam knew that was likely. And it was mostly her fault. But she wasn't convinced Terri would have given her a chance even if she'd stayed.

If they only had this one night, what did she have to lose by saying exactly what she was thinking? "You know I've liked you for a long time now."

Terri didn't let up but Sam knew she'd heard.

"But I didn't know you'd be this good." She laced her fingers through Terri's soft red curls. She wanted to hold off the orgasm she knew was coming. She didn't want Terri to stop. "You'd make a good submissive."

Terri's eyes darted up to hers for the briefest of moments, but she didn't respond. Sam knew the risk she'd taken using that word. Her still smoldering anger had made her reckless. But now she wanted to know what Terri was thinking.

Her tongue only worked faster, quick strokes and circles that Sam couldn't keep track of. Whatever magic Terri was doing threatened to leave her ruined for anyone else.

"Don't stop," Sam managed.

Terri doubled down, her tongue lashing faster and her face nuzzled deeper between Sam's legs. As hard as she tried to hold her orgasm back, wanting to enjoy Terri for as long as she could, she knew it was coming. Finally she gave up fighting.

A wave of pleasure came after the initial muscle clench and a moment later her knees went weak. She took a step back to balance against the bed. Terri followed and Sam had to hold her back. "That's all I can handle."

Terri wiped her lips and got to her feet. Standing there with her naked body on full display, Terri's beauty rocked Sam. "I know you didn't want me to say you were beautiful earlier so I'm going with gorgeous this time."

"You just came," Terri returned. "Everyone thinks their lover is good-looking in the afterglow."

"Yeah, but I'm right." Sam tried not to think too hard about Terri's word choice. Lover. She meant it in a generic way, but Sam wanted to earn that title more than ever. "My turn?"

"You think I want you again?"

Sam didn't answer. Her body still twitched with aftershocks, but her need wasn't satisfied. She opened the nightstand drawer and held up a cock. "Lucky guess."

"So predictable." Terri ran a finger from the bulb to the base of the shaft. "This better be clean."

"It's brand new."

"Do I want to know why you have a new dildo in your drawer?"

Sam reached for the leather harness. "I didn't think you were going to show up here, if that's what you're wondering. I figured I'd have to drive back up to Sac, but I wanted to be ready."

"It's not for some other woman?"

"You want to be my only submissive?" Sam grinned, but when Terri didn't answer, she regretted joking. "I bought it because I liked it. That's all."

Terri sat down on the bed as Sam fit the cock through the ring and then tightened the leather straps. When Sam drizzled lube over the tip, Terri pushed the comforter down and settled back on the pillows. She reached between her legs to finger herself. "I don't know if you'll actually need lube. But you're right. I want more."

"I know."

"You're annoyingly cocky sometimes." Terri's fingers glistened when she pulled them away from her folds. Sam reached for her hand and licked her fingers.

"Only sometimes?" Sam sobered for a moment, thinking of how Terri had gone quiet earlier. "If you're not into it, I won't bring up the submissive thing again."

"I didn't say I wasn't into it." Terri slid her tongue over her lips. "I've never really thought about it. I'm not exactly a submissive person."

"Not in the rest of your life, no. But you could be when we have sex. You might like a break from making decisions. From being the one who's always responsible."

"Maybe. Or maybe I just want that." Terri nodded at Sam's erect cock. "Don't go easy on me this time. I like it hard." When Sam arched an eyebrow, Terri added: "Please."

"You're a fast learner."

"This isn't my first rodeo, cowboy."

Sam leaned close and kissed her. She liked the way Terri casually dropped the word "cowboy." Gender games were a turn-on—not that she needed much help getting turned on at the moment—but she liked it anyway. With another kiss, she stroked her hand down Terri's chest and then lower to below her belly. She dipped her fingers and Terri responded by pushing into her hand.

Sam rolled her hand, coating her fingers in the warm wetness. When she shifted between Terri's legs, she had to fight the impulse to push right inside. Instead she dragged the tip of her hard cock over Terri's opening a few times, waiting for her to ask.

Terri gripped Sam's hips. She tried to catch Sam's lips for a kiss. When she couldn't get that, she arched up. After a few thwarted attempts, she said: "Tell me what I have to do. I'll do anything you want."

"Anything?"

Terri hesitated. "For the record, I'm still mad at you. But at the moment I'm so turned on I can't think."

"Is that a 'yes'?"

Terri tilted her head. "That's a 'yes please.'"

"Even better." Sam brushed her cock over Terri's opening again. "You want this?"

"I want it." Terri whimpered when Sam pulled back.

Sam kissed her lips. "I like you under me." She shifted a half inch and thrust her hips. The tip of her cock pushed inside, and Terri wrapped her arms around her, gripping tight as Sam slid all the way inside. When she pulled back to thrust again, Terri loosened her grip and eased back on the pillows.

"God, you feel good." She pushed her hips up to meet Sam. "I don't know if I'm going to come again, but you can keep this up all night."

"I will if you say please."

"Please."

Sam thrust faster and Terri's eyes closed. "You like saying 'please.'"

"Don't tell anyone." Terri closed her eyes and her lips parted, as if only waiting for a deep kiss.

The expression of bliss on her face made Sam heady. One night wouldn't be enough. But if that was all she got, she was going to make the most of it. She pulled all the way out and Terri opened her eyes. Before she could ask, Sam said, "Watch me."

Terri glanced from Sam's face to her cock. She raised her hips as Sam nudged her with the tip. "Show me what you got," Terri said.

"You sure you don't want me to be gentle?"

"Do I seem like the gentle type?"

Sam drove in hard.

Terri gasped and clutched Sam's forearms. "Again. Please."

With Terri watching, Sam pulled all the way out and then sank in deep again. Each time she thrust, Terri pushed up to meet her, moaning "more."

As much as Sam wanted to keep going for the rest of the night, her own approaching orgasm started to distract her. The base of the cock rubbed against her clit and when she sank in, the pressure hit exactly the right spot. She didn't stop thrusting but she found Terri's clit and clumsily rubbed.

"I don't know if I can wait for you." She was too close.

"Don't hold back. I want to feel you come."

Terri's words were all Sam needed to hear. She stopped fighting it and when her orgasm hit, she let Terri hear her pleasure. A moment later Terri screamed out her name and tensed. She shivered and then relaxed only to tense again.

Sam held her close, her own breathing still ragged. She hadn't been able to focus on Terri but somehow they'd both climaxed.

"Damn. That was hot."

"Tell me about it," Terri murmured. "Don't pull out yet."

Sam didn't want to move a muscle. She wanted to remember everything about the moment. How Terri felt in her arms, how a sheen of sweat coated their skins, and how the smell of sex filled her senses. She could stay this way all night if Terri wanted it.

Minutes passed and Sam kissed Terri's cheek. Her breathing had slowed and she looked as if she'd fall asleep any moment. "Okay if I come out now?"

Terri nodded and Sam eased out gently, pressing where she knew Terri would be tender.

"I don't want to sleep." Terri curled up against her, and lazily stroked Sam's cock. "I want you inside me again."

Sam wrapped an arm around her and pulled her close. "How about you sleep for a while and I wake you later?"

"What if you forget?"

"I won't." Sam knew she wouldn't forget anything tonight.

CHAPTER EIGHTEEN

Terri sat up, blinking her eyes in the sunlight. For a long moment she couldn't remember where she was. Then it hit her. Sam's bed. In Santa Cruz—fuck her for that. But what time was it? And where was Sam? More importantly, what was she going to do?

Get up, get dressed, and leave. That's what she should do. But she wanted to stay in bed and wait for Sam to come back. *God, what a night.*

There were good orgasms and then there was what she'd felt last night. Screw Sam for being that good and not telling her sooner. And screw her for leaving her to wake up alone. But what was she expecting? To spend the morning cuddling?

What they'd done last night was not the kind of sex that was followed by cuddling. Besides, they were still fighting. Sex hadn't changed that.

She fluffed her pillow and rolled on her side, still not ready to leave the space that smelled of Sam and carried a memory of everything they'd done.

Sam's dominance came as no surprise. She'd felt that under the surface even when they'd danced together months ago. But she hadn't expected to surrender so easily to it. When Sam had called her submissive, her first response had nearly been to laugh. *Submissive?* Was she kidding? Except Terri knew she wasn't.

And maybe she did want to be submissive this one time. If it meant being topped by someone who made her orgasm again and again and fucked her until she couldn't think, she'd take it.

Anyway, Sam was right. She loved not having to be in charge for once. Not being the responsible one. She'd given up control completely and hadn't regretted a moment of it.

Sam brought something out of her that she'd never felt with other lovers. Her desire was over the top and because of it Terri had been able to relax in a way she'd never done. She hadn't thought Sam would actually wake her up in the middle of the night for more. But she had. Anything she wanted, Sam would probably do to her without raising an eyebrow. And as crazy as it sounded, she could get used to Sam taking care of her needs.

But who was she kidding?

This wasn't the start of something. Last night was a one-time thing. Sam had officially quit the residency. Forget how much she liked being under Sam. She needed to get her butt out of bed and go back to Sacramento.

She stood up and wetness dripped down her thigh. That was Sam's fault mostly, but her subconscious hadn't helped. She'd dreamt all night of sex—a repeat scenario of Sam inside her with only the location changing. First they were in a grocery store and she was looking for olives but stumbled on Sam instead. Then they were in someone's car. She wasn't surprised that they'd ended up in the Residents' Office with her on Sam's lap riding her cock.

After she peed, she wiped tenderly. Were those bruises? Well, if they were, it was worth it. She wanted to be sore so she could remember everything that had happened.

* * *

"You found something to wear." Sam gave Terri a once-over that would have ruined any underwear—fortunately she wasn't wearing any. "That shirt looks better on you than me. I especially like it without any pants."

"It's a new style. All the rage. I also used your shower." Terri tried to sound casual, but she was tingling on the inside all over again and she felt a flush go up her neck when Sam didn't look away. Even after last night, she couldn't help feeling a little embarrassed by her response. That she was instantly wet wasn't a surprise, but that she wanted to tell Sam did give her pause. What would Sam do if she knew how wet she was? Take her again right here in the kitchen? She could handle that...

Sam handed her a coffee mug. "Extra cream, no sugar."

When Sam's hand brushed hers, Terri had to steady her breathing. She took a sip, avoiding eye contact. Sam was relaxed—like nothing was different between them. Somehow she had to pretend that's how she felt as well. "This is perfect. How'd you know how I like my coffee?"

"I paid attention in rounds—to all the important things."

"Very funny. You know I can tell when you're staring at my boobs." Terri had picked out one of Sam's button-down shirts, but she hadn't bothered with many of the buttons. "Didn't get enough last night?"

"Not even close."

Sam used the same low voice now as when they'd been in the bedroom. Despite the fact that they were standing in the kitchen, in the full light of day, she wanted to take Sam's hand between her legs and show her how easy it would be replay last night's act. Or maybe Sam had other things she wanted to try.

"Hungry?" Sam held up two packages wrapped in foil. "I thought we could go to my favorite breakfast spot and eat there. But you'll need pants."

"Hmm." Terri was starving, but she'd rather not bother with pants and by the way Sam's eyes kept tracking back to her body, she knew it wouldn't take much to get her back upstairs. But she was certain now that another round wouldn't satiate her appetite, and the rational part of her brain kept reminding her she should have already left. Finally she decided to follow Sam's lead and try to relax. Her brain and her clit could argue it out later. "Where's this spot?"

"You can see it out the front window. There's a bench across the street. Best spot in town."

Terri wrapped her hands around the coffee mug and went down the hall to the living room. Last night she'd only seen a fog-drenched street out the window. Now she could see what was on the other side. The ocean stretched as far as the horizon and the sun was already high. She spotted a bench not far from the cliff edge and figured that must be the breakfast spot Sam had in mind.

Sam came out from the kitchen. "What do you think?"

"You were right about the view."

Sam's gaze dropped and Terri wanted to take back her words. She hadn't meant to bring up last night's fight, but her comment had clearly come across that way. "I didn't mean anything by that. I promise. It's a nice view—that's all. More than nice. Million-dollar view."

"You're still mad?"

"What do you think?" Terri didn't know how else to answer and after a long pause, Sam seemed to accept that. "What time is it?"

"Quarter after eleven. The fog burned off a little early today, but it's still cool outside."

"Eleven? Shit." Terri went over to the sofa where she'd left her purse. She found her phone and checked for any messages. Nothing. Reed must have told everyone she was off limits after they'd talked. She dropped the phone back in her purse and looked over at Sam. "I never sleep that long."

"I got a new bed. The guy in the mattress store told me I was going to be sleeping like a baby."

"You bought a new bed for here?"

"That room's always been the guest room, but there was only a twin bed in there before and I like more space."

If Sam had bought a bed she'd known for a while that she wasn't going back to Sacramento. Terri fought back a swell of disappointment. She should have known better than to drive down. "You need a lot of space to work, huh?"

Sam held up her hands like she couldn't be blamed for that and Terri smiled back, but her heart wasn't in it. Who else would Sam have in that bed? Terri's mind flashed to the resident that had hung on Sam in the cafeteria. Megan Gresham. What if she'd already paid Sam a visit? Had Sam had sex with her in that bed too? She hated being jealous, but the bitter taste of it came all the same. And yet it didn't matter. Sam could sleep with anyone she wanted. She'd made her choice. She was leaving the residency and Sacramento. They had no future together.

Sam walked over to the sofa. She stood close enough to reach for Terri but didn't. Maybe she sensed the storm of emotions she was holding back.

"I'm not gonna lie. I was thinking of having you in that bed when I bought it." Sam caught the edge of Terri's shirt and gave it a soft tug. "Are we okay after everything last night?"

"Were we ever okay?"

Sam sighed. "What I meant was, are you okay with what happened?"

Terri nodded. She didn't trust her voice. With Sam close, jealousy had been replaced with need. Raw need. She wanted Sam all over again and was almost desperate enough to ask outright. But her pride wouldn't let her.

"About the bed...I didn't mean that I thought you'd sleep with me or want what we did last night. And I never thought you'd show up here. But you've been on my mind a lot and I know it's too late to take it back, but—"

"You should definitely not take it back," Terri interrupted. "I like that you were thinking of me when you bought the bed. We both know this can't go anywhere, but I like that it was me you were thinking of and not someone else." Terri reached for her purse again. She found her keys. "There's no way I'm wearing the underwear I was in last night, and since you're responsible for how wet I am at the moment, want to do me a favor and go grab the bag in the backseat of my car?"

"You're wet now?" Sam's look was priceless. She was the one who was embarrassed?

"Maybe I wasn't as obvious as I thought I was last night. You make me horny. It's annoying, but it's a manageable problem. My car's the blue BMW."

Without another word, Sam took the keys. Last night she'd had to park a half a block down because of all the signs for residents only, but she didn't feel bad sending Sam out on this errand. It was, after all, entirely her fault that she couldn't wear the clothes she'd come in. Plus this way she could gather her thoughts.

Terri watched Sam through the window. Instead of grabbing the bag from the backseat, she got into the driver's seat and pulled the car right up to the house. She parked in front and then got out with the overnight bag. Terri had reluctantly packed the bag, not wanting to admit she knew she'd need it.

Sam didn't make some joke about how of course she'd planned on staying. Instead she handed off the bag and went to find sweatshirts for them both. Terri tried not to think as she got dressed, but her brain wouldn't stop. She knew this didn't have to be complicated. Sam could simply be a diversion that came complete with mind-blowing sex. But no matter how many times she repeated that in her mind, everything about Sam, and who she was with her, made her dizzy with longing for more.

Sam pulled a ridiculous rainbow beanie on over her tousled hair and then picked up the sweatshirts she'd gone for. "Ready?"

Terri stared at a lock of unruly hair that jutted out one side of Sam's beanie. She wanted to lean close and tuck it into place, but she wasn't sure she trusted her body to make contact now. "Ready."

Sam cocked her head. "Why are you looking at me funny?"

"Somehow you pull off dorky and fucking hot all at the same time."

Sam grinned. "Gotta have some skills."

"I'm not sure I can handle all your skills." Terri moved forward and pushed the lock of hair under Sam's beanie. She stole a quick cheek kiss before she stepped back. "But I'm trying."

"Thanks." Sam opened the door and held it open, waiting for Terri. "After you."

Clearly the little kiss hadn't bothered Sam, but Terri's heart was still racing as she stepped outside. Why was she still a hot mess around Sam? They'd already slept together. She should have her senses about her now.

They crossed the street and the cool air sent a shiver through her. As soon as they got to the bench, she quickly decided on one of the sweatshirts Sam had brought. Summer lingered in Sacramento, but the chill of fall was in the air here. The view, however, was hard to beat.

The bench was perched at the edge of the cliff. Below, a narrow stretch of sand made a golden line and then nothing but shimmering blue ocean stretched beyond. The deep dark blue of the water perfectly matched Sam's eyes, but Terri stopped herself from saying as much.

Sam handed her one of the wrapped packages. "If you don't like what I made, there's a few restaurants we can walk to…"

Terri opened the foil and her mouth watered at the sight of toasted sourdough. Inside, cheese was melted over a scrambled egg, with avocado and tomato finishing it off. "This looks amazing." She took a bite of the sandwich and moaned. It was ridiculous to moan over a sandwich, but it was that good—or she was that hungry. Probably a little of both.

"I've heard that moan before."

Terri raised an eyebrow but didn't bother arguing. She knew how loud she'd been. She would have been embarrassed about all the noise she'd made, but Sam hadn't been exactly quiet. Every sound Sam had made had only turned her on more. After a few bites, she decided to ask what she didn't want to ask. The not knowing was harder in this case.

"Was last night typical for you?"

Sam finished chewing. She swallowed and then wiped her lips. "You're worried that I have sex that good all the time?" She shook her head before Terri could respond. "Nothing about last night was typical. Nothing about you is typical for me." She eyed the remainder of her sandwich. "I haven't made anyone breakfast in a long time."

"You've been holding this out from all the girls?"

Sam looked contrite. "Sometimes I'll make toast."

"No wonder you don't have a girlfriend," Terri teased.

"For the record, I've had plenty of girlfriends. And I did nice things for all of them."

"I believe you." Why any of them would have let Sam go, she couldn't imagine. But probably Sam had been the one to end things.

"I know I'm not supposed to say this, but none of them were as good in bed as you."

"You're right. You shouldn't say that." But a smug satisfaction filled Terri. Maybe it was wrong, but she wanted what they'd done to stand out in Sam's mind as much as it did in hers. She took another bite of her sandwich and followed the line of a wave until it crashed on the shore below. "Can I ask you another question?"

Sam didn't say yes or no, only waited for her to go on, but suddenly Terri didn't want to ask. She sensed that Sam already knew what her question would be. *Is there anything I can say to change your mind?* Finally, she decided not to ask it. The answer would only hurt more now.

"What is it?"

"Never mind. I don't want to ask."

Sam held her gaze for a moment. "I couldn't make the decision be about us. About if I had a chance with you. If it was only that, I would have stayed."

Terri shook her head. "I don't want to talk about it."

They finished their sandwiches in silence, though the thoughts in Terri's mind wouldn't stay quiet. Sam got up to toss the foil wraps, and when she came back to the bench, she sat a little closer to Terri and pointed out some seals playing in the surf. After a few minutes, she set her hand on Terri's thigh. Under other circumstances, Sam's move might have felt annoyingly possessive. One night of sex and Sam didn't get to act as if they were a couple. But her hackles didn't go up this time, and instead of pushing Sam's hand off, she traced her fingers. She wanted Sam's hand to still smell of her.

"You have nice hands."

"You have a nice tongue." Sam's tone lightened the mood. "How long do I get you?"

"I should probably have already left." But Terri didn't get up. When Sam turned her hand palm-side up, Terri traced that side too, distractedly following the lines as she wondered what Sam would say if she told her how the word "submissive" had done something to her. One word had triggered a whole cascade of emotions. She wanted to be submissive to Sam. But what did that say about her?

"Stay."

Terri met Sam's gaze. "Why?"

"Because you don't want to leave and I don't want you to go. Plus it's the perfect day to go to the beach and you're already here."

Terri looked out at the water. The tide was coming up, and in the short time they'd been sitting on the bench, the sandy beach had nearly disappeared. Dark brown rocks dotted the water below. If she left, she'd never get Sam out of her mind. Never. "Do you want to know the real reason I came?"

Sam waited for her to go on.

"After I talked to Weiss, I went to see Reed. I told her I thought you'd already made the decision, regardless of what you'd said to Weiss… She told me to get in my car and drive until I found you. She said it wasn't my job to convince you to come back, but that unless I had sex with you, I'd never get you out of my mind."

"Think we should tell Reed that's not how it works when you have good sex?"

Terri smiled. "You're so damn cocky."

"For good reason."

The dare-you-to-tell-me-I'm-wrong look on her face sent a shiver through Terri.

"So you really already knew?"

"A little part of me was holding out hope," Terri said. "I still am."

After a minute Sam brought Terri's hand up to her lips. She kissed her knuckles lightly and then let go. "There's no way having more sex will get you out of my mind, but I'd like it if you stayed. I don't think it'll hurt either of us if you spend one more night."

"It might if I'm lucky." The sentence slipped out before Terri could censor it, and then once she'd admitted that, she wanted to say the rest of what she was thinking. "I love that you made me sore."

Sam's look was sheepish. "I'm sorry if I was too rough—"

"Don't apologize. It was exactly what I wanted." She paused. "I like how you are in bed. I like the words you use…how you touch me. And although I'll deny it if you tell anyone, I like you topping me."

"I like you being my submissive."

Terri swallowed. "My submissive" was different than simply being submissive. But damn if Sam's words hadn't sent a tremor right to her clit. She wanted to spread herself all over again, beg for Sam's hand, and do anything to please her. Worried that her sudden need was obvious, she looked down to the waves crashing on the rocks. The sight of it did nothing to cool the blush on her cheeks.

"Can I take you further next time?"

Terri nodded without looking at her. What did Sam have in mind? A nervous excitement filled her body. She wouldn't ask what Sam was thinking or how long she'd make her wait. Sam had to know that she was at her mercy, but she liked that part of it almost as much as the reward for submitting.

Sam stood up. "Want to go for a walk?"

Terri stopped herself from asking if that walk could be back to the bedroom. "I might need more coffee first. Someone kept me up late."

"Okay, but we have to walk to that too. My grandma didn't believe in making coffee at home. She loved cafes."

"No coffeemaker?"

"Grandma was a little eccentric. Think of a crazy rich beat poet artist that likes to go swimming in the ocean fully dressed and you've got a pretty good image in your mind. She and my grandpa were complete opposites."

Sam held out her hand and Terri clasped it without thinking. It wasn't that she didn't have experience holding hands in public—hell, she'd been married twice—but she wasn't even in a relationship with Sam. So why did it feel so right to hold hands?

No one else they passed on the sidewalk seemed to care that they were holding hands. They turned off the quiet side street and onto a busy thoroughfare. It was Saturday morning, and with the sun shining everyone seemed to be heading to the beach. But Sam led her in the opposite direction. After a few blocks, Sam pointed toward a cafe. She let go of Terri's hand to open the door, then waved at the barista who looked up and smiled.

The place wasn't empty, but it was quiet compared to the bustle outside. A locals-only spot, Terri decided.

"Can we get a refill?" Sam handed the barista Terri's empty mug and then set her own mug in a bin of dishes to be washed. She stuffed some cash into the jar on the counter, but the barista shook her head.

"You know you can't pay here."

"But I can tip."

The barista mumbled "pain in my ass," but she smiled as she said it and then went to refill Terri's coffee. Sam only smiled and Terri wondered how well they knew each other. Sam hadn't been in town long, but maybe she made friends quick. Ignoring a pang of jealousy, Terri turned her attention to the artwork that covered the walls. In addition to dozens of paintings, sculptures and tapestries filled the spaces in between. Every available nook had something to notice.

"I love all the artwork in here. It's the kind of place you could spend all day in."

"Thank you for the compliment. I aim to please and take Yelp reviews." The barista smiled. "I'm Danielle, by the way. Any friend of Sam's is mine too." She handed Terri her refilled coffee and then pointed to the table with cream and sugar.

"Thank you." Terri smiled. She wished the coffee shop she frequented had staff half as nice. If she lived close, she wouldn't bother making her own coffee either.

"Some of my grandma's work is still up here," Sam said. "I can point it out to you if you'd like…"

"I'd like that."

"Make sure she takes you upstairs to see her work too," Danielle added.

"You have some of your photos here?"

Sam grimaced. "Yes, but you don't want to see them."

"Of course she does," Danielle said. "You show her or I will."

Terri smiled at Sam's meek look. It was nice to know that at least sometimes she could be made to behave. When she went to add cream, Danielle cornered Sam.

"You owe me new pictures. I sold out of the ones you hung last month in the first two days they went up. And I think you should charge more. You could make a killing if you actually—"

"I'll get you something soon. Promise."

Danielle huffed as she turned back to the counter. Terri could tell she wasn't actually mad however. Sam frustrated her. Apparently it was a common feeling. Terri walked over and Sam reached for her hand.

"Photos?"

"My grandma's paintings first. I want to show you one of my favorites. Danielle agreed not to sell it, but I don't think she'd let me take it home either."

At first glance, the painting was simple—a kid kneeling by a sand castle. In the background, the sun set over the surf and the waves were lit with gold. The longer she studied the painting, the curve of the hand around the turret held her attention. She found herself wanting to protect the castle from the waves as much as the kid did. "Is this you?"

"No. That's my father." Sam swiped her finger along the top of the frame, sweeping away the dust. A plaque on the wall listed the title of the painting as "Sandcastle" by Mary Ellen Samuels.

"But it was one of the last things she painted. She used an old photograph of my dad… I like this one too." Sam gestured to the next painting.

Work from several local artists hung on display all over the walls, but Terri was quickly partial to Mary Ellen Samuels' paintings. She liked the subtlety—the beauty in each painting wasn't the grandness of the cliffs or the expanse of the ocean but something small like the child's hand or the crack in a seashell. "Are any of your grandmother's paintings for sale?"

"Everything is except for the sandcastle. My dad hasn't even seen it."

"Why not?"

"He doesn't get over here often… Anyway, thanks for humoring me and looking at her stuff. It's good, right?"

"She should have been famous."

"She was to me."

Terri was caught by Sam's words. She wondered if Mary Ellen Samuels had appreciated her biggest fan.

"Want to go on that beach walk now?"

Terri shook her head. "You haven't shown me your stuff yet."

"I thought maybe you'd forget that part."

"No chance. Come on, I want to see your work." Terri glanced at Danielle and then at the other patrons. No one was looking their way. She stepped close enough to touch Sam but kept her hands to herself. Contact would only make resisting her harder. "Should I say 'please'? You know I will."

"I do like it when you say 'please.'"

Terri leaned closer and whispered the word into Sam's ear. Saying it in the middle of a coffee shop gave her a secret thrill and the look of desire on Sam's face was all the reward she needed.

"You say 'please' so nicely," Sam murmured. She clasped Terri's hand again and led the way to the back of the coffee shop where a narrow staircase was cordoned off.

Unclipping the rope with a closed sign, Sam said, "The ones of mine that Danielle usually sells on the main level are more G-rated. Surfers and ocean scenes. There's a reason the others are kept upstairs."

"Now I'm officially intrigued."

Sam started up the stairs. "Keep in mind, I shot all of these in my early twenties."

"Why should I keep that in mind?"

"You'll see."

They reached the top of the stairs and Sam stepped to the side. Terri looked at the wall in front of them and her jaw nearly hit the ground. First off, the woman was gorgeous. Second, aside from an open book that she'd strategically set across her breasts, she was entirely naked. And life-sized. The black and white photo covered most of the distance from the ceiling to the floor and easily measured three feet wide. "Holy shit."

Sam scratched her head. "Is that good or bad?"

Terri didn't answer. Hell, she'd let Sam stew for a minute after she'd pulled the rug out from under her with this. They were in a room clearly used for small concerts. Chairs and tables were set around a raised stage with sound equipment and a microphone. Along with the woman with the book over her breasts, there were four other photographs, all with a plaque listing Elizabeth Samuels as the photographer. One in color—a landscape shot of a surfer paddling on a board with a wave cresting behind her—but all the rest black and white nudes. Two naked men, two naked women. Not all beautiful but each one striking.

Terri walked around the room without saying anything, stopping in front of each picture. Sam didn't follow her. Instead, she went over to the raised stage and sat down. But Terri knew she was watching her.

In each shot there was a book, but Terri couldn't figure out the theme. "So I'm guessing you picked these particular books for a reason?"

"They're all banned." Sam added, "It was a statement. Everything's a statement when you're twenty-two."

"You took all these when you were twenty-two?"

"For a senior project. I double majored—art and biology."

"You didn't have a lot of free time."

"No… But art was my life. The bio degree was to make my grandfather happy. Back then I was still trying to impress him."

Terri had circled back to the first photograph and the largest in the set. She touched Sam's name on the wall plaque and then took a step back. "You have your grandmother's eye."

"What do you mean?"

Terri motioned to the woman's clenched fist. "This. It's not what you notice first, but it's what you remember." At first she'd stared at the woman's exposed crotch, and then she'd noticed the book, of course. Probably Sam had intended that, but clearly that wasn't all she wanted the viewer to appreciate. Although the woman was seemingly relaxed, reclining on a bed with the sheets casually rumpled around her, the white of her knuckles stood out. "These aren't for sale?"

"Danielle would never let them go. People call this place Banned Books Coffeehouse for a reason—although I doubt any of the tourists that drop in downstairs ever figure it out. There's no books anywhere and they only let people up here when they have a concert or it's open mic night. I keep telling Danielle she should set up a shelf of banned books. Like a little free library."

"You're really good."

Sam didn't respond.

As cocky as she was about sex, apparently that confidence didn't cross to other parts of her life. Terri walked over to the stage where Sam sat. "Thank you for showing me." She held out her hand, but Sam didn't take it. After a moment she dropped it to her side and exhaled. "I need some ground rules."

"For what?"

"You take my hand like it's no big deal. But when I try and hold yours…" Terri breathed out. How could Sam be so difficult and so much of everything she'd ever wanted at the exact same moment? "Do I beg for that too?"

"No—of course not." Sam shook her head. "I'm sorry. I got lost in my thoughts."

"I've seen that look in your eyes at the hospital. Like you were somewhere else. I assumed then that it was because you didn't want to be there. Do you want to be somewhere else right now?"

"Not at all. But if I'm being honest, a little part of me is still worried I'm making a mistake."

"You're a little late admitting that."

"I know. But this is the first time my two worlds have collided. With you here—in this room—all of a sudden it's all real. It's the right decision, but it's hard." Sam reached for Terri's hand as she stood up. "You can take my hand whenever you want."

"Except in the bedroom?" Terri arched an eyebrow.

"Then I like being in charge."

They were close enough to kiss, and the feel of Sam's body near hers made it hard to even think, let alone talk. Sam was a heartbreak waiting to happen. She knew that. And she should have left last night. As much as she wanted to pretend it was only the chemistry and the hot sex that had convinced her to stay, she was drawn to more than that.

"I like you in charge. But I'm not sure you know what you're doing."

"I know what I'm doing with you," Sam returned.

Sam's eyes held hers. She leaned close and met Terri's lips. The room where they stood, the sounds of the cafe below, everything else slipped away. Terri moved against her, parting her lips so Sam could deepen the kiss. Her knees went weak as Sam caressed her neck. It wasn't the fire of last night's kiss. This was sweet and tender and threatened to undo her.

When Sam pulled back, Terri nearly begged for another kiss. But she watched silently as Sam turned toward the stairs and started down.

Terri took one last look around the room. She didn't want Sam to be an artist if that pulled her away from medicine and from the world where a relationship could actually happen. And, yet, now she understood. And she wanted her more than ever. This Sam was someone she could fall hard for.

CHAPTER NINETEEN

"You okay?" Sam knew what she'd said in the cafe had upset Terri, had made her pull back, but she wasn't sure how to fix it. Despite the fact that they were walking right next to each other, she seemed miles away now.

"I'm fine. Still getting over that kiss." Terri's tone was light. "And I'm hoping it was a promise of more to come."

"It was." Sam didn't believe her entirely, but she understood the deflection. Outside, with the sun shining on a beautiful morning, she didn't want to restart a tense conversation either.

"Actually, I'm not totally fine."

Sam waited. When Terri didn't go on, she said, "What is it?"

"I can't seem to accept that you're quitting. You're a good doctor, Sam. And I know I need to let it go, but I can't… You've got less than two years of the residency left. The photography has to be on hold until that's over, but then you could swing both. You're enough of a rock star that I know you could make it work."

Sam nodded slowly. "I kept telling myself that. And I think I could make it work—if I actually wanted to be a doctor. I'm not really having second thoughts. I'm processing everything I'm giving up. And I wish you weren't part of that."

"What do you mean?"

"If I'd stayed in Sacramento, I think I would have had a chance for a real relationship with you. Eventually." Sam caught Terri's eye and smiled. "But now we'll be in two different worlds, three hours apart. I'm sure you're probably thinking—why start something?"

Sam hoped Terri would argue. When she didn't, she continued, "I'm hoping you'll consider it anyway. I know you're upset that I'm quitting, but you're the only part of the last six years of my life that I don't want to lose."

"Who said you ever had me to lose?"

Sam clenched her jaw. The anger she'd felt at Terri for trying to change her mind, for acting as if she was the only adult making sane decisions, came back full force.

"You made your choice," Terri continued. "I need to get over it."

They walked a full block before Sam's anger simmered down enough for her to think. She needed to restart the conversation on neutral ground if they were going to make it through the rest of the day.

Sam stopped walking and Terri did too. When she met Sam's gaze, she didn't look mad. More than anything else, she seemed tired. Sam stretched out her hand and Terri clasped it. "I don't want to fight."

"Me neither," Terri said.

"I'm sorry for quitting."

"I'm sorry too. And you're right. If you'd decided to stay, I was going to ask you out. I'd thought it all over while you were gone. Decided I'd take the risk." Terri exhaled. "I liked the game we played last night. Apparently I like someone telling me what to do. And, honestly, I'm still processing all that too. But we both know this is over when I leave."

"It doesn't have to be."

"Yeah, it does." Terri loosened her hand from Sam's grip. "And I don't think we should hold hands."

"Okay. Fine." Sam let go. The vibe between them was getting worse, not better.

They crossed the street and headed toward the beach. Sam avoided looking in Terri's direction and Terri seemed more interested in passing cars than anything else.

"'Game' is the wrong word for what we did," Terri said.

"I almost called you out on that."

"Why didn't you?"

"Because I didn't believe you anyway. This isn't just a game for you." Sam decided to push further. She didn't have anything to lose now. "You actually like me and it's freaking you out."

Instead of arguing, Terri gave a slow nod. "Not bad. You practice mind reading on the side? Along with stamp collecting, waltzing, and what else?"

"Surfing." Sam couldn't give up. Her heart wouldn't let her. "How do you feel about a drive instead of the beach? There's a spot I'd love to show you."

"You know you can do pretty much whatever you want with me today. After that…"

"I'm gonna change your mind."

"I don't see how," Terri said. "But I only get one more night and I don't want to spend any of that fighting."

"But we have good sex when we're fighting."

Terri rolled her eyes. "I'm serious."

Sam grinned. "So am I."

They were almost to the beach before Sam remembered she was the one leading. She pointed to the side street they'd come up and crossed at the intersection. Seeing Terri's car parked in front of the little blue house made her happy. But it'd be gone by tomorrow.

Instead of going inside, Sam led the way to the garage in the back. She punched in the code and waited. As soon as the sunlight hit it, the polished Aston Martin glistened. Terri sucked in a breath.

"Is this yours?" She walked past Sam to peek in the windows. "It's an Aston Martin, right? I so didn't picture you as a car geek. This thing's in perfect condition. What year?"

"1964. I didn't picture you as a car geek either." Sam opened the passenger door and waited for Terri. "It was my grandma's—came with the cottage."

"This is James Bond's car, right? Like the original Bond car." Terri circled the car, brushing a fingertip along the backside. "I love the silver. Do you have any idea how much it's worth?"

"No clue." Sam hadn't expected to impress Terri with the car. Clearly she had more to learn. She smiled as Terri leaned close to survey the inside. "You can get in, you know."

"I just can't believe you have an Aston Martin. My ex was totally into cars. He'd be flipping out right now if he were here."

"Unlike you?" Sam laughed when Terri gave her a look. "You getting in or not?"

"Oh, I'm getting in all right. I can't wait for you to take me on a drive. In fact, this car might be the only reason I'm okay waiting on more sex." Terri leaned over the car door and brushed Sam's lips with hers.

Sam's breath caught in her chest. Terri pulling her hand away earlier had hurt more than Sam wanted to admit, and now she desperately wanted to pull her close, to feel connected again. But was she imagining their connection? Was it only about sex now for Terri? Sam closed the door and went around to the driver's side, boxing away the emotions that rolled through her.

She settled in and started the car. "I used to joke with my grandma that she had a chick magnet. She never believed me."

Once they made it out of the city, the highway hugged the coast, curving along the edge of cliffs with sheer drops into the dark blue water and then coursing through stretches of rolling hills. The ocean stayed in sight, one gorgeous vista after another, with shades of turquoise and deep blue stretching to the horizon.

Sam tried to focus on the road but kept getting distracted looking over at Terri. Terri commented on the view but otherwise seemed content without conversation. She rolled the window down and stuck out her hand, letting her palm ride the breeze.

When Sam pulled off at a sign for a lighthouse, Terri's smile convinced her she'd made a good choice. They got out and walked around a bit, taking a trail down to the beach, then got back in and drove a little further to a farm stand. After they'd picked out strawberries, Sam's phone rang. She wouldn't have answered, but she noticed Doug's name.

"Mind if I take a call real quick? It's from my old business partner."

"Go ahead," Terri said, sorting through a table of local cheese. "I'll find us something to go along with the strawberries."

"Perfect." Sam clicked on the call accept button. "Hey, Doug. What's up?"

"Dude, you have no idea how many calls I've gotten since I sent out that email saying you were back. We're gonna need to talk dates. Things are booking up quick. You, my friend, are popular. Any chance you want a shoot tonight?"

"I can't. I'm kind of on a date." Close enough anyway.

Doug whistled. "You didn't tell me you had a girl."

"Well, I don't exactly. But I'm working on it. Hey, do you know a good picnic spot? We're almost to Half Moon Bay."

"Come to my beach. I'll make you a picnic myself. It's the least I can do considering the money you're gonna be making me."

No matter how Sam tried to convince Doug that making them food wasn't necessary, Doug ended the call saying he already had the food ready and she'd break his heart if she wasn't at his beach in a half hour.

Terri walked back to the car holding two small paper bags. "I couldn't decide between aged Gouda and Brie. So I got both. And a basket of blackberries. I shouldn't be left to my own devices at a farmer's market. Everything okay?"

"All good. You up for a little more driving?"

"Sure." Teri smiled and pecked her cheek.

Again Sam wished for more of a kiss, but again she kept her thoughts to herself. She pulled back on the highway heading north. Terri hummed for a while, than fiddled with the old radio.

"Does this work?"

"Sometimes. It's kind of a miracle this whole thing is still on the road. The mechanic who works on this car is this old guy named Otto. He keeps trying to get me to upgrade the radio."

"You're on a first-name basis with the mechanic?"

"Never a good thing, right?" Sam smiled. "By the way, we're almost there."

"Almost where?"

Sam pointed to a sign for Half Moon Bay and then pulled off the highway at the next exit. She turned onto a narrow lane and followed it to where it ended in a grove of eucalyptus trees.

"Is this a real parking lot?" Terri skeptically eyed the half dozen other cars parked in the dirt spaces between the trees.

"Officially?" Sam rocked her head side to side. "It's kind of a locals-only spot. But don't worry. We won't get towed."

As soon as they got out, Terri stretched and took a deep breath. "I love this smell."

Sam agreed. The salty ocean scent mingled with the sweet tang of eucalyptus was one of her favorites.

"But I am starting to wonder why you brought us here…"

"You'll see." Sam started to reach for Terri's hand but stopped herself. Terri noticed, her eyes darting to Sam's hand as she tilted her head.

"Sorry. Reflex." Sam jammed her hands in her pockets. "It's a short walk, but I promise it's worth it."

From the parking lot, they couldn't see the water, but the sound of the crashing waves carried. Sam led the way down the path that skirted behind a few houses and then dropped down a narrow gulch. When they reached the sand, the beach stretched out in a crescent with the cliffs behind them as a buffer from the rest of the world. Aside from a handful of surfers, the place was all theirs. Well, almost. Sam spotted Doug, complete in his ever-present tie-dye shirt, sitting on a cooler.

Terri didn't notice him, her gaze on the surfers. "The waves seem too high. Is it safe out there?"

"This crowd's got plenty of experience," Sam said. The next wave came in and three of the surfers got up. A moment later, all three spectacularly crashed.

Terri gasped and Sam quickly said, "They'll be okay." She pointed out as each one popped up to take a breath. They scrambled onto their boards and started paddling as the next wave rolled in. "These guys know what they're doing, but the ocean's moody today. You can feel it."

"Moody?"

"There are days when she acts like a teenager. Kisses you one moment and then throws you right on your face the next."

Terri shook her head. "I've always thought that I'd like to learn how to surf, but then I watch that—" Another wave crested and tossed another surfer. "And I'm not so sure."

"I'd get you up on something easy. Not these waves. These are tempting because they look nice and high, but the run's short and the drop-off comes quick. You watch these guys out here and they can't help nosing right off the face. Plus the undertow's strong. But I know a good spot, and I've got a foam board that you'd catch air on."

"I understood about half of that."

Sam smiled. "Sorry. I get excited about surfing. You'd really like to learn?"

"I would. Someday."

Sam didn't want to get her hopes up, but the look in Terri's eyes made her think maybe she could risk it. "I'd love to teach you."

They'd walked a few hundred feet further and were now close enough to Doug that he raised his hand. Sam waved back.

"Seems like you have friends everywhere," Terri said, glancing from Doug to Sam. "Do you know him?"

Before Sam could say answer, Doug hollered, "You two 'bout ready for lunch?"

Sam turned to Terri, "That's Doug. He comes across a little weird at first, but he's a super nice guy, I promise. He's been like a second dad to me. And the food will be good—he's a chef on the side."

"What's his main job?"

"I'm supposed to have a main job?" They'd gotten close enough that Doug clearly had overheard. He laughed and slapped Sam's shoulder, then pulled her into a bear hug. "Man, I missed you kid."

After he'd released her, he stretched out his hand to Terri. "Hi, Sam's gorgeous date."

Sam made introductions as Terri shook Doug's hand, hers tiny in his big paw. She didn't volunteer that Terri wasn't her date only because it seemed awkward to say.

"How long have you two known each other?" Terri asked.

Doug scratched his head and eyed Sam. "Ten years now?"

"About that. We met surfing. Right here, in fact," Sam added.

"I was surfing," Doug said. "Sam was floating around on her board snapping pictures. I used to fancy myself a photographer, but then I met the real deal." He laughed and jabbed his thumb at Sam. "This one here can make you cry over a shot of a damn dandelion someone stepped on."

"I take one dandelion picture and you never let me live it down." Sam shook her head. "Doug's a big baby. Cries all the time."

"Well, that's true. But anyone with half a heart would've cried over that damn dandelion." He launched into a description of the picture and admitted he'd literally bawled when Sam had given him the print.

Terri listened, a half smile on her lips, and then looked over at Sam. "She's an amazing photographer."

Doug agreed, then added, "Not the world's best surfer, however."

"Hey!" Sam laughed as Doug jabbed her side.

"All right you two, I gotta go." Doug tugged a ball cap on over his balding head. "Promised the wife I'd work on the pickup. Sam, can you keep the cooler until next Friday? We got two hundred and forty people at that wedding. Gonna be a long day."

"Yeah, sure. And thanks for all this."

"Anything for you, kid."

After he'd gone, Terri said, "He's lovely."

"You think so? Not too weird for you?"

"I like weird. But I am curious about what he made us."

"If it's not good, we have the Brie and blackberries as backup." Sam opened the cooler, wondering if she should apologize for letting Doug think they were a couple.

"So you take pictures with Doug. Is that a regular gig?"

"He's my business partner." Sam held up one of the containers and then peeked inside. Roasted potatoes with some assortment of delicious smelling spices. "He lives down the road. We were surfing friends for a while and then since we were both photographers decided to team up. Shot Mavericks together one year. But only my stuff ended up in a magazine, which got his nose bent out of shape. He wouldn't talk about it for weeks... Other than that we've always worked well together."

"Mavericks?"

"It's a big wave competition. Takes place pretty close to here." Sam pointed to where the beach curved in the distance. "Only happens every few years—when we get lucky. Everyone drops everything to come. The waves are huge. It's something you have to see to believe."

Sam handed Terri a Coke. "I told Doug no wine and he said he liked you already. Apparently wine at picnics is cliché."

"As opposed to a surprise picnic on the beach?"

Sam laughed. "Yes. Doug also happens to be sober so he may be biased."

Terri sat down on the picnic blanket and popped open the can. She took a long sip and then rested her chin on her knees. "It's pretty here."

Sam heard the change in her voice. The words didn't match her tone, and she knew something was wrong again. Probably she shouldn't have mentioned that she'd told Doug no wine. Terri's brow furrowed, but she didn't offer what she was thinking.

Sam sat down next to her. She'd grabbed a Coke too and clinked the can against Terri's. "Don't worry. I won't ask. You don't have to drink and you don't owe me a reason for why you don't."

Terri eyed her. "You did it again."

"Did what?"

"Mind reading. How'd you know that's what I was thinking?"

"I bet you get questions a lot." Sam paused. "Don't think I'm not asking because I don't want to know. If you ever feel like talking, there's a lot of things I'd like to know about you." She set out the three containers Doug had packed for them and read the labels on each one aloud: "Spinach salad. Roasted potatoes. Barbequed chicken. Here's a fork. Doug didn't give us any plates so we're sharing germs."

"I think it's a little late to be worrying about sharing germs, don't you?" Terri teased.

"Probably...I should have told you this already, but I get tested every six months and I'm usually a hell of a lot safer than I was last night."

Terri took the fork Sam held out for her. "I got tested after my last mistake was officially over and then six months later because of how it ended. There hasn't been a reason to get tested since."

"Mistake?"

"Otherwise known as marriage."

Sam opened her mouth but promptly closed it. She wasn't sure what to make of Terri calling her marriage a mistake, but then the significance of Terri staying over last night hit her. "Was last night the first time you've had sex since you got divorced?"

"Depends on your definition of sex. Technically?" Terri hesitated. "Let's just say it's been a while since I've done anything like what we did last night. Which is probably why I was dreaming about you taking me over and over again for the rest of the night. And why I've been distracted looking at your hands instead of the scenery for the past hour. My body seems to think I hit the sex jackpot."

"Maybe your body's right. I kind of love that you dreamed about it."

"And I love that sexy gravelly voice of yours." Terri laughed. She pushed Sam's shoulder. "I can't take you seriously when you sound that way, but it's amazing all the same. And thank you for blushing instead of asking how long it's been since I've been properly fucked."

"I blushed?"

"Yes." Terri laughed again. "And when you look at me that way, I don't know what I'm going to do with you."

"But you know what I'm going to do with you." Sam held up the container she was holding. "Salad?"

Terri shook her head. "Potatoes first. They look delicious."

"Not as delicious as your butt when I'm—"

"Stop." Terri said, laughing again. "Give me the damn potatoes. I'm having a hard enough time waiting for you."

At least they both wanted that. Sam handed her the potatoes and settled in with the salad, wishing again that sex would be enough for her. After they ate, they watched the surfers for a while.

Sam played commentator, adding in voice-overs for the waves as well as the surfers until finally Terri told she had to stop 'cause her cheeks hurt from laughing. She'd used the same voice Terri had called her sexy gravelly voice to make it funny and was pleased when it worked.

"Do you want to be out there surfing?"

Sam shook her head. "I'm happy right here. Maybe too happy."

"Hmm. Me too." Terri shifted closer to Sam and soon their shoulders bumped together. She rested her hand on Sam's knee and closed her eyes. "This is even better. I could almost fall asleep here."

Sam felt sleepy too, lulled as much by the sun and the waves as by the feel of Terri's body close. She breathed her in, savoring her scent and how Terri seemed to melt against her. "I can't remember when I've felt this relaxed."

"I was thinking the same thing. Maybe let's not think about it too hard," Terri said.

Sam sighed. "What do you usually do on your days off?"

"Work."

Sam laughed, but Terri gave her a look that made her realize she was serious. "Okay, let me try that again. When you're stuck in the hospital, what do you wish you could be doing instead? What's a hobby you'd like to have?"

"Does hot sex count as a hobby?"

"I love that you have a one-track mind, but I'm trying to get to know you here." When Terri didn't volunteer more, Sam said, "I like you. And I know we aren't dating, but I want to know what makes the famous Terri Anderson tick. Why'd you want to be a doctor?"

"I like taking care of people." Terri crossed her ankles. "Figuring out what's wrong and then fixing it... I love getting a diagnosis."

"The puzzle part of medicine," Sam said. She liked that part too. It wasn't enough, but she could understand at least.

"Exactly. And I love setting up a treatment plan and following up to see if it worked. I like all of it."

"So you always knew this was what you wanted to be? No turning point that pushed you into it?"

"Not really." Terri seemed to focus on the surfers, but Sam got the impression that her thoughts were far from the water. A long moment passed and when she looked back at Terri, she noticed tears welled in her eyes. Before they could fall, Terri swiped them away.

Sam touched her arm. "I'm sorry if I asked the wrong thing."

Terri shook her head. "It's fine. It's nothing really... And I'm sorry for getting all teary-eyed. For the record, I'm not usually a crier."

"You don't have to apologize. But whatever it is, it probably isn't *nothing*."

A tear slipped down Terri's cheek, but she didn't try to swipe it this time. She only stared out at the water. "All these years later and one little thing can pull me back into that car. Suddenly I'm hearing metal scraping metal, tires screeching..." She paused for a long moment. "I was seventeen. And drunk. I hit someone. Almost killed him."

"Oh shit. I'm sorry. That's awful." Sam reached over and set her hand on Terri's. Terri didn't go on, but she didn't pull her hand away from Sam's either. She went back to watching the waves and Sam followed her gaze.

The waves were gorgeous, perfect curls of white against a deep blue. One after the other came and went, but Sam had no desire to be surfing. More than ever, she wanted to be exactly where she was.

"My little sister was at a friend's house," Terri said quietly. "A sleepover. She called me to come pick her up 'cause she changed her mind about staying the night. But I'd been drinking."

"You started drinking young."

"I started drinking way before then. For a while *that* was my hobby." Terri's tight-lipped smile tugged at Sam's heart. The pain was obvious.

She took a deep breath and started again. "I went to pick her up. Knowing I shouldn't. On the way home, I got off on the wrong exit. I think maybe I'd blacked out for a minute. Went to pull a U-turn and didn't see anyone coming until it was too late. He was on a motorcycle…

"I can still see his body on the pavement. His leg was jackknifed and he wasn't moving. I took one look at him and was sick." Terri squeezed her eyes shut as if to clear the image. "Thank God he had a helmet. Probably would have died otherwise."

"If that happened to me, I think I'd give up drinking too," Sam said.

"Well, I did for a few years, but I picked it back up again. Guess you could say it was more of a bad habit than a hobby." She paused. "It took a few more close calls and lots of bad decisions for me to realize I can't drink. But that night, the accident, all of it, that's when I decided I wanted to go to med school. I wanted to save lives, not end them."

"You didn't end anyone's life."

"No. But it was close. And my kid sister was in the back seat. What if it'd been a truck I'd hit? What if the guy hadn't been wearing a helmet?"

"You must have been so scared."

"I was. I couldn't stop shaking."

Sam didn't press her to go on or ask anything more. They sat together, watching the waves, and then Terri slowly pulled her hand away from Sam's. She scooped up a handful of sand and let it slip through her fingers.

"I hated myself for a long time after that. For the accident, for drinking too much…"

"But it was an accident," Sam said. "You can't still beat yourself up about it. And because of it you became an amazing doctor. How many lives have you saved? I've heard the stories from Reed, from Weiss, from Shellhammer. You can ease up a little on yourself, you know."

"You don't need to try and make me feel better. It is what it is." Terri sighed. "Maybe we should go back to talking about hobbies."

"You really want to talk about hobbies or you want to change the conversation back to sex?" Sam joked.

"Definitely sex." Terri bumped against Sam's shoulder. "Thank you for bringing it back to that."

"You're welcome," Sam grinned.

"You're easy to talk to."

"So are you," Sam returned.

"I know I brought all that stuff up, but I don't want today to be a therapy session. And I'd rather we do more than talk about sex."

"That's fair. Maybe we should go somewhere with a better view?"

"I'd like that." But Terri didn't move to get up. "This still isn't a date, you know. When we get back to your place, I'm really hoping you aren't going to be all tender and sweet or anything because of what I told you."

Sam considered her response. In truth, she did feel a certain new tenderness towards Terri, but that didn't change what she wanted to do. If anything the closeness of the past hour only made her desires stronger.

"So I'm pretty sure you're asking me to fuck you until you can't stand up. Is that right, Dr. Anderson? I'm not sure if that's entirely appropriate considering three weeks ago I was your resident but—"

"Fuck you." Terri smiled. "And yes."

CHAPTER TWENTY

As soon as they got settled in the car for the ride back, Terri reached for Sam's hand and placed it on her leg. She'd held back long enough, and after their conversation on the beach, she wanted to feel Sam close. "That's better."

"Holding hands is off limits, but holding your leg isn't?"

"Right."

"Why?"

Terri considered her answer. "Because this is about sex."

"Then what's holding hands about?"

"Dating."

"Ah." Sam shifted her hand up a few inches. Instead of being above Terri's knee, her grip had quickly moved to the inside of her thigh. "I still want both."

"You'll get used to the disappointment."

Sam pulled her hand back to the steering wheel when they turned onto the highway. The frustration on her face was clear, but she played it off paying attention to the road.

"Will I distract you if I put my hand here?" Terri asked, setting her hand on Sam's thigh.

Sam shrugged. Terri shifted closer. "You know there are lots of reasons that only having sex is better than us dating."

"It doesn't have to be one or the other. We could have an open relationship."

"You know my answer." Terri slid her hand closer to Sam's groin. "But what if I tell you that when we get back to your bedroom, no part of me is off limits? You asked me earlier what I wanted. I want you to have your way with me. And I like it when you make it hurt a little."

Terri stroked her hand down to Sam's knee and then slowly made her way up to her groin again. Sam glanced at her hand when she fingered the top button of her pants.

"You do realize how hard you're making it for me to focus on driving, right?"

"I'm not worried." Terri traced down the center seam. "I know how much you want to get me in your bed."

"Fuck." Sam's forearm muscles were taut, her grip tight on the steering wheel. She passed a truck and then increased their speed, her eyes staying firmly on the road. "I think you should keep your hands to yourself until we get home."

Terri pulled her hand away and entwined her fingers in her lap. "What should I do with my hands then?"

"Exactly what I tell you to do."

Terri forced herself to look out the window. Already she was wet and she wanted Sam's hands on her. But the conviction in Sam's voice made her certain she wouldn't be disappointed later.

The drive home took too long, but they finally pulled into the garage and Sam cut the engine. "So what do you think of my grandma's ride?"

"I still can't believe you have an Aston Martin."

"Don't be too impressed. It's in the shop more than it's on the road."

"And yet you still don't know what it's worth?"

"The mechanic—Otto—could tell me. He babies this car. Polishes it up for fun. I'm sure he knows how much it'd go for." Sam swept a finger over the dash. No dust. "If he had the money, he'd buy it."

Terri guessed that number was two hundred thousand at least. The words "oblivious" and "rich kid" tumbled round in her head. But that wasn't news. Sam had grown up an only child with millionaires for grandparents. She had lawyer parents, an elite boarding school education, and spent carefree summers on the beach. Of course money wasn't something she thought of in the way most people did—hell, she was throwing away forty-one million dollars. But what bothered Terri wasn't that she had no sense of how privileged she was, but that she didn't understand the responsibility that came with it. From out of nowhere, she was pissed all over again.

Sam went around to open her door, but Terri got out before she could. "Thanks, but I don't need a gentleman at the moment."

Sam caught her hand as she started past. "What's wrong?"

"You're so damn privileged, and you don't even see it."

"Privileged? Okay." Sam's jaw clenched. "What else?"

"Us dating is a terrible idea. I'm at the hospital sixty hours a week and you know how often I'm on call. I can't drop everything and drive three hours to spend the weekend with you. And honestly it pisses me off that you'd even ask. You're the one who left."

"I'd come to you. I know how much you work—"

"No way. I wouldn't let you drive up. You chose this world. And if you're doing this—deciding to be a photographer—I'm not getting in your way. I'm not going to be something that sucks up all of your time." Terri hated that they were fighting again. And that she couldn't seem to stop. All over again it was her fault. "You know what really sucks? I do want to date you. You're perfect in so many damn ways."

"Gee, thanks."

Terri pressed on despite Sam's sarcastic tone. "You go out of your way for people you hardly know. You do kind things all the time that get you nothing in return. I've seen it. And you honestly want to help people. That's what makes you a good doctor."

"But I don't want that life."

"You could do both, Sam, and you know it. Work at your grandfather's practice a few days a week and take pictures the rest of the time. Forty-one million dollars. Think about how many people you could help with that. What charities would you give it to? Not some homophobic church foundation, right?"

"You don't know the whole story."

"Then tell me the whole story. Tell me what I don't know. Cause you don't make sense. Who throws away forty-one million dollars?"

"Can you forget about the money? Why is it so important to you anyway?"

Terri shook her head. She didn't want to answer given Sam's judgmental tone, but she couldn't let it go. "I've been broke most of my life, Sam. I have money now but only because I work my damn ass off for it. People who don't actually care about money—who would throw it away—are people who've never had to worry about it. I spent my childhood worrying that there wouldn't be enough money to buy groceries, that we'd be kicked out of the shitty apartment we lived in because we couldn't pay rent. And I couldn't do anything about it. You have no fucking clue."

"I'm sorry you went through that. And I'm sorry I suggested you were all about the money." Sam took a deep breath. "I'm also sorry I disappointed you. But I'm tired of trying to make everyone else happy. Doing the things everyone else wants me to do. I can't anymore. We need to drop this. We're not going to see eye to eye."

"Fine." Terri crossed her arms. Not only had she lost her temper again—which she'd promised herself she wouldn't do—she'd ruined their chances for a nice afternoon.

"Fine? That's it?"

"What else do you want me to say?"

Sam held her gaze. "God, you drive me crazy."

"Well, the feeling's mutual."

Sam stepped forward and pressed into Terri's lips. The kiss took away Terri's breath and all the arguments she was formulating against leaving before anything happened. Sam pressed against her, pushing Terri against the car. She moved down her neck, kisses trailing to her collarbones and then to her chest. Damn, what Sam could do to her nipples…

Terri couldn't keep track of Sam's lips, let alone her hands, and the realization that Sam was giving her a hickey came about two seconds too late. She pushed away enough to level her gaze on Sam. "You tried to give me a hickey, didn't you?"

"I didn't just try." Sam brushed the spot on Terri's neck where her lips had been. "I've never wanted to leave a mark, but I guess there's always a first time."

A thrill raced through Terri. She wanted to look in a mirror to see it for herself. Clearly she was too turned on to think straight. "I'm too old to be explaining hickeys."

"Then don't explain it. Let them wonder who had you."

Sam pressed into her again. This time the strength in her arms was too much to fight. Terri didn't want to resist anyway. She only wanted to give in. As Sam moved a leg between hers, expressing her desire in no uncertain terms and pushing up Terri's skirt, she had to grab hold of the car's door handle. Her legs were shaky and she wanted to suggest a bed, but she couldn't wait another minute.

Sam's kiss crushed her lips. She opened up and Sam made a low sound in her throat that only turned her on more. "I want to feel you," she managed, slipping her hands under Sam's shirt.

Beyond her sculpted shoulders and back, it was Sam's abs that anyone would pay good money to touch. Defined was an understatement. As she fought with Sam's T-shirt, she realized Sam had pushed her skirt up to expose her underwear. She held her breath as Sam grazed her hand over the silk. A second later she'd pushed the crotch to the side and plunged her fingers in.

"Fuck." Terri gave up trying to get under Sam's shirt. She had to hold on to Sam to keep her balance. But God did it feel good.

"I love that you're already wet for me," Sam murmured.

Every time Sam rocked into her, Terri wanted more. She wanted another finger, her whole hand even, and she wanted her deep. She had to bite her tongue to hold back her moans, leaning against Sam and silently begging her not to stop. How many fingers Sam had inside she couldn't tell, but the feeling of being filled was everything she wanted. The tenderness she'd felt that morning was gone. Now her body only wanted to be used, taking any pleasure Sam wanted to give her. She'd be sore later but she wanted that too.

"More."

Sam nipped her neck as she pulled back. "Please?"

Terri groaned. "Please."

Sam bore in hard. Terri doubted she'd still be on her feet if Sam's arm wasn't wrapped around her waist and she wasn't leaning against the car. She closed her eyes. The orgasm was building, blinding her. If she could only hold it back a little longer…

Sam plunged another finger inside, spreading her. Pain mixed with pleasure, and she sank her teeth into Sam's shoulder.

"You like that?" Sam thrust faster when Terri managed a nod.

Sam was rubbing her clit now too. Maybe she was using her thumb? Terri couldn't keep track. All she knew was that she didn't want Sam to stop. One more finger inside and she'd come. "More, please."

"You can't take my whole hand. You're too tight."

Terri clenched her teeth. She'd never been fisted. Never thought she could take it and never wanted it. But now she did. "Try anyway."

"No. I want to be able to play with you more later. I want you bent over my bed."

The thought of Sam fucking her from behind pushed Terri over the edge. Sam could have her any way she wanted. Knowing there was no point resisting the orgasm Sam would get out of her, she stopped fighting and sank down on Sam's hand. But Sam didn't let up. If anything, she pushed her further. Riding her hard until she gushed, Terri finally let out all the sounds she'd held back.

Sam held her through the climax with fingers still buried deep. She kissed Terri's cheek and whispered, "You know the neighbors are gonna wonder what I do in my garage."

"Good."

Sam pressed on her swollen clit. Again she couldn't stop the sound that came to her lips, her body clenching tight on Sam's hand. Let the neighbors hear everything. They'd only wish they had sex this good.

When the wave passed and Terri relaxed, Sam pulled out of her. The feeling of loss was enough to make Terri grab Sam's wrist. She needed something inside her again, but Sam shook her head. "You'll get more when I'm ready to give it to you."

A whimper escaped before Terri could stop it. Sam only pressed a wet fingertip to her lips in response. She sucked it in, tasting her wetness on Sam's fingers, then let it slip out of her lips. "I want to taste your cum, not mine."

"Enough to beg for it?"

The intensity in Sam's eyes took away Terri's voice. She nodded, but Sam held her gaze and she knew she had to answer. "On my hands and knees if I have to."

"That might get you something." Sam tugged Terri's skirt back into position. The seam was a little askew, but otherwise no one would know Sam's hands had nearly ripped it. "I was going to tell you that I liked your skirt. All day I've been having trouble not thinking about taking it off you."

"I think you made your point." Terri smoothed the fabric.

"You're so presentable. Almost like nothing happened."

"Then maybe you should take me up to your room and make it look like something happened." Terri stepped forward and lightly brushed her lips against Sam's. She pulled back and whispered, "I want to be sore when I leave so I can remember you."

"You'll be so sore you'll make plans to come back."

She knew Sam wasn't giving up. And maybe she needed to reevaluate things. They didn't have to date to meet up for sex. Without any commitment maybe it could work? Driving six hours for an orgasm like the one Sam had given her might be worth it. Plus, without any expectation that it would be a regular thing, they could escape the drama of long distance. Of course she'd have to get used to the idea that she wouldn't be the only woman Sam had in her bed.

Sam turned and headed for the side door. Terri followed. Her underwear was soaked but Sam would have it off in no time, and if everything went as she hoped, she wouldn't need clothes for the rest of the night.

CHAPTER TWENTY-ONE

Sam went to the kitchen and filled two glasses of water. Since Terri had come down the stairs that morning in nothing but one of her collared shirts, the buttons only halfway done, she'd wanted her. Being turned on all day was one part epic and one part torture. And what had happened in the garage had taken the edge off, but it wasn't enough by a long shot.

Terri waited for her to pass one of the glasses and then took a long sip. Sam watched her swallow, noticing again the red mark on her neck. It stood out against the paleness of her skin and reminded Sam of all the other things she'd like to do.

"I haven't gotten into BDSM much. But you make me think about it." Sam hesitated. They weren't dating, so why not really go for the sex? That was what Terri wanted anyway.

"I'm listening."

When Terri tilted her head up to Sam, it was hard to think of anything but kissing her. But if they were going further than last night, she needed to know how far Terri wanted to take things.

"You like it when I push you. When there's a little pain." Sam waited in case Terri wanted to disagree. When she didn't, she continued, "And you like it when I make you submit."

Terri reached for her glass again. She took another sip, but her eyes never left Sam's. The feeling of anticipation, eagerness, was undeniable.

Sam continued. "I'm not going to lie—I love it when you let me do what I want. I've always liked being a top, but I've never stopped to think about what I get out of it. It's always been about pleasing whoever I'm with. You make me want more."

Terri only waited for her to go on. But Sam knew she was on the same page even if she wasn't saying it out loud.

"Next weekend, after the wedding gig, I could drive up to Sacramento. I'd like to see you tied up."

Terri gave a half-nod, accepting the plan, and then shifted forward to touch Sam's chest. "What about tonight?"

"Tonight I have other ideas. But unless you want to make this a regular thing, I think you should leave now."

Terri swallowed. Her hand dropped off Sam's chest. She studied her glass for a moment and then said, "I want sex with you to be a regular thing."

"We're getting somewhere. That wasn't that hard to admit, was it?"

Terri raised her eyes to meet Sam's. "You're right. I like a little pain. And I never thought I'd say it, but I like you in charge. You telling me what I can and can't do does something to me."

"Then we agree that this can work for both of us." *Mostly.* Sam pushed away the nagging thought that the closer she got to Terri, the harder it would be for her to keep things only about sex. "I have to know that you'll say something if we're going too far. I don't want to really hurt you."

"I'll tell you," Terri promised.

"Then you should go sit on my bed and wait for me."

Terri's lips parted. She seemed about to argue but then reconsidered. When she obediently turned and headed upstairs, desire surged through Sam. Her arousal told her to forget their earlier fight and the compromise she didn't like.

She went over to the cabinet and found a matchbook. With the drapes drawn, candlelight would be nice and she had an idea that Terri would like the sensation of hot oil on her skin. Along with the new strap-on, she'd bought massage candles and extra lube. She kicked herself for not buying the handcuffs she'd considered. But at least now she had an excuse for another night.

While Terri had slept that morning, Sam had taken her harness and the cock downstairs to clean them. Now she grabbed both and dropped her jeans to assemble the package. As soon as the cock was fitted in the o-ring, the base pressed right where she wanted it on her clit, she pulled her jeans back on. The bulge was obvious even with the cock pointed downward, but she wanted Terri to see it.

Terri was waiting on the bed, her hands clasped in her lap and her ankles crossed. Her gaze went right to Sam's crotch and her tongue slid over her lips.

"Like what you see?"

"I do."

She started to get up, but Sam shook her head and Terri dropped back on the bed with a frustrated growl. Sam ignored her to light two of the candles—almond and sandalwood—and then closed the drapes. It wasn't as dark as she wanted it, but the change in the light turned on her other senses. She pulled off her shirt and eyed Terri.

"You should take off your shirt too."

Terri stood up and pulled off the shirt she was wearing. She waited for her next direction.

"And the bra."

Terri reached around and unclasped her bra. The pink tips of her nipples caught Sam's attention as much as the perfect fullness of her breasts. She wanted them in her hands, but waiting would make the reward even better. Her eyes strayed from the plum blossom branch tattooed above Terri's left breast down to the waistband of her skirt. The paleness of Terri's skin coupled with the softness of her belly tested Sam's resolve on delayed gratification.

"Now your skirt."

Terri found the zipper and tugged. She stepped out of the material and then straightened up. When she fixed a look on Sam, one part uncertainty and another part obvious pride in her gorgeous body, Sam wanted to rip the black silk bikini underwear right off her. But she didn't move a muscle.

Terri shivered like a chill had gone up her spine. The room was cool, but she'd be warm soon. Sam would make sure of that.

"Since I had my hands all over it, I know your underwear's already wet. You should toss it in my hamper."

Terri hooked her thumbs under the waistband and slowly pulled the black silk down her thighs. When she passed her knees, she stepped out of them. She bent to pick them up off the floor.

"I like the idea of you driving all the way back to Sacramento without any underwear…"

"You tell me and I'll do it." Terri held up her panties. "Where's your hamper?"

"Closet." Sam gave a nod to the closed door.

Terri had to walk past Sam. When she opened the closet door, Sam stepped behind her, stroking over her butt cheeks and then down her thighs. Terri held her breath as Sam made her way back up again.

"I didn't tell you to stop what you were doing."

Terri exhaled. She managed to open the hamper and toss in the underwear, then looked over her shoulder at Sam. When she'd shivered earlier, Sam had assumed she was cold, but her skin was warm. "You're nervous," Sam guessed.

"I shouldn't be. But I am."

"Do you want to stop?"

"No. Not at all."

Sam's grip strayed to Terri's hips. She wanted to pull Terri back a step to let her feel her cock against her butt, but she resisted.

"Can I turn around?"

"Not until I tell you." Sam gathered Terri's red curls and pushed her hair over one shoulder. She kissed her neck, her shoulders, and down her spine. Then she kissed the dimples above Terri's butt and straightened up. Her body begged to be let loose, to give Terri what she wanted, what they both wanted.

When she stepped forward, her chest pressed against Terri's back. The feel of skin against skin only cranked up her arousal. She shifted her hips and her cock pushed forward. Terri braced herself, one hand on the hamper, the other on the closet doorjamb.

"I want you inside me."

"I know you do." Sam stepped back, taking away the pressure. Her clit throbbed, reminding her exactly how ready her own body was for this. "Turn around."

Terri did. When she tried to kiss her, Sam stopped her with a hand between her breasts. She lightly caressed one of Terri's nipples, and the tip firmed with her attention.

"You don't have to be gentle."

Sam nodded, but let the nipple slip out of her grasp. "Take off my jeans."

Having someone undo her fly was an unexpected turn-on. Terri didn't rush it. She undid the top button. Then with a tug, slowly pulled the zipper down. Her hand brushed Sam's cock, but she didn't try stroking it. Sam would have stopped her anyway, despite how she wanted that.

Terri dropped to her knees as she pulled Sam's jeans all the way off. She ran a finger along the leather harness but stopped at the o-ring. "May I touch?"

Sam was too turned on to properly give orders now. But she forced herself to focus. "You forgot you're supposed to say 'please.'"

Terri licked her lips. God, she was eager. "Please may I touch?"

"Stand up."

Terri did and Sam spun the cock so it was pointed up. She took Terri's hand and placed it on the shaft. She had no doubt that Terri had given hand jobs before, but that only made what she wanted more real. When she closed her eyes, Terri was holding her cock—not something she'd bought in a sex shop but something that was part of her. She let Terri's hands work until her clit pulsed with need. As good as it felt, she wanted to come inside Terri. She stepped back and Terri let go.

"You know that idea you had earlier…" Terri's voice trailed. She looked from Sam's cock up to her eyes. "About you having me bent over your bed?"

"What about it?"

"I'd like that."

"Then go put your hands on the bed." Sam felt a rush of fresh desire as Terri walked past her. Keeping things only about sex might not be as awful as she'd thought. The arrangement freed them both to ask for, and get, exactly what they wanted.

Terri brushed the covers until they were smooth and then set both hands on the mattress. She looked back at Sam. "When do I say 'please'?"

"You'll know." Sam went over to the nightstand for the lube. She coated her cock and then squirted more into her palm.

When she spread the lube on Terri's slit, the sounds that came out of Terri were nearly enough to make her come. "You like that?"

"I like everything your hands do to me."

"Good." Sam stepped forward. The tip of her cock nudged Terri. "You like this too?"

"Too damn much." Terri dropped onto her belly and shifted her legs apart.

Knowing how much Terri wanted it turned Sam's arousal into a blaze. She forced her hand to go slow as she lightly traced a tattoo of the sun on Terri's back.

"You know you don't have to be gentle," Terri said.

Every muscle in Sam's body begged her to push inside, but she stepped back. "Close your eyes."

Terri looked over her shoulder. The challenge in her gaze only confirmed how much Sam wanted to push her. "Close your eyes," she repeated.

When Terri finally obliged, turning her face to the other side and closing her eyes, Sam went back to the nightstand and picked up the sandalwood massage candle.

"This might burn a little. But only a little."

Terri gripped the sheets as soon as the candle's oil hit her skin. A soft gasp escaped her lips, but then she clenched her jaw, her eyes still squeezed shut. Sam drew a circle with the oil and then massaged Terri's back and butt with it. The oil wasn't hot enough to actually burn, but she knew it would give Terri the pain she wanted. As much as she wanted to satisfy that need, she couldn't bear the thought of truly hurting her.

"More," Terri murmured.

Sam let one drip hit the back of Terri's thigh, and then a moment later, she let a drip slide into the crevice between her butt cheeks. Terri trembled under her. Regular candle wax hardened away from the flame, but this absorbed easily, and the sandalwood scent blended well with Terri's subtle musk.

As Sam worked the oil over Terri's back, the sounds of her pleasure filled the room. Terri's eyes were still closed and her lashes only fluttered when Sam kissed her cheek. "I like you bent over my bed. It's a good look."

"I should be annoyed with you for that, but I can't be right now. I want you inside me too damn much." Terri arched her back, pushing her butt against Sam's groin.

"Spread your legs more. I want to see all of you."

When Terri complied, Sam stroked up Terri's slit, causing a string of "Fuck yeses." As she dipped her fingers inside, the thrill was the same as when she dove into the ocean and took her first stroke over the breakers. God, Terri was dripping for her. She reached down to adjust her cock and then pushed the tip inside Terri.

The gasping moan that came from Terri's lips turned to a long "oh" as Sam shifted deeper. She pinned Terri under her, her chest pressed against Terri's back, as she changed the angle of the cock. When she pulled back and thrust again, she sank all the way in. Terri's butt cheeks pressed against her hips. Her clit buzzed as she started to pump.

"Please don't stop." Terri moaned again.

Stroke after stroke, Sam felt her body responding to Terri's sounds—the groans and the soft cries—all building her fire. She loved the sight of her cock disappearing between Terri's legs as much as seeing the length and width of it when she pulled back.

But nothing was better than the feel of pushing against Terri's butt every time she drove in all the way.

The base of the cock rubbed against her clit each time she went deep, and she rocked back and forth to increase the stimulation.

"You want it harder?"

"Please."

Terri kept her eyes closed and Sam sank in. She pumped her hips, bumping Terri's backside as she drove in with more force. She didn't want to stop, but suddenly she couldn't hold back her orgasm. One more thrust and she found her release.

She pulled all the way out, the overwhelming strength of her climax besting her attempts to keep fucking. Terri trembled under her. She hadn't loosened her grip on the sheets and her eyes were still closed, but she pushed back against Sam, still needing her own satisfaction. Sam reached between Terri's legs and fingered her swollen clit. She stroked fast, not letting up even when Terri arched her back and cried out.

Terri collapsed on the floor against the bed. She was still twitching when Sam wrapped her arms around her. "I need you," she managed.

"I know you do."

"Fuck you," Terri said, still breathless. "I mean I need your hand, asshole. God, what you do to me. Please—touch me."

Sam slid through Terri's wetness and found her swollen clit. Terri tensed, her thighs tightly clenching Sam, as she cried out again. Her scream was something some caged animal would make after it had busted free, and Sam took pride in knowing she'd brought that out. But it was nothing compared to what Terri had done to her.

After the waves of the orgasm seemed to ebb, Sam withdrew her hand. Terri curled up against her, resting her head against Sam's chest and sighing softly. Half in Sam's lap and half on the floor, she was finally quiet, all of her needs satisfied.

Sam wanted to admit that her own orgasm was the best she'd ever had, but she didn't dare break the spell with words. Minutes passed and she felt Terri shiver.

"Do you want to get into bed?" The wood floor was cold, and they were both naked. The only warmth came from their shared heat.

Terri shook her head. "Hold me a little longer. Right here. I don't want to fall asleep."

"You'll have me next week, you know."

"Next week is too long to wait," Terri complained. "And I think you mean that *you'll* have *me*. I'm going to be tied up… God, that sounds so damn good." She snuggled even closer to Sam. "I like you a lot, you know. More than I should."

Sam wanted to echo the same words. "It's only the afterglow. Come Monday you'll go back to being mad at me."

"Which is why you should take full advantage of me tonight."

"I think I just did." Sam smiled even though Terri couldn't see it. "But give me a minute and I'll be ready for another round. I might make you work for it this time."

"I don't know if I'll be able to move."

Sam caressed Terri's cheek. Her chest ached with an unexpected rush of tenderness, and she barely had time to think as the "I love you" came to her lips. Somehow she held it in. Even thinking that sentence was pure folly. She had to remember that this—whatever it was with Terri—was only about sex. No matter how much she wanted it to be about more than that, she couldn't think about falling for her.

CHAPTER TWENTY-TWO

Leaving the little beach house Sunday afternoon wasn't easy, and going back to work on Monday felt like a reality slap. The days passed, and Terri couldn't stop thinking of Sam, wondering what she was doing every minute and longing to see her again. Sam's frequent texts were a small solace, but she thought the weekend would never come. Then finally it did.

Sam: *I can't wait to see you tonight. What are you wearing?*

Terri: *A very unsexy lab coat. I'm at work.*

Sam: *I love you in that damn lab coat. You know it's Saturday, right?*

Terri considered her response. Telling Sam that she'd been counting down the days, had thought of her every hour, and needed her touch tonight more than she'd ever needed anyone sounded obsessive. Or worse, desperate.

Terri: *Had to help McReynolds with a case.*

Sam: *What color are your underwear?*

Terri couldn't help laughing. She quickly typed: *How old are you?*

Sam: *Thirty-one. You?*

That wasn't how she'd expected Sam to ask about her age, but now that it was out there, she couldn't ignore the question. Mostly Terri had stopped thinking about the age gap, but if it was an issue for Sam, she might as well find out now. She held her breath as she typed.

Forty.

Sam: *And the color of your underwear?*

Apparently she'd been worrying for no reason—or Sam was too horny to do the math. Shaking her head, Terri popped into the nearest bathroom and lifted her skirt. She'd been wearing more skirts as of late, giving the late hot spell as her excuse. The truth was she wore them because she wanted to hold onto the memory of Sam's hands sliding up her legs as she'd pushed her against the Aston Martin in her garage. How many times had she revisited that scene in her mind?

Instead of typing the reply, she angled the camera on her phone and snapped a picture. For a moment, she hesitated. She'd never sent any indecent pictures of herself to anyone.

A moment after she'd hit the send button, Sam replied: *HOT. Do you know how much I want to slide between your legs?*

Terri's finger hovered over the keys. What was it about Sam that made her feel reckless? Made her want to abandon her comfort zone? It wasn't that she was stodgy or had ever been a prude. But Sam took her to a whole new level.

Sam: *Are you wet? I bet you are. Check.*

Terri dropped her phone in the pocket of her lab coat and reached under her panties. She knew the answer, but she wanted to feel anyway. And now that she'd checked, she knew she'd soak her underwear. She wiped her finger off on some toilet paper and picked up her phone again, staring at the screen as she debated what to tell Sam.

All your fault. What time can I expect you?

Sam: *It'll be late. Probably nine.*

Sam had explained that the wedding gig was a two-day thing. She'd taken pictures at the rehearsal dinner Friday night and now was at some pre-ceremony photo shoot. The whole thing wouldn't be over until after seven. Fortunately the wedding was at some fancy country club in the East Bay and it wouldn't be as far of a drive up to her house. No matter how late she'd be, Terri wasn't going to tell her they should reschedule.

I'll be waiting.

Sam: *In lingerie?*

Terri didn't answer. Let Sam wonder. She stepped out of the bathroom and nearly ran into one of the nurses coming in. "Sorry."

"Oh, no worries, Dr. Anderson." The nurse smiled and got out of her way.

Probably she had no business being at work with her thoughts so distracted. She'd debated lingerie, felt ridiculous thinking of it, and then had gone to the store and bought something anyway. Now she was glad she'd gone for it.

Her phone rang, and she instantly hoped to hear Sam's voice. When she saw Reed's name, she masked her disappointment. "Hey you. What's up?"

"Do you think weddings need a color scheme?"

"You're not asking me to be a tie-break between you and Julia, right?"

The pause was long enough for Terri to guess the answer. "I'm going to give you some advice, Reed. Say yes to whatever she wants."

"Pink and purple. No joke. That's what she wants."

"And you say: 'I love pink and purple.' Trust me. It's not a fight worth having."

"You're probably right. But there are so many ridiculous details. And this only adds one more." Reed sighed. "What are you up to today?"

"I'll give you one guess."

"You work too much."

"Tell me about it." For the past year she'd felt a growing distaste for coming to work on the weekends especially. And she was tired of being tired all the time. But the other reason she wanted more time to herself, not that she'd admit it, was Sam.

"Have you heard from Sam?"

Right on cue. Reed seemed to have a sixth sense about Sam. Terri had done her best to be evasive on the subject of what had happened in Santa Cruz. She'd only admitted to spending the night—which drew a round of applause from Reed and made her blush way too much. If Reed knew the half of it, she'd do more than clap.

"She's coming to Sacramento tonight."

"Okay, you could have led with that. That's fantastic news! Will she be back in the hospital on Monday then?"

"She's only coming for the night. Weiss accepted her final resignation letter."

"Oh. *Oh.*"

"Yeah." Terri had made it down the hall to the elevator, and as soon as the door opened, she slipped in, hoping no one would join her. When the doors closed and she was alone, she said, "Reed, I know I shouldn't be, but…"

"You're falling for her."

Terri let out the breath she'd been holding. "I thought I was done falling for people. Been there, done that, you know? And I'm forty. I shouldn't be swooning when someone looks at me."

"I don't think age has anything to do with swooning. Can I say 'I told you so' yet?"

"No. It's only been a week."

"It's only been a week since you've let yourself consider a relationship. You've been fighting this for a lot longer."

Terri didn't have an argument there. "I can't stop thinking about her. I'm constantly checking my phone for a new message like some teenager. And what's worse—I love texting her. Love talking to her on the phone. All of it."

"You who hate being tied to your phone."

"Exactly. I can open up to her about anything. Already I've told her more than I ever told Kayla. Any of my exes actually." Terri thought of their last exchange and how simple it had been to admit her age. Everything she worried about turned out to be no big deal. "I finally told her how old I was. She didn't care."

"Course she didn't care. You're the only one stressing about numbers."

"She's basically ten years younger than me."

"Is that a problem for you?"

"I feel like it should be, but it isn't." Terri sighed. "*And* I probably shouldn't say this, but I need to tell someone—the sex is fucking amazing. I can't wait for her to come over tonight."

Reed laughed. "I'm happy for you. Not surprised, really, considering how cocky she is, but happy you're the recipient."

"But this is crazy. I can't do a relationship with her. She's three hours away, almost ten years younger than me, and she's completely changing the direction of her life. A month from now I might not fit in her world at all. I can't get attached."

"You're overthinking this. Maybe you won't fit in her world in a month, but you're the one always saying you don't want to deal with a relationship again. So who cares, right? Slow down and enjoy the ride.

Reed continued, "And not that this should change anything, but I think you're good for Sam. You know what you want and you won't compromise your ideals. That can make you a huge pain in the ass, but she needs someone like that in her life. Maybe she'll chill you out a little and you can push her to figure out her goals."

Even if those goals weren't in medicine. Terri sighed. "Maybe. But—"

"Maybe stop thinking so much. Seriously. For once in your life, do what feels easy." Reed paused. "You sure I should say yes to the color thing?"

Terri wished a color scheme was all she had to worry about. "Purple and pink are lovely together."

* * *

It wasn't until the doorbell rang that Terri felt her excitement turn to nervous energy. With a last cursory look at the living room, she went to open the front door. The house was sparkling, thanks to her cleaning lady, who hadn't minded an extra paycheck for a Saturday morning visit.

Normally, cleaning house and a quick trip to the grocery store was enough to be ready for company. This time she couldn't completely prepare. But not knowing exactly what to expect only turned her on more.

"Hey."

Sam's smile sent a warmth through her along with a clench of undeniable longing. "Hey yourself."

She'd missed her way more than someone she was only supposed to want for sex. She hated the fear that came with that realization—the fear that she might be a temporary attraction for Sam, someone to be caught and then let loose again after a need had been satisfied. Sam hadn't done or said anything to deserve that suspicion, but old baggage was hard to lose.

Terri pushed her misgivings aside. Tonight was about sex. She'd save Sunday for telling Sam she wanted to reopen the discussion about dating. "I like the suit."

Sam glanced down at her outfit and then tried to smooth a wrinkle in her shirt. "It looked better ten hours ago. I've had a long day."

Terri opened the door wider. "Then you should come in and relax."

As Sam stepped inside, Terri had a hard time not reaching for her. She waited as Sam slipped off her black dress shoes and set them in line with Terri's shoes. When she straightened up, she smiled again. "It's really good to see you."

Terri didn't echo the words even though she wanted to. Between the black slacks that fit like they'd been tailored for her, the crisp white button-down shirt rolled up to the elbows, and the narrow black tie, Sam was positively edible. "Is that your camera stuff?" Terri asked motioning to the bag Sam had.

"That and other things. I asked Doug to grab one of my lenses for me and he may have seen a few of those other things." Sam grinned. "He enjoyed giving me a hard time about the handcuffs. Would it be weird if I asked to use your shower?"

"Not at all. There's a bathroom up the stairs, first door on the left. Right next to the guest room. I figure we could use that room tonight for…things."

"Things?" Sam stepped in front of Terri. "I should make you say it. Make you say exactly what you want me to do to you." She leaned close and met Terri's lips with a light kiss.

Before she could pull back, Terri caught her tie. She deepened the kiss, feeling her body respond with a resounding yes. The way her body wanted Sam overpowered any thought of trying to control her desire. She'd let Sam have her in every bed in the house if she asked.

When Sam pulled back, she opened her eyes. "Don't take too long in the shower."

"I won't." Sam shouldered her bag and headed upstairs.

Terri tried to occupy herself in the kitchen, fussing with already clean counters and pouring two glasses of water. Some nights she still wanted the calm courage that came with alcohol, but it wasn't worth the price. Especially not tonight. She hoped Sam didn't care that she didn't even have wine to offer. One thing was certain—Sam didn't have any problem overcoming inhibitions entirely sober.

When she couldn't think of any other excuse to delay, she went upstairs. She passed the guest room, not letting herself peek in on Sam, and went to her own room.

The condo had three bedrooms—two of which were master bedrooms each with their own bathroom. She had more space than she needed, and although she rarely had anyone staying over, she'd fully furnished all of the rooms. After some deliberation, she'd decided not to use her own tonight. Partly that was because she thought she could relax more if they weren't in her bedroom, but also the guest master had a rod iron headboard that made her wet just imagining Sam slipping a rope around the rods.

She turned on her stereo, letting "Lady Marmalade" blast, and slipped off her skirt and blouse. As she checked her reflection, a nervous excitement filled her. She'd worried about the lingerie, but with all the lace and the hooks and strings, it felt now like a strangely empowering sex costume.

"Hot damn." Sam stood in the doorway.

"You don't knock on a woman's door?" Terri smiled despite how her heart pounded in her chest. "You never know what you might see doing that."

"I did knock. Your music's loud."

"Nice excuse." Terri didn't move to turn down the music. The way Sam was openly appraising her made her feel unbelievably sexy. All the workout classes were entirely worth it to have someone lick their lips like they couldn't wait to taste her.

"It's a good thing you're not married anymore."

"Why's that?"

Sam leaned against the doorjamb. "All that about coveting someone's wife…"

"You covet me?"

"I'm sorry. Was it not obvious?" Sam raised an eyebrow. "I'll do better."

Sam had exchanged the suit for a white T-shirt and a pair of boxers. As good as she'd looked before, Terri liked this even better. But the clothing had less to do with it. The fact that Sam was here, leaning against her bedroom door, and had only come for one reason, eclipsed everything else.

"You gonna invite me in?"

"You already opened the door. Looks like you're doing whatever you want tonight."

Sam came up to her and without preamble, reached for one of the straps connecting the bra to the panties. At her light tug, the material pulled taut between Terri's legs. Terri wondered if Sam could smell her arousal. Could sense that she was already wet. Sam had enjoyed plenty of women before—she had to know how hungry Terri was for her.

"I'm going to have trouble not coming as soon as you touch me."

"You'll come when I tell you," Sam said. Her tone was light, almost careless, but the words were an adrenaline shot to Terri. She felt keyed up and weak at the same time. Anything Sam asked, she'd do.

With one fingertip, Sam followed the strap up to the lacy bra. She traced the curves, sending shivers through Terri when she brushed over her nipples. "I like this. Maybe I'll let you keep it on for a while."

"Keep me decent?"

"That's not happening tonight." Sam let her finger drop off the lingerie. "Do you want me to tell you about what comes next?"

Terri wondered if Sam sensed how nervous she was. Regardless, there was no use pretending she knew what she was doing. She'd tried to prepare, even read online sites about D/s relationships and bondage. All of it only made her want Sam more. "It's probably silly but...I decided on a safe word. Since I've never let anyone tie me up before."

"It's not silly. But you know I'll untie you as soon as you tell me."

Terri nodded. She trusted Sam, but this was still her first time. "Hamster."

Sam's lips turned up in a half-smile. "I won't ask why." She caught Terri's hand and took a step back toward the door. "All I'm gonna say is that I've been thinking about this all week."

Every step felt charged. Terri kept her eyes on Sam, trying not to question if the tingling sensation was fear or desire. When Sam opened the guest room door, she noticed the restraints right off.

Black leather handcuffs were on plain display in the middle of the bed. Sam had stripped the bedding down to the white fitted sheet, and aside from the cuffs only one pillow remained, pushed up against the headboard. A black rope weaved between the rods of the headboard, and another was slipped around the footboard. She hadn't thought about Sam restraining her ankles as well. She wouldn't be able to even move her legs—she'd be completely at Sam's command.

"We don't have to put any of this on you," Sam said, somehow guessing her indecision. She caressed her arm. "Maybe we're not ready..."

Terri appreciated that Sam had said "we" as if it wasn't only her who wasn't ready. Sam might not be a BDSM expert, but Terri could tell she wasn't nervous. The realization that this probably wasn't Sam's first time was a relief in a way. Terri didn't want to know details, but she appreciated experience. She eyed the handcuffs again. "I want to try it."

"Good."

Sam pulled her into a kiss that blocked out all other thoughts. For the moment, this was only about sex. About blinding desire and a satisfying reward. About pleasure mixing with pain.

She let Sam lead her to the bed and didn't resist as she fitted the first handcuff on her wrist. The soft leather didn't bind or chaff, but still she couldn't help pulling back when Sam went to buckle the other handcuff.

"Only one?" Sam asked.

"No…I want both. And the ankles too." Terri held out her hand so Sam could tighten the strap. She had trouble relaxing as she lay on the bed. Her arms were tethered above her head, and although she could move them a little, there'd be no way she could free herself. Sam moved from one side of the bed to the other as she attached a second pair of cuffs on her ankles. Soon she wouldn't be able to resist anything Sam did to her.

She closed her eyes and took a deep breath, reminding herself that she trusted Sam. And she wanted this. In the background, pop music filtered in from her bedroom speakers. Taylor Swift. The song didn't fit the mood, but something about not being able to control even the music amplified everything that was happening.

Only one light lit the space—a little lamp on the nightstand—but she could see Sam clearly. And Sam could see her. Terri tried not to feel self-conscious when Sam paused to appraise her work.

"I'd love to shoot you like this…maybe someday you'd let me?" Sam traced a line down the outside of Terri's thigh. "You're gorgeous."

Nerves fired when Sam's hand left her skin. She wanted to reach for Sam, to pull her on top of her, but when she tried to even sit up, she couldn't. A lock of hair fell between her eyes as she tried to settle.

Sam reached over and pushed the curl back into place. "You'll have to ask for what you need."

Terri tugged against the restraints again. She wasn't sure how long she'd last. Sam would untie her, she knew that, but she didn't want to ask yet. "I need you."

"I know you do."

But she needed to feel more than Sam's light touch. She needed to feel her weight pinning her. And she wouldn't say it, but she was desperate to be covered. To have Sam protecting her. She was at Sam's mercy because of restraints that she'd put her in and yet her need for Sam had only intensified.

Sam took off her shirt. She wasn't wearing a bra, and her breasts made perfect little peaks on her chest. Terri knew she wasn't packing. She would have felt the cock when she'd pressed into her earlier as they'd kissed. But she didn't want that tonight anyway. She wanted fingers pinching her nipples, lips bruising hers, and a rough hand holding her down. She sucked in a breath as Sam dropped her boxers.

"I love your body."

"My body loves yours," Sam murmured.

There was nothing she could do when Sam moved on her. She couldn't even grip her shoulders or run her hands through her hair. After a few failed attempts to at least try to touch Sam, she finally dropped her head back on the pillow. Sam's lips distracted her some—kisses that moved from her lips to her neck and then trailed down to her cleavage.

Sam found the snaps along the side of her panties and a moment later she'd torn them off. There was still a mess of straps and the lace bra still covered her breasts, but Terri had never felt so exposed.

Sam met her gaze, as if knowing her thoughts. "I could do anything to you right now."

Sam drug her finger from Terri's belly button down over her mound and then parted her slit. A shiver of need rushed through her. "I need you there."

Sam didn't push inside, only lightly stroking Terri's thighs. "Are you wet for me?"

"I've been waiting all week." Terri pumped up her hips, needing Sam to touch her.

"You could have had someone else." Sam parted her folds.

Terri braced for Sam to thrust a finger inside, but she didn't. She lazily circled her opening, only making Terri want her all the more.

"I could have had someone else but I only wanted you." Terri knew Sam wanted her to say that. But it was also the truth. She wasn't playing a part in a game tonight. "I don't want anyone else to touch me."

"Good."

When Sam bent her head to taste her, Terri strained against the ties. She bucked, but Sam only held her down. There was nothing she could do as Sam's tongue coursed roughly over her clit. Terri clenched her fingers into fists. God, it was ecstasy, but she had no control of it. She cried out, but Sam didn't stop. Thank God she didn't stop.

When she bucked her hips again, Sam was more forceful, and Terri let herself give in. She'd had plenty of lovers go down on her, but not being able to do anything except lie there and take it made the experience entirely new. She had to accept every attention to detail that Sam seemed intent on giving and that was a mind fuck all to itself.

Minutes passed and Sam didn't let up. Terri thought she might not come at all, despite how relentless Sam was with her tongue and how her clit twitched with pleasure. But her mind held her back. She couldn't reciprocate, couldn't even rake her nails down Sam's back or hold her face against her.

Now she wanted Sam to have a strap-on so this wouldn't be all about her. She could let Sam get off fucking her, but relaxing enough to let her own body come was another subject entirely. And still, as her doubt swirled, Sam didn't let up with her tongue.

Sam's hands moved from Terri's breasts, pinching the nipples through the lace, to her hips and then back up to her neck. She loved the roughness in Sam's touch and how she didn't seem to have any pattern. One minute she was gripping Terri's arm, the next she was slipping under her butt to reposition her. When Sam's finger slid inside, Terri moaned. The pressure on her G-spot forced her to consider that she might come after all.

One finger, then two, then three. Terri could feel the pressure increasing. She was able to move her legs enough to pull her knees up and spread herself more. When Sam murmured, "That's four. I think you can take all five tonight," Terri wanted nothing else.

She felt Sam shift and then suddenly pull out. "Where are you going?"

"I brought lube."

Terri waited for Sam to come back, her thoughts jumping from wanting to ask to be untied to wanting to force her body to come this way. When Sam came back to the bed, she kissed Terri's lips.

"Have you done this before?" Sam asked.

"Been fisted or been tied up?" Terri shook her head. "Neither."

"You have to relax for it to work. Want me to untie you?"

"No."

Sam coated her hand in lube and then dripped some on Terri. The coolness made her clench, but a second later Sam was on her, stroking her clit and parting her folds.

"Show me how much you want this."

Terri closed her eyes and pumped her hips up. When Sam didn't enter her, she dropped her hips and then tried again. "Please…"

Sam's fingers slipped in her then, and she murmured "thank you," which seemed ridiculous but felt entirely right.

"You'll thank me again later," Sam promised.

By the stretching pain, Terri knew all four fingers were inside her again. Sam was riding her in slow strokes, easing her open. She wanted to watch when Sam's thumb moved in, but when she looked down to check, Sam had dropped her head and all she could see was her tousled brown hair. In the next moment, she felt Sam's tongue circling her clit again.

"I'm gonna come if you keep that up," Terri panted.

"Don't come."

Terri tried to fight back the orgasm, but Sam's tongue felt too good and her muscles wouldn't stop rhythmically clenching around Sam's fingers. She'd been worried that she wouldn't come and now she couldn't stop it. "I don't think I can help it."

Sam lifted her head, breaking the spell of her tongue. Terri felt her clit quiver. Dammit, she was so close. "Please let me come."

"Not yet…I love how slick you are, how open…" She turned her wrist, her thumb raking over Terri's swollen clit. "But you can take a little more, can't you?"

Terri bit her lip. She wanted more, but she wasn't entirely sure she could take it. Finally she nodded. Sam didn't change anything she was doing; her fingers stayed in place and her thumb kept up the slow back and forth over her clit. Wetting her lips, Terri forced herself to say the words aloud. "I want you to fist me."

"Even if it hurts?"

Terri nodded, hoping Sam would accept that. Words wouldn't come to her lips and her mind was a mess of emotions. She looked up into Sam's eyes, steel blue in the candlelight.

"After you come, you're going to want me again."

Terri nodded again. She'd do anything to please her. If Sam only knew…

"You like belonging to me."

Terri's breath quickened as Sam changed her angle. She was so close to coming, but Sam didn't seem to care how her thumb was torturing her clit with pleasure.

"Say it."

Terri wanted to say the words. Wanted it out in the open and wanted Sam to hear it. "I love being yours. Only yours."

"Good girl." Sam leaned over her and kissed her lips. "Now you get your reward." She shifted back and pushed her thumb inside.

Waves of pleasure rolled through Terri as her muscles clenched on Sam's wrist. She had to bite the inside of her cheek to hold back her moan and then even that wasn't enough. When she let out the sounds she couldn't hold back, Sam only pushed in another half-inch, letting loose a new shock of nerves.

"Fuck me." Terri panted.

"Look."

Terri opened her eyes. Sam's forearm was between her legs. Everything below her wrist was inside her.

"You feel amazing."

Every slight movement Sam made was pure pleasure. "Please don't come out." Terri closed her eyes and dropped her head back on the pillow. *Filled.* That was the only word that came to mind, but the sensation of having Sam's hand in her was so much more than that.

"Now you can come for me."

"I think I'm past that." As good as it felt, she didn't think an orgasm was on the horizon anymore. She was fine with that. This alone felt perfect.

"We have all night," Sam said. "I'm not going anywhere."

"Good." Terri murmured. "I love your hand inside me."

"All you have to do is let go. Let me take you all the way."

Terri wanted to argue that she was tied up and Sam's entire fist was inside her. What else was left to let go of? But she didn't say anything, and she was aware after a moment of Sam's tongue on her clit again. Then she felt Sam's thrusting, subtle at first, but building enough to almost be uncomfortable before her body relaxed into the motion.

Fine, Sam could do whatever she wanted. It felt too good to tell her to stop. She stopped tugging on the restraints and let her head sink into the pillow. Sam rocked into her, over and over, sending pleasure through her. She closed her eyes, thinking she never wanted Sam to pull out, and the pulse at her clit started up again. She didn't understand how it could be possible, but all of a sudden there was no denying that Sam was going to get what she wanted.

Without warning, she came. She arched her back, called out Sam's name, begged her not to stop, then tried to squeeze her thighs together to hold her in place. She felt Sam's caresses as she writhed against the ties.

"I got you."

She heard Sam's voice as if it came from somewhere far away, felt a gentle brush against her cheek when she strained again, then light kisses on her belly. But the orgasm didn't let up. Wave after wave rolled through her body and she couldn't do anything but let it happen. As soon as she was sure it was over, another rush swept over her. It happened again and again until she was certain she couldn't handle anymore. What had Sam done to her? She'd never had any orgasm last this long, never been this undone.

When her body was finally spent, she collapsed back on the mattress breathless and shaking. Sam had loosened the straps and now wrapped her free arm around her. Thank God she didn't try to pull her other hand out. Minutes passed and the shaking gave way to a surreal calm.

Sam touched her cheek, and she realized she was crying. "Was it too much? Did I hurt you?"

Terri rocked her head side to side. Not too much. No. But how could she explain what she'd felt? "Don't come out." Her words were slurred and slow. She could hardly swallow and there was no point trying to move. She knew her muscles wouldn't obey.

How many minutes passed before Sam pulled out? She didn't know. But she complained when it happened even still, not wanting the emptiness she felt without Sam's hand inside her. Sam only touched her lips, telling her to rest. The handcuffs and ankle straps were undone completely and then a blanket was pulled up to her chin. Terri didn't have to move—Sam took care of everything.

She told herself that she'd only rest for a minute. Then she'd try to pleasure Sam. Try, because nothing could compare to what Sam had done to her. When Sam pulled her close, tenderly kissing her cheek, she felt the last little bit of herself that she'd held back let go. It was useless fighting it. She'd already fallen for her.

Tomorrow she'd ask her out on a real date regardless of all the reasons it didn't make sense.

CHAPTER TWENTY-THREE

Sam woke at the sound of a car honking. She tried to fall back asleep when the honking stopped, but then the realization that she was back in Sacramento hit her. Back, yes, but not to stay. That thought came with such a mix of emotions she knew there was no chance she'd get any more rest.

It was morning, but early, and the rays coming in through the blinds cast only a weak light to the room. Terri's arm was draped over her, and when she rolled carefully on her side, easing her arm off, somehow she didn't wake.

Sam breathed her in. The scent of her sex mixed with sweet vanilla lotion. Terri was as breathtaking in her sleep as she was awake. Sam let her eyes wander from the curve of her jawbone down her smooth slender neck. She'd already taken account of all the tattoos—a favorite being the plum blossom branch with the white dove about to land among the flowers. It wasn't only the location that she liked, an inch above the swell of Terri's breast, but the intricate detail of the pink flowers and the bird's spread wings. The interlocking Celtic band on her right forearm was also nice, along with the pair of fish swimming in opposite directions at one bicep and an Egyptian third eye on the other. The sea of colors and patterns were mesmerizing and she envied the artists for the time they'd spent on the bit of skin Terri had granted each one.

Someday, maybe, she'd get Terri to tell her about the tattoos. She had a feeling there'd be a story—at least of which one she'd gotten first and why.

Finally Sam looked away and took in the room. She'd hardly noticed the space the night before, but there was little to note, as it turned out. Aside from the bed and a dresser that looked unused, there was a reading nook by the window with a high-backed chair and a small table with a lamp. Typical guest room. Even the wall art felt sterile—a tapestry of greens and golds on one wall and a photograph of a sunset over snow-capped Sierras on another.

That they were in the guest room instead of Terri's room shouldn't have bothered her, but it did. Clearly Terri hadn't wanted what they'd done to happen in her bedroom. She was proving her point that this was still only sex and nothing more. Sam had fooled herself thinking they were connecting in all the messages they'd exchanged that week. Nothing had changed.

As frustrating as it was to be the one wanting more, Sam wondered if it wasn't some cosmic payback. How many times had she been the one who was detached and only interested in sex? With Terri she'd thought they had a deeper connection. Whether Terri wouldn't let herself feel it or simply chose to ignore it made Sam alternatingly want to give up completely and work harder to convince her they had something worth risking heartbreak.

But, damn, she couldn't complain about the sex. What they'd done last night had loosed something wild in her. Seeing Terri tied up had been the stuff of fantasy. And what she'd let Sam do...

Her cell phone buzzed and she slipped out of bed to quiet the call, searching the pockets of her suit until she found it. Doug. Wondering why he'd call at this hour, she carefully opened the door and stepped into the hallway.

"What's wrong?" She kept her voice low, hoping Terri would keep sleeping.

"Sorry to call so early. I've been up all night trying to rip out my stomach lining." He groaned, then coughed and groaned again. "I think I'm gonna be sick again."

"You sound awful."

"I need a favor. I've got a family photo shoot in San Francisco at ten. Any chance you can stand in for me? Now that your name is back on the website, everyone's asking for you anyway."

Sam checked the time. She needed a shower, but if she skipped breakfast, she could make it to the city barring any traffic. As much as she didn't want to leave Terri, maybe it was best not to spend another day with her. "Text me the address—and feel better."

"Thanks." Another groan. "Next time I go back for a third plate of prawns, tell me I've had enough."

Sam ended the call and glanced at the closed door behind her. She decided to shower in Terri's room to let her sleep a little longer. If that was crossing any lines, let Terri say something. She wasn't going to shy away from an argument, but she didn't want to be the one to bring it up again.

It wasn't until after she'd dried off from the shower, dressed, and brushed her teeth that she saw movement under the rumpled covers. Terri yawned, then stretched and rolled on her side as if planning on slipping back to sleep. But she rubbed her eyes and looked in Sam's direction.

"Why are you dressed?"

"I have to leave. I was hoping you'd wake before I had to go."

Terri ran a hand through her tousled curls. The sunlight streaming through the blinds turned her locks a breathtaking red-gold. She sat up in bed and stretched again. "What time is it?"

"A little after nine." Sam finished buckling her belt.

"Wait, did you say you were leaving?"

"Yeah. Doug texted me. He thinks he's coming down with something. Either that or he ate too many prawns at the wedding. He needs me to do a family photo shoot."

"This morning?"

"I know the timing sucks, but word gets around if you cancel on people." Sam went over to the bed and sat down. Terri reached across the covers and brushed her hand over Sam's.

"I really don't want you to leave."

"I know. I'm sorry." Sam couldn't leave though without checking in first. "Can I ask you about last night?"

"About the crying," Terri guessed.

Sam nodded. "Should we have not gone that far?"

"We definitely should have gone that far. It was fucking amazing." Terri sighed softly. "I think my body was overwhelmed—as cheesy as that sounds. I've never completely let go like that. And now you're leaving and I can't even try to return the favor. Not that I'd be able to match you."

Sam breathed out the worry that had built up. They were fine. She had to stop thinking so much. "We could make plans for next weekend. I don't mind driving up again."

Terri started to nod but then stopped. "I can't. I'll be in Costa Rica."

"Costa Rica? Wow. That's great." *Not great.* Why hadn't Terri even mentioned the trip? Sam answered her own question: because they weren't actually dating. But in all the hours they'd chatted that week, how had Terri not thought she'd want to know?

"Well, after you get back you can text me if you want to meet up again."

"If?"

Sam nodded, trying to keep an impartial look on her face. She started to get up, but Terri grabbed her wrist.

"Give me a minute. My head's still foggy from everything you did to me last night…" She scooted closer to Sam, blinking away the rest of her sleep. "I hate that you're leaving without me being able to thank you. Not properly anyway."

"You don't need to thank me. I promise I had as good a time as you did."

"Not possible. I wish I hadn't fallen asleep."

Terri stroked up from Sam's wrist to her forearm in a gentle caress. Sam had to fight the impulse to pull her arm away. Her earlier touch had felt sweet, loving even, but she had no reason to think Terri meant it that way.

Terri continued, "You keep making every night amazing. I'm gonna get spoiled. And as much as I need a vacation, I don't think I'm going to have a good time without you." She let go of Sam's arm. "I should have told you about the trip. Believe me, though, I've had better things on my mind lately."

"Than a vacation in Costa Rica?"

"Yes. You."

Maybe Sam was making a big deal out of nothing. Terri had a lot on her mind with work and everything. But she still could have mentioned it. "How long will you be gone?"

"Ten days. But then I go right back to work. It'll be two weeks at least before we could see each other. I don't know if I'll be able to go that long without you."

"You'll manage. It's just sex, right?"

Terri narrowed her eyes, but before she could say anything, Sam stood up. She didn't really want to fight—not now when they wouldn't see each other for two weeks. But did it even matter if they settled this? "I hope you have a great trip."

"Sam."

"What?"

"Sit back down."

"I have to go." She knew she was screwing up, but she couldn't say the words to fix it. The "I'm sorry" wouldn't come to her lips, and she hated that she felt so needy. Was it crazy to want Terri to cancel the trip and spend the time with her?

"Please?"

The note of uncertainty in Terri's voice made Sam pause. Was Terri scared that she'd leave? After everything she'd said about not wanting a relationship? As soon as she thought she'd figured her out, she was left questioning everything all over again.

"I don't want you to leave mad."

"I'm not mad."

Terri tilted her head. "You're a bad liar—which is something I appreciate—but how 'bout you don't even try. Tell me what's going on. I know you're pissed."

"I'm not pissed. I'm frustrated. Mostly at myself." She wasn't going to sit down. She didn't want to be that close. That would only make her want Terri again. "Obviously you don't have to tell me everything that goes on in your life. It was dumb of me to think I deserved to know about your vacation. You can do whatever the hell you want to do. And I shouldn't have brought up the 'just sex' thing. You've been clear about not dating from the beginning."

"I know what I said, but we could still talk about it."

"What's the point? Nothing's changed. You live here, I live in Santa Cruz. You don't want to get in the way of my career, and there's no way I could get between you and the hospital." Sam knew any conversation would only be spinning wheels. "I have to go. I can't be late to this photo shoot."

"So go. It's a good excuse."

"A good excuse?"

"You want to leave."

Sam exhaled. Was it that obvious? Well, she might as well say everything then. "I'm mad that you didn't want me in your room last night—that we're in your guest room. And I'm mad at myself because I'm getting too damn attached to you."

Terri looked down at the covers and then at the open bedroom door. "Come to Costa Rica with me. We could have ten days together."

"I can't go to Costa Rica, Terri. I'm broke." Sam shook her head. "And I really have to get on the road. It's not an excuse." She leaned down and kissed Terri. No lingering deep kiss like all the ones that had come before it, only a soft brush of lips.

A moment later she shouldered her bag. She didn't look back. One foot in front of the other until the front door shut behind her and her stomach clenched. What had she expected Terri to say? That she'd changed her mind about the dating thing and that maybe she was getting attached too?

But what Sam had expected was exactly what had happened. And now she had the feeling she wouldn't be back. It wasn't fair to her own heart to keep hoping for something that Terri didn't want.

CHAPTER TWENTY-FOUR

Sam coasted over a low wave and then rounded behind another surfer to stake out her spot. With the sun warming the back of her wetsuit and her cheeks cool from the ocean spray, she didn't have anything to complain about. She'd already had a handful of solid runs but was waiting for the right wave to try out some tricks. Even if it didn't come, however, she told herself she should be happy paddling around on a crystal clear morning. Should be, but she wasn't. She hadn't been happy all week. The fact that everyone else around her seemed to be in a good mood only annoyed her more.

"Looking hot, Samuels." Danielle paddled over. "Saw you get some air on that last one."

"Anyone could get up on these waves."

"Does your girlfriend surf? If she does, you better keep a close eye on her. The boys out here will be pulling out all the stops. She's hot enough for me to consider."

"Not my girlfriend," Sam said, forcing a smile to volley back the playful banter that Danielle expected.

"Not yet or not anymore?"

Steve, one of the locals and possibly the best surfer of the bunch, overheard and whistled. "You got a girlfriend, Sam? Why's she not out here?"

Sam eyed Danielle. "Now look what you started."

Danielle scooted close enough to bump the nose of Sam's board with hers. "So what is it? Is she a bad kisser? I dated this guy for a while that was so damn nice to look at but terrible at kissing. It was awful."

"She's good at kissing. Among other things."

"Sounds like a girlfriend to me," Steve hollered. "Hey, heads up. Who's taking this one?"

"Me," Danielle said. "I gotta get back to the shop." She'd already started paddling and Sam was happy to have a break from the inquisition.

The wave was flawless and Danielle rode it nearly to shore. She stumbled in the shore break and then got to her feet and waved. Not many people were lucky enough to be able to put up a CLOSED sign when they wanted to surf. Danielle didn't have a bad thing going. But was it enough? Sam had never wondered before if Danielle wanted more out of life, but now she found herself questioning everything.

Terri had texted her a handful of times on Sunday after Sam had left her house. The first text was a picture of the handcuffs she'd left and then:

Thanks for an unforgettable evening. Still sorry we left things the way we did. Also sore in the best possible way.

After deliberating on a response, Sam had finally gone with "You're welcome," which sounded equal parts uninspired and weirdly off-putting. After several more texts from Terri that ranged from jokes about dildos to her vacation itinerary, Sam had sent a curt reply saying she needed a break and some time to think.

No more texts came after that, and Sam kicked herself when the next several days passed without a call. She'd asked for a break, but she hated it all the same. More than once she considered driving up to Sacramento. But what good would that do?

A wave jostled her thoughts and nearly pushed her off her board. If she'd been paying attention, she would have taken it. As she watched it crest, she knew it was exactly what she'd been waiting for. She kept her gaze trained on the water, waiting for the next in the set.

The only way to get Terri off her mind was to make a decision to end things. But she didn't want to do that. What she wanted was for Terri to come to the same realization that she had—they had a real connection that was more important than the sex. Or at least *as* important. Ending things simply because Terri didn't want to see that was ridiculous. But if Terri didn't want more than sex, she'd never be satisfied.

She needed to tell Terri that even though she'd agreed to it, a sex-only relationship wouldn't work for her. Maybe that meant they'd have to break things off, and although the thought of not seeing Terri made her sick, prolonging it would only make everything harder. What she finally decided, mostly because she didn't want to decide at all, was to wait until after Terri got back from Costa Rica to have any conversation.

The next wave rose up behind her and she knew it was going to be bigger than the others. Without questioning it, she started kicking. Whether it was luck or the fact that she had more than a little frustration to vent, her timing was right on. She pushed up on her board and as soon as she was steady on her feet did a quick bottom turn and then a roundhouse cutback. Her heart bounced up to her throat when she managed a snap that sent a spray of water soaring above her. She heard someone cheer and couldn't help smiling.

Although she could have tried more tricks, she simply carved the rest of the ride because it felt too good to do anything else. When she saw the shore coming, she stepped off her board. Nothing flashy—only a nice end to a perfect ride. Everything went dark as she let her body sink below the rolling water. When she surfaced, she saw Steve paddling a few yards away. Not only was he one of the best surfers, he also watched out for everyone.

"How'd that feel?"

"Like a walk in heaven."

Steve grinned. "You got that right."

"Catch ya later."

"You're leaving now? With these waves?"

"I'm done. That last one was too perfect." Surfing was all about knowing when to call it quits. The significance of that thought weighed on her, but calling it quits with Terri was a lot more complicated.

The walk home included a detour for pizza. She didn't rush, stopping to chat to the neighbors she'd now become friends with and then stopping again at the bench across from her front door.

She thought of the last text Terri had sent—her vacation itinerary. She'd probably meant it as a peace offering, but then Sam had gone and sent the text about needing time instead of simply saying "have fun" or whatever the normal response should have been.

Regardless, now she knew that in a little under an hour, Terri would be boarding her flight to Houston. After a two-hour layover there, she'd board a flight to San Jose, Costa Rica.

The thought of Terri getting on a plane and flying hours away made Sam's stomach clench. It was only a vacation, but the rift between them would widen, she knew, even more than it had over the last five days. She wanted to at least say goodbye. As soon as she had that thought, she worried it was too late. She hurried to rinse off her board and her wetsuit, then ran inside to find her phone.

"Hi, Sam."

"Um, hi." Sam's mind spun. The rush at hearing Terri's voice was quickly dispelled by the clipped sound of her words. No doubt she was upset. But she'd taken her call. "Should I not have called?"

"It's fine. What is it?"

Sam took a deep breath. "Well, I wanted to talk."

"Can you hold for a minute? My sister is on the other line and we were just saying goodbye."

"Yeah. Okay." Sam paced as the seconds ticked by. She should have called sooner. But still she didn't know what to say. Should she really break things off simply because Terri couldn't give her what she needed? She'd already asked for more and been turned down. What else could she do?

Finally Terri came back on the line. "So what's up?"

"I wasn't going to say this but...mostly I called because I missed hearing your voice." She'd been desperate for it all week but hadn't wanted to give in. "And I thought we should talk before you left."

Silence.

Sam pressed on. "How are you?"

"Fine. You?"

Terri's "fine" sounded anything but. "Everything okay with your sister? Was it Kelly or Bianca?"

There was a pause, and then Terri said, "Kelly. Everything's fine. Has anyone ever told you that you've got a really weird ability to remember names? I think I mentioned my sisters' names one time."

"I pay attention to little things. It's not only names." Sam could draw all the tattoos on her body, could list every place she'd touched that had made Terri moan, could recall her smile when they'd sat on the beach watching the surf. "Are you at the airport already?"

"Yeah...Sam, why are you really calling me?"

"I wanted to hear your voice."

"You already said that. That's the only reason?" There was another long pause. "It's good to hear your voice too."

"You sure about that?"

"I'm sure. Although there've been a few days this week that I wouldn't have felt that way."

"Why is today different?"

"I don't know. Because you finally called?" She gave an exasperated sigh. "Sam, I've gone through two divorces, but you win the prize for taking me on the biggest rollercoaster of feelings in one damn week. You know, I wasn't looking for this. I didn't want to fall for you."

"You didn't fall for me. We had sex. Good sex, but that's all."

"Don't fucking tell me what I did or didn't do, Sam. How the hell do you know?"

Sam's chest tightened at the sound of hurt in Terri's voice. "That was a dumb thing to say. I'm sorry. But you said you wanted this to only be about sex."

"And did you stop to think that maybe I changed my mind?"

Sam didn't know what to say. Hadn't she wanted Terri to feel the same way she felt? So now they both felt like crap. Mission accomplished.

"I needed you to check in with me after what we'd done." Terri's voice had softened, but the hurt was still there. "And, I don't know, maybe act like you cared? Something happened on Sunday. I knew you were upset, but then…then you got cold. And fucking left. I know I'm an adult and I can handle that, but… Ugh. I don't even know what to say to you now. The truth is I knew better. I tried not to fall for you, but it happened anyway."

"I'm sorry."

"Sorry? Whatever. You wanted me to fall for you." Terri cussed under her breath. "You know the worst part? I never trust people. Not people I barely know. And certainly not people that could hurt me. But I trusted you. I thought after all the texts and everything we talked about that I knew what to expect. But you totally blindsided me."

"I didn't know—"

"No shit you didn't know. And you didn't ask. You just walked out. And then you text me to tell me you need a break. We're not even dating. Screw you."

Sam pinched the bridge of her nose to stop the tears from coming. "Don't get on the flight."

"Don't go to Costa Rica? You're kidding, right?"

Sam knew it was too much to ask, but she had to anyway. She had to see Terri tonight. "Change your flight to tomorrow. I'll pay for the change fee. I can meet you at the airport and we can get a hotel room for the night."

"The flight's about to board. It's too late to change anything."

"Then I'll find a flight to Costa Rica and meet you there. It'd be worth it even for a few days…" It was crazy, but she'd do it if Terri agreed.

"You coming to Costa Rica doesn't make any sense. Not for only a few days."

"Does it have to make sense?"

"Sam, Costa Rica isn't the point." The line went silent again for a long moment before Terri said, "We both made mistakes. I should have told you how I was feeling Saturday night, and you cutting me off like you did…well…you know how I feel about that. But I got to thinking that maybe you were right. Maybe we do need a break. We can both take the next two weeks to figure out what makes sense for us. What we really want."

"Is 'us' still a possibility?"

"I don't know."

If possible, Sam felt worse. Did Terri have to be so logical about everything?

"I gotta go. We can talk when I get back."

"Okay. Have a good trip." What else could she say? So many things. But the line clicked and Terri was gone.

Minutes passed and Sam only stood in the hallway staring at her phone. When she looked up from the screen, her body reminded her that she was standing in the same spot where Terri had first kissed her. She glanced at the wall she'd pushed Terri against, her lips tingling. When Terri had walked through the front door that night, she'd had no idea what to expect. She'd blown everything now.

Waiting until Terri got back to tell her how she felt wasn't possible. She pulled up her recent calls and tapped on Terri's number. Voice mail picked up and she steadied her thoughts. There was a chance Terri would check her messages on the layover in Houston. There was also a chance she wouldn't want to listen to any messages when she saw it was Sam who'd called.

"First off, I really like you." Sam knew she had to be honest about her feelings. All of them. "I know we have something and I've known that for a long time now. But you kept holding me at arm's length and…I started to think you didn't want what we had." She ignored the tears on her cheeks. "Second off, I'm sorry. I'm sorry I thought I knew what you were thinking. And I'm sorry I left the way I did last weekend. Especially after what we did. I screwed up and I want to make it up to you."

Sam had circled from the hall through the living room and back to the hallway. Now she stopped pacing and brushed off her tears. What if Terri was done? She didn't want to consider that possibility, but it was there all the same.

"I get it if you can't give me another chance. But if you get this when you're in Houston, can you call me? I'm going to look up flights. And I know it doesn't make sense to fly down for only a few days, but I want to see you. I need to make things right…" Sam stalled. "I know this sounds cheesy, but if I have a chance with you still, I'll do anything."

CHAPTER TWENTY-FIVE

On either end of the smooth, white, sandy beach was dark green jungle. The only other thing in sight was the ocean—turquoise water stretching as far as the horizon. Terri adjusted the angle of the umbrella, leaned back on her towel, and tried to soak in the view along with the sun on her legs.

The resort excelled on what the website had promised. Relaxation. But all that relaxing only let her mind wander to Sam whenever it wanted. At the moment, she had the excuse of the surfers. An afternoon breeze had brought high waves and a half dozen surfers were out on the water trying to catch a ride. Most were tourists from the resort, and if they managed to stand up at all, the ocean quickly tossed them. So of course she wondered how Sam would fare. Then she wondered what the whole day would have been like if Sam had joined her like she'd wanted to.

Four days had passed since their conversation in the airport, and she still wasn't sure what her next move should be. She'd listened to Sam's message twice in Houston, then twice more when she'd landed in San Jose. But she hadn't called her back. She knew they needed to talk, but she wasn't sure what to say.

On the long bumpy ride out to the coast, she'd decided that she didn't blame Sam for pulling back. Her timing was crap, but she understood. And she wasn't upset anymore. In fact she felt guilt more than anything else—guilt that she'd held Sam at arm's length, exactly like she'd said on her message, when all she'd wanted to do was pull her closer. But she couldn't get past the question of how they could make it work, especially if Sam's first move was to run rather than to talk through a problem.

Terri pulled her knees up to her chin and rested her head. The beach vacation should have been paradise, but everything was marred with what-ifs. What if she'd said yes and Sam had come? What if she'd never kissed Sam? She'd wanted everything they'd done together, but if she'd never made the trip to Santa Cruz, maybe she could have easily forgotten about her. Now nothing about her was easy.

That morning Terri had gone on a hike to a waterfall—the trail cutting deep through the thick of the jungle—and stopped at a lookout, only to think of Sam. Butterflies as big as her hand and brilliant blue flitted close enough to touch while howler monkeys called to each other and toucans soared above. She wondered what Sam would notice and what she would take a picture of. And instead of enjoying it all, she'd stood there trying to ignore a gnawing loneliness.

What if Sam was the one? After being married twice, she couldn't believe she'd even ask that question. This wasn't her first solo vacation, and yet it was the first time she'd truly wanted someone to be with her. And not just anyone. She wanted Sam.

Tomorrow she was set to take another bumpy jeep ride inland to see the volcano and then the cloud forest. But all she wanted to do was be transported to Sam's doorstep. A huge wave came up and the surfers disappeared from view. She stood up, suddenly worrying that they'd be swept out, but then a moment later the wave crested and she spotted them again. She let out the breath she was holding and looked behind her at the resort. The nagging sensation that she was in the wrong place was growing stronger. If she skipped the volcano and the cloud forest, could she call this enough vacation?

* * *

Once she'd made the decision, the pieces came together quickly. Suddenly she was in Houston five days early. Compared to the calm of the remote beach where she'd thought this all through, Bush International was a jarring wake-up call. She hadn't even talked to Sam yet. All she could do was trust that Sam hadn't changed her mind.

"Sorry for the hold. How can I help you?"

Terri smiled at the professional sound of her sister's voice. She'd never called her at work and never asked for a favor, but she couldn't show up at Sam's door. They needed a neutral space. A little hotel in San Francisco might be perfect. "Do you have any rooms for tonight?"

"Tonight? Let me check... We have one left."

"Great. I'll take it."

There was a short pause and then, "Is this who I think it is?"

"Hi, Kells."

Kelly's hoot made Terri's smile widen.

"I thought I recognized the number, but then I told myself I was imagining it. Aren't you supposed to be in Costa Rica?"

"I decided to come back early."

Kelly hmmed. "This has to be about a woman. No way would you cut a vacation short for a guy."

Terri laughed. "You know me too well."

"I want the full story, but let's get you set up with this room first."

After the details were solidified, Terri hung up with Kelly, promising to tell her more later, and then debated the text she wanted to send to Sam. She decided to send the link to the restaurant from the hotel's website and then added a quick note:

Any chance you could do dinner at seven? Would love to see you.

After a moment of indecision, she hit send.

A minute ticked by without a response and then another. Terri knew there was a possibility Sam would have other plans. A photo shoot even. When she was about to toss her phone in her purse, the screen blinked with a new message.

Sam: *I'll be there.*

Terri's heart pounded in her chest. All the questions rattling round in her mind raised their hand at once. For now, she had to accept that she'd see Sam tonight. Everything else would have to wait.

"You're really here!" Kelly came out from behind the reception desk and gave Terri a bear hug. "I can't believe my big sis came to see my hotel!"

"I should have come sooner." San Francisco wasn't even that far away from Sacramento. She simply hadn't made the time for a visit.

"Uh-uh. No feeling guilty—I see those wheels of yours turning. We both know you're too damn busy to breathe let alone come to a random hotel where your little sister works. I'm excited to have you here. That's all. I promise. Now, give me a minute to get you checked in. And then we'll talk about why you're here." Kelly spun back to the reception desk. "It's not the best room. If you'd given me a little warning I would have set you up in the suite with the skyline view."

"Next time." This time she wasn't here for any view. But seeing how happy Kelly was, she was glad she'd thought of coming at all. "We should pop in on each other more."

"We should." Kelly looked up from the screen and grinned. "You totally made my night. And we're all set." She held up a card key and then knocked on a door behind the reception desk. "Hey, Andre. My sister's here. You're on."

Andre opened the door and leaned back on his chair. "Hi, Kelly's sister. Wow. Holy red hair Batman. You two have the same DNA or something?"

"Very funny." Kelly stuck out her tongue at Andre and then turned to Terri. "Ignore him. He's nice to look at but..." She turned to wink at Andre. "We're still on for skeeball tomorrow, right?"

"'Cause I'm nice to look at?"

"That and I like skeeball."

Terri had to laugh. Fortunately, Andre did as well.

"Follow me, sis."

It wasn't the first time someone had commented on the family resemblance. Bianca had dark brown hair that was straight as could be, but Kelly and Terri had the same red curls, and side by side, there was no doubting they were sisters.

As soon as they were out of the lobby, Terri said, "So is Andre the new boyfriend?"

"One of them." Kelly smiled. "You're not the only one who stays busy."

Terri laughed. "I guess not. Does he know he's not the only one?"

"Yes...but he also knows I like him better than the other one."

"Then why keep two?"

Kelly shrugged. "Variety?"

"I think I'm too old for variety."

"Some days I am too. But I'm not sure I'm ready to propose to Andre." She pointed out a painting of a dark blue triangle on the wall. "We've got a deal with one of the galleries in town and have some of their art on display. This one's called 'The Other Night.' I've stared at it for about an hour and still have no clue what the artist was thinking."

Terri smiled when Kelly looked back at her. "I've missed you."

"Me too." Kelly slipped her arm around Terri's waist. "But now you know where to find me."

As they walked, Kelly explained that the hotel had two dozen rooms—which was a good thing if one wanted a quiet upscale place to stay in a prime spot in the city, but a challenge in the busy season when they were always turning away guests. She also pointed out a few other paintings and then some of the new decor. Terri could feel Kelly's pride, and she wished again that she'd taken the time to drop in on her sooner. The short tour ended when they reached her room.

"Here it is." Kelly walked in, turned around, and then looked back at Terri. "What do you think?"

"It's nice." Maybe too nice. Definitely romantic. "Now all I have to do is not freak out."

Kelly flopped on the bed. "Okay. Spill. I want the whole story."

Terri set her purse on the table by the door and wheeled in her carry-on. The room wasn't big and there was only one bed. For some reason she hadn't even considered the sleeping part, but clearly they weren't going to simply have dinner and go their separate ways. But she wasn't sure it was a good idea for them to have sex. Even if they planned on sleeping on opposite sides, what were the chances they'd keep their hands to themselves?

"You are going to tell me, right? I mean, you left your vacation early for this chick. It's gotta be serious." Kelly arched an eyebrow. "Or someone screwed up. You or her?"

Nothing got past Kelly. Terri sighed. "A little of both. But I don't think I'm up for telling you all the details."

"Why not?"

"Because I can't have that conversation with my little sister."

"Ooh, was it a sex problem?"

Terri rolled her eyes.

"You do realize I'm thirty-one, right? I've probably had more partners than you."

"I'm aware of that possibility." She also was well aware that Kelly was the same age as Sam—and there was a good chance that Sam had more experience than she did as well. "Unless there's a medical reason I need to know, I really don't want to hear about your sex life. Do you honestly want to hear about mine?"

Kelly bopped her head from side to side. "Depends. How cute is she?"

Terri sank down on the bed. "I lose my train of thought when she walks in the room. And, no. Sex isn't a problem. She's almost too good."

"Mm. Yeah. I want to hear more."

How was it possible that Sam was the same age as her little sister? "Too bad. I'm not telling you."

"What kind of sister are you?" Kelly teased. "Okay, at least tell me you have a plan. You left your vacation for this woman. That's all I know. Does she need to do something to fix things or is it all on you?"

"I think it needs to be a joint effort but maybe mostly me. I blamed her, but…that wasn't fair."

Kelly nodded. "Do you love her?"

The answer was waiting on the tip of her tongue, but Terri didn't say it. Had she really fallen in love despite everything? She closed her mouth and swallowed, wondering how she could be so overcome by one word.

"Speechless, huh? That answers that. Does she love you back?"

Terri lifted her shoulders. She thought she knew, but what if she was wrong? What if she was only a good time for Sam? And yet every time they'd had sex, Sam had held her afterwards and the tenderness in her touch was undeniable. Sam focused on her like no one else was around, like nothing else mattered. Even in the stream of texts they'd exchanged, Terri had worried Sam was too attracted to her. *Worried.* No wonder Sam had pulled back. Meanwhile Terri had focused on the sex and pretended she wasn't falling for her.

Kelly touched Terri's hand. "You don't need to have it all figured out tonight. When does she get here?"

Terri glanced at the clock by the bedside. "She'll be here at seven."

"In twenty minutes?" The urgency in Kelly's voice was endearing. "Are you going to change?"

Terri glanced down at her travel clothes. She was wearing a comfy knit shirt and loose pants—perfect for travelling but not what she wanted to be wearing on a date. Although she wasn't sure tonight qualified as a date. "I'd love to shower…I hadn't really thought about clothes. I packed one dress, but it's probably wrinkled."

"I'm a whiz with the iron." Kelly pointed to the carry-on. "In there?"

"You don't mind?"

"Are you kidding? For the first time I'm helping my big sis. Do you know how many times you've helped me?" Kelly motioned to the bathroom. "Go shower. We don't have time to argue."

Kelly distracted Terri from thinking about seeing Sam by keeping up a running monologue about her relationship woes not only during her shower but as she was toweling off and changing into the dress. Andre sounded like a keeper, and Terri told her as much, but the other beau had plenty of good attributes as well. Only when her cell phone buzzed with a text did Terri feel a twinge of nerves.

She glanced at the screen and took a steadying breath. "She found a parking spot."

"Where are you meeting her? Here at the hotel? Did you already pick a place for dinner? 'Cause I can totally give you recommendations. You're going to let me meet her, right?"

"Hold your horses." Terri typed out a quick response: *Meet you in the hotel lobby.*

She set down her phone and considered Kelly's request. She didn't want to tell her no, but she was already anxious.

"Please let me at least say hi. I promise I won't say or do anything to make you regret it. Please?" Kelly batted her eyelashes. It was a classic Kelly move, and Terri knew there was no point fighting those eyelashes.

"Okay, but only a quick hello."

"Thanks!" Kelly squeezed Terri's arm. "You know, this is the first time I'm meeting someone you're seeing before you're marrying them. By the way, your dress is perfect. Not too fancy—you don't want to seem like you're trying too hard—but sexy enough to get her attention. I wish I had your boobs."

Terri grinned when Kelly tried to squeeze her own breasts to make more cleavage. "You're gorgeous and you know it. Now stop fondling yourself, goofball. Did you really not meet Kayla before we went to the courthouse?"

"No. You didn't even think about the fact that I might want to judge who my sister was marrying before it happened." She pursed her lips in a mock petulant look. "And since you and

David didn't have an official wedding either, it wasn't until that Christmas that I met him."

"I've made a lot of mistakes." Terri laughed when Kelly gave her an "I could have told you that" look. "Does it make it any better if I say that this is honestly the first person I've slept with that's worth introducing?"

"Now that I understand."

"But I don't know about the relationship part. We seem to be really good at sex and not much else." She glanced at the bed and imagined Sam pushing back the covers. "I was thinking we could come back here after dinner to talk, but I don't know if that's a good idea. There's a chance we won't do much talking."

"I knew you and I were related." Kelly handed Terri her purse. "Come on. I want to be introduced to the woman that's got my tight-ass sister all hot and bothered."

"Hot and bothered" was one way of putting it.

CHAPTER TWENTY-SIX

"That's your girlfriend?" Kelly whispered. "Damn. I might be gay after all."

"Don't even think about stealing her," Terri said under her breath. Her pulse had started racing as soon as they stepped out of the elevator, and when she spotted Sam, chatting with Andre at the reception desk and looking perfectly handsome in a dark gray suit, her heart jumped up to her throat.

"Too late. Already thinking about it." Kelly grinned when Terri shot her a look.

Kelly was as straight as could be, but anyone could appreciate an attractive woman. Especially one in an expensive suit that looked like it had been made for her. God, Sam was gorgeous.

Sam pulled her hands out of her pockets and straightened up. Her tentative smile carried all the uncertainty Terri had felt over the last week. She didn't know where things stood. Neither did Terri.

Kelly walked right up and stuck out her hand. "Hi. I'm Kelly."

"I'm Sam." Sam clasped her hand. "Nice to meet you. Terri's told me about you."

"She's told me about you too." Kelly raised a knowing eyebrow, and Terri cringed. Hopefully Sam wouldn't guess what Kelly was thinking.

"You've got a nice hotel," Sam said. "The location's perfect."

"But a pain in the ass to find parking near," Andre added.

"True." Sam met Terri's gaze. "It's good to see you."

"Likewise."

"You look amazing."

"So do you." Terri wanted to take away the uncertainty in Sam's eyes, but there were no magic words to say. They had to figure out their next step together.

"Is it getting hot in here or is it just me?" Kelly fanned her face, not so subtly winking at Terri.

Little sisters were always little sisters, no matter what they promised. "Aren't you supposed to be managing a hotel or something?"

"Oh, I'm done for the night," Kelly said, her mock innocent tone fooling no one. "Fortunately, I hire amazing staff like Andre so I don't have to live here twenty-four seven." Andre blew Kelly a kiss and then laughed when she pretended to dodge it. Kelly continued, "But I do need to go home. It was nice meeting you, Sam." She turned to Terri, pecked her cheek and, as she pulled back, murmured, "I like her."

So do I, Terri thought. Seeing Sam again after all the ups and downs of the past two weeks made her certain of that at least.

When Kelly left to get her things, Terri turned to Sam. She felt lightheaded as Sam held her gaze. If she held out her hand, she knew it'd be shaking—so much for her reputation of being ice-cool during a crisis. She tried a smile. "Thanks for driving up."

"Thanks for asking me."

"So…dinner?"

The restaurant was attached to the hotel but had a separate street entrance. When they went out, Sam held the door. Terri had to step close to make it through the doorway, and a hint of

Sam's cologne sent a tingly sensation through her body—as if she needed another reminder for how much she wanted her. God, it was hard not to turn and kiss her.

Outside the street was teeming with cars and pedestrians hurried past on the sidewalk. Terri started toward the restaurant entrance, but before she could reach for the restaurant's door handle, Sam opened it. She almost said that she could open a damn door, but when she looked up, her breath caught in her chest. Sam's dark blue eyes held her gaze.

"Is it okay if I open doors for you?"

"I can do it myself."

"I know. That's why I'm asking."

This was an official date. There was no arguing that. She'd asked Sam to dinner and now here they were. And Sam was taking a risk too.

"Thank you." Terri stepped past Sam and into the foyer, reminding herself to breathe. The maître d's greeting was warm and immediate, asking for their patience as their table was readied. As they waited, Sam stood at her side, close enough to touch but seemingly careful to keep from doing so. Her gaze wandered from the maître d's desk to the handful of candlelit tables and then to her shoes. She was nervous too. Terri could feel it. As smooth as she could talk, always seeming so confident, Terri knew some of that was an act.

"I didn't know if I'd hear from you," Sam said. "You have no idea how many times I've wished I could go back and do that last Sunday all over again. I'm so sorry for all the ways I screwed up."

"Yeah, that was impressive."

Sam's smile was faint.

"I meant it when I said we both made mistakes. And, by the way, I listened to your message so many times I think I have it memorized." Terri paused. "I forgive you. You forgive me?"

Sam nodded.

Terri held out her hand. A quiet voice in her head warned her that she didn't know what she was doing. *Playing with fire*, she returned.

Without a word, Sam clasped her hand. The noises of the restaurant funneled away. The candles all blurred. Sam's grip tightened and Terri felt like she was floating. If only she could stay in this moment, holding Sam's hand and not thinking about what might happen or what should happen.

Too soon their table was ready and a waiter came to lead them to a quiet back corner. Sam kept hold of her hand until they reached their table. She let go then and Terri felt jostled awake from a dream.

Once they were seated, the waiter cleared his throat. "Would you like to see the wine list?"

"Water's fine for now," Sam returned.

"Of course."

The waiter slipped away, and Terri said, "You know you could order wine even if I don't drink."

"Turns out I don't like it. Beer's nice on a hot day, but I really only drink to be sociable." Sam paused. "But thank you for telling me it's okay. How was Costa Rica?"

"Beautiful. Unfortunately I couldn't stop thinking about how much I wanted you there with me."

Before Sam could say anything, the waiter returned to fill their water glasses and then, when it was clear they weren't ready to order, slipped away again. Sam scanned the menu and Terri tried to do so as well, but she couldn't focus.

"I really hoped you'd call me back when you were in Houston."

"I wanted to," Terri admitted. "But then I didn't know what to say."

Sam set down her menu. She glanced at the other diners and then back at Terri. After a moment, she said, "I need to know what you want out of this."

It was a reasonable request, given everything, and the intensity in Sam's words made her realize that she couldn't get out of answering. She also knew Sam wouldn't accept a "maybe." But how were they going to make this work?

"You left your vacation early. You asked me out to dinner and then wanted to hold my hand. As excited as I want to be about all those things, I need to know what we're doing here. I don't feel like that's too much to ask."

"It's not." Terri swallowed. How was Sam the mature one in all of this? And why the hell was it so hard for her to say what she wanted? Because if Sam broke her heart, she knew she'd be done for good. There was no coming back from someone like her. "I want a relationship with you. A real one. But I honestly have no idea how we can make it work."

"We're both pretty smart. I bet we can figure it out." Sam stretched her hand across the table palm up. When Terri placed her hand on top, Sam gently clasped it. "I missed you."

"I missed you too."

Sam continued, "You know, some things are easier than you'd think. We could go on a date—without written orders or any treatment plan."

"Some of us like plans." Terri dared herself to go on and say the rest of what she was thinking. "I'll try it your way, but do me a favor and let me down easy when we break up. If I let myself love you, I know I'm going to have a hard time getting over you."

"Ditto."

Maybe it was all the travel messing with her sense of time or maybe it was being with Sam, but when they finished dinner, Terri didn't feel tired. She also didn't want to send Sam home despite the fact that she wasn't quite ready to take her up to the hotel room. Somehow knowing they'd both acknowledged this was the start of something made what they did feel more significant. Sex wouldn't be a game this time.

They stepped outside the restaurant and instead of heading back to the hotel, Terri caught Sam's hand and started down the sidewalk in the opposite direction. The traffic had thinned and there were fewer people out walking now, but the city, with its blinking lights, still had a pulsing energy. When they stopped at an intersection, waiting for the light to change, Sam's arm wrapped around her shoulders.

Terri leaned into her embrace. "How does it work when we have sex now?"

"What do you mean?" Sam asked.

Terri bit her lip, trying to put to words the tangle of questions she'd thought of at dinner. Sam had kept the conversation going asking about Costa Rica and then work, but still her mind had wandered to sex every time Sam reached for her water glass or picked up a utensil. She kept returning to the thought that the last time they'd been together, Sam had tied her up and fisted her. And it was more than the act—more than what she'd let Sam do. Something she'd held back from all her other partners, she'd finally given in to Sam. That was why Sam pulling back when she did had hurt so much.

"I'm not going to be submissive the rest of the time. I mean I want to be that way in bed, but…"

"But you won't be in our relationship?"

Terri nodded.

"I wouldn't want you to be. That's not you." After a moment, Sam continued, "You're used to being in charge—used to telling everyone else what to do. And you're so good at what you do that everyone listens. All of that is incredibly sexy. But so is what I get in the bedroom—the part that wants to be slowly stripped and fucked until you can't stand up. The part that doesn't want to be in charge."

The light changed and they crossed the intersection. Terri's heart thumped in her chest as Sam's words replayed in her mind. *"Slowly stripped and fucked until you can't stand up."* When they reached the other side of the street, she stopped. Her clit was pulsing, and she was certain that if she checked she'd find she was already wet.

"I didn't really have a plan for what happens next. I figured we'd do dinner and talk and then…"

"You want to take me up to your hotel room?"

"Does reading my thoughts ever make you uncomfortable? Because sometimes it should."

"Not yet but keep trying." Sam winked. Terri started to turn toward the hotel, but Sam tugged her back. "I'm not quite ready."

"You're not ready to go up to my room?"

"Not quite." Sam leaned close and met Terri's lips. One long kiss and then another. Someone whistled and still Sam kept on with the kissing. Terri didn't want her to stop even when she finally took a step back, a sheepish grin on her lips. "Okay. Ready."

Terri batted her chest. "You."

"What?"

She shook her head, laughing. "I thought you were going to tell me you wanted to wait on sex or some bullshit like that." She started walking again, her body still zinging from Sam's lips.

"You in a hurry for something?" Sam said, catching up.

"Yeah, I got a hot date."

"Oh, really? You want to be in charge tonight?"

Terri glanced at Sam. "Why do you ask?"

"Some people are switches. I didn't want to assume you always wanted to be one way if you didn't…"

"Do you like to switch?" Terri wasn't even sure she was using the word correctly.

"No, but I'd do it if you wanted it."

"I don't want to switch. I like you on top. And don't tease, but I read up on Dominant/submissive sexual relationships while I was waiting at the airport in Houston."

"Sounds like a good use of time." Sam grinned. "What'd you learn?"

"All sorts of things."

"Want to elaborate?"

Terri pushed herself to talk about it, knowing the conversation had to happen sooner or later. "I kind of fell into this with you. Our roles, you know? But I was reading and thinking and, well, I realized it's right for me. It's not only a game, like I said it was the first time." She paused. "I like that I can be me around you. You don't ask me to be anything or anyone I'm not."

"So we can agree that we like our roles in the bedroom, but we're a work in progress on the relationship?"

Terri nodded. But there was still more she had to say. "I'm going to say this now because I don't want it to be an issue later—I don't want you coming up to see me every weekend. I'll feel too much guilt about you not focusing on photography."

"And I won't ever expect you to show up at my house. I know the hours you keep."

When they made it back to the hotel, Terri let Sam open the door, deciding she didn't actually mind. If Sam wanted to open every door for her, she could do it. Sam's term for them—a work in progress—made her feel hopeful and somehow relaxed her too. They didn't need to have every detail figured out. Not yet.

Andre waved from the reception desk. "How was your meal?"

"Delicious," Sam said.

Terri nodded. She hadn't thought she was hungry, but she'd enjoyed every bite of the pineapple chicken.

"Kelly wanted me to tell you she popped into your room to leave you a little surprise."

"Uh-oh."

Sam looked over at Terri. "Uh-oh?"

"I know my little sister. Surprises from her are usually inappropriate or dangerous."

"So trouble runs in your genes?"

Terri caught the front of Sam's shirt and pulled her close. "Yes." She kissed her, nipping Sam's lower lip, and then stepping back before Sam could deepen the kiss. "You're in for it."

They took the stairs up to the second floor, and Terri wondered what surprise Kelly would have gifted. There was no telling, really. She'd one time let her pet rat loose in Terri's bedroom when Terri had a boyfriend over and another time left a bag of peas to defrost under her sheets. And that was before her teenage years when she got really mischievous.

"Chocolate?" Terri almost didn't trust the box of chocolate candies on the corner of the bed. She glanced around the room, but nothing else seemed amiss—except for the fact that Kelly had tidied everything and put the clothes she'd changed out of back into her suitcase.

"I think she left you this too." Sam held up a folded slip of paper that was next to the chocolates.

Terri scanned it, smiled, and then decided to read it a loud: "T, I like Sam. You have good taste. But if it doesn't work out,

I got you chocolates—and can I have her number? Mostly kidding. Love, Kells."

Sam laughed. "For the record, I don't want to date your sister, but I love how she teases you."

"Yeah, don't get any ideas." Terri smiled. She set the note down and opened the box of chocolates. "Want one?"

Sam picked one of the dark squares and popped it in her mouth. "Almost as good as a Reese's."

"You and your Reese's." Terri shook her head, picking one of the dark squares as well and then setting the box and the note on the nightstand. She took a bite, letting the rich bittersweet chocolate flood her mouth. "Mmm, that's good."

"Wait, how was it?"

"Mmm," Terri repeated. "Almost as good as how you taste."

Sam stepped forward and circled her arms around Terri. "So did we talk enough about feelings tonight to make you feel comfortable about making out with me?"

Terri smiled. "You're the one who wanted a damn relationship, remember? I've always been fine ignoring the feelings."

"You thought you were fine, but now that you're dating me, you're gonna realize it's better having sex *with* feelings."

Terri didn't try to argue. When Sam leaned down to meet her lips, she pressed in, slowly opening for Sam's tongue.

"You taste like chocolate," Sam murmured. "Can I take off your dress?"

"Do you practice these lines?"

"I got a whole list I'm working on."

"Mmm. You should keep working."

Sam stepped back. "All right, you think you can do better? Let's hear it."

Terri reached for Sam's belt. She slid her forefinger along the edge of the leather and then stopped at the buckle and looked up at Sam. "May I take off your belt?"

"Does that line usually work?"

"First time I've tried it. You've been my first for a lot of things."

Sam smiled. "I like being your first."

Terri slowly worked the loose end of the belt through the buckle. She took her time with each loop, wanting to race ahead so she could finally touch Sam but at the same time wanting to savor every moment.

When she had the belt free, she slipped it around her neck and then dangled the ends in front of Sam. "Wanna hold this for me?"

"You know I do." Sam gripped the leather and pulled her in. Terri closed her eyes, more ready than ever to give herself to Sam. She lost herself in the kiss, the crush of Sam's lips only adding to her desire.

Between kisses, Sam managed to get her dress off and then her bra. It wasn't long before she was standing in front of Sam, who was still fully dressed, in nothing but her red underwear and the leather belt. Sam's warm hands moved up and down her sides, and she shivered with need. She longed for Sam to push aside her panties and feel how wet she was for her. Instead she only kissed her lips again, then her neck and each of her breasts.

"I want you so much," Terri murmured.

Sam caressed her neck and then tilted Terri's chin up to her. "What else?"

"May I take off your pants?"

Sam nodded and Terri immediately reached for the top button. Once she had that undone, she tugged on the zipper and then worked the pants down. Sam stepped back, pulling her pants off all the way and her underwear as well, then took another step back and pushed back the sheets. She sat down on the edge of the bed and pulled Terri to her.

Sam took one long kiss from her before letting Terri pull back. Terri wanted nothing more than to drop to her knees and press her tongue between Sam's legs.

"I want to make you come."

"Tell me more." Sam smiled.

"I'd rather show you." Terri knelt. "May I?"

Sam parted her legs. When Terri bent her head, Sam's fingers combed through her hair. Terri slipped her tongue over Sam, found her swollen clit and sucked. Sam's salty taste, the scent of her, filled Terri's senses. She let Sam's clit slip out of her lips and then stroked her tongue over and around her opening. She loved oral sex, knew she was good at it, but she had something to prove this time, which made her all the more willing to drive Sam insane.

When she started circling the clit faster, slipping in hard strokes over the tip, Sam grabbed her hair. She pumped her hips to push into Terri's mouth and moaned. Terri shifted back on her knees and looked up at Sam.

"Will you come in my mouth? I want to be good and lick up everything you give me."

"Oh, fuck." Sam murmured, pushing herself into Terri's mouth again. "Don't stop until I tell you."

Those were orders she couldn't wait to follow. Terri took Sam into her lips again, sucking and then stroking and then pausing to lap everything up before starting the pattern all over again. When Sam's rhythmic pulsing of her hips increased, her hold on Terri's hair almost painful, Terri knew the orgasm was coming. She increased her speed and gave Sam everything she could. Sam's hips pushed up one last time and Terri held onto her, sucking hard.

After the climax raced through her and Sam relaxed, shifting her butt back on the bed, Terri pulled her back to her mouth. She wasn't done yet. Sam didn't fight, letting her take her back into her mouth, drinking her in. She moved from Sam's slit to rim her asshole and got rewarded with a low, long moan. She knew she could give Sam another orgasm if she'd let her. Terri wanted her to have every satisfaction possible. She pressed her fingertip on Sam's clit as she rimmed her again. She didn't let up until Sam clenched her legs, trapping Terri in place, moaning. A moment later a tremor rushed through her and then finally she relaxed, collapsing back on the bed.

Terri kissed her way up Sam's body—a soft brush of her lips on the inside of Sam's thighs, the swell of her mound, then pushing up her shirt to kiss the side of her ribs, then her neck and last the smooth softness of her cheek. She settled on the bed, wrapped against Sam, and waited for her breathing to slow.

After a long while, Sam shifted onto her side and rested her palm on Terri's chest. "Well, that was fucking amazing. I never have two orgasms in a row like that."

Terri smiled. "I was trying to impress you."

"You did."

"You know...what you did to me the last time when I was tied up...I don't even know how long that orgasm lasted. I think it was about a month."

Sam chuckled. "That was fun."

"You're a hard act to follow."

"It's not a competition."

"Thank god." Terri snuggled closer to Sam. "I love how you taste."

"Also thank god."

"I'm up for anything, you know. Anything you've ever wanted to try with someone." Terri pushed herself to go on. "I found this one site with whips...and some nice collars."

"You'd want that?"

Terri nodded. She was embarrassed to admit it, but she wanted to get past the embarrassment and past her old sex hang-ups too. She'd been told that she thought of sex too much, but Sam's appetite had already made her feel better about that. She'd also been told that she was boring—Sam had no idea how much she'd helped her ego in that regard. And although it didn't seem to make sense that one could want sex too much but also be boring, she'd worried it was true.

"I like how you push me. Trying new things has always kind of intimidated me. I hate messing up so I stick to what I know, but you make me feel like it'd be okay if I screwed up and something wasn't perfect."

"I'm not exactly sure how you'd screw up sex."

"My ex could give you a list." Terri thought of all the fights she'd had with Kayla. Mostly it was about her not being adventurous enough. Not being creative. Not being poly was part of all that too. She knew she hadn't changed so much as Sam made her feel safe in a way Kayla never did.

Sam stroked a warm hand over her breast. "I know this shop not far from here. Maybe tomorrow we can go buy some things?"

"I'd like that." The anticipation alone of what Sam would want her to try made her wet.

"But right now you'll have to be satisfied with only my hands."

"It's your hands I love best."

"Not me?" Sam grinned.

Terri sucked in a breath. "I know you're joking right now, but you have no idea how much I want to answer that."

Sam brushed her fingertip over Terri's lips. "Me too." She leaned close and kissed her. Then she murmured, "But I think we're done talking for now."

"I like talking to you."

"You also like me fucking you." Sam nipped her neck. "And tonight I get to convince you I'm someone you want to keep around."

Sam pushed Terri onto her back and then moved on top of her, kissing her lips. Terri closed her eyes, savoring the feel of being pinned, the smell of their sex, and Sam's lips trailing down her chest and over her belly button. When Sam's hand parted her, she pushed up her hips. She'd never been so ready.

CHAPTER TWENTY-SEVEN

Surreal. That was the word that kept bouncing round Sam's head as she lay in the hotel bed contemplating the past twenty-four hours. Not only had Otto found a buyer for the Aston Martin at a price that nearly matched what she owed in student loans, she'd gone on an official date with Terri and her father had called to set up a meeting to talk. She wasn't sure which of the three things she could have least expected.

But Terri was stretched out next to her, as beautiful as ever, and proof that last night really had happened. She hadn't woken when Sam got up the first time to pee and she'd only rolled from her side to her back when Sam had slipped into the shower. She hadn't even woken when Sam had stepped out to make a few calls.

Her first call was to reschedule Sunday's meeting with her father. After stressing about how to tell her parents she'd quit the residency, she'd finally decided to send her dad an email. He hadn't freaked out like she'd expected. Instead he'd called up and said, "You gotta be happy in this life, but we should talk about your finances." It was so unlike her dad—both that he thought happiness mattered and that he'd called at all—that the only thing she could think to say was "thanks" before agreeing to the meeting. Now she'd have to reschedule. Not surprisingly, she didn't reach him in person and had to leave a message with his secretary.

Considering that she could count the number of conversations she'd had directly with her dad, she didn't know what to expect and she wondered how he'd take the news that she was selling the Aston Martin. Aside from selling the beach house, she couldn't see any other options, however. No way she'd make enough money shooting pictures to pay off her med school loans and she still had the taxes and the insurance on the house to consider. Along with the fact that she had to eat.

She hoped her father would pass the news on to her mother and that she wouldn't have to talk to her directly. But since she hadn't received any irate voice mails from her mom, she figured he was avoiding the conversation. She didn't blame him.

The next call she made was to the hotel reception desk to ask for a late checkout. Kelly had answered and her voice was so similar to Terri's that Sam had nearly forgotten what she wanted to ask. They'd ended up chatting about restaurants, and Sam had promised to bring Terri back to the city so they could all go out to dinner together.

Sam glanced at her watch and then gently brushed Terri's shoulder. She let out a soft moan but didn't open her eyes. Finally Sam leaned down and kissed her cheek.

"Mmm." Terri's eyes fluttered open and then closed again.

"I hate to wake you, but it's almost checkout time."

"Not possible," Terri mumbled. "We have until eleven."

"It's ten minutes 'til."

"Your watch must be wrong." Terri rolled over on her stomach, tugging the covers with her. "Maybe it's on the wrong time zone."

"I wasn't the one who went on vacation."

"But you should have. You should've come to Costa Rica with me."

"I can think of a lot of should've." Sam pulled the covers back and kissed Terri's shoulder blade, then pushed her hair aside and kissed the nape of her neck. Kelly had stressed that they had to be out by noon because the room was booked for tonight, but now the desire to have Terri one more time battled with wanting to make a good impression on her family.

"If you keep doing that, I'm going to make you put your hand between my legs to see how wet I am."

"You're gonna make me, huh? I like this version of you. All relaxed and dazed. Post-sex hangover?"

"Your fault entirely." Terri moaned softly when Sam kissed her neck again. "If you felt me, you wouldn't make me get out of bed."

"You're right. Which is why I'm not giving into that temptation." Sam kissed her one last time and then stood up. "I don't want your sister to come up here and kick us out."

"Oh, buzzkill. Did you have to mention my sister?" Terri sighed and rolled over. "And how is it that you're the adult in this relationship?"

"I think we take turns pretty well on that bit." Although she was happy the tables were turned for the moment. They'd gotten past all the conversations about the residency, but she still wondered if the fact that she didn't have her life together or even a good plan to get there bothered Terri.

"This bed is almost as nice as yours." Terri shrugged the covers off the rest of the way and stretched. "I love waking up sore in all the right places."

"I was worried we took things too far last night." Sam had asked more than once if she wanted to stop, but Terri had only begged for more.

"You worry too much." Terri got out of bed, brushing her hand over Sam's chest as she passed her. "Don't start getting soft on me now that we're dating. I want a repeat of everything we did last night as soon as possible." Terri went to the bathroom and flipped on the light. "Ugh. I really need a shower. Can you call to get us a late checkout?"

"Already done. We have until noon, but your sister told me I wasn't supposed to tell you that."

"That's Kelly for you." Terri peed and then turned on the shower. She didn't seem to care that Sam was watching her, even sticking out her butt and wiggling it as she waited for the water to get warm.

"I still can't believe we're dating now."

Terri looked over her shoulder at her. "It's all because you're stubborn."

"I know."

Terri stepped into the shower, and Sam wondered if her butt was one of the things that was sore this morning. She'd stuck her butt up in the air, daring Sam to spank her, after Sam had told her to roll over. It was hard getting past her own concerns about hurting anyone—there was a big difference in her mind between power plays and pain—but there was no question Terri had liked getting spanked.

Terri stuck her head out of the shower. "Are we still going to that toy store you mentioned?"

"Are you in the shower thinking about sex toys?"

"If I was, would you come join me?"

Before Sam could answer, Terri popped her head back into the shower. What were the chances that Terri would want all the things Sam had only fantasized about before? She kicked off her shoes and started to unbutton her shirt. It wouldn't take long to get what they both wanted.

* * *

"Where are you taking me next?" Terri swung the bag from the sex shop on her wrist. Her other hand was latched on Sam's.

"I was kind of hoping I could take you home. You could spend the rest of your vacation in Santa Cruz." Sam glanced at Terri. "It's not Costa Rica, but we have some pretty nice beaches and I hear the bed in my house is really nice."

"I don't have to go back to work until Tuesday. That's four days. I'm sure you have other things you've planned to do."

"I already rescheduled one of them." And, yes, she had a photo shoot, but she thought Terri might be up for going along and keeping her company.

"In four days there's a good chance you'll get tired of me. I mean, how many different sex positions are there?"

"Are you actually worried about me getting tired of you?"

Terri shrugged. "I don't know. Maybe?"

Sam stopped walking. Terri tried to keep going and then looked the other direction when Sam tugged on her hand.

"Hey. Can we talk?"

Terri avoided Sam's eyes. "Talk about what?"

"I like you. I want to spend as much time as I can with you. And I'm not going to stop liking you because I'm with you too much. So far that's only made me like you more." Sam waited, hoping Terri would say something. When she didn't, she added, "We might not get another four days in a row again."

"I know."

"Can you not pull back right now and instead tell me what's going on?"

"That's funny coming from you." Terri was clearly still trying to joke as a cover-up.

Sam exhaled. "I made a mistake not telling you why I was upset when I left your house. And not calling you back until you were about to get on the plane was just plain dumb. Blame butch ego. But now that I know you want this, I'm all in."

"Okay." Terri held Sam's gaze. "I want to learn how to surf. Will you teach me?"

"I know the perfect place. But we have to go back to Santa Cruz for that."

"I'd love to spend the rest of my vacation with you. Your bed is amazing. Almost as amazing as you." Terri stepped in front of Sam and brushed her lips with a soft kiss. "Be patient with me? It's gonna take me a while to get used to someone liking me as much as you do."

CHAPTER TWENTY-EIGHT

Nothing was quite as sexy as a woman in a wetsuit. Terri had spun around for Sam to help her zip up; she had had no trouble with the zipper, but it was impossible to not caress Terri's neoprene-hugged ass. When she did, Terri only looked over her shoulder and winked.

"You'll get me later."

"That's what makes it even harder. I know everything you'll let me do."

Terri turned back around and put her hands on Sam's shoulder. "And there are things I'm still waiting for you to try."

"Really? What?"

"Not telling you yet." She gave Sam a deep kiss. When she pulled back she laughed. "You can open your eyes now."

Sam opened her eyes. Terri was looking at her with a smile still on her lips. Behind her the ocean stretched. Deep blue blending into a pale sky blue with the sun overhead and not a cloud in sight. Gentle long waves rolled one after the other. "I can't remember when I last felt this happy."

"That's sweet," Terri said. "But don't get too gushy on me."

"Why not?"

"I need you focused. Remember, I'm scared of sharks and I've never done this before. I don't want to die out there."

"You know I'm not gonna let anything happen to you. But I'd be a lot more focused if you tell me that sex thing you're waiting for me to try."

Terri shook her head. "Surfing lesson first."

"Why is it that I'm drawn to femmes who like to be in charge?"

"Because you know we only like to be in charge sometimes. Now let's do this." Terri picked up her board and started down the beach. The long foam board teetered awkwardly, the nose dipping first and then, when Terri offset that, the fins dragging in the sand. She looked back at Sam. "How do you even walk with this thing?"

Sam jogged over. "First lesson: your board is your friend. Get cozy with it." She shifted Terri's hold so the board was against her hip and balanced. Then she dropped to her knees and latched the leash on Terri's ankle.

Terri looked down at her. "I'm having a little deja-vu here. Although the last time you tied something around my ankle I was wearing a lot less material."

"Trust me—this is just as sexy." Sam stood up. "But we're focused on surfing right now, remember?"

"Mm-hmm. Totally focused."

Sam ran through the same points she'd already told Terri about getting through the breakers and then picked up her own board. She'd also brought a waterproof camera that she liked when she wanted to snap some shots for fun and swung this over one arm. "I'm gonna let you get in the water first, but I'll be right behind you the whole time."

"Promise?" Terri's expression was determined, but she was clearly nervous.

"Yep. You got this."

Terri took a few tentative steps into the water, then held her board out, balancing as a wave rumbled past her knees. "Fuck, you didn't warn me it'd be this cold. You're watching out for sharks, right?"

"Of course." Sam positioned her camera and snapped a picture. "But you'll be fine. They don't like redheads."

"Seriously?" Terri glanced back at her and Sam couldn't help smiling. Terri shook her head. "You."

"Me?"

"Yes. You." Terri took another step forward, keeping her eyes on a cresting wave. "You're a terrible liar."

"You've told me that before. What else?"

"I like you."

"I like you too. Wait, is that a shark?" Sam couldn't help smiling when Terri looked back at her with her tongue sticking out. Sam was quick to snap the picture. "That one's going on the wall."

Terri held up her middle finger. "How about this one?"

Because she could, Sam took that shot too.

By the end of the afternoon, Sam knew she had several good shots, including a perfect one of Terri standing up on her board with a big smile plastered on her face. Danielle joined them for a while, surfing for a half hour or so and winking at Sam when Terri said something about how she liked that her girlfriend privileges including surfing lessons.

Girlfriend. She hadn't had an official girlfriend since before med school. And Terri was nothing like the women she'd dated before. She liked that Terri was already using the word, but it struck her how different things felt this time. As they walked back to the house, she wondered again what Terri's past relationships had been like.

"How long were you married to your ex-wife?"

"That's out of left field," Terri said. "Why do you ask?"

"I was thinking that I liked hearing you call me your girlfriend."

They'd gotten back to the house, but instead of going inside Sam led them to the side yard where the outside shower was. "We have to wash off the boards." She turned on the water and helped Terri rinse her board first. "If you don't want to talk about exes, we don't have to. My ex stories are all pretty boring, but I was never married. An ex-wife or an ex-husband is a lot bigger deal."

"Some are. Some aren't." Terri leaned her board against the side fence as Sam rinsed hers. "Kayla and I lasted three years. With David it was all of nine months. You've probably dated people for longer than that."

"My longest relationship went almost four years. She left me for an actress. Then called me up a week later wanting to get back together again."

"She broke up with you?"

Sam nodded. "We'd been done for a while…and the actress was hot. I didn't really blame her." But that all felt like a different lifetime now. "So what went wrong with you and your exes?"

"With David I always say we were too young to know what we wanted, but the truth is he was too nice and I walked all over him." She paused. "I've started to realize I need a challenge."

"Someone who frustrates you a little?"

"And tells me what to do," Terri added. "David and I met in college. I should have dated him and then moved on. Instead, he proposed and I didn't want to break his heart… We still keep in touch. He's a dentist down in LA and I've gone to see him and his family a couple of times. I love his wife. She bakes cookies and does crafts. About as different from me as you can get."

"So would you say the ex-wife was the bigger deal?"

"For sure. Kayla and I met at the hospital. She was a resident too."

"Technically I'm not a resident."

Terri raised an eyebrow. "Not anymore."

"Strip. We need to rinse the wetsuits too."

"You just like to tell me to strip." But Terri spun around, waiting for Sam to unzip her.

"Why'd you and Kayla not work out?"

Terri peeled off the wetsuit. Underneath she had on a striped white and black bikini and if she wanted to spend the rest of the day only wearing that, Sam wouldn't complain.

"Do you really want to know?"

"Unless you don't want to tell me." Sam held out her hand for Terri's wetsuit and started rinsing it. She definitely wanted to know, but she didn't want to push. "There are towels inside if you want to go grab one."

"I'm fine." Terri folded her arms. "I'm kind of surprised you didn't hear the stories. For a while, it was all anyone wanted to gossip about."

"I heard that you were in some kind of love triangle. Honestly I didn't really believe it 'cause what people said didn't really fit with what I knew about you." Sam unzipped her wetsuit and tugged it off.

"Long story short, Kayla wanted someone more exciting than me. She started sleeping with another one of the residents. Rebecca." Terri looked over at Sam. "Sorry you asked?"

"Not yet. But do you want to stop there?"

Terri shrugged. "I guess I'd rather you know the whole story. Rebecca wanted us all to have a threesome. Kayla did too. I wanted Kayla to have her fun and decide she liked me better. That's not how it played out."

"No wonder you didn't want to date a resident." Sam opened the side door and grabbed two towels from the stack she kept by the door. She handed one to Terri and wrapped the other around her waist. "So in the end Kayla picked Rebecca?"

"They lasted about two months. Then Kayla came back with her tail between her legs. Wanted to get back together with me. When I said no, she lost it and started telling everyone what had gone down. Of course she added quite a few fun details that never happened. Apparently I'd made a sex tape of all of us together—and sold it online."

"Shit. What a mess."

"Exactly. I started the divorce process and told myself never again." Terri paused. "The funny thing is, back then I was really only comfortable with vanilla sex, and I was so scared of messing something up that I hardly let myself enjoy it. No way would I have made a sex tape. I barely pulled off the threesome."

"Huh. You've changed."

"You think?" Terri grinned. "I decided that with the next person I slept with, I'd stop worrying about messing up so much. I wanted to have fun."

"So basically I had good timing?"

"That and you are so damn sure of yourself that I kind of let myself get swept away. You make me stop thinking so much."

"From vanilla to ass-slapping and restraints." Sam clicked her tongue. "You sure you're okay with everything we've been doing?" She thought of the whip and the clamps Terri had picked out. She couldn't go that far if Terri wasn't certain it was what she wanted. "I don't want you to wake up one morning and realize this isn't really you."

"This is me." Terri touched Sam's wrist and then trailed a light fingertip up her arm. "I've never felt sexier. Or more in control. Which I know sounds weird, considering."

"It's not weird. I'll only ever do what you want me to do."

"I know. Speaking of…" She unwrapped her towel and took a step closer to Sam. "What do I have to do to get you to put on your strap-on tonight?"

"Hmm. Well, for starters, you can stay in that bikini."

"And?"

"For the rest of the night you do exactly what I tell you to do."

"That sounds like a perfect evening on a perfect day of vacation. Why didn't I decide to spend all ten days here?"

"That's a very good question." Sam pulled Terri into a kiss. Dinner would have to wait.

CHAPTER TWENTY-NINE

"Look at this little one go!" Terri clapped her hand over her mouth as one of the hermit crabs launched himself at another crab. The two tumbled shell over shell into the tide pool with a dramatic mini-splash.

Sam had her camera angled on a group of sea lions basking on a rock not far from where they sat. "I love that everyone else comes here to watch the sea lions and you're smitten with the hermit crabs."

"I keep hearing Sebastian from *Little Mermaid* and wondering if these guys can sing." One of the crabs with a bright orange shell that had been warily watching Terri since she'd sat down on the rocks scampered a few inches closer. "I think this one likes me. She keeps giving me the eye."

Sam laughed. "You are so weird sometimes."

"Which is why you like me."

"Completely true." Sam switched out her lens and then scooted back a few feet. She settled back on the rock, lying on her belly with her camera focused on the tide pool.

"Can you take a picture of Shelly?" Terri pointed to the crab that was still eyeing her.

"You named the crab?"

"Of course I named her. Look how beautiful she is."

Sam snapped a shot and then peeked around the camera at Terri. "It's nice to know your type. I feel like I can measure up to that."

"Don't get too complacent. I like you when you're trying hard."

Sam angled her lens on Terri. She snapped a few shots and Terri mostly ignored her, watching the crashing waves, sun glinting on the spray, and then the barking sea lions perched on their rock. Usually she was self-conscious when someone photographed her, but Sam had a way of making her feel like she was only one part of the scene. And she knew Sam didn't expect her to smile or even necessarily look at the camera.

Last night she'd let Sam shoot her naked. Parts of her were covered by the sheets, but it was the first time she'd ever had someone take a picture when she wasn't hiding behind any clothes. Although she'd been nervous at first, Sam had quickly relaxed her, talking her through everything. But Sam was like that with everything. Calm and reassuring. She would have made a damn good doctor. Terri sighed. No matter how many times she told herself to let go of it, she still worried Sam was making a mistake. *A forty-one million dollar mistake.*

Sam put away her camera and her lenses, carefully tucking everything into place in her bag. "Ready for our next stop?"

They'd woken early to surf. After, Sam had made breakfast and with very little effort, Terri had convinced her back into bed before they left the house again. As far as she was concerned, the rest of the day was all bonus, but it was sweet that Sam had an itinerary and wanted to show her the sights.

Terri eyed the orange-shelled hermit crab still peering at her. "It's gonna be hard leaving Shelly, but I am looking forward to that caramel apple you promised."

"Sometimes you have to let those hard-to-get girls go."

Terri shot her a skeptical look. "When have you ever done that?"

"Well, that's what I've been told. Fortunately for you, I don't like to do what I'm told." Sam got up and stretched out her hand. "This caramel apple will be every bit as good as you can imagine. Tart apple, sweet caramel, salty nuts… And it's all on a stick so you can keep your fingers clean. We both know that's the real reason you like to put everything in your mouth."

"Sure. That's the reason." Terri clasped Sam's hand, accepting the help up. As soon as she was standing, she leaned close to Sam. "And now I'm going to be thinking of all the other things I'd like in my mouth as I eat that caramel apple."

"That's my goal."

Sam kissed her, silently reminding her as she nipped her lip that it wouldn't be long before they were back in bed.

* * *

Terri waited for Sam to unlock the front door, eyeing a little hand-painted sign next to the doorbell that read "Paradise is a beach house" along with a sketch of a dog running on the beach. She pointed to the sign. "Did your grandma make that?"

"No…I found it online."

"You bought it?" Terri laughed. "Okay, didn't see that coming."

"Why not? It's cute. I want a dog like that to take the beach. I'm going to get one when I'm old. He'll run around chasing sticks and I'll just sit there smiling."

"You might already be old enough for that. I mean, you did buy a cute little sign to go over your doorbell."

Sam's grin was sheepish. "Remember, I also have a stamp collection."

Terri opened her mouth in a mock gasp. "How'd I forget about that?"

"My ballroom dance moves were so good you couldn't remember anything else." Sam winked. "But it is a little bit like paradise here."

"True. And someday you should get a dog. You'd be a good dog parent."

"You think?"

The sincerity in Sam's question surprised Terri. "Definitely."

"I never had a dog. When I was a kid, we had these two Siamese cats. They were kind of like dogs I guess. At least that's what my parents always said whenever I asked for a dog."

Every time Sam mentioned her parents, she got a clouded look in her eyes. Terri wanted to ask about it, but she got the sense that she'd have to find the right time. "I love dogs. My last one passed a few years ago and I haven't had the heart to get another. Turbo. I know he's not resting in peace. That little booger's probably barking at everyone up in heaven."

"Turbo? Sounds crazy."

"Oh, he was. Totally wild. That's why I loved him." Terri paused. "What about kids?" It was weird to bring it up except she wanted to know where Sam stood on the subject.

"What about them?"

"Do you want them?"

Sam hesitated. "If I had the choice, I'd definitely pick dogs. But I guess I'm not completely opposed. Do you want kids?"

"No. I thought I did for a while, but it turns out I'm an awesome auntie and dogs are cuter."

"You had me worried there for a minute." Sam opened the door. "Probably good to know these things before you get in too deep."

"How deep?" Terri stepped past her, slipping in a kiss right as Sam started to laugh. The taste of the caramel apple still lingered on her lips, and after one kiss Terri went back for another.

After getting back from the tide pools, they'd walked to a candy shop specializing in caramel apples and all things dentists would hate. The place was dangerously close to Sam's house, as was the pizza place that they'd gone to for lunch. With all the sex on top of surfing, Terri thought she could eat everything in sight. On Tuesday she'd go back to healthy eating.

Unfortunately Tuesday would come way too soon. She'd had to check her phone to be sure of the day when she'd woken that morning. It was Sunday, which meant she only had one more day with Sam. On Monday she'd leave and she'd wait 'til then to face the fact that she didn't live in paradise.

Terri followed Sam into the living room which, second only to Sam's bedroom, had quickly become her favorite place in the house. She loved that Sam didn't have a television or any screens in the house and instead sat and stared out the window at the ocean.

"I forgot to tell you—I've got a shoot at six tonight. It's right down at the beach. One of my surfing buddy's kid needs senior portraits. He surfs too so I figured we'd see if there were any waves. I'm hoping to catch some good light right before sunset." Sam kicked off her sandals and sank down on the couch. "You're welcome to come, but if you want to stay here and relax that's fine too."

"I'd love to watch you work."

"Really? Okay, cool."

Sam patted the couch and Terri sat down, snuggling close. She felt a swell of contentment when Sam wrapped her arms around her. "I'm gonna miss this."

"Then don't leave," Sam whispered.

"I'm glad you didn't cancel the shoot because of me. I've been worried that you might have dropped everything so we could hang out. And it's been lovely but...I know you said you were short on cash."

"Broke, actually." Sam sighed. "But not for long. I got plans. Don't worry. And I have credit cards."

Since they'd gotten to Santa Cruz, they'd walked everywhere and made all their meals at home. Terri had wondered, but didn't want to ask, if partly it was because Sam didn't have any money to go out. And then she felt bad that Sam might be skipping work to spend time with her instead. "You know, I can pay for things for a while. We could go back to splitting when you become that famous photographer."

Sam shook her head. "I'd rather miss out on something than have you pay for all of it." She seemed about to say more, but the doorbell interrupted her. She loosened her hold on Terri. "That's weird. You're the only person who's rung my doorbell since I moved in."

"Maybe a neighbor?"

"Maybe." Sam got up and went to open the door. "Oh… Hi…Did you not get my message?"

A woman's voice answered: "He got your message. Whatever your plans were, you can be late."

From her angle on the couch, Terri couldn't see who she was talking to. Sam stepped back, opening the door wider, and then shot a look in Terri's direction. It was hard to decipher much in a quick glance, but Sam's shoulders had tensed and clearly something was wrong.

A well-dressed older couple, the man in a tan suit and the woman in a dark blue dress with a shawl over her shoulders, entered. Terri immediately stood up. It wasn't hard to see the family resemblance. *Shit.* What were Sam's parents doing here?

"Uh, Mom, Dad, this is Terri. Terri, these are my folks. Lynn and Mark." Sam turned back to her parents. "Dad, I said I couldn't do today. You show up anyway?"

Sam's smoothness had gone out the window. Terri stepped forward. "Hi. It's nice to meet you. Maybe I can get drinks while you talk?"

"That'd be great. I'll take a seven and seven," Mark said, loosening his tie.

Sam shook her head. "I don't have any alcohol. And Terri, you don't need to get anyone drinks. I think maybe we should go out—"

"Why don't you have any alcohol?" Lynn interrupted. "Is that why you left the residency? Were you drinking too much?"

"No, Mom. I wasn't drinking too much." Sam clenched her jaw.

"We do have Coke and orange juice. And water, of course." Terri waited for someone to respond. She could have cut the tension in the room with a knife. "Can I get a glass for anyone?"

"We?" Lynn looked from Terri to Sam. "Is she living here? Did you drop out of the residency for her?"

"No." Sam's voice was tight. She lowered it even further and added, "Look, can we not do this right now?"

"Do what exactly?" Lynn crossed her arms and with her head cocked, she looked like a force to be reckoned with. "Find out why my daughter is throwing away her future? I think I deserve to know."

Mark cleared his throat. "I think we all need to sit down and talk."

"I'll go for a walk," Terri suggested.

"That'd be great," Lynn said, giving Terri a tight-lipped smile.

The dismissive tone in Lynn's voice made Terri's skin crawl, but she started toward the door anyway.

"Wait—I don't want you to leave." Sam caught Terri's hand. She glanced at her dad. "You know that dinner we had with Dr. Weiss and his wife? Right after I started the residency?"

Both Lynn and Mark nodded.

"This is Dr. Terri Anderson. The pediatric internist that Dr. Weiss was raving about. The one he said practically ran the whole place. And, yes, she's my girlfriend." Sam let go of Terri's hand. "But she's not why I left the residency. In fact, if you asked her, she'd be on your side. So don't fucking stand there judging her, or me, when you have no clue what's going on."

"Elizabeth, watch your language," Mark said. He glanced again at Terri. "This has nothing to do with Elizabeth dating women. Lynn and I have never had a problem with that."

"The problem is with her throwing her future down the toilet," Lynn added.

Terri touched Sam's arm. "I'm going to the kitchen to get everyone water. Maybe you could all sit down and talk?"

Terri took a deep breath when she reached the kitchen. Sam had lowered her voice, but she could still hear her. The tone was unmistakable—she was pissed—but the words were hard to decipher. Terri filled four glasses with ice water. She knew Sam had beer in the house along with a bottle of vodka in the freezer. Her choice to not offer this to her parents would be a question for later. At this rate, Terri was going to have a whole list of questions. When had Sam told her parents about leaving the residency? Her father seemed to be taking the news better than her mother, but no one looked happy.

She headed back to the living room, carefully balancing all four glasses. Sam's father had sat down in the love seat and Sam was sitting on the couch. Lynn had decided not to sit, apparently, and was in the middle of delivering her assessment on Sam's current situation.

"And I doubt you've gotten a real job. How exactly do you plan to buy food? You'll need to pay back all of your student loans. Not to mention eat. And you think you have a roof over your head but this—" She motioned to the wall nearest her. "Isn't free. The outside needs to be painted, and I can only imagine all the other disasters waiting with a place this old. You do know you have to pay homeowner's insurance right? And do you even know when the taxes are due?"

"I'm thirty-one years old, Mom. I know the bills I have to pay."

Terri wondered if she should have lingered in the kitchen. She glanced from the sofa to the rocking chair in the corner of the room and then decided to sit by Sam.

"So what's your big plan?" Lynn held up her hands. "Your father said he thought you had a plan. God help us if it's that you're going back to photography. That barely paid the bills before."

"I'm selling the Aston Martin." Sam eyed her father as she delivered this news. "Otto's already found a buyer. Even with him taking a cut, that will cover my student loans. And, yes, I'm going back to my old job."

Terri took a sip of the water, hoping not to show any surprise. She wasn't shocked that the car was fetching a good price, but she couldn't believe that Sam had decided to sell her grandmother's car. A car like that wasn't simply a car. And she hadn't even known Mary Ellen Samuels, but she felt the pang of the loss anyway. She'd kept the car in mint condition for that long, only ever driving it to the beach, and then passed it to her granddaughter, which meant either she was quite attached or she'd always wanted to have a Plan B. Some way out if investments got tied up maybe. Now Sam had a Plan B.

"It's probably a good call on selling the car," Mark said. "Prices on those old collectors won't hold forever. Might as well make your money now before the market for them tanks."

"I was worried you'd be upset because it was Grandma's."

"She gave it to you for a reason. It's yours to do what you want with."

Lynn cussed under her breath. "If she'd finished the damn residency, the loans would have been paid off when she'd started working. And instead she's selling your mother's car and you don't care? Well, I do. Elizabeth, you're making a huge mistake. I don't even want to think of what your grandfather would have said."

"He'd say he was disappointed," Sam volunteered. "But I don't think he ever actually wanted me to be a doctor. Or even thought I could do it. He wanted the control."

"We're all disappointed. And then some." Lynn turned her glare on Terri. "Do you know what she's giving up? Has she told you?"

"Mom, don't go there."

Lynn ignored Sam. "Forty-one million dollars. And all she has left to do is finish the residency. That we're even having this conversation is—"

"What did you think you were going to accomplish today?" Sam interrupted. "Did you actually think that coming here and reminding me that I'll have bills to pay and that I'm throwing away forty-one million would make me change my mind?"

"Yes," Lynn said. "Because we didn't think you were a complete idiot. Your father set up a meeting to talk to Dr. Weiss."

Sam shook her head. "I'm not a kid with a problem you can fix because you know people."

Did they not know that Sam had quit over a month ago? Even with a special favor from Weiss there was no way Sam would be accepted back to the residency. Terri almost said as much, but then Sam spoke up again.

"I quit the residency and I'm not going back. And honestly I don't care who I disappoint anymore. Dad, you told me before that Grandma had some money in stocks set aside for me if I needed it. I need to know how much and how I can get it. I know things are going to be tight, but I'm going to make it work."

Mark nodded, but before he could say anything, Lynn cut in, "Dr. Anderson, I'm sure there's something you could do. Some other option. Does she even have to finish the residency to work in general practice?"

Sam shot a look at Terri that clearly said "stay out of this." "The residency isn't the point. I don't want to be a doctor."

"Why the hell did you even go to medical school then?" Lynn fired back. "Why waste that time and money if you weren't ever planning on finishing? This is what you always do, Elizabeth. You're so headstrong. You never listen to anyone. And as soon as something gets hard, you quit."

"That's not true," Mark said. "She said from the beginning she wasn't sure this was right for her. But she stuck it out anyway. And she's stuck with a lot of things. Women for instance—as much as you hoped that was a phase. And photography."

"That's a hobby," Lynn argued. "Not a career."

Terri wasn't sure if Lynn meant women or photography or both. It was almost funny, but the look on Sam's face took the humor out of the situation. Her parents continued to argue and her expression smoldered. Terri didn't blame her for her anger one bit. Not now.

"I wanted to make Grandpa proud," Sam said, interrupting the bickering. "And I wanted to prove that I could do it. Go to med school, be a doctor. But then I realized the person I was trying to make proud wasn't just dead, he was a pretty shitty human being. And I started to question everything." Sam looked over at her father. "Why'd you let me believe he was this great guy?"

"What are you talking about, Elizabeth? Your grandfather was a great man." Lynn's tone sounded defensive now, instead of simply angry. Mark didn't say anything, only holding Sam's gaze.

"I found a box of letters from your brother, Dad. It was in one of the closets I was clearing out. All these letters and receipts. From Paul Samuels. Grandma saved everything." Sam's voice cracked. "Your brother that Grandpa disowned. Because he was gay. You never even told me that I had an uncle."

Mark studied the floor.

"A gay uncle. I always knew Grandpa was a big homophobe, but you aren't. At least I didn't think you were."

"I don't know what you read in the letters, but there's always two sides," Mark said quietly. "Your grandpa and Paul never agreed on anything."

"Two sides? The side that gets disowned and the side that does it?" Sam's voice was as quiet as her father's, but her words scathed. "I always knew how horrible Grandpa's church was. But that doesn't excuse this. He let his own son die. Didn't try to help him at all. Didn't even visit when he got sick. I know—I read it in the letters. Paul asked to see him. Wanted to make things right before he died. But Grandpa wouldn't see him because he was living with his lover and he didn't approve. And Grandpa was supposed to be this amazing fucking doctor. But his own kid got AIDs and he did nothing. Didn't even help him die. Just cut him off.

"I read every letter your brother sent to Grandma. It was all in that box… She paid for his apartment in San Francisco. Did you know that? Grandpa ordered her not to. Told her to disown him. But she didn't. And she paid for all his medical bills too. What'd you do, Dad? Where the hell were you in all of this?"

Mark looked up, and Terri saw tears well in his eyes. "I held his hand when he died. It was the hardest thing I've ever done. And then a week later you were born." He took a shaky breath. "We were all a wreck. All of us. You have no idea how much your grandfather regretted his decision."

"You could have told me."

Mark nodded. "I couldn't talk about him without breaking down. I thought one day your grandma would tell you. But she said it didn't seem right to weigh a kid down with that. And then the years passed."

"And Grandpa didn't say anything because Paul was gay," Sam guessed.

"Or because he regretted what he'd done. I don't know." Mark sighed heavily. "I know you hate him right now. I hated him, too, for everything that happened. But I got over it. Woke up one day and realized Paul was gone and nothing would bring him back."

"You could have told me about him."

"It's still not easy talking about it. Even now. You know there are other ways to get the money. You could get married. That's always been the case."

"I don't even care about the money anymore. And I'm not marrying a man—even if it's only some sort of business transaction."

"That's in the will? That you could get the money if you married a man?" Terri couldn't imagine Sam marrying a man, but she also couldn't believe that was one of the stipulations. And yet from everything she'd just heard about Sam's grandfather, she wasn't entirely surprised.

"It's not happening," Sam said. "I'm not marrying some dude."

Mark cleared his throat. "Well, then you have some things to figure out."

Terri imagined how hard it must have been deciding on medical school. She could have found a guy willing to sign a contract and gotten the money the easy way. But that wasn't Sam's style. And now she was willing to give it all up. Had already made the choice even.

Lynn spoke up finally: "We're not helping you out financially, Elizabeth. You're thirty-one. You blew your chance to be a doctor. Fine. Don't be stupid. Find someone to marry—I'll draw up the contract for you myself. You've only got three more years." Her gaze was fixed on Sam, and Terri was struck by the fact that there was no sympathy in her eyes. Sam was a problem to be fixed, nothing more.

"There's a timeline on top of it?" Of all the dumb things she'd heard, Terri thought that might top the list.

"It doesn't matter." Sam eyed her mom. "I'm not asking for financial help. Or any help. Dad was the one who wanted this meeting."

"And maybe today isn't the best day for that," Mark said softly.

"No shit. That's why I cancelled." Sam cussed again under her breath and then exhaled. "I'm sorry, Dad. I don't want to yell or be in a fight right now. I cried when I read those letters, and I didn't even know him. I can only imagine what it must have been like for you. And Grandma."

"You're a lot like him. That's what your grandma always said. Just as headstrong. Just as smart. You even have his same eyes." Mark took a deep breath. "We all did what we thought was right, Sam. But I'm glad you finally found out anyway." He glanced at Lynn and then stood. "We should go."

"You shouldn't have brought up Paul. All you've done is hurt your father. You can't read some letters and think you understand everything." Lynn's words stung. "If you want to make this about an uncle that you didn't even know, fine. Use that excuse. But the truth is, this is about you throwing away your future."

Sam didn't respond. After a moment, Lynn shook her head and followed her husband to the door.

Terri walked them out, awkwardly exchanging goodbyes and then closing the door. Sam didn't move from the couch. She'd dropped her head in her hands.

"I guess it's meet-the-family week," Sam said. Her tone was joking, but she kept her gaze on the floor.

Terri sat down on the couch and rested her hand on Sam's leg. "I'm sorry about your uncle."

"Me too." Sam sighed. "I wish I could have known him. He seemed so cool in all the letters. Even though he was dying, he had a sense of humor about everything. It's funny how you can miss someone you never knew."

Sam didn't say anything more for several minutes, and Terri wondered if she wanted her to leave. She debated asking, but then only stared out the window at the calm blue water. It didn't seem right that the ocean was so smooth now.

"I looked up to my grandpa for so long. Then reading those letters and putting the picture together..." Sam's voice trailed.

"It must have been awful to realize who he really was."

"I kept thinking, why am I trying to follow in this asshole's footsteps? Why try and make him proud when he wouldn't even help his own dying kid?"

Terri rubbed Sam's thigh. "You don't have to hold everything in, you know. You can tell people what's going on before you reach a breaking point."

"I've never had anyone to tell. I love my dad, but the conversation you heard was more words than we've ever exchanged. And my mom and I have never gotten along." Sam was quiet for a long moment and then said, "Fuck. Maybe she was right. Maybe I shouldn't have brought up Paul. Maybe what's in the past is in the past and we all need to move on."

"I don't think there was a right way to have that conversation, but I think it needed to happen. They shouldn't have kept that from you. Not for this long."

Sam straightened up. "I've got a photo shoot to get ready for."

"Can I make you dinner? We haven't eaten any real food since breakfast."

"I don't think we have anything left."

"There's peanut butter and jelly in the cupboard. And we have a few slices of that sourdough. Or I can go get some take-out. What do you feel like?"

Sam shrugged. After a moment, she said, "Maybe you should go. I'm not going to be any fun tonight."

"Turns out I want to be around you even when you're not fun." But she wished Sam would tell her if she wanted her to stay or not. Maybe Sam wanted time alone but didn't want to hurt her by saying that. Or maybe she wanted company but didn't want to admit she needed it.

Sam leaned back on the sofa. "I shouldn't have called my dad out like I did. But I didn't know. It must have been awful losing a brother and then never talking about it. And they never talked about it because of me. They were trying to protect me. How messed up is that?"

"Their decision not to tell you isn't your fault. Don't take that on."

Sam didn't respond.

"Can you reschedule the photo shoot?"

"Steve only has his kid part-time and the deadline for the senior photos is next week. I promised this. God, I feel like crap."

"Parents do that to you."

"No kidding." Sam took a deep breath. "Maybe you're right. Maybe I need to eat something…"

Terri leaned close and whispered. "Tell me to go make you a damn sandwich and I will."

Sam gave a wry smile. "Naked?"

"If I didn't know how shitty you were feeling right now, I'd think you were serious."

"What if I am serious? I'm pretty sure I'd feel better if we had sex."

Terri couldn't help laughing. "You're the only person I've ever been with that wants sex as much as I do."

"It's 'cause we're meant to be." Sam reached for Terri, pulling her back on the sofa and into another embrace. "Sure you still like me after all that?"

"I'm sure." There was no question in her mind. Sam's words circled in her mind. *Meant to be.* That's how it felt, but she didn't trust the universe enough to say it aloud. "I'll be in the kitchen making sandwiches." She slipped out of Sam's hold, giving her a kiss on the cheek as she did.

As soon as she headed down the hall, she longed to be back on the sofa still in Sam's arms. She didn't want to think of leaving. Too soon she'd be back at the hospital, back at the job that consumed her, back to falling asleep alone without Sam nestled against her. She'd lost track of the number of times she'd sworn she'd never marry someone again, never commit, never risk her heart again. But here she was, falling in love, and she couldn't seem to help it.

CHAPTER THIRTY

In the four days they were together, Sam got used to the beach house with Terri in it. She liked waking up early, going down to start breakfast, and then slipping back into the warm sheets to wait for Terri to wake. They'd made love every morning. Breakfast in bed came after.

As soon as she'd gone, the cottage felt empty and too quiet. Sam skipped breakfast and spent hours staring out at the ocean in her living room. Sacramento felt a lifetime away and she knew Terri would be slammed with work after her time off, so she tried not to bother her.

They shared one nightly call but agreed not to meet up until Reed and Julia's wedding. Sam tried to keep busy, knowing three weeks would pass faster if she didn't have time to think about it. She scheduled several new photo shoots, edited a backlog of pictures, and even managed to get some prints framed and delivered to the coffee shop. But Terri popped into her head whenever she had a still moment, and for the first time she could ever recall, despite how many years she'd lived alone, she had moments of being truly lonely.

After too many days berating herself for not simply focusing on her own work, she decided to write a letter. Not an email, but an actual letter.

For the stamp, she went up to the attic to get her collection and then she agonized over which sheet to part with. Finally she decided on some national park ones and hoped Terri would smile when she saw the line of stamps plastered across the envelope. The stamps were worth more if she'd sold them online, but that wasn't the point. Then she'd added a note on the back of the envelope saying she'd like to visit each place and hoped Terri hadn't already planned next year's vacation.

A week passed before she saw a bright red envelope arrive in the mail. Terri had picked an ocean stamp and a heart was drawn on the back. Sam brushed her finger over the tiny wave and then carefully opened the envelope, fully intent on saving it. Terri could tease her later for being old-fashioned.

Along with a slip of paper, there were two photos inside. One was of her surfing and another was a funny selfie they'd taken together. Terri had brought her phone to the beach on the last morning, saying she didn't feel like surfing but only wanted to watch Sam. In the picture, Sam was in a wetsuit and dripping wet after getting tossed in the breakers, and Terri was bundled up in one of Sam's sweatshirts and her rainbow beanie. She smiled at the picture and then read the note.

The words made her long to call Terri, but she resisted. Instead she taped the note to the door, quickly memorizing the last few lines: "How about that national park in Hawaii next time? No wetsuits needed." It wasn't signed "Love, Terri," but she hadn't dared to sign hers with that tempting word either.

When the day for Reed and Julia's wedding rehearsal dinner finally came, Sam couldn't keep herself occupied with any task around the house. She decided to drive up early, with the excuse of wanting to scope out the scene before the others arrived.

The day was picture perfect and even the freeway traffic didn't get to her. Reed and Julia had picked a boutique winery in Napa that doubled as an inn for the ceremony and the rehearsal dinner as well. She didn't know how many people they'd invited, but as soon as she arrived at the address, she realized the place couldn't hold a big crowd. That was a plus for her. Big weddings were hard to shoot without backup and she'd be solo for this.

She didn't rush to check in, grabbing her camera instead and walking the vineyard. The plowed rows between the grapevines were littered with gold and brown leaves, but the plants themselves still had enough green and yellow clinging on to be gorgeous. Huge oaks lined the perimeter, and Sam set up under one of the trees, figuring out the light and snapping a few shots of the rolling hills.

Her phone rang and she answered it when she saw Terri's name. "Hey."

"Hi, you," Terri said, her smile coming through the phone. "Where are you?"

"Somewhere beautiful. When are you joining me?"

"I'm still at the hospital. Depending on how fast I can wrap up things here, I'm thinking three, maybe four hours."

Sam's hopes for some time alone with Terri sank. "So, dinnertime?"

"Probably. Is that a problem?"

Sam hated feeling needy and wanting more than Terri could offer. She looked up at the sky. Puffs of clouds drifted overhead in the pale blue. "No, it's fine. Just wanted you sooner is all."

"You'll have me all weekend, you know."

"Might not be enough. I've worked up an appetite."

Terri laughed. "Good. So have I. You have no idea how much I've thought of you. And of what you'll do to me this weekend."

Well, that was something. Sam could hear the desire in Terri's voice and wanted to tell her to leave work early.

Terri added, "I promise I'll get there as fast as I can."

After she'd hung up, Sam went back to exploring. Beyond the view from the inn, she found a perfect spot for pictures of Reed and Julia alone—the side of an old barn with rough-hewn wood planks and a tipped-over wine barrel left to be taken back by the earth. All around the gold and brown leaves were scattered, but near the barn there was a maple adding in some red. Sam snapped a few pictures of the spot, planning where she'd ask Reed and Julia to stand. As much as she loved photographing people, catching a coy smile, or a pensive look, or the moment someone slid a ring over a finger, she loved the part of her job when she was alone scouting out how and where to set the scene almost as much.

When she'd settled on where to take group pictures and scoped out the site for the ceremony, a vine-covered trellis on a hill overlooking the winery below, she headed back to the inn. Reed's car was parked out front, and she heard the racket of kids as she approached. She hadn't expected Terri to ask about kids, but she'd been relieved to know her answer. It had hit her then that they truly did fit together.

Too easily she could imagine walking hand in hand with Terri, years from now, a dog racing ahead of them on the beach. That's all she wanted. But she couldn't expect Terri to give up the hospital to move in with her.

And they weren't getting married either. Terri had made it clear that she wouldn't do it again. Although Sam had denied wanting to ever get married, she'd thought of it plenty. And she'd taken pictures of enough weddings to have a plan for her own. It was some kind of irony that when she finally found someone she could imagine spending the rest of her life with, she knew that she couldn't get down on one knee to ask her.

"Sam, over here." Reed waved. Her two kids scrambled between her and the fountain in front of the inn, obviously in the midst of a game of tag.

"Where's the bride?"

"Inside getting us checked in. I think she needed a break. These two are a lot on a long car ride."

Reed's kids both stopped running. "A lot of what?" The one with the blond braids—Carly—had spoken up, but they both looked expectantly at Reed.

"A lot of energy," Reed said.

"Nice save." Sam winked.

Bryn—Sam had no trouble remembering her name right off—put her hands on her hips as she narrowed her eyes at Sam. "I remember you," she said. "You're scared of kids."

"I'm only scared of some kids. The scary ones," Sam teased.

"And you tried to kiss Aunt Terri."

Sam opened and closed her mouth. Her first thought was to tell Bryn that she would have kissed her if they hadn't been rudely interrupted.

"From what I hear, you've both gotten better at the kissing," Reed said under her breath.

Despite how quiet she'd said it, both kids heard. They looked at each other, made faces and screamed "Ew!" In the next breath, they'd gone back to chasing each other around the fountain.

"I didn't think they'd hear," Reed apologized.

"As long as Terri is okay with them knowing, it's not a problem for me."

"Oh, she is. She's been talking about you a lot."

Sam wanted to ask what she'd said, but Reed was Terri's friend first. "How are you holding up? Nervous?"

"You have no idea. But I don't even know why, exactly. Logistics, I guess. It's not like I'm worried that Julia won't say yes. I've checked to make sure I have her ring about a dozen times. And every time I try to run through my vows I sound like I've got marbles in my mouth."

"You brought your dancing shoes, right? I can't wait to catch a shot of that waltz."

Reed pushed her glasses up her nose. "Yeah, about that…"

"No waltz?"

"I convinced Julia to go with a song that we could kind of sway to. No waltzing required. Actually, I think she was as relieved as I was. But maybe you can miss that picture anyway? I still think there's a good chance I'm going to trip and fall."

"You reserve the right to delete any picture that you don't like. But if you trip, I'm getting that shot."

"Gee, thanks." Reed laughed. "Joking aside, I really appreciate you doing this for us. And I know you didn't want me to pay you, but I think you should reconsider. Now that you're not working at the hospital and—"

"Now that I'm broke?" Sam smiled as she said it, but the words pinched at her pride. She wondered how much Terri had told Reed aside from the kissing. But even if Terri hadn't mentioned it, Reed could guess the money wasn't flowing at the moment. "This is my wedding present to you, remember? I don't want you to pay me."

Reed sighed. "Okay. But I'm getting your room and don't argue about that. Julia and I already talked about it. Trust me, there's no changing her mind once she's decided something. You haven't checked in yet, right?"

"No. I wanted to scope out the vineyard while there was still good light." She wished she didn't need a free room, but reality was, she did. And if she accepted that, Reed wouldn't press to pay for the pictures. Plus if the room was already covered, Terri wouldn't try to pay for it all.

"I've missed you around the hospital," Reed said. "But Terri says you seem happy."

"I am." For the most part that was true. "I've got some guilt about quitting, but I know it was the right decision. I feel lighter. Like I've let go of all these expectations and can go back to being me."

"Good for you. This job takes too much out of you. It's not worth it if you don't love it. And you and Terri?"

"We're good. Really good, actually." If Reed wasn't Terri's best friend, only another butch she could confide in, she'd elaborate. Not only was she having the best sex of her life, they connected on so many levels. She almost didn't trust that it could be real. If only she could have her every night.

"Terri had more to say... Apparently you're pretty much amazing in bed."

Sam grinned. "You two talk about stuff like that?"

"We've been friends forever. But I've never seen her this happy. I've also never heard her talk about sex quite this much. And I hope you're not planning on taking pictures all weekend 'cause she's convinced you'll be working on some new positions together."

"I didn't think Terri was the kiss-and-tell sort."

"She isn't usually. You've brought her out of her shell, my friend." Reed patted Sam's shoulder. "I'm thinking I could use some pointers. You working off of a lesbian Kama Sutra book?"

"A lesbian Kama Sutra? Is that what you two are talking about out here?" Julia had stepped out of the inn at exactly the wrong moment. But she was smiling and looked pleased at what she'd overheard. She looped her arm through Reed's and added, "Are you taking pictures for that too, Sam?"

"Uh, can I plead the fifth?"

Reed and Julia laughed. The two kids stopped racing around the fountain and one hollered, "What's so funny?"

Julia raised an eyebrow at Reed and murmured, "Not it."

"Something adults find funny that you would say is gross," Reed answered. "Like armpit hair."

Both kids made faces as if they'd tasted something disgusting and then were off running again.

"Armpit hair?" Sam asked.

"Works every time. I'm not sure why. As soon as I say armpit hair, they're out."

"You also happen to be magical and can fix everything," Julia said, going up on her tiptoes to kiss Reed's cheek. "Let's go get our bags, hun. And, by the way, Sam, I checked you in. Your room is on our card and don't try anything funny to get out of letting us pay. Reed and I already decided."

CHAPTER THIRTY-ONE

Terri texted at six to let Sam know she'd made it to their room, but there was no time even for a hello kiss. The rehearsal dinner started at six-thirty and Sam was in the dining hall early to snap pictures as guests filtered in. She'd gotten a few shots of Reed, Julia, and the kids before any meltdowns could happen and then moved on to greeting the other guests and explaining the combinations of family she wanted to shoot tomorrow. Reed's three brothers all looked vaguely like her, tall and studious but warming up quickly. Her father was shorter, laughed a lot, and sported a tweed coat, and unruly wispy gray hair. After a quick shot of all of them together with a promise to corral them again tomorrow when everyone was in a tux, she moved onto Julia's family.

"I didn't realize you were an only kid like me," Sam said, catching a shot of Julia with her hand in her mom's, her father in the background beaming.

"And what they say about only kids is completely true," Julia said. "We're amazing and a total pain in the ass."

Sam laughed. "Couldn't have said it better."

She snapped a few more pictures when Reed greeted Julia's mom and then stepped back to let them talk. No one new entered the hall, so she took a moment for quick review of the pictures she'd taken. The lighting in the space wasn't great, but she spotted a few shots that she liked right away. With a little editing, they'd capture the unstaged moments perfectly.

"There you are." Terri's arms encircled Sam's waist from behind. The scent of her perfume caught Sam's attention, bringing all of her wandering thoughts into fine focus. "Am I going to throw you off photographer mode if I tell you how much I want to be fucked tonight?"

Sam lowered her camera and turned around. Terri's lips were waiting for hers. She didn't intend for a crushing kiss, but one gentle brush wasn't enough. Terri parted her lips as Sam deepened the kiss. One hand pressed against Sam's chest as the other held onto her belt. When Sam pulled back, suddenly remembering they were in the middle of a crowded hall, Terri's eyes were still closed.

"Mm, I missed that," Terri said.

"There's probably some quiet little nook we could find for a quick, but more thorough, hello…"

"Probably. But I don't want anything quick. I want to wait for an extra long hello. And I want to sit all through dinner thinking about what your hands are going to do to me later."

As much as Sam didn't want to wait, she knew it'd be worth it. Terri's green eyes sparkled with a mischievous glint.

"I did as you asked, by the way. Haven't touched myself for a week. It wasn't easy, but I knew the reward you'd give me for being good would make it worth it." Terri drew a line down Sam's chest. "I should let you get back to work. I love it when you're in photographer mode…makes me want to do anything to get your attention."

"Let me get back to work and you'll have my full attention sooner."

Terri dipped her head and then joined a crowd heading for the dining room. She was gone so quickly that Sam would have lost her except for her hair. Ringlets of red. And the dress. Dark green to give her gorgeous eyes competition. She looked amazing. And later she'd be all hers.

"How's it going, Sam?"

"Hey." Sam smiled. Mo and Kate, Julia's friends that she'd met at the barbeque ages ago at Reed's house, stood arm in arm. They made a truly gorgeous couple and Sam vowed to ask later exactly how they'd gotten together. Terri had said it was a long story. "It's good to see you two."

"You too," Kate said.

"We didn't know you were a photographer until Reed just mentioned it," Mo said. "We might have to get your number. Kate and I were thinking of taking some pictures before the baby comes."

"Belly shots," Kate clarified, an immediate blush on her cheeks as she rubbed the bump Sam hadn't noticed.

"Congrats, you two! How far along?" Sam had no idea they were expecting but was thrilled for them.

"Fifteen weeks." Kate sighed. "And I've spent most of that time vomiting."

"I'm sorry. They say it gets better?"

Kate raised a skeptical eyebrow. "Next time Mo is carrying."

Mo gave a vigorous head shake, and Sam couldn't help laughing. "Maybe one and done?"

"Maybe." Kate looked over at Mo. "What do you think, babe?"

"We'll see how cute the first one is." Mo leaned down to kiss Kate. She was as tall and athletic as Kate was petite. Sam thought again how well matched they were. It wasn't only the difference in their skin, Mo's deep brown against Kate's pale cream, but they looked like they could be models on the side. Sam wondered if the sperm donor had been as good-looking. The baby was gonna be one lucky kid regardless.

"Usually I do a package. Pictures of the baby bump when you're ready to send out announcements, then again when you're closer to your due date. And we'd do one more shoot with all three of you after the baby's born."

Mo looked at Kate. "All three of us…I can't wait."

"That's exactly what we're looking for," Kate said.

Mo agreed. "Do you have a card?"

Sam reached into her back pocket. Fortunately she'd come prepared. "I also do a first-year series. Those are my favorite." As much as she couldn't handle kid energy, she loved babies, loved photographing them, and loved watching the new parents proudly snuggling them. "You're friends with Terri, right? We're dating so you can find me through her if you lose the card."

Mo turned to Kate with a smug look. "Called it."

"You did. Okay. I owe you five bucks." Kate turned to Sam. "At Julia and Reed's barbeque we were placing bets on whether you and Terri would hook up. Mo said it'd be more than a hook-up."

"And then you teased me about being a soft-hearted romantic."

"I did. And you are." Kate shook her head, but a smile played on her lips. "But I love you for it."

"Not as much as I love you."

The look in Mo's eyes as she reached for Kate's hand, the other hand across her chest as she dramatically, albeit jokingly, pledged her undying love, made Sam think there was nothing wrong falling for a soft-hearted romantic. Mo laughed at her own antics, and Sam angled her lens. She caught a great shot right as Kate leaned close.

After they'd gone, Sam snapped a few more shots, but the crowd in the hall had thinned. She peeked into the dining area. Nearly everyone had taken their seats so she stowed her camera, happy to be done for the moment. Later she'd need to get her camera out again, but all she wanted now was to find Terri and enjoy a fancy dinner together. If only that, and the sex they'd have later, could be all that was on her mind. Instead there was a nagging question about what their next step would be. If the past three weeks had taught her anything, it was that she wasn't cut out for long distance. And seeing everyone around her in love only made her doubt that it would work out as easily for her.

* * *

"I didn't know dinner could last that long."

Terri had kept a casual distance through the meal, as if aware that an accidental touch would make it harder for Sam, and still she managed to slip into their room without brushing close.

Sam set the cardkey on the dresser and undid the top button of her shirt. She longed to reach for Terri, but something unspoken kept her hands to herself. "You seemed to enjoy dinner."

"Oh, I enjoyed it. Although not as much as I liked watching you work the crowd." Terri smiled. "You charmed everyone tonight."

"I got a few skills."

"More than a few," Terri said, stepping out of her heels. She reached for the zipper at the side seam of her dress. "Mind if I shower?"

"Go ahead." Sam could tell Terri was tired. She wondered if maybe she'd rather go right to sleep. "You had a long day. We could wait 'til tomorrow for—"

"Are you kidding?" Terri's hand stalled. "Please tell me you're kidding."

"It's okay to be tired. You worked today and had a long drive in probably shitty traffic. Tomorrow's your best friend's wedding and…" Sam's voice trailed when Terri stepped in front of her. She'd unzipped her dress and slipped it off her shoulders, but it still hung around her hips. The half-undone look along with a sexy black bra cupping her breasts into a line of perfect cleavage had Sam wondering what she'd been about to say.

"And what?"

And nothing. God, she couldn't wait another minute. "You can shower later," Sam murmured, closing the distance to Terri's lips.

Sam didn't wait for Terri to catch her breath. One kiss and then another as she pushed her back a step toward the bed. She unhooked Terri's bra while she distracted her lips. Another kiss and she had the dress all the way off. One more, crushing this time, and Terri readily submitted, her lips parting as Sam's tongue pushed against hers.

They tumbled onto the bed, Sam on top quickly pinning Terri's arms. She didn't need cuffs or restraints. Terri gave in. She panted between kisses, murmured Sam's name, and then begged. "I need you. Please."

Sam shoved aside her panties and pushed inside.

"Fuck, yes." Terri was too loud for the next room not to hear. She tensed, squeezing Sam's fingers, and then splayed her knees, opening herself to Sam. "I love what you do to me."

Sam slipped out, letting the panties slip back into position, demurely covering Terri's mound. When Terri whimpered, she held the same fingers that had been inside Terri up to her lips. "I should tell you to stay quiet, but I like your sounds too damn much."

"Tell me and I will." Terri's tongue slipped over Sam's middle finger.

"You need more than my hand tonight."

Terri nodded.

"Close your eyes and don't move."

When Terri gave a second nod, Sam got out of bed and went to her suitcase. She'd purposefully left her harness and cock on top, guessing that she wouldn't want to dig for it later. She quickly undressed, keeping one eye on Terri.

In only the black panties, her breasts on display and her eyes closed, Terri was truly breathtaking. Sam pushed a bullet vibe into the base of her cock and tested it. The buzz made her clit pulse in anticipation. She grabbed lube, coating her tip and then squirting some more in her palm.

Terri took a sharp breath when Sam pushed her panties aside the second time. Remembering her orders, she kept her eyes closed, only tilting her pussy up and murmuring her pleasure as Sam spread the lube over her folds.

The bed creaked as Sam kneeled over Terri. She thought of sliding into her with the panties pushed to the side, but then the desire to have her completely naked won out. She tugged the silk off and pushed Terri's knees up. Her own clit pulsed at the sight of Terri, glistening wet and ready for her.

She drew a slow circle, lightly grazing her fingertip over Terri's slit. "Do you know how much I want you?"

Terri opened her eyes and met Sam's gaze. She continued the slow circle pattern on Terri's skin. Having Terri watch only spiked her arousal.

"Who said you could open your eyes?"

"Mmm." Terri closed them again, a smile on her lips. "Sometimes I want to misbehave so you'll punish me."

"But you've been so good all week." Sam parted Terri's legs further and shifted between them. She leaned down, kissing her way up Terri's thighs until she reached the apex. "Waiting patiently for me."

"I have been good," Terri murmured. She pushed her hips up. "And now I get my reward."

"You do." Sam dipped her finger inside—not far enough to sate Terri's desire, only enough to enjoy the slickness. "Reed told me you talked to her about the things we do…that you kiss and tell."

"I don't talk about everything. Some things I'm too shy to admit. Even to her."

"I like that answer." Some things they'd keep between them. Sam trailed up Terri's body with light kisses, then positioned the tip of her cock. She didn't try to push inside but pulled a nipple between her lips instead. She circled it with her tongue and then sucked, nudging her cock forward an inch.

Terri gasped, her arms wrapping around Sam as she tried to spread herself more. Sam reached down and felt the cock. The bulb was at Terri's rim, but she couldn't take it any deeper. Shifting back, Sam let off the pressure, then moved back down, kissing a path over Terri's belly and lower to her folds.

"Why'd you take it away?" Terri pumped her hips. "I want you inside."

"You're tight."

"I'm only tight because I haven't had you. Three weeks is too long." Terri whimpered.

Sam moved up to Terri's lips. Her own body begged her to drive the cock inside, to open Terri with the force she wanted. But she made herself hold back, savoring how her clit pulsed with need.

"Please?"

When Terri pushed up against her again, Sam gave one gentle nudge to part her. This time there was less resistance. With a slow thrust, she slid all the way inside and Terri let out a long, low moan.

"Oh, yeah," she breathed. "Like that."

Sam pulled out, repositioned, and then thrust her hips. She buried the cock deeper this time, feeling Terri's belly brush against hers.

"Again." Terri moaned, her face flushed with desire. "Please."

Sam pulled out faster the third time and drove in hard enough to make Terri groan with pleasure. She repeated the move a few more times and then felt Terri straining to hold her inside.

"I want a little vibration. Tell me if it's too much." Sam reached down to turn on the bullet vibe and a tremor raced through her. Her own orgasm wasn't going to take long. "You okay if I come inside you?" She brushed her fingertip over Terri's swollen clit.

"I love it when you use me to get off," Terri said, her eyes still closed. "But fuck me hard enough and I'll be good and come for you too."

Sam shifted her position and started pumping faster. Terri matched her rhythm. Every time Sam pulled back, she pushed up. Sweat coated Sam's back and her arms trembled from holding her weight off Terri's body. But she couldn't stop now. The wetness between her legs was her cum and not the lube and her clit was firing. "I can't hold off much longer."

"Use me. That's what I want," Terri said.

Sam gave in then and felt the climax hit. Squeezing her thighs, she let the wave roll through her. Before it was done, while her body still buzzed with an orgasm, she started thrusting again. Her muscles complained, but she fought through it, then reached down to press her thumb on Terri's clit.

Terri bucked hard, arching her back and screaming out as her orgasm took hold. Her nails gouged Sam's back, and she cried out again.

Sam pulled her close, kissing her neck, her chest, her lips, anything she could reach. God, she loved her. Loved everything about her. How strong she was...how hard she fought...and how beautiful she was when she surrendered.

It didn't seem possible, but she knew Terri was hers. Finally she could feel it. *She's mine. And I'm hers.* Tears welled, but she didn't rub them away. She pressed into Terri's lips again for another long kiss.

Minutes passed before Terri's tremors finally stilled. Sam tried to relax, but her heart banged in her chest and she was still tingling from the orgasm that hadn't exactly finished. And she didn't want to pull out. Hopefully Terri wouldn't ask.

They lay together as their breathing slowed. Every passing minute, Sam became more aware of the tightness in her chest and the words she longed to whisper.

"I love having you like that," Sam said. It was almost what she wanted to say. Not quite, but close. "You're so damn hot..."

"I love you," Terri murmured. "I know I'm not supposed to say it right now, but I can't help it. I love you." She sighed softly. "I wasn't supposed to fall for you at all."

"I love you too." Once the words were spoken there was no going back, but Sam didn't care.

Terri clutched Sam closer to her. "Don't pull out yet. I like this part. Having you inside me. And I think I already knew, but thanks for saying it. The 'I love you' bit. I like hearing it."

"Me too."

CHAPTER THIRTY-TWO

Terri tried to lie still. For once, she'd woken first and she couldn't fall back asleep. Not as soon as her mind reminded her of what she needed to tell Sam. And of everything that had been said last night. She stayed on her side, watching Sam's slow, even breathing, and tried to convince herself that what came next wasn't a big deal. She loved Sam and Sam loved her back. The rest would be only logistics. Unless it wasn't.

Sleep smoothed Sam's features, relaxing muscles that were usually tense. But even at rest Terri doubted her mind wasn't busy. Determined, Reed had called her. And focused. But the day Sam had left the hospital, turning her back on everything she'd worked for, Terri had questioned all of that. In fact, she'd thought Reed had been plain wrong about her. Months later she now realized that she'd been the one who was wrong.

Sam hadn't taken the easy way out. If anything, she'd done exactly the opposite. And when she talked about photography and the goals she'd set for herself, her focus and determination were more clear than ever. Terri hoped she could help her reach those goals. But what if she'd only be in the way?

Last night they hadn't bothered closing the drapes and light poured in with the sunrise, catching the flecks of gold in Sam's hair. Terri had to hold herself back from brushing a few wisps that fell across Sam's forehead.

Her eyes opened and closed. She reached for Terri, snuggled closer, and then eased back to her slow, even breathing. Several minutes passed before she opened her eyes again.

"Morning," Terri whispered.

"You're awake?" Sam murmured. "How's that possible? I always wake up first."

"I used to be a morning person before I met you. Hard to believe, I know."

Sam rubbed sleep from her eyes and yawned. "I'd blame whoever you were sleeping with for that."

"That was definitely part of it." Terri kissed Sam's cheek. "I gotta go pee. I didn't want to move and wake you up." She scooted out of bed. It wasn't only that she had to use the bathroom. She suddenly felt anxious, thinking of what she had to say.

When she got back, Sam lifted the covers so she could slip back in. She tried to settle in Sam's arms, but her mind leapt from one what-if to the next.

"What's wrong?"

"Nothing's wrong." Terri breathed in Sam's scent. The musk of sex and sweat mixed with a faint memory of her cologne. Was it possible to want someone too much?

If she asked, Sam would make love to her again. Right now. They wouldn't have to talk.

"Something's on your mind." Sam kissed her shoulder. "I can tell. What is it?"

Terri shifted, rolling on her back to look at Sam. "It's weird being with someone who's maybe more intuitive than me. I'm not sure how I feel about it."

Sam ignored the deflection. "Is it about what we said last night? The 'I love you' part? We can go back to saying 'I like you' if that's what you want."

"I do like you, but I also love you. It's not about that. However. While we are on the subject of how much I like you, this morning hair of yours is really sexy." Terri ruffled Sam's already tousled hair and smiled. "It looks like you spent all night fucking someone."

"Nice try, but I'm not letting up on this even if you try to distract me with sex." Sam pecked Terri's cheek. "Is it something about Reed and Julia's wedding?"

"No..." Terri took a deep breath. "There's something I need to decide. But I'm nervous about telling you. There's a chance you'll freak out, and then things will be weird, and we'll both pull back, and I don't want that to happen."

"I only pull back when I don't know where we stand."

Terri had noticed that. But this news could change that pattern. She hoped she wasn't making a mistake starting the day with it. "I went for an interview last week. Actually it was a second interview. And it went well." She took another deep breath. "Yesterday morning I got a call saying they want to hire me."

"I didn't know you were looking for a new job."

"It's been on the back burner for a while now. About six months actually. But other things distracted me." She smiled and caressed Sam's arm. "And before you say anything, I promise that I wasn't trying to keep this from you. A friend told me about this job, but I wasn't sure it'd be what I really wanted until I checked it out myself."

Sam still didn't say anything. Terri pushed her pillow against the headboard and shifted up on her elbow. "You know I love my job, but it's too much. The days are long and I rarely get a weekend completely off. I'm always on call. There's no real break. Not without worrying about what might be going wrong or what I'll come back to."

"What's the position you interviewed for?"

"Medical director. It's a group practice. Ten doctors now and it's growing. I'd have my own patients and oversee the other doctors. But no residents, no stress from being in a crazy busy hospital. At five, everyone goes home." That part was possibly the most appealing. Well, other than how close she'd be to Sam. "Plus they offer four weeks vacation every year. To start."

"That sounds perfect. Why were you worried about what I'd say?"

"Your dad wrote the offer letter."

"My dad?" Sam's brow creased. "Wait, you interviewed at my grandfather's practice?"

"I didn't know it was your grandfather's practice when I sent out my resume. It was months ago. And I didn't even realize it when I went for the first interview. It was only when I got the official offer and I saw your father's name listed as the CFO. I hoped maybe it was a different Samuels, but it's not."

"He does financial law mostly...but my grandfather asked him to help with the business end of things at his practice." Sam sat up in bed. No part of her looked relaxed anymore. Terri might as well have dumped a pail of ice water on her head.

"Are you mad? I really had no idea. You made it sound like your grandpa had this little solo practice."

"He did. Then he joined with another doctor and it grew from there."

Terri didn't miss that Sam hadn't answered the question. Was she mad or only thrown by the news?

"I sent my résumé in before we ever got together. I didn't know..." Terri waited, wondering if Sam would argue that once she'd figured out it was her grandfather's practice she could have moved on and looked for another position. But Sam didn't say that. "I'd have to move if I took the job. I couldn't commute all the way to San Jose every day."

"I don't understand why you didn't tell me you were going for an interview. Even if you didn't know it was my grandfather's practice."

Terri met Sam's gaze. "What if an offer never came?"

"Then we'd talk about it. Process it together." Sam reached for Terri's hand. "If we're really trying to be in a relationship, I want you to tell me what's going on in your life. Obviously I don't need to know everything, but we've talked every night for the past three weeks—not one of those nights did you think it might be a good idea to say you had a second interview at a practice in San Jose?"

"I should have told you." Certainly when she'd gone for the second interview. But even when she'd driven down for the interview, considered how close she was to Santa Cruz and Sam, she'd held back. "Don't laugh, but I was scared."

"Scared of what?"

"Of not getting the job and disappointing you." She was embarrassed to admit it, but it was the truth.

Sam gave her hand a gentle squeeze. "You are not going to disappoint me. There's not even a chance." She let go of Terri's hand and stared out the window for a long moment. "When do you have to tell them your answer?"

"Monday. I wanted to talk to you before I made any decision. They want me to start as soon as possible, but I want to give at least two months' notice at the hospital. I won't take the position if you don't want me to. But I am going to keep looking for something like it. I finally reached a breaking point."

"This could be perfect for you," Sam said. "You won't have to work as much, still have patients but you'll be in charge…"

"Exactly." Terri felt a glimmer of hope. Maybe Sam wasn't mad. Maybe she'd only needed a minute to digest everything. "I didn't realize how unhappy I was working so much until I spent four days in paradise with you." Terri touched Sam's arm. She needed to feel her, needed to know they were still okay. "You kind of ruined me, you know. I don't like to be away from you."

"Don't tell Weiss," Sam joked. "He's already mad at me."

"It can be our little secret." Terri stroked down Sam's arm to her wrist. Sam spread her palm and Terri traced the lines on her hand. "I don't want to go three weeks without seeing you. But I don't have to take this job. It's your grandfather's old practice and your father's the CFO. The whole thing is messy."

"Messy is a good word for it." Sam's hand closed around hers. "Is it okay if I ask for some time to think?"

Terri nodded, feeling doubt settle back in. She'd hoped Sam would immediately agree, but it was fair to ask for time to think it through. "Just so you know, if I take the job, I was planning on getting my own place. I'm not suggesting we'd move in together. At least not at first."

"The practice is only a forty-minute drive from the beach house. I tried the commute when I was still thinking about taking the job."

Was that Sam's hesitation? That in some small way, Terri was taking *her* job? Of course it wasn't the same position. Being the medical director was a lot different than joining the practice as a newbie doctor. But still.

Sam brought Terri's hand up to her lips and brushed her knuckles with a kiss. "I love you."

"I know. And it's amazing." Terri felt tears prick her eyes. "But the weird thing is I love you more."

"Weird?"

Terri laughed at Sam's scrunched eyebrows. "I've never really been in love before. Infatuated, yes, and swept away for sure, but this is different. Before the other person liked me and I went along with it. But with you…when we aren't together I'm thinking about you all the time. I can't wait to be with you. And then when we are together everything feels perfect. I feel happy and sexy and loved. And you're smart and funny and so damn good looking."

"And?" Sam grinned. "Feel free to go on."

Terri laughed. "And really fucking good in bed."

Sam trailed her toes up Terri's leg. "I could be even better, you know."

"I don't think that's possible."

Sam pulled Terri closer. "Are you mad that I can't be excited right away?"

"I'm not mad."

"Disappointed?"

She sighed. "Maybe a little. But I understand. And I want you to take your time."

CHAPTER THIRTY-THREE

The wedding ceremony went off without a hitch. Unfortunately, Terri hardly spoke to Sam before, during, or after. She was in constant motion, with her camera always in hand, and as much as Terri longed to distract her from her job, she knew she couldn't.

Dinner was nearly over when Reed finally dragged Sam over to Terri's table. "Sit. Eat. And no arguing."

Reed greeted everyone else at the table with a wide smile. She'd had the same smile on her lips since Julia had said yes under the canopy of pink and purple flowers. "You all have to help me out here," Reed continued. "I told her she's not allowed to take any more pictures until she puts something in her mouth."

"In her mouth, huh?" Terri said, raising an eyebrow. "Did you mean to be intentionally vague with those orders?"

"No," Reed said, chuckling. "That was an honest mistake. For all of you with your mind in the gutter, I meant get her to eat something."

"Yeah, that still could be open for discussion," Mo joked. But she pushed a plate toward Sam. "Either way, Reed brought you to the right table."

Kate spoke up, "I feel like maybe Terri should be the one feeding her."

"They'll save that for later," Reed said.

As the others laughed, Mo said, "Hey, Reed, congrats. I've never seen Julia look so happy."

"Yeah, so far so good." Reed glanced back at the table in the center where Julia and the rest of the family were seated. "Now all I have to do is get through that first dance."

"You got this," Sam said. "And if you don't, I'll delete the pictures."

"Thanks. And the rest of you have to promise to forget."

After several vows not to forget, Reed left laughing. She whispered something to Julia when she took her seat, and then Julia gave the whole table a scolding finger shake. That only got more laughs.

As beautiful and touching as the ceremony had been, Reed overcoming her shyness for a kiss that left no question as to how good Julia's wedding night would be, Terri had trouble focusing on that or anything else. Her thoughts kept circling back to Sam. She'd slipped in and out of her line of sight all day, the camera an ever-present reminder that Terri couldn't distract her. And she'd only seemed to sit down to eat to appease Reed. Maybe their morning conversation still weighed on her? The plate of food in front of Sam remained untouched as she took the free moment to scan the images on her camera screen.

"Did you get some good shots?"

"So many. Reed and Julia are both great—they're making this easy on me. And those kids." Sam held up the camera so Terri could see a shot of the kids peeking out on either side of Julia's dress. "I have to say the kids are growing on me. They're both trouble. And adorable."

"I think that's the definition of kids. Julia and Reed are going to love that picture."

"Sam, put down the camera for a minute and eat," Mo said. "Otherwise in about two seconds Julia's gonna come over here and chew us out."

"It's true. Give it here." Kate held out her hand for the camera.

Sam seemed reluctant, but she handed it over, eying the plate of food. Along with a filet of teriyaki salmon there was a side of rice and another of stir-fried veggies. "I'm not used to relaxing when I'm shooting a wedding."

"But you do eat, right?"

"Usually standing up in some hallway or in the back of the dining room." Sam sighed and picked up her fork. "Mo, you up for placing a bet on who's catching the bouquet tonight?"

Mo grinned at Kate as she jabbed her thumb Sam's direction. "Check it out—I got a new gambling buddy!" She turned back to Sam. "Tell me you like football and we're golden."

Sam grinned. "I'm a Raiders fan."

"You do realize this is the Niners table, right?" Mo shook her head but said, "Twenty bucks says one of the twins catches the bouquet."

"I don't know. They're pretty short." Sam scanned the crowd, but her eyes came back to their table. "I'm betting twenty on Kate."

Kate held up her hand, flashing a ring. "Someone already put a ring on it. But you'd have lost anyway—I never go near flying bouquets."

"Sam's used to losing. She's a Raiders fan." Mo winked as she said it, and Sam feigned an indignant look.

"I'll go twenty on Terri," Kate said. "I got a feeling about this."

"Those type of feelings need to be kept to yourself," Terri said, laughing. "I'm not going anywhere near that bouquet either."

"Sounds like you got your work cut out for you, Sam," Mo said.

"Oh, she's done all the hard work." Terri shifted her chair closer and set her hand on Sam's leg. It was the first time she'd been able to touch Sam since they'd had the sheets tangled around their legs that morning, and in an instant, she wanted to be back in bed. "Besides, if I was going to marry anyone again, it wouldn't be because I caught a bouquet."

"Why would it be?" Sam held Terri's gaze.

They'd been joking before, but Sam's serious tone changed that. Terri stalled for a moment, wondering if she dared to be honest. "I'd marry someone if I could imagine spending the rest of my life with them."

As soon as she'd said it, Terri realized she could imagine spending the rest of her life with Sam. That hadn't been the case with Kayla or with David. Sam only stared back at her, as if waiting for her to say more. But she couldn't say more, and her heart thumped in her chest so hard she thought Sam must be able to hear.

"Sam, I've seen that look in a girl's eyes," Mo said, her tone still joking. "Now's your chance to ask. You got a ring in your pocket, right?"

Before Sam could say anything, Terri said, "I think we both know I'd be the one doing the asking."

Sam's gaze didn't waver from Terri's. "Why do you say that?"

"Because after two marriages, you'd think I'd say no if you asked. And you wouldn't want to be turned down. So you wouldn't ask."

"You know what they say—third time's a charm." Mo clinked her wine glass against Sam's and turned to Kate. "For the record, a courthouse wedding is the way to go."

Kate leaned close and kissed Mo's cheek. "Totally agree."

"Is that what you two did?" Sam asked.

Terri was glad the focus was off her now. She still felt unsettled. Surely Sam, for all she could guess about her, had sensed what she hadn't said.

"It was perfect, really," Mo said. "None of the hassle, but you still get the wedding night. If you know what I mean."

"We can all guess what you mean," Kate teased.

As Mo and Kate went back and forth on the merits of wedding night attire, Terri resettled her hand on Sam's leg. She wished they were alone, not in a crowded dining hall with the festive crowd all in a good mood.

The tablecloth hid her hand, but she wouldn't risk moving any further up Sam's thigh. Before they made love again, they needed to talk. Taking the new job wasn't only a career move. She wanted it for their relationship. But were they ready? And what did Sam want?

"When did you say the baby was due?" Sam asked.

Terri had lost track of Mo and Kate's conversation but tried to refocus now.

"April," Mo said. "With luck, on my birthday."

"I can't wait to see Mo try and deal with another Aries." Kate patted her belly. "You hear that? No showing up late for the party."

"When's your birthday?" Terri asked Sam, surprised that she hadn't thought to ask before.

"July 9th."

"Cancer. Of course. That explains a thing or two." As much trouble as they were, Terri had a soft spot for Cancers. But she realized now that also meant Sam had only barely turned thirty-one when they'd gone to the dance class together. Why'd she have to be thirty-one? Could she even ask her to think about forever? All the times she'd shied away from conversations about commitment, and now she wanted that from Sam?

"What she means by that, Sam, is that we're irresistible," Kate said. "I'm a July baby too."

"Completely irresistible, loyal, and more than a little stubborn," Terri added.

"Now they tell me." Mo smirked. "So your sign explains why you're so damn stubborn, huh?"

Kate smiled. "It's the irresistible part you're supposed to remember. And Aries are more stubborn anyway."

As Kate and Mo argued who was more stubborn, Sam looked over at Terri. "You sorry you didn't ask my sign before you kissed me?"

"I knew what I was getting into with you."

Sam entwined her fingers with Terri's. In a lowered voice, she said, "I wish I could take a break and we could go somewhere quiet for a minute. But they'll be getting the cake ready and coming for me soon."

In the same low voice, Terri said, "Can't wait 'til tonight to have me?"

"That too." Sam smiled. "But mostly I wanted to talk. I've been thinking about our conversation this morning—the job offer."

Just then, one of the waiters walked up to Sam's chair and leaned down to whisper something in her ear. Terri shifted back in her seat, thinking again of how much was still undecided. She wished she knew what Sam wanted.

Sam set down her fork and stood up, reaching for her camera. "Time to cut the cake. Save a dance for me later?"

After the cake was cut, a few of the tables were cleared to make room for dancing. The DJ switched off the classical music that had played through dinner and then announced the new couple as the opening chords of Billie Holiday's "It Had to be You" filled the room. Reed stepped out into the cleared space, her hand latched on Julia's, and the twins cheered.

All through the wedding, Terri had kept it together, but now she didn't stop the tears. She went over to where Bryn and Carly were standing and put a hand on each kid's shoulder. Bryn scooted up against her and Carly leaned into her hand.

"You two have the best moms."

Bryn nodded. Carly looked up at her and smiled. "We know."

Terri squeezed Carly's shoulder. "And they have the best kids."

"Maybe now they won't practice kissing so much," Bryn said.

"Hmm. I don't think that's gonna change."

From the dance floor, Julia caught the twins' attention and beckoned.

"I think she wants you to join them."

Carly didn't hesitate, but Terri had to convince Bryn. After a moment, all four were dancing together. It wasn't a waltz, but it was perfect.

"Hey," Sam said, suddenly standing next to her. She held out a handkerchief. "I was wondering when you were going to need this."

Terri took it and dabbed her tears. "So chivalrous."

"That's me." Sam raised her camera and went back to taking pictures. The first song ended and other couples filtered onto the dance floor. Terri expected Sam to leave, but she stayed close, snapping pictures.

"You know earlier," Sam said, still looking through the viewfinder of her camera, "when you said you'd only marry someone if you could imagine spending the rest of your life with them?"

"Yeah?" She felt the flush on her cheeks and was glad Sam wasn't looking her way.

"I've imagined that with you," Sam said. She lowered her camera and held Terri's gaze. "Does that freak you out?"

"No. I've imagined it too. You and me, walking on that beach by your house, holding hands…with our little dog chasing after a stick."

"Big dog," Sam said, a half-smile edging her lips. She raised her camera again and snapped another shot. "If you want to take the job, I'm okay with it. But I want you to move in with me."

"You can't hide behind your camera when you say something like that." Terri pulled Sam's arm until she lowered the camera again.

"You weren't supposed to notice I was hiding."

Terri smiled. "You're not the only one who can mind read. I want to move in with you, Sam, but I'm not sure we're ready."

"When you say 'we,' do you really mean 'you'? 'Cause I'm ready. It's the job I had to think about."

"And?"

"I want you to take it. If that's what you really want. My grandpa's practice needs someone like you." Sam paused. "Move in with me?"

"I want to, but…"

"But what? You worried about living in sin?"

"Sure. That's it." Terri bumped Sam's shoulder. "Leave it to you to try and joke right now."

"Still think I'm irresistible?"

"Yes. For better or worse." Terri steadied her racing pulse. As nervous as she was, she had to say the words on her lips. "I love you, Sam. I love us together. And I'd love to move in with you. I know it's too soon, but I already know you're the one. This time there's no maybe."

"You already know, huh?" Sam's tone was still joking, her smile making her all the more handsome.

"Marry me." After the words slipped out, Terri held her breath. *Please say yes.*

Sam held her gaze. "Are you serious? You know I really don't care about the living in sin part, right? We don't have to get married at all."

"I know. And I'm serious."

Sam leaned close and met Terri's lips. The tenderness in her kiss took Terri's breath away. She forgot about the rest of the room and eased into another kiss. And then another.

Finally Sam pulled back and straightened up. "Okay. Sorry about that. I couldn't help myself. Ask me again. I'm ready this time."

Terri smiled. "Will you marry—"

"Yes," Sam said immediately. "And yes again. You're the one." She set her camera down at one of the tables and held out her hand. "Dance with me?"

EPILOGUE

Sam tucked in the corners of her side of the sheet. "I'm not sure how I feel about you and my mom hanging out."

"Her office is only a few blocks from the practice. We went out for lunch."

"And then shopping," Sam said. "You have to admit it's a little weird."

"We were shopping for you. It's not that weird. Besides, your mom's not awful when you get to know her. You two are about as opposite as they come, but she's not always difficult. She loves you even if she has trouble showing it. You know, she was the one who asked me what you'd want for your birthday."

Sam shook her head. "She doesn't need to get me anything. You didn't have to either. Turning thirty-two isn't a big deal."

"People actually like you. You're gonna have to get used to the fact that we might want to show it." Terri tossed Sam one of the pillows and then fluffed hers. "Besides, this is the first birthday I get to spend with you. And you're going to love your present. I promise."

Sam came around to her side of the bed. "That's what you keep saying. I'm getting a little nervous."

Terri wrapped her arms around Sam's shoulders. "You should be."

The doorbell rang and Sam sighed. "Let's hope this goes better than the last time they came here."

"If it doesn't, I'll make it up to you later. Naked." Terri met Sam's lips for a quick kiss.

Sam wanted another, but Terri tugged her to the hallway. Lately things had been better with her parents, and she wasn't dreading today's planned lunch as much as she would have a year ago. Most of that was Terri's doing. After Terri had won over her father, Sam had watched in amazement as she'd worked on her mom. More than a few family dinners later, she'd accepted that as long as they weren't trying to fix her, or manage her life, her parents weren't bad company.

Terri opened the door, hugging Lynn and then Mark. Sam stood to the side, wondering at the big box on the doorstep.

"I don't think we can wait on the surprise," Mark said, hefting the box. He carried it into the living room and then once it was on the coffee table, turned to Sam with a big smile. "Happy birthday, kid."

He patted her shoulder and then stepped back. "I wouldn't wait too long to open it."

Sam looked over at her mom. "So I hear you and Terri got this together?"

Lynn smiled. "It was her idea."

"Open it," Terri said, motioning to the box. "The suspense is killing me."

"You already know what's inside."

"But I don't know if you'll like it," Terri returned.

Aside from the big red bow on the top and a card, there was nothing special about the box. Just a plain brown shipping box.

"Save the card for after," Mark said. "That part's from me."

Sam set the card on the table and then pulled off the bow. The box wasn't taped, only folded in, and as soon as the bow was off, the top pushed up.

"What the…" Sam glanced from Terri to her mom. "No way!"

Sam yanked the box open and a black puppy nose popped out. Paws landed on her chest a second later as a tongue lapped her chin. She scrambled to catch the puppy when it jumped the rest of the way into her arms.

"You got me a puppy?!" Sam couldn't stop smiling as the puppy wiggled and licked. "I can't believe it."

"It gets even more unbelievable. Mark, go get Tilly," Lynn said.

Mark went outside and came back a moment later with a crate. "This one's ours." Another black puppy, nearly identical to the one in Sam's arms, burst out as soon as he unlatched the gate.

"Terri picked out the puppy and I picked out the collar," Lynn said, stepping forward to scratch the head of the puppy in Sam's arms. "I know how you love rainbows. And I set you up with training classes for him too. That was the plan. Then Terri convinced me that Mark and I needed a puppy too…" She went over to take the other puppy from Mark, kissing its head as she did. "But look at this face—how could I say no? She looked so lonely sitting in the cage after we took her brother. The woman at the shelter said it was a good idea. This way they can have play dates."

"I'm not sure what's crazier—you two with a dog or me with a dog." As Sam watched her parents coo over their puppy, she realized maybe Terri was right. Maybe she needed to change her perception of them. Terri hung back a little, her hands pressed together.

"Do you like him?"

"He's exactly what I always wanted." Sam grinned as the puppy tried to hug her with one paw on each shoulder. "Best present ever."

"Happy birthday." Terri stepped forward and kissed her cheek.

"I think you're going to like this too," Mark said, reaching for the card.

Terri held out her hands to take Sam's puppy. "I'll hold him while you read."

"Do you know about this too?"

Terri shook her head. "This is all your dad. But he's been acting like he's got something up his sleeve."

"He only just told me on the drive over," Lynn added. "And, trust me, I tried everything to get it out of him earlier."

Sam opened the envelope, wondering what surprise her dad would come up with. He wasn't one for presents. Then again neither was her mom. Every year for as long as she could remember they'd either taken her to a store so she could pick something out or given her cash.

A slip of paper fell on the ground when she opened the card. She reached for it, realized it was a photocopy and quickly scanned the lines highlighted in bright yellow.

"I probably should explain," Mark said.

"This is a copy of Grandpa's will?" Sam guessed.

"One of the pages from it. He wrote that letter to you, saying what was in the will with all the restrictions, but then I got to wondering…" Mark waited for Sam to finish reading before he continued. "I decided to read the original will. There's nothing in there about a husband. Only that you have to be married by the age of thirty-four. Gay marriage wasn't legal when the will was drawn up so that's probably why he didn't specify."

"But it's legal now." Sam finished. "So I could marry anyone I want?"

"And the money would be yours. Of course you wouldn't have to get married at all. But seeing as how you're already engaged, all you'd have to do is show Grandpa's lawyer a marriage certificate."

Sam read the highlighted sentences again, still doubting it. "You sure about this? There isn't a different section in the will that contradicts this part?"

"I went over every line."

Sam sank down on the sofa. She folded the paper and set it on the coffee table by the box the puppy had come in. Her puppy. "My life's been so much better since I wrote that money off. Maybe I shouldn't take it."

"I had a feeling you were going to say that." Mark sat down next to her. "This isn't only about you," he said, picking his words slowly. "It's about Paul too. My brother wouldn't want the money going to that church foundation. Neither do I. Think of who you could help instead. Maybe donate some of it to AIDS research. Set up a scholarship for local kids."

Sam looked over at Terri, searching her face for some hint on how she felt about it all. If she decided to accept it, the money would be her responsibility too. But she already knew Terri would leave this decision to her.

All along she hadn't believed the promised inheritance would ever be hers. Even as she'd gone through the steps to become a doctor, she didn't truly believe that one day she'd have forty-one million to show for it. That was partly why she'd been able to walk away from the money. "I want to do right by your brother, Dad. But life's pretty perfect right now. What if this screws everything up?"

"You won't screw it up," Lynn said. "As hardheaded as you are and as much as we don't often understand you, in the end you make the right decisions."

Sam looked at Terri again. "What do you think? We'd be together in this."

"Money won't change how I feel about you, Sam."

Sam knew the same was true for her as well. She nodded and then glanced back at her dad. "It's not a puppy, but that's some card, Dad."

"Well, I can't exactly compete with a puppy."

Terri and Lynn set both puppies on the ground and they sprang at each other, tails wagging as they fell to wrestling. Everyone was quiet for several minutes, watching the puppies play, and the reality of what she was taking on settled on Sam's shoulders.

"Where's your camera, sweetie?" Lynn said. "I want a picture of the two of them playing together."

"And then we need to talk about names," Terri added.

"Names?" Sam watched the puppies roll on the ground. "I just found out I'm a dog owner and forty-one million dollars richer. I'm not sure I have the brain space to come up with a name."

"You're not forty-one million dollars richer until after the wedding," Terri said. She winked when Sam looked up at her. "Good thing you already found someone willing to marry you, huh?"

"Good thing." Sam held out her hand and Terri clasped it. "I love you. Thanks for the best birthday present. And for asking me to marry you."

"I may have asked, but we both know who belongs to who."

Sam smiled. "I know I'm all yours."

Bella Books, Inc.

Women. Books. Even Better Together.

P.O. Box 10543
Tallahassee, FL 32302

Phone: 800-729-4992
www.bellabooks.com